NEWDON KILLERS

Simon Farrant

Edited by Gemma Newey (The Crucifix) and Cat Chester at Pink Proof (Famously Ordinary and Death Dolls): info@pinkproof.co.uk

Covers:

The Crucifix and Famously Ordinary by Michael Bray
Death Dolls and Omnibus artwork by Amanda: www.letsgetbooked.com

First Edition 2018

Farrant Fiction, Corby, Northamptonshire

ISBN:
Ebook: 978-1-9999791-2-6
Paperback: 978-1-9999791-4-0

Acknowledgements

It takes more people than just the author to get a book from inside the head to the mean shelves of booksville!

I am very grateful to Gillian Craddock for her law expertise in Death Dolls

A big thank you to my patient beta readers, you know who you are.

Thank you to Book Connectors FB group for your encouragement and advice. A huge thank you to Cat Chester of Pink Proof for her top notch editing skills, and Amanda at Let's Get Booked for editing the short story.

Last but by no means least, my Family for your ongoing love, support and encouragement.

Table of Contents

THE CRUCIFIX

Prologue

Mason's Last Sermon

Mason Grey was very popular in his church. Having been their leader for many years, his congregation followed him without question. Over those years, he had established a firm authority. He was just another pastor at first, but his strong charisma soon shone through. After the first twelve months or so, his attention to studying the Bible started to dwindle, but his sermons were so packed with biblical references that the congregation could no longer keep up. While frantically looking through their Bibles for the passages Mason read out, they had to assume he was using them as they were written and in the correct contexts.

His ego was huge, but he was clever enough to avoid being arrogant or smug. When his parishioners spoke to him about issues that were bugging them, he always listened carefully to discern what they wanted to be true. Mason would then pray with them, telling them that he was lifting them up to the Lord. By then, they truly were in the palm of his hand; he could've told them anything with the killer sentence of, 'Jesus is telling me that...' He always made sure that the person who had come to see him believed that God was letting them have things their own way. *Why make them think too much into things and start to doubt their faith?*

Mason loved appearing as though he were speaking in tongues, the mysterious ancient tongue. The Bible tells believers that tongues is all about worshiping God. In words that Man cannot understand, it is the soul praising God, and Mason told people regularly that God had given him the power to translate tongues to allow him to be closer to God and guide the people to keep on the holy path.

Mason's clear love for God was infectious, and the zeal in which he delivered his sermons and 'messages' was infectious.

People came from many miles around to Mason's church; his closest followers really believed that he could've been a famous missionary like Billy Graham if he had so wished.

He always dressed immaculately, his beard was trimmed with precision, and the length was *just so.* Mason's hair was large, slicked back with product but not greasy looking, almost like it was stored in a box between Sundays. Each time he encountered his male parishioners, he shook their hand with tailor-made precision. If a man preferred a limp lettuce, they got a limp lettuce. A firm, 'manly' handshake was met by a 'manly' handshake. The more senior men or those that had known him for a long time were treated to a hug with the mandatory pats on their back. All the men were called 'Brother' by Mason. *Make them feel part of the family and I bet they'll toss more coins into the collection tray.*

The women were all hugged and kissed on each cheek, even those who would normally shrink away from personal space invasions. Their partners never objected. Mason had that special skill of making everyone feel special, but he always allowed the person he was talking with to take the lead so his own character wasn't put in the spotlight.

He wore a quite strong aftershave, the odour of which, along with the aura of fame he cloaked himself in, gave him the metaphorical smell of alpha male. That was powerful. Many, if not most of the women in the church were drawn to him in more ways than simply the sense of a Father figure. If he'd made notches on his bed post, it would've looked like the prison wall of a criminal using five strip gates to count the days he'd been inside.

The power of prayer played out each week in his church. Prayer gave him the power to know people's innermost hopes and fears. He wished well for his followers; after all, he had got to know them all reasonably well.

Tithing was one biblical feature that Mason became particularly skilled at ensuring his followers practiced. At one point, not long after he'd become the pastor, he gained a flash of inspiration when a man called Jeff Lucas came to him to ask for prayer. Jeff hadn't been blessed with parents who understood much about money, so he was never taught the basic life skills of handling finances. He had no savings, and seemed to live hand to mouth despite having a decently paying job as the manager of a large book store.

He had the confidence to ask for help from Mason, because the pastor was very approachable, and Jeff felt that his confidential situation wouldn't be compromised by a man of the cloth.

Mason prayed with Jeff for a good twenty minutes before saying, 'Jeff, the Lord is asking me to help you. Come to me tomorrow after work with the last year's bank statements and I will teach you how to manage your money. Is that okay?'

Jeff beamed, delighted that Mason could help. 'Yes, I'll say my child has a dentist appointment so I can knock off a bit early, and then I'll come here. See you then!' He practically skipped out of the room, and skipped back in the next day.

After a good hour working out what was what with Jeff's finances, Mason clicked the end of his Parker pen with a triumphant grin. He said, 'Right. We'll ring round where you owe money to, and I'll negotiate with them to spread your repayments. I see that if you tithe, which is to gift the church ten per cent of your income, as the Bible tells us to, God will bless you. He has given me the gift of being good with money. After the tithe, you will have five hundred pounds per month more in your wallet than you do now. I know that you're afraid of the money lenders, but God is more powerful than an institution of man. So they absolutely *will not* refuse my proposal.'

Mason sat back in his top-of-the-range office chair and grinned widely, making sure that he didn't look smug. Lightheaded with relief and excitement, Jeff said, 'Mason, you are a lifesaver. Honestly, this was getting me down so much. I wasn't sure how much more stress I could take from the credit card people ringing me and sending me so many letters.'

Wow! I'm going to start a course for any other folk struggling with their finances. If I can use tithing to get two grand or more from fifty people, that will be enough to hide leaking money dripping into MY account! I can't see how people could object; they give money to me, well, God really, and they have more money to spend. Okay, this is essential to get the quote right for the sermon.

Sunday that week, after a very loud worship, Mason put his hand in the air and said, 'Thank you. God is loving worship this morning! It is time to talk about money and God's Word. Have you ever wondered what the Bible says about how He wants you, as a disciple of Christ, to handle your money? I won't embarrass anyone, but one of you came to see me this week, and

I helped them to understand about how He requires you, that's right, *requires* you, to look after your pounds and pence. I looked to the Lord with the person. Guess what, people? I worked out how to pay his debts, give ten per cent of his money to this church, and still have *five hundred pounds* more in his pocket at the end of the month. Five hundred pounds, people.' Mason paused, allowing that to sink in. Gasps rang out around the room, and people were shouting, 'Amen!' and 'Thank you, Jesus!'

'All we have to do is to look in the Bible, folks.' Mason paused again, looking around the room and nodding every time he made eye contact with anyone. He took a breath and said, 'Leviticus, chapter twenty-seven, verses thirty to thirty-three. Numbers, chapter eighteen, verses twenty-one to twenty-eight. It also says that tithes were used to meet the needs of foreigners, orphans, and widows. Deuteronomy, twenty-six, verses twelve to thirteen.

'In addition, everyone was to be generous with those in need. If there is a poor man among your brothers in any of the towns of the land that the Lord, your God, is giving you, do not be hardhearted or tight-fisted toward your poor brother. Rather, be open handed and freely lend him whatever he needs. New International Version, Deuteronomy, chapter fifteen, verses seven to eight.' Mason again scanned across the faces in his congregation, looking as many people in the eye as he could.

'It's all there! God has opened my eyes, thanks to my visitor this week. I am going to help each and every person who wants that help. On Tuesday at 6pm, I shall help anyone and everyone who comes to my house.' Looking round, he saw that more heads than he could count were nodding. *This is going to be epic!* As it turned out, more people arrived than his lounge could hold, so he sent half of the attendees home to return the following day.

Over the next week, he printed out around sixty tithe direct debit forms. *Might as well make it as easy as possible for them to give generously!*

Mason hadn't always been a pastor. Truth be told, he wasn't even a firm believer. However, he knew religion had been around for probably as long as people had been on Earth, so it was surely a solid career to follow. Before he went to Bible college, his life was far from holy. *Going into a church should be a great way to escape from the past. I hope I get the chance one day to get revenge on people who crossed me.*

Even now, years after turning his back on his old life, he'd involuntarily laugh or scoff with incredulity that he'd even been accepted into the Church. Of course, he hadn't disclosed his criminal past in his application form. His path had crossed truly dangerous men, gangsters, drug dealers, and all kinds of other shady people.

This is like being a rock star, being a pastor. People are throwing money at me, and women, so many of whom are star-struck, literally throw themselves at me. I don't know why more people don't take it up as a career!

One sunny Sunday, Mason woke up feeling like death. The news had been full of stories of people getting hit with a new mutation of Austrian Flu; he assumed he was one of the casualties. All Mason knew was that he'd never felt this ill before, sweating like an Eskimo in the desert.

After a week or so, the flu itself had gone but other symptoms remained. Mason was beyond knackered all the time, and any exertion wore him out even further. His body could barely move, and he knew there was no chance of making it to church.

Over the next few weeks, he got to know who his friends were; twenty of his followers stayed loyal to him, checking up on how he was each day. One of them, Abbie, slipped into the role of carer for him. For that, he would always be grateful.

The Church was tolerant of his time off, but after a number of months it had become clear that he wasn't going to be well enough to work as a pastor any longer. When a replacement pastor was recruited, he slipped seamlessly into Mason's sermon shoes.

Most of the congregation were happy with the new guy, Donald Sopel, but that small core of loyal worshippers missed Mason terribly. His personality was bold and bright, loud and charismatic. Compared to Donald's thoughtful and discreet ways, the two were like night and day.

The church was in an excellent financial position thanks to Mason, and they compensated him handsomely for his services to see him into as comfortable a retirement as possible.

Getting to the doctors was a challenge for Mason; someone had to drive him and had to use a wheelchair to get him around. Finally, he was diagnosed with fibromyalgia. Mason had not heard of it before, but the doctor provided him with a good amount of information material to learn from.

Being at home alone was fast losing appeal; he felt that he was being wasted and his pastor skills needed to be used.

One day, Abbie sat on a comfortable chair in his lounge and told him she wanted to talk to him. He wondered what on earth she wanted to talk about. *This feels a bit weird.*

She said, 'Mason, the new pastor isn't a patch on you. His sermons are dull, and the excitement for the Holy Spirit just isn't there anymore. I know it would be hard, but might you consider running a church from home? I don't mean attached to the Church of England or anything, just Mason's place of worship. We all miss you so much, being our pastor.' She looked at his astonished face, and misread it. 'I'm sorry. It would be too much, wouldn't it?'

Mason grinned. He hadn't felt a flash of happiness like this for a long time. 'Abbie, you are a bloody genius! This sounds great! Get some other people like Mikey and Pete to come round tomorrow and we'll see what we can sort out.'

And lo; the cult of Mason Grey was born.

Chapter One

Mason Grey sat in his LA Z Boy armchair, watching Bargain Hunt.

I want to hate daytime television.

He breathed out the final pungent cloud of roll-up cigarette smoke. The fumes spiralled to the ceiling; a spider enjoyed the passive smoke.

At 5'5", Mason wasn't very tall; his hands deformed and painful with arthritis. His face sported a large beard which covered a spreading double chin. He most usually wore jogging trousers and a loose t-shirt, which he found to be very comfortable. Normal trousers tended to rub on his hips after a while and make him sore.

He could walk, just a few paces, but didn't go out of his home much. He liked to try and make a joke of it; 'My bins go out more often than I do.'

Agoraphobia had taken hold of him in the last year. Mason couldn't go out for fear of being unable to escape danger; panic attacks crippled him when he remembered how independent he used to be. He would sweat when he thought about going too far from his home.

Mason looked around his comfortable lounge, happy with life despite his tormenting disabilities. It was quite unremarkable, except for a couple of features. The rooms lightly coloured painted walls helped make the room seem larger than it was. The furniture was good looking and comfortable; expensive too.

One wall featured an extra-large oak bookcase. Upon it rested hundreds of books, most of them religious and all of them he'd read. Mason enjoyed turning the corners of the pages; making it clear to his friends that he was always reading.

There wasn't a single book on it that hadn't been read at least twice, most of them many times. There were several bibles of varying interpretations, the pages blackened from overuse. Other books about Hebrew and of the ancient world sat ready for their next reading.

Scattered amongst them, where space allowed, were tens of trinkets; miniature statues of saints, twee quotes on small plaques and several ornate crucifixes. All were souvenirs of Mason's travels, which he looked back on with fond memories.

He remembered a holiday to the south of France often, visiting places nearby and the north of Italy. Monasteries and vineyards summed it up well.

Mason looked out of the practical French doors towards the garden and admired the gardener's handiwork. She had kept the lawn so well that it resembled a golf course green; trees marked the boundaries and the flower beds were stuffed with foliage. He tried to smell the outside aroma, but his cigarette smoke masked the fresh air.

The weather had been nice for two weeks and today was another day of sunshine. There was a pair of pigeons walking around the lawn pecking at the ground, the male one trying to steal bits of food from his partner. Something startled them, and they flapped noisily into a neighbour's tall conifers.

Mason tried to stand, with the ambition of ambling to his patio sofa. He put his hand onto his desk to steady himself. Slowly he rose; his leg muscles screamed with pain and his knees creaked audibly. He felt his back shuddering with unsteadiness.

With a sigh he resigned himself to sitting again. All the willpower in the world couldn't help him, much to his chagrin. He let himself drop to a sitting position, which he regretted when a sharp pain shot up his spine.

The effort of standing had taken the wind out of his sails.

Mason popped a couple of painkillers out of an almost empty strip; opiates were the ones he used the most for the best pain relief. He yelped then cursed when the foil backing sliced his thumb like a paper cut. He licked the wound to stop it bleeding, remembering something about saliva clotting blood. He enjoyed the metallic tang as his tongue lapped at his wound; Mason loved the taste of his own blood.

How can such a small cut sting so much? I'll be feeling that for a while.

To his relief, a packet of assorted size plasters sat within easy reach. They were sat on his notebook along with a pen, already opened so that Mason wouldn't have to struggle to open them when he needed one. Packets like that proved tricky for his arthritic fingers.

With a jolly knock on the front door, and cheery call of 'Hello', a visitor let herself in and breezed into the room.

Abbie Hepburn cared for Mason. She did all the daily chores and never complained, even about washing his smalls. She was devoted to him and had persuaded him to keep preaching from his home. To be fair, that hadn't taken much.

When Mason had been the pastor at the village church, followers came from miles around to hear him speak. Since becoming housebound, Mason had invited twenty parishioners to join him as he launched a new church at his house. It hadn't taken long until he held charismatic authority over them all. He loved the attention and the look of adoration in their eyes.

I might as well be called Jesus by them.

He based his preaching on the bible, but his sermons represented nothing that had been taught in a bible college. Mason loved the ego bolstering that his followers gave to him. As such the church had evolved into a cult, much to his delight. They always gave generously in the collection, many of them providing ten percent of their income tithe plus more on top.

He wanted to create a permanent home for all of the cult members, with a following akin to David Koresh before the Waco siege in 1993. When an old chapel came up for sale, he bought it and his followers adapted it into a home, and place of worship.

Abbie saw herself not only as his carer but also as Mason's deputy. Caring for him had made a bond between them. It wasn't as intense as being lovers, because Abbie held Mason on a pedestal. To cross the line between carer and partner was taboo to her.

Abbie dusted the expansive bookcase and said, 'Mason, you know you should quit smoking.'

Mason glanced across at her, 'I know, I know, but it's the one thing I can enjoy. Having a chronic illness is no fun.'

His attention resumed on watching the television.

'How's your sermon coming along for Sunday?'

Abbie knew this was safer ground, all the attention had been given back to Mason.

Abbie didn't see Mason glance back at his dog eared notebook, 'Almost finished'.'

Mason turned down the volume of the TV, and turned to continue speaking to Abbie. He changed his expression to look more sincere, which he was fond of using; it gave himself more gravitas.

'I've been meditating on the Word of God and fasting this week.'

Abbie's smile lit up her face, 'You are so holy Mason. I love how you keep close to God.'

He lifted his lighter to yet another roll-up that he had put between his lips; the flame flickered mesmerizingly for a brief moment before Mason put the lighter back down on 'the arm of his chair. The tip of the cigarette glowed intensely red as he took a deep drag.

Though his disgust was plain to see, Mason casually asked, 'Abbie, did you see on the news about another paedophile priest from Ireland being sent to prison?'

'Yes, I saw that.'

'Prison is too good for them; they should be handed down a death sentence.'

'I agree, totally. Fancy a cup of tea?'

Mason smiled and his eyes lit up. 'Yes, that would be smashing.'

Abbie stood and walked to the kitchen to make the drinks.

Bringing two steaming mugs of fresh hot Yorkshire tea from the kitchen, Abbie sat down on the large sofa next to his chair, and as close to him as possible, 'Here you are, two sugars just as you like it.' She handed him the cup, which he took happily, and looked him in the eye, 'Please think about quitting smoking, Mason. It's terrible for you.'

Mason knew she was right, but instead of answering or making eye contact, he stared out of the French doors.

'Let's go outside, it's far too nice to be in here. Got to make the most of the sunshine, you know what England is like with its changing weather.'

Abbie was happy. *Great, I thought he would ask me to go home.*

She retrieved Mason's well used wheelchair from the hall, the mechanism was stiff making it difficult to unfold for use. A wheel squeaked as she pushed it over to Mason; it smelled musty from being sat unused for five weeks.

'Thanks.'

'No problem. Why don't you buy an electric one, then you can go in the garden when you like?'

'Maybe, they are expensive though'

'I'll organise a whip round with the congregation, I'm sure that everyone will be happy to contribute'.

"What a good idea, Abbie, get me a blue one please." The rest of the afternoon flew by, with small talk flowing, as did the tea. They must have drunk about seven mugs of the hot beverage each. They didn't talk about anything of consequence, mainly about programmes on the television.

Mason felt exhausted; a crash of energy wiped him out. He was annoyed with his body for being so lethargic after doing nothing strenuous, 'Abbie, I need to go to bed now, the stupid fibromyalgia has caught up with me.'

She smiled with sympathy and pushed him back into the house. 'I've finished the chores; I'll leave you in peace. See you tomorrow, Mason.'

She hoped that Mason would ask her to visit before then.

Mason smiled at her as she left the building, 'Bye. Be careful out there!'

She is a godsend; I don't know what state the house would be in without her. The flock would not appreciate having to do the housework before a service could take place.

Chapter Two

Sunday
Mason's House

Great, everyone has come today. I hope they like my plan. He wanted to shock his followers, to stir up passion and hate.

'God abhors paedophiles.'

The congregation muttered, 'Amen.'

Pete Taylor growled through gritted teeth, 'Bastards should swing!'

At 6′5″ and built like a proverbial outhouse, the words he uttered made the hairs on everyone's arms stand on end.

Mason knew he had the congregation in the palm of his hand, just as he liked it. He spoke with authority, commanding the attention of every person present. He took his time and looked each of them in the eye; he knew they would see and hear only him. Mason had a steely look in his eyes, no one doubted his sincerity. As he turned his head he nodded slightly to each member of the congregation. He made a grim face as if about to deliver terrible news.

'I have been in prayer, worshipping in Tongues, and asking the Holy Spirit for Divine guidance. This is what *He* told me, from *His* word, the Holy Bible.

Fornication is among the 'lusts of the flesh', Galatians chapter 5, verses 16 to 21;' Mason paused and looked at the congregation making sure they were all engrossed in his words, his mouth lifted slightly at the corners with a knowledgeable smile and he nodded as if he knew his words were the truth, "and among the evil things that come from the heart of a man apart from God, Mark Chapter 8, verses 21 to 23." He glanced around the room quickly, wanting to push his speech home. Taking a quick intake of breath he pointed at the ceiling as he said,

"He gave this passage to me: From Romans, chapter 13, verse 4 - For he is the minister of God to thee for good. But if thou do that which is evil, be afraid; for he beareth not the sword in vain: for he is the minister of God, a revenger to execute wrath upon him that doeth evil.' Mason breathed out deeply, the speech seemed to have taken a toll on his emotions, the passion with which he had spoken was palpable. He seemed to sink into his chair a bit as the speech had come to an end.

A hubbub passed round the room; half of those present nodded their heads and uttering "Amen" or "Thank you Jesus", the rest were transfixed by him, their whole concentration focussed on the bearded man

Mason knew how Pete felt about paedophiles, 'Pete, tell me what you think this means.''

Pete growled, 'It couldn't be clearer, Mason. It means, with no doubt whatsoever, that God is asking us to execute his wrath and kill paedophiles.'

Mason nodded his head and gave a grim smile, 'I agree, Pete.'

A murmur rippled around the room. For Mason, time seemed to stand still. *Are they going to think I've gone crazy?*

He took a deep breath and said, 'Let's have a show of hands to see who agrees. There must be unanimous agreement.'

All twenty members present raised a hand. A discernible chill passed through the room, causing everyone to shiver. *What the fuck was that? I hope God isn't showing me that he is pissed off.*

Pressure had built in the room; everyone was in a complete zone of only thinking of and seeing Mason.

'Great, 'now we're like the musketeers – one for all and all for one.' A chuckle rippled through the room, breaking the tension.

The transformation into a killing cult was complete. Mason was both shocked and delighted that it had been so simple to convince the flock. *Maybe my leadership skills are immense.*

He decided that he needed to allow the group to take ownership; to cement in the commitment to summary rough justice.

He smiled with determination and asked, 'Any ideas on what we should do to them?'

I could do with a smoke, I bet Pete does too.

To his surprise, it was Abbie who spoke next. 'The Lord wants us to execute his revenge, let us kill with methods used in the Bible. People will know death was vengeance from Him.'

Another ripple of approval. A frisson passed through everyone, tense energy making each person experience goosebumps. The hair on the back of Mason's neck stood erect, which he assumed was the same for many of the people present.

This is amazing.

'Praise the Lord!' Expressions of worship burst around the room, the volume increasing with each expression of love for their God.

'Thank you Jesus!'

'Pour down your Holy Spirit!'

Mikey 'Taff' Graham strummed his well worn guitar; he was a talented musician. The room seemed full of real joy. The congregation was content to worship and praise for another ten minutes. Everyone was lost in the moment the highly emotionally spiritual energy making them elated.

Some people had their eyes closed and hands held out with their palms facing up to heaven ready to receive whatever their Lord sent to them. Others couldn't keep still; three people had picked up flags and were waving them with vigour.

When the worship naturally lulled, Pete spoke, 'We need a calling card; so everyone is in no doubt that we are doing the work of the Lord.'

Mikey spoke next, with his strong Welsh accent and his blonde hair flopping over his eyes, 'What about those crucifixes on your bookshelf, Mason? There is no stronger image of Christ than the crucifix. Those ones are gorgeous too, whoever finds the bodies will know that a real follower of God has carried out his will. My favourite is the wooden one because Jesus was a carpenter, with the leather cord. When I look at it I really am reminded of the sacrifice that he made for us. '.

Genius, Mikey, wish I'd thought of that. You're a great man.

Mason said in a solemn voice, reflecting the gravitas of the situation, 'Does EVERYONE agree?'

All twenty of the flock nodded as one, some with more enthusiasm than others.

'Maybe we need to make a note to say God abhors paedophiles to leave on the bodies.'

Mikey, you're on fire mate.

'All right, Mikey, good idea. Can I leave that with you?'

Mikey beamed; thrilled to be included in the plans. 'I'd be delighted. It'll be a piece of cake.'

Mikey was 21 years old; Mason thought Mikey was perfect to be moulded into a successor to him. *He's dedicated to the cult; charismatic and good looking like me. Perfect to take over when the time comes.*

'Mason, there are four crucifixes there, are we going to use them all?'

Damn right.

'I think that will be the best thing to do. We must be seen to be determined to follow the wishes of God. Guys, I'm crashing out again. We will have to meet again later this week. My fibromyalgia means that my energy just vanishes at the drop of a hat. How about tomorrow, 7pm?'

All of the congregation nodded, with sympathetic noises being made. 'Oh, bring ideas everyone please'.

As everyone left, Mason thanked them all one by one for coming to the meeting. He knew that doing that, despite feeling even more ill than usual, cemented everyone further into their mission. The quiet of the house compared to how noisy it was when it was full was staggering, it made him feel like his ears were ringing for a while. Mason did like the smell of the house after the church meetings, perfumes lingered for quite a while as did the smell of food, if somebody had brought something like an apple crumble to share with anyone who wanted some. That was quite a regular occurrence.

Stupid illness, we could have got more sorted out.

He reclined in his chair where his feet just about reached the footrest, and slept soundly.

****

Mikey was excited to be included in the emerging plans. He slipped quietly into his house so as to not disturb his father who Mikey knew would be snoozing on the sofa in front of the television. As he expected, the elder man was asleep, with a cold cup of coffee sat on a stained coaster. Mikey smiled affectionately at the slumbering man, his dad had brought him up as a single father since his mother died when he was twelve. *That coffee does smell nice, I'll make us both a fresh one in a bit.*

Mikey stepped as quietly as he could up the stairs to the home office that a spare bedroom had been converted into. On the walls were photos of the family when his mum was alive, he like the school photos a lot because they reminded him of his happy childhood growing up in Wales. The familiar odour of home satisfied him, there is no more comforting smell than your own house.

It took just a few seconds for the computer to fire up, Mikey knew his way around the programmes and made the ransom style note in less than fifteen minutes.

The printer whirred noisily as it woke up and spat out the results of his work.

His dad called up the stairs in a groggy voice, "Hello? Mikey? Is that you, son?"

"No it's the ghost of Newdon, course it's me, Dad!"

"I didn't hear you come in, sorry."

Mikey smiled to himself, pleased that his entry into the home was quiet enough to not wake his dad.

"What you up to anyway?" came the voice from downstairs.

"Just printing off some music notes for church, dad." Mikey's face suddenly felt hot and he felt his body freeze as if he had been caught out doing something he shouldn't be doing, "I'll come down and make a fresh coffee in a minute, your one smells delicious!"

He took care in folding the paper so it didn't crease the note, and slipped it into his wallet.

The rest of the evening was pleasant, Mikey enjoyed spending time with his father as he was a kind hearted man. *If I'm half as great a guy as he is, I'd be happy.*

Mikey realised that the evening was keeping him from thinking too much about what he and the other member's of Mason's church had decided to do, it was easier for him to just think about other things than what he was helping to do. He realised that he was worn out when he was battling his eyelids from closing before 10pm, "Goodnight Dad, I'm knackered,"

"Night night, don't let the bedbugs bite!"

Mikey laughed at his dad, "I'm 21 you know, no need to talk about the bed bugs."

"You're never too old," Laughed his dad, and Mikey walked away, shaking his head a small amount with amusement at how his dad always said the same things to him.

Chapter Three

Mikey made a tray of hot drinks for everyone who wanted one Mason had made more of an effort in his appearance than on a usual Sunday, and was dressed in a plain dark blue suit instead of casual trousers and a loose fitting shirt.

'How are you feeling, Mason?'

'Good today, thanks for asking. I'm determined that we can all come up with a plan to erase paedophiles.'

Pete opened a packet of chocolate digestive biscuits and took a couple before passing them to his neighbour, 'Don't worry Mason, by the end of the evening we'll know what we're doing. We have enough muscle power'

Abbie chipped in with a laugh, 'We need brains *and* brawn, Pete.'

Pete winked at her, 'Good job we have you then, love,'

A chuckle rippled throughout the room; Mason noted that the flock seemed as relaxed in the company of each other like any other Sunday.

Mason cleared his throat and spoke in an authoritarian tone, 'Is everyone ready? We are here to make a plan on how to execute God's will.'

Twenty expectant faces looked at him waiting to hear what he was about to say.

He sipped from a glass of cold water, and relished the refreshment before asking, 'Mikey, how have you got on with making a note to put with each crucifix?'

Mikey handed Mason an A4 sheet which he took out of his wallet and unfolded, 'Here, Mason, this is what I've come up with.'

On it, in the style of an old ransom note, was written: ''

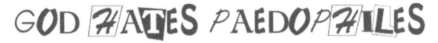

'Mikey that's great. Short and to the point'.'

Mason handed the note to Abbie, who looked at it and nodded. She passed it on to her neighbour, who in turn nodded and passed it on, until it had made its way around to everyone and back to Mason. The atmosphere in the room was solemn; the joviality had slipped away, a couple of people were wriggling a little as though their nerves were stopping them from keeping still

Jesus, Mikey could have written anything and they would all agree. I suppose that is a good thing, too much time could be wasted on little details like this.

Abbie broke the silence with a quiet cough to bring attention to herself. 'I've been looking online to find targets.''

Mason encouraged her with a nod of his head, 'Go on.'

Her face flushed deep red with a mixture of embarrassment at being the centre of attention, and hate towards the targets. 'We have four crucifixes; 'four targets. I found a Facebook page that shows what paedophiles have been released from prison. There's a few who live near here; there are four in the Newdon area.'

Pete spoke after Abbie, in a rough voice, 'We can easily find out where they live, by looking on the electoral roll. Abbie, did you make a note of their names?'

She passed a piece of paper to Pete, 'I have them here.'

'Thanks. Obviously, Mason can't take a practical part in the eliminations, so I'll be in charge of that. If that's ok, Mason'?'

Mason nodded in agreement. *Excellent, Pete, I need not nominate anyone now.*

Pete looked at the names and growled them out, 'Ian Murray, Jack Barker, Ed Miles and Dave Harvey. Has anyone heard of these people before? It might make it easier if we know something about them beforehand."

Not one person put their hand up, shaking heads filled the large room as people looked at each other. Some of them shrugged and a blast of chatter flowed for a few seconds while it became clear that these people all seemed to be unknown to them all.

Mason picked up his notebook and made a show of writing each name in it. His eyes lit up with a purposeful glint as he wrote, even though his arthritic hands looked to be stiff. It seemed to Mason that Abbie, Pete, and Mikey were the keenest to take a lead.

'All right everyone. I think Abbie, Pete and Mikey should be in a small group to take care of each target. Everyone agree?'

A murmur of consent echoed round the room. Heads nodded and Jane Davidson clapped her hands. Spontaneously, everyone in the room clapped too, in a crescendo of noise escalated by some cheers

Genius! The trash will be disposed of soon. Mason was feeling exhausted again, but didn't want to lose the momentum of the meeting. With a deep sigh he tapped the side of his mug several times with a spoon making a loud tinging noise.

'Ladies and gentlemen. I'm handing over to Abbie for half an hour; I need to take a break.'

With no further ado he pulled on a black lever and his chair reclined into a very relaxed almost horizontal position. Mason soon fell into a light but essential slumber.

****

Abbie took over the meeting with confidence. Clearing her throat she commanded attention, 'Let's get organised. First, we need to find where the targets live. Maybe me and Jane could volunteer ourselves for this task?" Jane nodded determinedly, the two women looked round the room to lots of confident smiles.

Pete had a cheeky smile, he winked at Mikey and said, "I'm sure that these two can manage to be nosy enough to find out where they live…"

Mikey smirked, as did a few of the other men at the sexist banter. Jane pointed at him with mock indignation, "How very dare you Pete? Ok, I think you are right."

It was a wonder that the laughter that came from the room didn't wake Mason.

Abbie relished being the unofficial second in command. It was an occurrence each week that Mason needed to rest for a while during the Sunday meetings.

'I suggest that we look to the Holy Bible. There is no mention of people being killed for specifically being a paedophile; however, we cannot allow that to dishearten our resolve.'

A solemn air returned to the room, nods moving most heads present.

'The Bible has quite a few examples of killing. Does everyone think we should use those to make it clear that it's God's wrath?'

Mikey chimed in, his Welsh tones soothing the harsh ideas into an acceptable proposal. 'Abbie... everyone... I've made a list of four practical killings. Although, personally, I would like to crucify them, we wouldn't be able to do it.'

A positive and happy laugh spread through the flock, which to an observer would seem surreal.

Abbie nodded her agreement and encouraged him, 'Go on, Mikey, tell us what you have found.'

'Leviticus, chapter 20, verse 27; death by stoning. That one is easy as long as we make sure that the paedo can't run away. I'm sure that they were buried up to their waist first and I believe that they still kill people that way in the Middle East'.

Judges, chapter 4, verse 21 a tent peg was driven through the victim's temple until it went into the ground. Kind of gory, but sounds great fun as long as we remember a mallet

Judges, chapter 3, verse 12, a sword driven in so far that the handle was hidden in fat; that seems messy but not too hard to do.

Leviticus, chapter 21, verse 9, burned to death; again easy but will stink of cooking flesh.'

Mikey looked out of the French doors into the garden, where light rain had started to drizzle, 'This is serious guys, if we get caught we're in deep trouble. We'll be incarcerated 'til we're ancient. Anybody want to back out?'

The tension in the room had become palpable; Pete wriggled on his chair, which in turn made everyone fidgety. He looked round the room, into each person's eyes for a few seconds. Some seemed determined, some afraid, some steely, but not one person looked as though they wanted to back out.

In his, unmistakeable, Yorkshire accent, Pete broke the silence of the room, 'Right folks, we have the targets, and how to kill them. I reckon we should have a brew, before working out how to execute the plan.'

With his words the tension lifted and Mikey chimed in, 'I shall write the relevant verse on the bottom of each note, too.'

Pete was impressed and smiled at Mikey, 'Another good idea, mate.'

Abbie had a smirk on her face, her eyes lit up and she waved one arm to grab everyone's attention. Pete wiped a trickle of sweat from his forehead, "God, it does get hot in here with all these bodies. What's up Abbie?" He looked at her with curiosity.

"Mason has asked me to sort out getting an electric wheelchair for him in blue. I bet he doesn't think that we'll be able to sort it out without him knowing about it." More or less everyone was smiling and laughing, Abbie lifted a finger to her lips, "Shush guys, let's not wake him up!"

Mikey laughed with affection, "Not even that earthquake from a few weeks ago woke him up, when he is asleep he may as well be a rock for how much life he has in him," he grinned, obviously pleased with his description of Mason.

Abbie scratched the top of her head, and the grin of happiness couldn't be suppressed, "I think if we all chip in a hundred quid then we'll get a decent one for him. Let's keep it a surprise though."

She grinned even wider when it became clear that this wasn't going to be an issue, some people were digging into their purses or wallets and handing a bundle of cash to her. A quiet man who always sat at the back of the room on his own put his hand in the air which amazed Abbie, "Yes Ronald?"

"What's your paypal details please? I can contribute two hundred and fifty quid,"

"That is super generous of you," Abbie grinned, her face flushing with happiness and relief that the congregation had fulfilled her expectation that getting a wheelchair for Mason that he could use by himself to get into the garden had been fulfilled.

Jane eagerly put her hand in the air, and wriggled with excitement like a child being told she can have some sweets, "Abbie, my sister in law works in the mobility shop in Newdon town centre. I'll get her to sort it out with a staff discount so we can get Mason the best spec we can. He deserves it afterall."

Abbie seemed a bit non plussed by this, *I never knew that you have a sister in law, every day is a* school *day.*

****

Abbie spoke softly 'Here, Mason, have a cuppa, love.'

He awoke and smiled, his eyes struggled to focus; the glasses that were perched on the end of his nose didn't exactly help him to see.

I must pluck up the courage to go to the opticians. I could always get Abbie to take me there. Mason saw the enormous mug of tea, and smiled with gratitude as he knew it would be just how he liked it. The drink smelled perfect.

'Thanks, Abbie. What's happened while I grabbed some beauty sleep?' Abbie brought him up to speed. Mason had felt the plan had taken on a life of it's own.

Jane raised her manicured hand in the air. *I'm surprised that she's taking part so much tonight; she's usually as quiet as a church mouse.*

'Yes, Jane, what would you like to say?'

'Mason, I think we should take out one a week to put the fear of God, pardon the pun, into other paedophiles. Maybe starting on the next Saturday.'

'Fabulous idea Jane, thank you. It's no good just talking, we need actions. Doing it a week apart means it should be easier to plan, too.'

Jane hadn't finished, and interrupted Mason in eagerness. 'Mason, while whoever is going to do the... err... eliminating, the rest of the church should meet and pray hard that the attacks are successful, and that the executors keep safe and return back unharmed'.

The congregation, as one, nodded and voiced their agreement. Calls of 'Amen' echoed around the room, some even clapping.

'Thanks, Jane, wonderful idea. Prayer cover is essential, and will help the executors because they will know they have God beside them.'

Pete interposed, 'Listen, Mason, I think me, Mikey, Abbie, Jane and you should meet tomorrow to talk in more detail about the nitty-gritty. Everyone else should keep praying for God's blessing for our mission. We should all get together on Friday to praise him, ready for Saturday. What do you think?'

Mason passed his gaze over Mikey, Abbie and Jane, and asked them in unspoken words if they agreed.

They nodded in unison. 'Then it's agreed.'

Mason wrapped up the meeting by speaking loudly, "Thank you everyone for coming," He placed his hands together as if he were praying, "Please remember to pray throughout the week, that is really important." There was excited chatter, people were standing and stretching themselves before putting their coats on. Five minutes later and his home was, once more, empty of visitors. He took several deep breaths, before draining his mug of tea. *I wish I could drink something a bit stronger; I think I need a stiff drink.*

Abbie and Jane were the last two to leave the house, it always seemed to be the way for the past few months that no one else stayed longer.

Jane was a faster walker, and was soon at her car door.

Abbie suddenly remembered that her and Jane were to find out the addresses of the men that were going to die in the next few weeks. She trotted after Jane, "Hang on, when do you want to meet up to find out where the guys live?"

Jane smirked, which Abbie found odd, "Don't worry about it; my cousin is a cop and I'll ask her to find out."

"Really? I'm sure that they aren't allowed to look up people's details without good reason or they'll be in big trouble,"

"My cousin will find a way, don't worry. I didn't mention it in there because I just thought it would be better that way," *More like I'm good at improvisation,* "I'll call you if there's an issue."

Jane looked at Abbie as if she was daring the other woman to suggest another course of action. Abbie looked away first and fidgeted with her fingers, "Alright, if not then I'll see you here on Tuesday,"

With a nod and tight smile, Jane slithered into her car and closed the door.

Abbie cast her eyes at the pavement and kept walking to her vehicle, *that was a bit weird, I've never known her to be bossy like that before.*

Chapter Four

The doorbell chimed a cheerful tune. Jane, Mikey, Pete and Abbie entered the house in a quiet line. Abbie went straight to the kitchen and switched on the, limescale encrusted, kettle and put a tea bag in five matching mugs. A splash of milk followed, accompanied by a spoon of sugar' but just for the men, she remembered that Jane didn't like sugar in her tea. Abbie was well known amongst the church for having a fabulous eye for the smallest of detail.

Everybody else sat in contemplative silence; there was no need for small talk. Mason put a hand rolled cigarette to his lips, lit it and took a long drag. The smoke exhaled upwards towards the ceiling. *At least no one is asking me to put it out.*

Abbie handed out the cups of tea, before taking her seat in a comfortable arm chair. He peered at the other people, "Abbie, are you available to take me to the opticians in a couple of weeks?"

"Sure, Mason, that's no problem at all. I'll always help you where I can."

Mason nodded his thanks, and then said, 'Thank you all for coming today. I thought it would be difficult to get anybody to volunteer for the task in hand. Thank you all for proving me wrong.'

He opened his notebook at the page where he wrote each target's name. 'Ian Murray, Jack Barker, Ed Miles and Dave Harvey.'

Mason took a big swig of his tea, relishing the heat being introduced into his body and running towards his stomach. His fibromyalgia meant that his normal body temperature was only 35.6 Celsius, and he often felt chilly, even having to wear two pairs of socks at the same time quite regularly. The pause would give his words more drama after when he spoke again. He'd been speaking in public for as long as he could remember so knew all the tricks of the trade.

'Death by stoning; a tent peg driven through the target's temple until it goes into the ground; a sword driven in so far that the handle is hidden in fat; and finally burning to death.'

'Anyway, what order are we going to kill them in?'

Pete pulled his sweater arms into shape, 'I think we should just kill them in the order in which they are written. 'It's simple and avoids the headache of creating some sort of order.'

After a few moments of thought, not to mention frowns as they all thought about what Pete had just said, everyone present smiled and nodded their agreement, no one could think of a good reason to disagree. There was a feeling of relief in the air that a task could have easily taken a long time to try and decide upon had in fact had a simple solution.

Jane said, in between sips of her tea, 'I agree, let's do that; kill them in the order of methods written down.'

Mason grinned, 'Right, that's decided then. This is turning out to be a straightforward affair.'

Good job that I won't be actually doing the crime. I doubt I could do any of them, I'm too squeamish. Think of all the blood and the stench of death, too – if they shit themselves it'll be even worse

The atmosphere was positive, like they were talking about doing the accounts and not the impending murder of several people. *One for all and all for one,* Mason concluded.

Abbie collected the still warm empty mugs and Mason heard them tinkle together as she put them into the washing up bowl.

'Abbie, leave them and come and sit down. This meeting is vital.'

She sighed, return to her seat and sat down with her eyes cast towards the floor, 'When will it start, Mason? Who's actually going to do the deed? I don't think I will have the stomach for it.'

Mason gave her with sympathetic look, 'Don't worry, you can help lead prayers here, if you like.'

The expression on her face brightened and Mason thought she seemed happier, but something in her eyes made him feel she wanted to do more., 'No, Mason, I will go and play my part'. Her posture improved and she seemed to sit up straight as if she was proving to herself how determined she was.

Pete spoke next, 'I'm up for it. Are you Mikey and Jane?'

Mikey and Jane did not hesitate for even the briefest of moments and agreed too, nodding with enthusiasm.

Mason stroked his beard, 'So, next Saturday we will stone Ian Murray to death. I'll send a group message to all the church members, asking if anyone else wishes to take part later.''

With an excited smile that showed in his voice, Mikey agreed, 'Good idea, it's not going to be easy. We need some muscles to dig the hole and throw the rocks.''

'Fair point, Mikey. I'll message them now.'' Mason opened a messenger app on his brick-like mobile phone and sent a request for anybody who wanted to help to meet at his house on Saturday at 7pm. He added that everyone must come anyway to pray, if they were not going to take part. His phone repeatedly pinging and vibrating almost off the arm of the chair as the members of his flock replied. Within twenty minutes, every member had confirmed their attendance. . Mason rolled another cigarette; the edges of his index and middle finger yellowed from continuous nicotine. His hands seemed to tremble a touch as he lifted it up to his mouth.

Mason watched as Pete took a packet of cigarettes out of his shirt breast pocket. He seemed to briefly look at the graphic image on the front of the packet. 'Sod it; you never know when you are going to die anyway. Might get hit by a bus tomorrow. Shit, at least it's not us getting stoned to death on the weekend.'

Macabre laughter, well known to go with black humour, filled the room as did the acrid smell of cigarettes

Jane pushed her collar length mousey hair behind her ears. Determination filled her normally defeatist looking eyes, 'How are we going to do it?'

A pregnant pause filled the air. Mason and Pete took synchronised deep drags of their cigs, neither man wanted to look at anyone else, Mason coughed a hacking smoker's cough and looked out into the garden. Pete appeared to be examining something on the sole of his shoe as he had his legs crossed

Abbie looked at the floor, feeling determined but out of her depth. She started to bite her bottom lip, absentmindedly and her eyebrows knitted together. Mikey rubbed his face and eyes, covering them with his hand.

Pete grinned and tapped the side of his large nose with a Cumberland sausage-like finger. 'I have a cunning plan'.

Mikey and Abbie smiled and they looked at each other exchanging a glance of relief that Pete had come up with an answer. Mason smiled, 'Alright, Pete Blackadder, you can be team leader on this mission. More tea, Abbie?'

****

Fifteen minutes later, and the plan was complete. Mikey stood and strolled over to the large bookcase. He picked up one of the crucifixes and crossed himself. Something that he had never done before, but felt the right thing to do.

Mason shivered, 'Someone just walked over my grave.'

****

I wonder if God is telling me something.

'Here's your tea, Mason. Get it down your neck; it'll help you keep warm.'

The friends simply sat peacefully, enjoying their drinks. There was an air of calmness, now that the fine details had been ironed out.

Mason broke the quiet, 'This is going to be amazing guys. I can't see how we could be caught. It's the perfect crime; we will rid the streets of paedophiles, so no one will care.' He smiled smugly and absentmindedly ran his fingers through his beard.

The others simply nodded, smiled and looked out of the open French door at the sunset. A murmuration of starlings formed in the near distance and danced mesmerizingly in the darkening sky. Soon after, they roosted in the trees, in a cacophony of noise.

Chapter Five

Every time a meeting was called at the church, every single member would arrive within ten minutes of each other. Today was no exception; there was an air of excitement that seemed to flow from everyone. Chatter and laughter filled the air.

Mason spoke in a loud voice to open the gathering. 'Folks, thank you all for coming on this important evening. Let us pray together for our amazing volunteers.'

Whispers of 'Amen' made their way round the room.

'Heavenly Father, we pray that you will give Pete, Mikey, Abbey and Jane, your divine protection tonight as they execute your will. Bless them with courage, Amen.'

Once again the room echoed to the sound of many more 'Amen's'.

The team were feeling confident, excited even. With relish, Mikey said, 'I have the crucifix and note in my pocket in a food bag I've made sure that there are no fingerprints on either thing. I've been so excited waiting for this night to come.'

Positive noises from the rest of the congregation filled the room, the atmosphere buzzing.

Pete lit a cigarette and puffed out a well crafted smoke ring. Mason followed his lead and lit up a roll up.

Abbey tutted at the two smokers and shook her head in mock anger before opening the French doors to let some fresh air in. Both Pete and Mason chuckled at this.

I'm glad that I don't need to worry about laws in the workplace.

Abbey nodded over to Mikey.

What are they up to? Hope they haven't been thinking, their brains will overheat. Mikey walked out of the doors, and vanished around the corner. *Curiouser and curiouser; I hope he isn't taking his eye off the ball.* Mason heard a door open from the driveway, a few unfamiliar noises and then a door closing. A sense of excitement permeating the air in the room. 'Mason, close your eyes,' ordered Jane.

She is never bossy. I had better do as I'm told. He closed his eyes tightly, still trying to smoke his cigarette but missing his mouth and nearly setting fire to his beard.

Abbie admonished him with a motherly tone. 'Mason! That has to be Fibro brain fog, trying to smoke with your eyes closed.'

Mason chuckled, he was' used to doing strange things because of the cognitive impairment that fibromyalgia brings. Putting the tea bags in the fridge was a recent one, as was making a cup of coffee without boiling the kettle first

Jane's was the next voice that Mason heard, 'Open those blue eyes, Mason'.

He did as he was told. A brand new, blue, electric wheelchair was sat in the centre of the room. Mason was speechless, a rare occurrence indeed.

'What do you think, Mason?'

'It's amazing, Abbey!'

'I told you that we'd have a whip round. It takes weight up to 20 stone so you will be fine.'

Yeah, only just though. Maybe I should go on a diet.

'Thank you all, I am humbled by your kind donations. I hope that a driving test isn't required.'

Brief laughter was followed by a ripple of applause which pulsed around the room. With a smile Mason changed the subject. *Going out? I hope I can avoid it; I can't cope with crowds.*

'Ok folks, I think it is time for the amigos to go and fight the good fight.'

Pete agreed, 'It's time to go.' The man-mountain stood and the other three followed suit. The small group filed out of the building without further ado, and closed the door with a soft click.

Mason looked around the room, he asked in a quiet voice, 'Is everyone feeling alright?'

All of the remaining members nodded, a few even smiled. None of the remaining worshippers had wished to take part in the killings.

'I think we should have quiet, personal time with the Lord. Pray as you feel you need to pray, we need to give prayer cover to our brave warriors.'

The congregation murmured approvingly. Some made small groups of between two and four people, others sat on their own, deep in contemplation and prayer.

Chapter Six

Mikey's van
9pm

The friends sat quietly inside the anonymous white van which smelled of Pete's sweat. Mikey had affixed false number plates, just in case someone reported suspicious behaviour to the police. Jane had changed into a Newdon Pizza Palace uniform, out of sight in the rear compartment. Abbie exited the van, and went into the pizza shop.

'It's getting very real now, are we all sure that we are doing God's will?' Asked Mikey.

Pete nodded, 'Yes, it's time.'

Abbie had made sure that her face was hidden from the CCTV camera, by wearing an oversize hat. She kept her eyes down and her head low, so the only thing that the camera saw was her petite frame.

'Ham and pineapple, small thin crust, please'

No point spending loads of money on a decoy. It smells nice in here, it's making me hungry.

Ten minutes later, she clambered back into the van, 'Ready?'

The others answered as one, 'Ready.'

Pete, with a low voice laden with menace stated, 'Ian Murray is going to be meeting his maker soon. Mikey, empty out the snatch bag, I want to make sure you all know what to do.'

Mikey took out all of the items and looked through them again, for the twentieth time that day. 'Collapsible shovel, gloves, towing rope, a blindfold, four balaclavas, a gag and gaffer tape.'

Pete gave his approval with a nod. 'Good job that Ian is a Billy-no-mates, so this will be a doddle.'

Abbie, with a slight hint of doubt in her voice, agreed. 'I hope so. I have watched his house a few times over the last couple of days, no-one but him goes in and out of it. I'm glad that Jane's cousin is in the police and got the address for us.'

"That was a good idea petal, I don't remember anyone talking about checking out the targets. How did we not think of that?" Pete shook his head in wonder, as it dawned on him that maybe the plans weren't as thorough as he thought.

"Yes, thanks Abbie it's a good job that we have you on the team," Gushed Mikey, smiling widely at her.

"It's ok lads, I just want to get it right for Mason." She blushed and looked out of the window to try and hide her embarrassment.

"Ooh Abbie and Mason sitting in a tree k-i-s-s-i-n-g!" Grinned Mikey, Pete laughed along and ruffled Abbie's hair.

"Piss off Mikey," She mumbled and pulled her hood over her head to hide from the men.

****

Five minutes later, the van coasted to a halt several metres from Ian Murray's home. The brakes squeaked a fraction, but sounded much louder than it actually was to the occupants. Pete fastened his jacket to the top then put on a Balaclava, and baseball cap, before pulling the hood of his jacket over his head. A look in the rear view mirror satisfied him that his identity was safe from the prying view of any CCTV cameras or neighbours. With a twinge of butterflies in his stomach, he got out of the van. Slowly he made his way towards Ian's home. A temptation to look at his mobile phone made his hand delve into his jeans pocket. The screen glare would be too risky; a covert as possible approach was essential. He didn't want all their hard work to go to waste.

In the van, Abbey slipped over into the driver's seat. She keenly kept her eyes trained on her companion walking away from the vehicle. Mikey put the snatch bag onto his knees. The weight of it felt several times heavier than it actually was. It was like the weight of the world was on him.

Pete walked past the target's home. The blinds were closed, illuminated by the light that shone in the living room. He quickly turned into Ian's drive and pressed himself into deep shadow by the front door. Abbey started the van, and keeping the lights turned off, parked right outside Ian's home.

Here we go.

Mikey and Jane alighted through the same door to minimise noise. Mikey joined Pete in the deep shadow. Jane pulled down her hat to hide her eyes in case there are any CCTV cameras, even though Abbie had checked during the week and spotted none.

She walked up to the front door and using the brass door knocker, knocked with a rat-a-tat-tat. She didn't hear footsteps, but she did hear a bolt being opened and keys turning in the lock. The door opened slightly, with the chain engaged. An uncertain male voice came from behind the door. 'Hello?'

Jane said in a confident voice, 'Pizza for Ian.'

She stepped to the left of the door, so that Ian would see her and her friendly smile.

Ian released the chain and stepped forward. 'I'm sorry, young lady, but I haven't ordered any pizza. This is quite extraordinary.'

He smiled softly at Jane; who thought that he seemed to be a quiet and thoughtful man.

They say it's the quiet ones you have to watch.

'Can I use your loo, please?'

'Of course my dear,' he said, stepping aside, 'it's at the top of the stairs.'

Jane handed the pizza over then went up the stairs, whilst the men remained hidden in the deep shadows. Ian walked away from the door towards the kitchen, happy that a Good Samaritan had bought him a pizza. In the kitchen, he opened the fridge door and gave a rueful smile at the lack of food inside it. After selecting mayonnaise and closed the door softly, he looked at the pizza with satisfaction, and walked back into his lounge.

Ian didn't expect to see Jane, or the two balaclava clad men that were standing in his lounge. The shorter of the two said in a surprisingly camp Welsh accent, 'Come with us. Now! We can do this the easy way, or the hard way.'

Ian considered running past them but knew that resistance was futile He nodded his elderly head in defeat, as the colour drained from his face. Despite the house being chilly that evening, a bead of sweat appeared on his forehead. The television was till on, although electricity being wasted was the least of Ian's worries.

Pete grabbed hold of Ian with a strong grip, who pleaded in a a weak voice, 'Please, that hurts.'

Pete said nothing in return, instead fixing his hardened glare onto Ian's frightened, teary eyes. 'Rope.' Pete demanded with a grunt''

Mikey retrieved the rope quickly and bound Ian's wrists together tightly. *Good job Pete didn't do that; he would have cut the circulation off.*

Abbey decided that she couldn't bear the terrified look in Ian's eyes any longer. 'Mikey, put the blindfold on him. He shouldn't see where we are going'.

The Welshman did as he was asked, without hesitation. Abbey walked out of the house, and looked up and down the street to make sure that there were no prying eyes. The coast was clear.

The trio bundled Ian towards the van. He was very afraid; being bound and blindfolded, he semi-walked and semi-stumbled towards the vehicle. The painful sound of a shin slamming into the side of the van made everyone pause momentarily, before throwing the man into the back. Ian whimpered, but got no sympathy. He didn't ask for help because he knew that he wouldn't get any.

Mikey closed the rear door with a quiet click, to lessen any chance of anyone hearing an unfamiliar noise. They 'didn't want to risk a keen neighbour nosing around where they were not welcome.

Tension inside the vehicle was palpable; body odours and perfume cloying. The journey was silent. Ian was far too afraid to speak, and prayed silently to himself. Abbie expertly drove in a way that did not draw attention.

She spoke half to the others, and half to herself, 'Don't want to get stopped, it would be hard to explain.'

Jane chuckled, 'We won't get stopped; we have God on our side'.'

Nothing was said after that and they all continued on in silence.

After fifteen minutes, Abbie brought the van to a standstill and applied the handbrake. The engine pinged as it cooled in the still, warm summer air. There was still a modicum of daylight.

'Get the shovel.' Pete said coldly to Mikey.

In the blink of an eye, the Welshman got the shovel from the snatch bag. He quickly assembled it and handed it to Pete. Mikey then reached into his coat pocket and pulled out a GoPro video camera.

'Abbie, make sure you video the dirty paedo being slaughtered. We'll have the proof to show everyone in the church ,and we'll have to work out how to email it to other paedophiles when they come to our attention so they see what will happen to them if we track them down"

'Fantastic idea, just make sure none of us make a starring appearance,.' Jane added, her growing confidence surprising Abbie.

Dark horse is Jane. I thought she only came to church and knitted teddy bears for the hospital. How she came across, coming out of Mason's the other day scared me too. Something's a bit strange there.

They stopped at a local country park, which was usually the scene of pleasurable times. The trees stood guard to the woodlands, protecting Mother Nature. Tall, dark shadows blanketed the ground. Recent rain had made the pleasant woodland smells even fresher. Mikey and Pete walked through the car park to the nearest path.

'Mikey, we need to be out of sight of the car park, but not too far in case we have to carry the old boy."

They come across a barbecue area, after walking for two or three minutes. 'Perfect, Pete. There's plenty of space to get rid of his last breath here. Do you mind digging the hole? I think it will take me twice as long as you.'

Pete grinned, a glint lighting up his eyes. 'Give me the shovel.'

Mikey pulled the shovel from his bag, and handed it to Pete. 'Tell you what Mikey. While I dig, you can find some rocks to throw at Ian. Put them on that picnic table.'

He pointed to a nearby table; trestle construction, dark brown in colour, and a bit unsteady on it's legs. Someone had scratched graffiti into the wood. Actually hundreds of people had; "I ♥ U 4eva, Matt", "luvs Cock, Fuck" and the inevitable mobile phone numbers just a very small sample of people's scribes.

Mikey was keen to complete his task, and soon had an impressive pile of stones of various sizes piled on the table. With barely a bead of sweat troubling his forehead, Pete finished digging a hole with a flourish.

He winked at Mikey, 'Let's go and get the paedo, boyo.'

Twenty minutes later, Pete and Mikey pushed their blindfolded and wrist bound prey into the hole.

'What the hell is going on?' Ian defiantly shouted, although a tremor in his voice gave away his fear.

'Stay where you are and it'll all be ok.' Abbie said in a soothing voice.

Her words seemed to reassure him, for a moment at least, until cold and damp earth covered his feet and legs to the knees. He tried to step up, but the earth proved too heavy and anchored him down

Jane laughed at him cruelly, 'Stop trying to escape, old man. It isn't going to work.'

The wind visibly left Ian's sails. His shoulders dropped, his body relaxed to the point of collapse. The earth was up to his chest, heavy and threatening to arrest his breathing. Pete stopped shovelling the earth, and carefully folded the tool before giving it to Mikey to stow away in the bag.

'Make your peace with the Lord God Almighty, you are about to pay the price for attacking kids. There is no place on the planet for paedos.' Jane sneered.

She bent down and whispered to him, 'I'm going to enjoy killing you, Ian. You're going straight to hell.' She removed Ian's blindfold, with a flourish.

He looked confused and terrified. 'You've made a terrible mistake. I'm not a paedophile. You have the wrong man." His voice gained a fragile strength, on the edge of an imminent breakdown.

The so-called 'God's Messengers' looked at each other; disgust etched upon each of their features. Mikey nodded almost imperceptibly to Abbie, who raised the GoPro and activated it; pointing the lens at Ian. He had a blank look in his eyes; resigned to imminent death. Jane cast the first stone with ferocious heft, which struck Ian with terrific velocity in the ear

Rounders practice has come in handy.

Ian was totally unable to defend himself, buried up to his chest in the earth. His last conscious moment had come; ended by the second rock, hurled by Pete. With a sickening noise, the rock smacked Ian between his eyes. His nose shattered, and his skull fractured. Blood sprayed across the picnic area, decorating the table and dog shit bin in vivid crimson.

With just the third rock, Mikey delivered the fatal blow.

Abbey turned off the camera and gave it to Mikey. She had turned a very pale colour, sat on the table and muttered, 'Thank God that's over.'

Mikey smiled at her, humourlessly. He retrieved a food bag and a pair of petrol station plastic gloves from his bag. The gloves easily pulled onto his hands, the knot in the bag proved a bit trickier. He ripped the bag open, and pulled out the note and crucifix. Mikey put the bag into his pocket, then stuffed the crucifix and note into Ian's shirt breast pocket.

'Good work, Mikey.' Abbie said with palpable relief.

He smiled a tight smile; his lips barely rose beyond the horizontal. A murder of crows cawed in the trees, making the scene even more gruesome. They flapped ominously; the branches and leaves shook noisily when they flew away.

The killers walked away from their victim and didn't look back at him.

'At least some kids are safer now that vermin is dead.' Pete growled.

The others joined in, trying to justify their act, 'He deserved it.'

'I wish we could have done it sooner,' were among the some of the words uttered.

The drive back to Mason's house was done in silence; the initial adrenaline surge had ebbed.

****

'Is it done?' There was no need for Mason to elaborate.

Mikey nodded and brought the brutal stoning up onto Mason's flat screen television.

The sound of rocks striking Ian's skull filled the comfortable room. Ultra High Definition had captured the separation of scalp from skull deliciously. Gasps filled the air. No one was able to wrestle their eyes away from the screen. Shock and disgust turned into euphoria; adoration feted on the warriors of rough justice. The remainder of the evening passed by in a blur, wine flowed freely as did the chatter.

As the clock chimed midnight, the last supporter bade the warriors of Godfarewell.

'Thank you all.' Mason praised. His eyes were red raw from being rubbed many times, fighting fatigue, 'Mikey, rest tonight, this will exhaust you all mentally and physically, alright?.'

The young Welshman simply nodded; exhaustion descended upon the assembled group.

Abbey looked at Jane, 'Come to mine on Monday, to start to plan for next week?'

'I'll be there at ten. Banana bread is in a tin ready.'' The ordinary arrangement was an extraordinary juxtaposition to the subject at hand. *Maybe I imagined some kind of friction between Jane and me.*

Mason slowly and painfully arose from his chair. 'Good night, see you all here on Thursday at 7 pm.'

Pete offered his elbow to support him, which Mason gratefully accepted.

Pete, Mikey, Jane and Abbie left Mason's house and went their separate ways, into the night.

****

Monday.

9am Abbie's house, Jane arrived on time with the promised banana bread. She knocked on the door, which Abbie opened within three seconds.

Jane smiled with seemingly genuine warmth, which caught Abbie off guard, "Hi Jane, come in. I saw you walking from your car, that's why I opened the door so soon after you knocked."

Handing the food across to Abbie, Jane grinned with a dramatic wave of her hand, "My famous banana bread,"

"It smells delicious!" Abbie almost drooled as she took in a deep breath savouring the smell.

Jane had a twinkle in her eye, "I've made Mason some for after church later. He's asked me if I'd like to stay afterwards, how could I say no? I like him a lot."

That statement took Abbie by total surprise, and her jaw dropped open for a moment before she regained her composure, "Do you? I wonder if he knows, wow this is exciting,"

She had better stay away from him, he's mine. Shit, he's not mine, this is awkward.

Jane smirked, looking like the cat who had got the cream, "If he doesn't know yet, then I'm sure he will do in no time. I think he's only asked me to stop behind because he feels sorry for me being a quiet old spinster,"

Abbie made a noise somewhere between shock and amusement at what Jane had just said.

Damn I need to change the subject, I haven't felt jealous like this for donkey's years.

"Right. Let's have a think about how we can find out what we can do about Jack..."

Jane squinted and looked out of the window, "We know where he lives, so we could go and scope him out. He is a lot younger than Ian though, so he might be away over the weekend. Let's look him up on Facebook and see if his privacy settings allow us to check him out,"

"Great idea," Abbie picked up her iPad from the coffee table, and soon delved into social media.

"Oh my God, look Jane, he is going to be away this weekend."

Over the next twenty minutes or so, they worked out Jack's plans for the weekend and wrote them down. The earlier friction that Abbie felt had melted away, and she felt much happier. With a sigh she sat back on her sofa, "Any banana bread left?"

The two women laughed and gossiped for half an hour or so before Jane left and went home.

Chapter Seven

Thursday

7pm

Mason's house

Rain gently pattered against the French doors. A cool breeze made the evening feel autumnal. Jane and Abbey arrived together and in contrast to the weather, were in a sunny mood. Their cheer lifted Mason's gloom; his body seemingly melded into his armchair.

Abbie smiled and headed into the kitchen. 'Want a brew, Mason?'

Jane sat on the sofa, smiling at Mason.

'You're looking pleased with yourself, Jane'.'

'Wait until you hear the research on Jack, 'our next target,'

The two remaining attendees came into the house, allowing the comment to hang in the air.

'Got that kettle on, Abbie?' Pete called out.

She walked into the room holding a tray of drinks. 'Maybe you should make them next time, Pete.'

A relaxed chuckle came from the men. Everyone looked at Mason, before the meeting started.

'Thank you all for coming, again, and on such a rainy evening. We seem to have found a good system; I don't need to say much. Jane, what have you and Abbie discovered?'

All eyes were now focused on Jane, anticipating what she would say next.

'We found that this weekend is going to be the perfect time to kill this paedo.'

Jane picked up her steaming mug of tea and dunked a hobnob biscuit. Her eyes brightened, as she smiled at Abbie; who took the lead. 'Jack Barker loves fishing. His Facebook account links him to lots of fishing groups all over the UK. This weekend he is attending a competition at High Hill Reservoir. It's about a half an hour drive from here.'

'It sounds crowded; there will be too many people around. Is it really a good plan to kill him there?' Pete asked.

Jane pulled a box out of her handbag and placed it on her knees. 'We have registered you, under a false name, to join in the competition. Abbie found these bad boys on eBay.'

She took a tent peg out of the box. 'Blue Diamond hard and stony ground tent pegs. Twenty and a half centimetres long, heavy duty; perfect for nailing him to the spot. A tent, chair and fishing tackle are coming in the week.'

'I'm doing this alone?'

Jane grinned; a psychopathic glint in her eye. 'I'll be there too, as your wife. Mikey will hide in the tent, we're setting up early to get ready. Abbie is going to be the driver, again.'

Mason blew on his cup of tea, the steam blowing outwards on his breath. 'Sounds like a great plan you have there, ladies.'

He smiled warmly at everyone, before asking Mikey to text the rest of the congregation to come together again on Saturday evening. The Welshman was happy to be given a task, to cover the butterflies that had invaded his stomach, as he thought about the looming doom. 'No problem, Mason.'

After another half an hour or so, the group went their own way home. Mason was too exhausted to go to his bedroom, instead deciding to sleep in his armchair.

Chapter Eight

The second meeting, before their next killing, had already seemed part of the weekly routine. Pete looked at the tent and the mallet amongst the equipment on Mason's floor.

'I hope you have read the instructions, Jane, I have no idea how to erect a tent'.'

'Don't worry, me and Mikey will soon sort that out. He was in the Boy Scouts after all.'

'I bet I catch a fish. Jeremy Wade from that programme River Monsters; I taught him everything he knows about catching a trout!'

Mason laughed. 'Like hell you will, I bet you don't even catch an old boot'.'

The mood in the room was once again jovial; the weather matched the sunshine in the room.

3:30pm

Pete, Abbie, Jane and Mikey once again embarked on their extraordinary journey. Mikey had double checked that he had the murder note and crucifix, in a food bag, along with some petrol station gloves. Pete had double checked they had all the gear that he had been bought for the weekend.

After precisely 30 minutes they reached High Hill Reservoir. Pleasingly, they were the first to arrive. Not even the organisers were there. Jane looked at a map that she had printed off from the competition organiser's website, noting where she had marked a cross, signifying their pitch. *Damn I am good.*

It took them only about twenty minutes to set up. An elderly VW camper van purred into the gravel car park. A middle aged man got out of the driver's door. He had an extravagant handlebar moustache and slicked back hair. It had so much product in that it looked greasy.

His tee-shirt was a size too small, presumably to show off his muscles. A cheesy cliché of a tribal tattoo peeked out of the sleeves of his top, down to his elbows.

'My God, look at the state of that guy!' Whispered Mikey to Jane.

She whispered back through gritted teeth. 'That is Jack Barker, what a narcissistic prick.'

'Shit, he's in a campervan, what shall we do, Jane?'

'Don't worry. He put on the Facebook page that he wished he could sleep in it, but was going to use a tent to be close to his rods.'

'Thank goodness for that, we would have had to cancel otherwise.'

Jack, with a glint of amusement in his sky blue eyes, spoke to them. 'Hi people, a lot of you here for one pitch.'

'Yeah got my son and his friend helping me to set up. This is my wife'.' Pete was trying his hardest to be friendly, although, a 'don't mess with me' slant to his voice closed the conversation. *No small talk would be weird.*

Jack smiled affably and retrieved his tent from his van.

Jane added. 'It's our first competition, I think we're a bit early, no one else is here yet.'

'I'm always at events early too, good to be ahead of the competition. No one else will be here for another hour I think..'

Pete and Jane looked at each other, then at Abbie and Mikey. An unspoken message went between them. Abbie got her mobile phone out of her jeans pocket.

'I'm just going to text work; I'm going to throw a sickie'.'

Thirty seconds later, Mason's phone made the tone that told him that a text had arrived. He rubbed his eyes, as he had just started to snooze. Once he could focus, he read the concise message.

'Mason, we have an opportunity to kill him soon and avoid other people. Text the rest of the church and get them to pray.'

Mason was immediately wide awake. He simply texted back, *'ok'*. He then sent a simple text, to the rest of the flock.

'Barker about to die. Pray hard and meet here at six.'

A flurry of 'ok' messages almost vibrated his phone off the coffee table.

Jack quickly erected his tent, with an air of well practiced ease. Jane called to him, 'That's a nice tent, it looks comfortable, too.'

'Yeah, no point in being cramped up. I like my creature comforts. I go to lots of these competitions; gives me some peace and quiet from the wife.'

He looked over at Pete with a twinkle in his eyes.

Pete looked back, forcing a smile. 'Maybe I'll fly solo next time too, mate.'

He had to look out over the tranquil reservoir to let his simmering rage cool. A duck swam along the edge of the water, before it disappeared into reeds. Within minutes, a calm had settled over the area. Jack had already cast his first line and sat in his olive green camp chair. Pete was trying to tie a hook to the end of his line. He had selected a totally unsuitable size, not unintentionally.

Jack looked across, 'Don't think I'm being funny, but that hook is way too big. Fish won't bite on that monster. I've got some spares in my tent, hang on a moment and I'll get one for you.'

He deftly rose from his chair and reached his tent in a couple of strides.

Mikey sat between the fictional couple and Jack. He sprang to his feet and held the mallet close to his thigh. Jack bent down to grasp his tent zip. It was about halfway raised when Mikey struck the back of Jack's head with all his might. The impact made a painful crunching noise. With not even a gasp, Jack fell forwards, in an unconscious state, into his tent.

'Take that you dirty fucker.' Mikey muttered under his breath.

He stood and looked behind him. Ashen faced, Abbie passed the GoPro to Mikey. In turn, he pulled the sandwich bag from his pocket containing the note and crucifix. Pete pulled on the petrol station gloves and opened the box of Blue Diamond tent pegs.

'Ready, Mikey?'

'When you are, Pete.'

Mikey switched on the camera, making sure that only Jack's face was visible. Pete picked up the note and skewered it on the tent peg. He carefully placed the sharp end of the peg on Jack's temple. There was a chilling silence; Pete's vision narrowed as he raised the mallet. Time seemed to stand still. His concentration purely focused on hitting the peg as hard as he could.

The mallet swung down and struck the peg. In the blink of an eye, Jack's head has been effectively attached to the earth. Surprisingly, not much gore erupted from Jack's penetrated skull; just a small spattering of blood erupted against the canvas.

Once the camera had been switched off by Mikey, he placed the crucifix onto Jack's ear. The two men shuffled out of the tent and closed the zip. To the innocent observer, there was no hint of the horror inside. Pete looked out onto the reservoir, seeing Jack's luminous orange float bobbing and then vanishing beneath the still water. Curious, Pete picked up the rod and began to reel in whatever had bitten onto the hook. He slowly turned the handle and felt the line snag under the water. A light tug and he felt that it had freed. A very light breeze was picking up. Nearby, a sole magpie sat on a branch looking at the people watching Pete.

Pete whispered, 'It's something quite big, but it's weird... it's not trying to swim away.'

Click, click, click, click, the line wrapped around the reel.

'I can see something dark near the surface, almost got it!'

With vigorous jubilance he quickly reeled in the remainder of the line.

Pete yelled, 'What the fuck!'

Mikey, Jane and Abbie stared in disbelief; the hook had captured a human head; firmly embedded in the hole where an eye should have been.

'She must be quite freshly dead, or the rest of the body would be floating.' Mikey speculated.

'What should we do with it?' Abbie asked. 'Cut the head off the line and chuck it back in, or let it dangle from the line back in the water?'

Jane laughed. 'Swing it in, Pete.'

Pete swung the head across to within grasping distance. Jane without a thought about forensics took hold of the head, as if it was a melon from the supermarket shelf. With a swift yank of the line, the hook ripped out of the eye.

Jane seemed to relish in the gruesome discovery. 'Mikey, open the tent zip. This will really confuse the cops.'

She threw the head into the tent and after a single roll it came to rest against Jack's body. It lay on its side as though the body were asleep and hidden by Jack's dead body. Mikey took a photograph of the bizarre scene on his mobile phone, before pulling down the zip.

They swiftly took down their tent and carelessly deposited it, and the fishing tackle, in the boot of the car. *I hope we haven't left too much forensic evidence. Mikey thought to himself.*

Abbie tackled the drive back to Mason's home carefully, so as to not draw any unwanted attention to themselves. It seemed to take an age before they parked on Mason's driveway, the engine pinging as it cooled.

The rest of the congregation were not waiting for them when they arrived; for this the small group were thankful, as it gave them time to have a very *British* cup of tea to regroup before everyone's arrival at 6pm.

Chapter Nine

As Mason had expected, every member of the congregation had assembled.

'Thank you all for coming,' He sipped some tea to milk the moment before continuing. 'Thank you all for your prayer cover for our holy warriors. God gave them the opportunity, as you know, to kill Jack earlier than expected. It is done. Praise Him. He allowed them to kill him before more people arrived. I imagine that a lot of people will be meeting together and not have a clue that a paedophile lays dead nearby.'

A murmur of agreement and positive words rippled around the room. 'Mikey made sure that the good deed was captured on film for prosperity. Mikey, play it to us please young man.'

Mikey switched on the footage, playing it on Mason's television

A hush descended in the room; the television screen was filled with the image of a man in a tent. He was apparently sleeping. Tension became palpable and time seemed to stagger. Some averted their eyes when the mallet was lifted. A droplet of blood momentarily obscured the action, before falling away to reveal the freshly deceased victim. There were gasps, followed by a few people applauding, followed by a brief silence and then unanimous applause. Excited chatter filled the room.

Mikey coughed loudly to catch the assembled people's attention.

'As we were about to leave, we saw Jack's fishing float submerge. Pete reeled in the catch.'

The photograph from his mobile phone showed on the TV screen. Stunned silence engulfed the room.

Ash from Mason's cigarette dropped into his cup of tea. 'Who the hell is she?'

'We have no idea, Mason, the head was attached to the fishing hook; there was no sign of the body. We decided to throw it into the tent to confuse the police.' Mikey elaborated.

No shit, Sherlock. Mason let out a nervous laugh, 'Good work, all of you. Let's not worry about the woman.'

The congregation continued chatting, as if what had been shown on the television was simply fiction. Wine and tea flowed; pizza arrived from the local kebab shop.

There is no doubt, killing celebrations rock.

By the time that midnight crept by, most of the assembled flock had left and Mason had fallen asleep in his chair.

Jane smiled, and picked up his notebook. A biro was close by; she turned to the page with the list of victim names and scored out Jack Barker. Jane gave Mason a gentle kiss, on his forehead and left the house to make her way home.

Chapter Ten

Abbie had just finished vacuuming and dusting when people started arriving for the church service. 'Thank you, Abbie. I do appreciate your hard work.'

'It's no problem, Mason, especially as you pay me for it.'

'You on about the housework?'

Mason gave Abbie a cheeky wink to emphasise the innuendo. She blushed and laughed. Jane went to stand at the French doors and look out at the garden, so that she didn't have to listen to Mason's attempts at humour.

Five minutes later, and the room was full. Mason couldn't remember the last time that his house didn't hold a Sunday church. He was grateful that his weekends were not lonely.

'Welcome, everyone. As you know, both of our paedophile hunt missions have been a success.'

A ripple of positive noises made its way around the room.

'We still need to seek protection from the Lord. We can't be complacent, who knows when the police will track us down.'

Mason reached for his cup of tea, leaving the thought hanging in the air.

Jane only let a single heartbeat pass before speaking, 'God has everything in hand, there's no reason to worry. Both, erm, events went totally well. In fact, Jack met his maker earlier than we had planned as you know.' She smiled sweetly at Mason; a silence fell on the room.

Positive noises soon swelled again and suddenly the unsureness that was smothering the room dispersed. Worship spontaneously started; instruments played quietly. Some people sang, others prayed. Most had their hands in the air, reaching out to God.

Mikey started playing his guitar more loudly; he launched into the latest praise songs that the congregation loved. The music naturally lulled and Mason took control of the meeting, launching fully into a regular Sunday sermon. It was natural, Mason didn't need to refer to notes, he could easily remember his bible and lessons from years gone by, it was his memory for things that have happened in recent times that was more patchy.. These days, the congregation were thankful that the sermons were no more than fifteen or twenty minutes in length. He wasn't able to talk for long, his concentration soon slipped into a soupy fog. *Should really hand over to Mikey soon and take a back seat.*

'Thank you all for coming today, folks. We are halfway through our mission. Next week, Ed Miles is going to be the lucky devil meeting the musketeers.'

Soft chuckling washed through the congregation and all of them smiled.

'He is to have a sword driven into him so far that the handle gets stuck in his fat. With that nice image, please go and pray throughout the week to support the mission. Jane and Abbie decide between yourselves when to meet and research about Ed.

Meet here on Thursday at seven thirty with Pete and Mikey and we'll talk about what is going to happen. Everyone else, are you happy to support in prayer?'

Of course, this was a rhetorical question; no one was ever going to even think of proposing a different course of action.

'See you all here on Saturday at seven thirty, to support our brave warriors in prayer.'

Mikey gave a few final strums to his guiatar, as people were saying goodbye to each other, leaving only Mason, Pete, Jane and Abbie in the house. 'Thank you all for your amazing hard work on *our* mission. God will reward you greatly.'

I'll be thankful when this is all over.

Again Mason felt exhausted; the excitement of the weekend was really catching up with him. The others saw how tired he was and bid their farewells.

Chapter Eleven

Thursday
7:30pm
Mason's house

Mason stubbed out his rollup cigarette at the exact moment that the front door opened – Abbie and Jane had arrived.

'Mason, you're still smoking?'

'Sorry Abbie, I keep forgetting. Maybe I'll phone the doctor tomorrow and ask for advice. Maybe.'

'Make sure that you do, or I'll hide your tobacco.'

Despite the threat, both Mason and Jane laughed.

'You are incorrigible, Mason!' Abbie found herself laughing as she opened the French doors to let some fresh air into the room.

Without a knock, the front door opened. A breeze rushed through the room, the remaining two crucifixes falling onto the floor.

Is that another sign? Don't be stupid Mason, of course it isn't.

Mikey and Pete appeared at the door, looking happy with themselves.

Mikey said in his sing song voice, 'Hi guys, check out this bad boy we got online.'

Pete seemingly conjured into his hand an awe inspiring knife. 'It's a Tech Machete 3 with its seventeen inch blade; perfect for Ed Miles to get his comeuppance.'

Pete grinned, 'I won't let Mikey hold it, or he might try to catch a sheep with it!' Despite it being such a poor stereotypical joke, everyone laughed, including Mikey.

Pete passed the machete to Mason. Mason felt the weight in his hands, but couldn't properly grip the handle. It slipped out of his hand and fell towards the floor.

'Don't grab it!' Called Jane, alarm ringing in her voice.

Mason resisted the temptation to grasp the knife; it sliced his thin trousers as it was pulled by gravity towards the floor. The cruel pointed tip tore the skin on his leg. Mason shrieked; the pain intense and vivid. 'Fuck!'

Abbie and Jane rushed to his side; Pete picked up the weapon and sheathed it. Colour drained from everyone's face, as though slapped with the wet fish of reality.

Jane naturally took on the role of team leader. 'We need to sort this out, right now. Guys, get him on the floor; Abbie, go and get a clean towel.'

Pete and Mikey only struggled slightly to put Mason on the floor; the same gravity that had helped the knife assisted them in their task. Pete grasped Mason's foot and, assuming a kneeling position, he put the foot onto his shoulder. Abbie appeared with a plain white towel, and a pair of scissors.

Handing the scissors to Mikey she said, 'Mikey, slice his trouser leg from the ankle up to his waist'.

It was done in a heartbeat. The trouser leg partitioned, like stage curtains, and revealed a slight cut on his thigh. Although not deep, it was at least seven inches long, in the shape ofa semicircle on his thigh. Jane pressed the towel onto the wound for a couple of minutes. Once she removed it, it had stopped bleeding. Abbie pottered into the kitchen and returned with a hefty first aid box.

Mikey laughed, 'Planning for a war, Mason, with a first aid kit like that?'

'Well, got to spend the collection money somehow.'

'Mason, mate, don't give up your day job to become a comedian.'

Abbie found a tightly packaged bandage dressing roll. She and Jane quickly, and efficiently, sorted out dressing the wound. Abbie affectionately spoke in a soft voice to Mason, 'There you are butter fingers, let's get you comfortable in your chair.'

She stood and motioned for Mikey and Pete to put Mason back in his chair. 'I'll make us all a cuppa, extra sugar for you Mason,'

Mason picked up his painkillers, slicing his thumb on the foil backing, 'Fuck's sake! What's next, these things happen in threes.'

Pete chuckled, 'Old wives tale mate. It's our job to cause pain.'

The man-mountain leant towards Mason, passing him the box of plasters.

Everyone was sat, with a mug of tea steaming by their side.

Mason naturally took the lead, 'Here we are once more. We are halfway through our paedo hunting missions. Thank you all for listening God's will, and taking it to fruition.'

He stared out of the French doors, towards the garden but didn't really look at anything. The magnitude was starting to weigh on his shoulders. *Got to shake that off, work has to be done.* Mason took a sip of his still steaming Yorkshire tea, the others mirroring him by doing the same.

'I don't need to say anything further, you ladies and gentlemen are truly exceptional.'

Pete chuckled again, in an ebullient mood. 'You'll make us blush Mason.'

'I think you'll need to save some of that enthusiasm for this Saturday, when Ed Miles meets his maker. Ladies, fill us in on your research.'

Mason peered at Jane and Abbie with blurring vision. *Really must get to the opticians, I'll ask someone to take me after all four are dead.*

Abbie cleared her throat. 'Ed is a creature of habit. Eat, sleep, work, repeat. We haven't had chance to see what his weekend routine is like, which is a worry. He has a nine-to-five job. In effect we have a choice; option one is to execute the job on Friday, when he gets home from work. He lives in a suburban street, which is fairly quiet because it is a cul-de-sac. Option two is to watch him on Saturday, and go with the flow.'

She sat back in her chair, picking up her drink, and looked patiently at Pete and Mikey.

They looked at each other, then at Mason. 'It seems to me that Friday must be the better option, Saturday is too much of an unknown entity. Jane, tell us the Friday plan.'

Mason looked at Jane and smiled a thin smile; the stress starting to show on everybody's faces.

'Guys, try not to worry that the plan to kill on a Saturday has gone out of the window. You've shown that you can adapt your plans before and this is no different.' Mason took another sip of his tea.

That should do the trick.

Jane smiled, this time a confident one, even if she didn't feel completely comfortable. 'Ed gets home from work at between five fifty and five past six. He drives a black Ford Mondeo. Ed parks in the same position every time on his drive, then goes into his house. He doesn't go out again, once he's home. It gets dark by five, now autumn is underway. Pete, Mikey, I think that either you need to break in when it's dark or kill him on the doorstep.'

Pete spoke next, still gripping his cup of tea like it was an extension of his hand. 'Mikey, we'll break in so there's no chance of being spotted dropping him on the doorstep.'

'But Pete, if we do that then there'll be a chance of being spotted breaking in and there'll be some hard questions to answer if the police arrest us.'

'You're right boyo, what do you suggest?'

'I've got it. We'll wait until seven thirty, and then make a special pizza delivery again. It'll be easier this time, we've done it before and don't need to worry about taking him alive.'

Abbie surprised herself hearing her voice making a suggestion, 'Maybe we should buy five pizzas and bring the other four back here afterwards.'

The palpable tension in the room lifted; it seemed to be back to business as usual. Mason lit a rollup cigarette, Pete followed suit filling the room with a smoky fog. Abbie stood and opened the French doors enough to ventilate the room with fresh, cool, autumn air. Mason exhaled sending smoke towards the ceiling followed by a deep, chesty, hacking cough. Abbie and Jane looked at each other, and shook their heads at him. Mason and Pete chuckled; Mikey looked on impassively.

'Alright, ladies and gentlemen, tonight's meeting is concluded. I'll let you four arrange between yourselves tomorrow's action. Mikey, can you text everyone from church to pray for you guys and meet here for a post killing meeting at eight fifteen?'

'Sure Mason, no problem.'

Mason reclined his chair and closed his heavy looking eyes, and within a heart beat was asleep.

Pete grinned. 'Old boy is knackered,'

He stubbed out his cigarette in an ashtray sporting the legend 'Jesus Saves'. 'Whoever designed that had a good sense of humour.'

Despite themselves, Jane and Abbie couldn't help to chuckle.

Mikey pulled a sandwich bag from his pocket and carefully placed the penultimate crucifix into it. He smiled a carefree smile. 'Like the shepherd said to the sheep, let's get the flock out of here.'

Pete laughed. 'Good Welsh joke there, mate. You're right though, let's meet at my place at six thirty on Friday.' The others made affirming noises, shrugged on their coats and left the building.

Chapter Twelve

Friday
7:20pm
Mikey's van

Abbie settled into the driver's seat, and passed the stack of pizzas she had just bought to Jane.

'Feels like déjà vu.' Jane muttered.

'Is everyone ready?'

Abbie didn't wait for an answer and pulled away from the kerb. Three minutes later, she parked close to the cul-de-sac entrance. Without speaking, Pete and Mikey alighted. They looked like burglars, with their balaclavas and baseball caps. A glance up and down the road confirmed they were alone, apart from a handful of cars parked outside neat suburban homes.

They walked confidently into the cul-de-sac, bolstered by clouds covering the moon and stars. Without a glance back, the men manoeuvred onto the gateless drive and knelt down. No one would see them, draped in shadow and shielded from the house by a car.

Seven thirty precisely, the van parked outside the neighbour's house. The men watched Jane get out, pulling her Newdon Palace pizza cap to cover her face from any prying cameras. She walked confidently to the door, and pressed the doorbell button. The door opened fully.

Ed looked at her. 'That was quick! It says on Just Eat that there's a thirty minute wait, you've only been ten.'

'We aim to please, I'm really sorry to ask, but can I use your loo please? Don't tell the boss, but I'm pregnant and need to go a lot.'

Ed grabbed the pizzas and moved out of her way, 'Sure, it's at the top of the stairs.'

The door closed. Mikey looked at Pete with wide eyes and pointed to his watch. Pete nodded and unsheathed the evil blade.

'Wait the camera.' Mikey whispered.

He pulled it from his pocket and pointing it away from the men, pressed the record button. Pete held out his free hand, and turned it off. Mikey looked quizzically at him. Pete winked and stood up. Mikey followed suit and they walked silently to the door. *Good job there is no gravel.*

Pete looked at Mikey and gave an almost imperceptible nod. He held the camera in his left hand, switched it on then placed his right hand onto the door handle. The next second seemed to take an eternity. Pete pushed down the handle, alarmed at the how noisy the mechanism was. Their sneaky approach had been blown; he rushed into the house with Mikey a couple of steps behind.

Ed sat on the sofa, and looked at the hall not computing what was happening. Frozen to the moment in time; a slice of Hawaiian pizza raised halfway to his gaping mouth. Pete was on him in less than two seconds, Ed's fight or flight reaction had gone AWOL. In an autonomous motion, with no room for thought, Pete in an over-arm motion thrust the machete as hard as he could into Ed, before pulling it back out. Blood sprayed with each breath; the blade had surely penetrated the lung. Blood soaked his fashionable shirt, making it cling to his body. He looked shocked and although his eyes were vacant, he didn't die straight away. He tried to stand, but Pete delivered a second stab into his gut.

Almost robot like, Pete stood tall, all the time keeping the camera pointing at his victim. He lifted his foot and mercilessly pushed the knife with his foot until the handle was ensconced in Ed's belly fat. Pete prodded the button on the camera to stop recording. 'Fuck you, you dirty paedo bastard.'

The toilet flushed and Jane appeared in the doorway. 'What is going on? I thought we were going to kill him together?'

Pete was struggling to control his breathing and clearly still riding the wave of adrenaline.

Mikey sighed. 'Ed was sat on the sofa, so we didn't get the element of surprise. Luckily he was like a deer in headlights.'

'That's lucky, Pete, he's a mean looking mother. I bet the kids were petrified of him.'

'Certainly better off dead.' Pete snarled, his top lip curling upwards giving him the appearance of a wild wolf.

Mikey quietly took out the crucifix and note from his jacket pocket. He made short work of putting them on top of Ed's now still body. 'Let's go, guys.'

It was raining heavily when let left. Keeping their heads low, they quickly left the house and got into the van and not a moment too soon. As Abbie pulled away a moped parked up where the outline of the van's footprint was marked by dry tarmac.

Pete grumbled, 'I bet that this rain isn't God's tears.'

The others were relieved that his intimidating dark mood had started to lift.

Chapter Thirteen

As always, the whole congregation was assembled by the allotted time. Abbie and Jane made tea for everyone. They never reflected on if they just did it as a so called woman's job. Mason tapped a spoon against his mug, which bore the legend 'More tea, Vicar?' A gift from a loyal follower, but he couldn't remember who.

'Welcome, ladies and gentlemen. Today has seen the attempted extermination of target three.' He paused for effect. The whole room collectively seemed to hold their breath. 'Success.'

The room erupted into cheering and clapping. 'Praise Jesus!' and 'Hallelujah' calls rang round.

Good job this house is detached or people would think we're going crazy.

'Take it away, Mikey.'

The television screen suddenly filled with unsteady motion, silencing the room with intrigue and a hint of fear. The machete filled the screen and vanished out of the top of the screen.

Like during the previous screenings of their murders, time seemed to stand still. Suddenly, like a surprise – judging by the gasps – the knife appeared back on the screen, much faster than it had gone upwards. Shocked silence momentarily filled the room. A quiet ripple of applause tentatively motioned round the room like waves of the sea.

The musketeers, as Mason had nicknamed them, remained focused on the screen. Blood pulsed from the wound, much more than Pete remembered. Now, the vicious blade was being pulled from the wound.

'I thought you said…' The tension's palpability silenced Mason. Ed's gut filled the screen, the buttons on his shirt ready to fly off from the tension put on them by the girth of stomach.

STAB!

The shock of the second puncture prompting more gasps from the congregation. The musketeers kept watching the television. Mason watched transfixed; his eyes wider than in recent memory when Pete's Doc Martin shoe filled the screen. The final thrust of Pete's foot against the end of the knife burying it in Ed's lard completed the footage.

Shock blanketed the room.

This killing somehow seemed more brutal than the previous. The gravity of the situation pushing the atmosphere down and seemed to suffocate the room.

Fuck, I need to smash the tension.

'Fantastic, musketeers!' Mason said and clapped respectfully. The soft applause took on its own momentum, and within seconds the room thundered with noise.

The swell of applause naturally quelled, colour returning to a number of people's cheeks. Mikey needed no prompting and began strumming his guitar.

Perfect; the atmosphere was too intimidating. Surprisingly, Pete looked stunned.

Singing didn't feel right; Mason closed his eyes and raised both of his palms as if in a meditative trance of worship. Some people hummed, some prayed aloud. All of them with their eyes closed.

Good job. The next one is the last one; I'd have a stress problem with more.

Mason let about five minutes pass, until everyone was in a good place – mentally. 'I think tonight's meeting is finished now. Feel free to talk amongst yourselves and see you all here on Sunday, as usual. Oh, by the way, we have plenty of pizza!'

His infectious smile lit up the room.

Pete asked with a glint in his eye, 'How's your leg now, Mason?'

'Healing nicely, thanks for asking.'

The following hour sped by; the mood was back to how it was after the first killing. People slowly drifted away.

'Bye Mason.'

'See you Sunday, God Bless.'

'Night, everyone.'

'Sleep tight.'

It was almost midnight when all the musketeers had left the building.

Chapter Fourteen

Every member of the flock was present, as Mason had expected. 'Once again, thank you all for coming today. This is the final service before we do God's will and kill a paedophile. The lucky man who will suffer our wrath is a Dave Harvey. He has Abbie to thank for finding the Facebook page that told us who required God's wrath.'

Mason looked at Abbie with an amused look. She squirmed and looked at her shoes. 'Just kidding, Abbie.'

Mason chuckled, 'Sorry, I didn't mean to embarrass you. Let's hear the Word of God.'

Most of the assembled followers picked up a very well worn copy of the bible. He spoke from memory; his eyes let him down by not focusing on his notes. Most of the flock had noticed, but none of them would speak what they thought; such was the authority that he held over them.

Following the familiar routine, after the preaching came singing and praising God. His charismatic authority was even stronger than ever before.

'Wow, the Holy Spirit has been with us today in great strength. Take that with you this week, as we plan our final killing. Pray regularly each day for our brave musketeers; for protection and that they escape from earthly authorities. Now, go in peace and serve the Lord; Amen.'

'Amen,' echoed the flock.

'Righteous warriors, Jane and Abbie, talk between yourselves to arrange your research into Mr Harvey. You ladies, Pete and Mikey please come here on Wednesday to put the plan of action together. Seven thirty, as usual.'

'That's fine, Mason, I'm collecting my new crew cab van on Tuesday,' said Mikey.

Jane asked, 'What's one of them?'

'It's like a regular van, but instead of space for three people in the front, there's two rows of seats, then the wall behind them then the cargo compartment.'

'I see, should be more comfy than sitting in the back of your old tranny!'

Chuckles once more filled the air; the friends stood up, said their goodbyes and then left the house.

Chapter Fifteen

Tuesday

Noon

Mason's house

Abbie was doing her regular housework at Mason's house. 'Your hand welded to your phone today, Mason?'

He had only put it down a few times, to drink tea. 'Yeah, just been catching up with friends, I've been too knackered up until today. Got to say, though, it's a struggle even now. I'm getting tired and my focus is blurry. Typical.'

'Have a nap, Mason. It'll help you no end.'

'I think you're right. Wake me up before you leave.'

Mason pulled the lever to recline the chair back and fell into a slumber almost immediately. The television played a music channel that Abbie didn't like. She turned it to a rolling news channel; the presenter catching Abbie's attention.

'Now we cross to hear from the news conference taking place about the recent murders targeting paedophiles.'

A high ranking police officer, Abbie noted that he was an Assistant Chief Constable, started with the usual pleasantries.

"Good afternoon, thank you all for coming today, we are here to talk about the horrific murders that have taken place recently in the town of Newdon.

The Police have thoroughly searched each victim's home, and computers. Vitally, we reassure the victim's families that there are no traces of any links to paedophilia whatsoever.'

Abbie dropped the tin of polish, the noise dampened by carpet. On a hunch, she slid Mason's mobile from under his fingertips.

Hope he hasn't got round to password protected it; probably not with his short term memory.

She let out a quiet sigh of relief when the phone let her in. The icons on the home screen showed a new text. Holding her breath, Abbie pressed the icon. Jane had a lengthy conversation thread. A quick scroll revealed that Jane and Mason had texted each other every day for many weeks. From about 8 weeks ago, a particular conversation caught Abbie's horrified eye:

'I love you Mason'
'Prove it to me'
'I will do anything'
'Even kill for me?'
'For you, anything'

Abbie couldn't believe her eyes, she cast her mind back to her conversations with Jane in their time together doing their tasks helping to work out the fine details of the killings. *"I'd do anything to be with Mason, he's the perfect guy for me."* Blimey, that's a hell of a thing to do for someone's love.

With a flick of her thumb Abbie came forwards to the day that the congregation had agreed to start their killings:

"See Mason, I told you that I'd do anything. Killing people for you is nothing."

"I couldn't believe it when they all agreed, I've hated those guys for years. Death is nothing less than they deserve. Your idea of making them looks like paedophiles was inspired."

"I love you Mason, I know you feel the same about me."

"Do I?"

"Stop being such a tease, I'll convince you of it soon"

'What *the hell to do? I'd better contact the boys.* She went into the kitchen and dialled Pete's number.

'Hello, you ok?'

'Did you see the news?'

'Yes, I don't understand. We need a meeting, I'll call Mason.'

'Pete, I'm at Mason's house cleaning. He's asleep. I had a hunch to look at his phone; it's too much to talk about now, but he and Jane are in it together.'

'You're fucking joking!'

'Couldn't be more serious, Pete. Look, I'll leave him asleep and come to your house now.'

'Good, I'm working from home today anyway. I'll call Mikey and tell him to come over.'

'Alright, see you soon.'

'Bye.'

Abbie hesitated and contemplated taking Mason's phone. *No, he'll wonder where it is. I'll take photos of the texts.* She took photos of the incriminating text messages, hoping he would stay asleep.

Mason started snoring loudly. Abbie could help but look at him with contempt.

His notebook caught her eye. With trepidation she opened it. Amongst the doodles of penis' and breasts, she found the page listing the victims. Each of them, except Dave Harvey had their name scored out.

~~Ian Murray~~

~~Jack Barker~~

~~Ed Miles~~

Dave Harvey

Abbie turned the page, to the final page. In Jane's handwriting she read:

Need help to kill - how? Church?

Facebook page for targets

Why would ppl kill?

Kiddy fiddlers?

~~Maybe money?~~

Paedos, evry1 hates them!

I Love You Mason xxxxxxxxxx

Paedo Hunters r us!!

Abbie quickly photographed the two pages, then put the notebook back carefully, exactly where it had been. Quietly as possible, she put on her Sketchers and shrugged on her coat. Without a look back she left the house.

Chapter Sixteen

Mikey and Abbie both arrived within five minutes of each other, the smell made them both have to hold their breath when they could until they got used to it. Mikey gave a side ways look to Abbie and pinched the bridge of his nose. She squinted, and held back a laugh that was trying to sneak out. Pete didn't see them do that, but he wouldn't have been bothered anyway. He gathered his scattered paperwork, so the others could sit somewhere.

The Welshman asked, 'What did you find, Abbie?'

'Mikey, you won't believe your eyes.'

She opened her phone and navigated to the photo gallery. 'Here, just swipe and you'll see.'

He swiped through the images; his eyes widened as he shook his head, 'I can't believe it.'

He passed the phone to Pete. 'Mother fuckers. Using us to do their dirty work! We have to get revenge.'

'But how, mate? Do we call the police, Pete? I know an officer, a friend of my sister. Laura Love, she's great.'

Pete and Abbie shook their heads.

'I think we have to take them out,' said Abbie, with renewed fire in her eyes.

'I agree,' growled Pete gruffly. 'Let's burn the fuckers, make them die in pain.'

'It has to be today, Pete. Otherwise Jane or Mason might see the news and know they could be rumbled. Any ideas guys?' asked Mikey, before adding, 'Why would Mason need to leave the house? He never leaves the property.'

Abbie broke out into a grin. 'What, Abbie, come on love, share.' Urged Pete.

'I'll tell him I booked him an optician's appointment at six. He should still be asleep if I go back now.'

'What about the bitch?' The harsh words sounding out of place in his sing song voice.

'I'll text her from Mason's phone, to meet at his at five thirty to lend some moral support. I'd better go, to make sure I'm back before he wakes. You two make a plan then meet at Mason's at five thirty. Ok?'

'Ok, Godspeed.'

Chapter Seventeen

5:30pm

Mason's house

Jane arrived a couple of minutes after the guys. 'Hope I'm not late. I got here as fast as I could after work.'

'We should still be there on time, but we have to leave now.' Mikey said.

Mason chipped in, 'How come you didn't tell me about the appointment before, Abbie?'

'Oh, it was just luck they had a cancellation, and I didn't tell you because that would have given you too much time to ponder it and then cancel.'

Mason chuckled. 'You know me too well, Abbie.'

Not well enough mate.

Pete gruffly spoke, 'I've come to give weakling Mikey help to put your chariot in his van. He forgot to get the ramp out of the old van.'

Mikey made a show of rolling his eyes. 'Thanks for your kind words, Yorkshire pudding!'

Everyone laughed. Mason walked with a slow pace, using his walking stick, to the van. Pete opened a rear passenger door and helped Mason in.

'Good job Mikey got a new works van, I don't need to shell out for a taxi.' Mason had a look of anxiety, obviously trying to hide behind words.

Pete just grunted and slammed the door. 'Oi! Don't break my new beast.' Mikey said, jokily waving a fist in Pete's direction.

Abbie grinned, 'Bagsie shotgun.'

'No chance, I ain't sitting next to Jane she might try to kiss me.' chuckled Pete. 'Besides, I already claimed passenger rights.'

Abbie smiled. 'Alright grumpy, I can't sit in the middle though, cos I'll be travel sick.'

Jane sighed. 'Don't worry, I'll sit next to Mason in the middle.'

Pete and Mikey lifted the gleaming electric wheelchair into the back of van. 'Ready Mikey?'

'Ready.'

The town centre was close to Mason's house, ten minutes by car. 'I need to get some diesel guys, she's nearly empty,'

Before anyone could answer, Mikey pulled onto an Esso forecourt. He made sure that the filling cap was on the opposite side to the cashier's window.

Abbie announced, 'I need a wee wee.'

She left the van, walking meaningfully towards the shop.

Mikey said in a loud voice so that Mason and Jane would hear as he got out of the vehicle, 'Pete can you fuel up please? I need to use the cash machine inside the shop.'

Pete grunted and alighted from the van, the vehicle rocking slightly when his huge frame moved outside. Mikey walked to the shop. Unseen from the van, the massive windows obscuring the sightline, he stood by the magazines and got the GoPro camera from his pocket. The final crucifix and note were retrieved too, and placed on top of a pack of tea bags.

Not wanting to draw unwanted attention he browsed the magazines while watching Pete in his peripheral vision. Pete looked into the van and saw Mason in deep conversation with Jane. He selected the petrol pump. *Diesel isn't flammable.*

After ten seconds of pouring petrol into the tank, he pulled the nozzle out and doused the rear tyre in the foul smelling fuel. Continuing to pump fuel, he aimed the nozzle at the floor, grimly watching a small lake forming. Pete splashed the sides of the van too. The final act was to make a trail of fuel as far away from the van as it would spray.

Pete replaced the nozzle and grinned at the readout. '£82.94.' *That's a lot of fuel.* He looked to the shop, and gave a thumbs up. The click of the van's lock and then deadlock. Locking remotely made Mason and Jane look up, startled from their conversation.

They looked at each other, confusion etched on their faces. Pete's face appeared, grinning. 'Funny Pete, unlock the doors!'

He lifted a cigarette to his lips, 'I don't have the key.'

'What the hell are you doing, Pete?' Jane shouted.

'We found out your plan, bitch, and you're both paying the price. Make peace with your maker, you're about to meet him. Abbie did tell you Mason that smoking kills.'

Chuckling at his joke, Pete walked over to the pavement and lit his cigarette. He smoked it, taking long drags so the tip glowed red for seconds at a time. Mason and Jane banged on the windows and yelled. Other motorists were looking over, bemused. In the time honoured British way, no one wanted to get involved – not wanting to know why people in a van were banging on the windows.

Abbie spotted that the cigarette was almost finished and hid at the back of the shop by the fresh milk. Mikey lifted the GoPro and pressed record. In one motion, Pete flicked the glowing cigarette towards the trail of petrol and started to run.

Time seemed to freeze, at that moment Mason shit himself with fear and screamed uselessly, 'No!'

The petrol ignited and burned furiously. Within a fraction of a second the van was engulfed in flames. Mikey stopped recording, and as quick as he could joined Abbie. The tyres exploded one by one, in ferocious fireballs, before the van finally, with a huge bang, exploded. The windows in the shop blew in, glass showering all around.

Sirens wailed in the distance, Mikey looked at Abbie and nodded; they ran out of the shop, as fast as they could.

Chapter Eighteen

Thirty minutes later
Red Lion public house

Abbie, Pete and Mikey sat around a small round table, on plush upholstered, well worn stools – The stereotypical type, with red cushion and brass studs around them.

A bottle of champagne sat incongruously in the centre of the table.

Pete poured each of them a flute, 'I propose a toast.'

Mikey knew exactly what Pete was going to say and so interjected, 'One for all and all for one!'

The friends laughed and tapped their glasses together.

Amen

While writing The Crucifix, the tension built in my head. I needed a break-out. What better way than to write a fun, swear word filled, story?

Here is the result.

Enjoy it, a free bonus story from me.

Tony Tomato

Part I

Tony sat on the vine. He loved life, growing next to his best mate Toni.

She's so fit.

The tomato plant grew and grew. Tony loved looking down on less fortunate vegetables. Paolo Potato had it bad; he had to grow underground. He moaned about it every day. 'Hey Paolo, what lovely weather today,' called out Tony.

'Fuck off, asshole!'

'Ignore him; he won't be laughing when the rain is rolling down his red face.' Brenda, the runner bean, shouted.

'Shhhh, I can hear Henry the human!' Toni yelled at the other veggies and fruit.

Anna Apple chuckled. 'Well, we're ok up here'.

'Fuck off, Anna,' yelled Paolo. 'It's alright for you being right up in a tree; you can see for miles'.

All the veg laughed; Paolo was the world's grumpiest potato.

Henry smiled with warm happiness, matching the warm sun. *What a lovely day at the allotment.* He couldn't see the vegetables faces, nor hear their voices. Good job; what would he have said to Paolo, 'Shut the fuck up, spud!'?

The old man adjusted his floppy sun hat to shade his neck and with his sleeves rolled up to his elbows, he was ready to set to work.

Henry pulled a bright green Co-op carrier bag from his pocket and shook it to unfold it. He hummed the theme to the Archers and reached up to the ripe tomatoes. Pluck! Tom was dropped into the bag. Pluck! Toni was next to drop into the plastic bag. Cut! Kerry the lovely green cucumber was next. Snip! Pluck! Dig! Soon the bag brimmed with lovely ripe vegetables.

Soon, all the veg sat on the counter in the kitchen. Tony, Toni, Kerry and the others tried hard to keep their veggie faces hidden.

'I have a bad feeling about this!' Toni cried red, tomato tears.

Tony broke out into a sweat.

'I'm sure I haven't rinsed the tomatoes yet, must be going mad.' Henry said aloud to himself.

'This one is super beefy, I think I'll have its seeds!' Henry liked talking to himself.

Kerry smirked; she had seen the massive sharp shiny knife first. Cucumbers know more than tomatoes. With a chuckle, inaudible to the human ear, she watched Henry put down the chopping board.

'Nice knowing you, Tony!'

'What do you mean, Kerry?'

'You are about to be chopped up to be eaten, blushing boy.' This comment resulted in more wailing and angst from Tony and Toni.

'Henry! Please! No!' Toni was terrified, but it was pointless. Henry couldn't hear vegetables talking.

At that moment all the salad items saw *the knife*.

You didn't need to be a cucumber to know that trouble was ahead. They didn't clock the colander though. It was a huge surprise to them being heaped together in the colander and then shocked beyond words when water struck in a torrential river from the tap.

'Good job that we aren't animals, or we'd all shit ourselves!' Aubrey Aubergine yelled.

'Funny fucker!' Paolo had found his voice again.

'Fuck off Paolo!' The rest of the veg shouted in unison.

Seconds later, Toni was going under the knife. Chop! Chop! Chop! Tony couldn't believe his eyes. The last he saw of her, she was being tossed into a large salad bowl. He cried buckets of invisible tomato tears.

Henry sat a smaller knife onto the work surface. A plant pot, with fresh soil appeared and put on a saucer. *What's this fucking wise guy doing now?*

'PUT ME DOWN, ASSHOLE!' Of course, Henry couldn't hear Tony. He sliced Tony in two. 'No! Put me back together!' With horror, Tony saw his seeds being scooped out and deposited into the plant pot. 'What is happening? I hate you, Henry!'

Tony was amazed and relieved to see Toni in the bowl right next to him. 'Hey girlfriend, nice to see you again.'

Toni didn't reply. He was horrified to realise that she had drowned; mayonnaise smothered her.

Just a few minutes later Tony passed away.

Part II

Henry looked with pride at the fresh stalks sprouting from the tomato seeds. *Can't beat home grown.* The moment the new shoots broke through the clag of soil, and reached for the sky, Tony awoke. *Fuck me, I'm back!*

Tony's heart sank as he realised that he was at Henry's house.

Henry carried the plant pot out to the greenhouse. Tony perked up realising that things were hotting up.

It wasn't long before Henry had set Tony down into a comfortable gro-bag. Whistling to himself, he left, and Tony let out a sigh of relief.

'Yeah, fuck off back to the house, tosspot.'

'What's your problem?' A disembodied voice caught Tony's attention, and he realised that he wasn't alone in the greenhouse. He looked around and spotted a courgette.

'That guy is growing us to eat.'

'Whatever, that's bullshit. He's growing us because he loves us.'

'Look, this is what happened to me.' Tony told the Courgette at length what happened to him in his past life.

'Oh my God!' quivered the Courgette, 'I don't yet have a name and I'll be dead soon.'

'We need to kill that twat.' Tony and Courgette looked high to see where the new voice came from. 'I'm Barry Banana. He deserves to die for giving us such puerile names. Courgette, I will name you. I name thee Juliette'.

Tony and Barry laughed, Juliette didn't get the joke.

The penny dropped a moment later, 'You're a funny cunt.' Tony and Barry were in hysterics, and so Juliette stuck as her name.

'Banana boy, whatcha think we should do,' Juliette asked in a passive aggressive voice.

'Leave it to me, we need a spy.'

Andy the King of the Ants crawled round the greenhouse with his army. 'Psst Andy!' 'What you want big boy? No funny business or I'll call Cousin Diego. He's a leaf cutter ant, with an army of a million. He'll cut you up and make you wish you'd never lived.' Barry had to bite his tongue to not laugh.

Tony told Andy what he knew about Henry. 'Son of a bitch. How can I help?'

'Go in there once he's asleep and look up on Google to how we can bump him off.'

'Consider it done.'

'So, Andy, what did you find out for us?'

'You won't believe it, but I found that if you crush enough cherry stones you can make cyanide.'

FAMOUSLY
ORDINARY

James Dean hated his name.

Several times a week he thought about why he didn't have a regular name. James blamed his father; he more than likely took charge of naming him. Like most things in his parents' relationship, his father liked to think he was 'the man of the house' and dominated all the decisions. He decided what companies to use for utilities, and everything else. Denise sometimes asked to be more involved, but she got nowhere.

Dean Dean, his father, was hung up on his name, but unlike his son, he tried to not let it show to the outside world. Being from an older generation, it wasn't the done thing to let your emotions shine through. James survived school and college unscathed; youthful ignorance meant most of the kids didn't connect to the movie star, and those who did thought having the same name as a famous person was cool. Still, he had a lot to be happy and content about. James had a nice job in the same warehouse his father worked in that paid well, a nice car he had chosen because it was what he wanted rather than just being what he was able to afford after scraping the money together to buy it, and a nice detached house with an integral garage. He could buy nice new clothes as and when he wanted, which he was grateful for because he didn't like to wear the same clothes repeatedly. *Nice. Such a small word,* James thought, *but damning by faint praise.*

James believed his life was normal, like other successful people. Yet he aspired to be something more. His mind was always on fast forward, daydreaming. He was fascinated by the adverts on television for the RAF Reserves. That looked extraordinary; he just needed a push in that direction. He hoped Dean would dare him to apply and say he thought James wasn't cut out for it just so he could prove him wrong.

To entertain himself when he saw someone on the street, he would often invent a story about them for a few minutes. These stories were detailed, and they came to life in his imagination when he saw them play out in his mind's eye.

Facebook didn't yet have a group for 'Normal People with a Famous Name'. Maybe no one wanted to start one for fear of the unknown and the inevitable ribbings, or maybe because they just wanted to keep a low profile. Perhaps they didn't even pay their moniker any attention at all. Maybe James needed to see a psychiatrist to help him with his problems, but he was in denial that his mind was a swirling pit with unseen depths. In his daydream world, which he was sure was created by having the hated name, the characters he created were normal people with the curse of stupid famous names. James had always been bitter, even as a schoolboy. He hid behind a mask of fake smiles for everyone outside the shop floor he lorded over. Somehow, he covered up his arrogance when he was talking to people like Mrs Khan in the local newsagents, who didn't know him as well as his family did. His belief was that most of the other non-famous, famously named people must have received their name because their parents loved the celebrity. And they didn't think of the impact on their beloved offspring's mental health, maybe not even realising their child shared their name with a famous person. James often looked at Facebook when he had some spare time and typed random famous names into the search bar to look for other 'normals', as he liked to call them. There were lots: David Beckham, Richard Branson, even Cat Deeley. However, there was never any contact with them; James somehow needed to hang on to that bitterness and perceived rejection for himself. It was an obsession. His fingernails were a testament to the stress he caused himself; he had bitten them all right down to the quick.

Sometimes, when James was at work, people dared to smirk or take the piss about his name. If anyone went too far, he flashed the political correctness card. 'I'll have your job for bullying if you don't pack it in,' was his go-to phrase. It always worked; no one would have tried to bully him. In fact, him being the bully was the truth.

It had helped James' rise through the ranks, of that he was sure. The higher management seemed to like his way of threatening the workers to keep them under control. He would do things like turn down holiday requests and hold back new uniform from the workers who needed fresh clothing, and if one of the workers was vociferous, he'd make a point of annoying them as much as he could. James liked the power he had, as though he were entitled to it.

James knew he was memorable. Not only for his name, but also for his physical stature and the gregarious air he put on. He was over six feet tall, and broad shouldered too. Unlike his slobby father, James loved going to the gym. Feeling sweat pour down his face made him happy and gave him the opportunity to show off his body. *These massive mirrors are awesome!* James often wore a great deal of hair product, splashed on designer aftershave and wore expensive suits to make himself look important. He liked to wear shoes that made a loud noise as he clicked along the corridors of the warehouse, intimidating anyone and everyone within earshot. It was a good job his parents didn't charge him rent, or he would have had to cut back on his fashion purchases.

His boss knew James was a tough taskmaster to his underlings, which he found amusing, much to the chagrin of the shop floor staff. James would set targets he knew were unrealistic for the workers to achieve, so he'd have more opportunities to berate them. Seeing people squirm in meetings delighted him, and sometimes, he could almost smell the fear from particular members of staff. There wasn't a union in place in the warehouse, and although some members of staff were trying to persuade the management to put one in place, their efforts were without success. He knew too that James was determined to succeed and not sink into a life with a below-average job.

James confided in his boss about his family. He didn't want to end up in a below-par marriage like his parents. They never seemed to see eye to eye on anything, like it was some kind of battlefield rather than a relationship. Quarrelling was the normal conversation in their house when Dean was involved in the discussion. He was stubborn and could never be wrong, even when he knew he wasn't right.

James had resented them for years, ever since being a teenager, and he often wished he had been adopted. That wasn't a flash in the pan feeling either; it had haunted him for as long as he could remember, and he was sure the feeling was reciprocated.

Denise walked away from Dean last January, having had enough of his arrogance and overbearing dominance. He liked to belittle her, but she knew she deserved better than being treated like that. Dean commented daily on her clothes, which were good quality high street items, saying they looked like charity shop bargain specials. He couldn't or wouldn't understand that taking care of one's appearance is an attractive trait, and he even stooped to making untrue comments such as saying she should take a shower more than once a day. He was a believer in the old fashioned ways that housework was a woman's job, and unless he had no choice at all, he always managed to avoid doing chores.

She had her sights set higher and knew she was better than being stuck in the dead end marriage with Dean Dean. She thought James was a chip off the old block, except he had more ambition and took much more pride in his personal appearance. Dean only showered when he really needed to and often smelled of onions. No matter how often James or Denise tried to encourage him to take better care of himself, he laughed them off and told them it was his personality that counted.

Denise was an office clerk at an accountant in Newdon, but she liked to tell people who didn't know her overly well that she was the manager. She wanted to aim high in life. Denise rented a decent flat in a new build area of town, which she organised before leaving the marital home. *So much better than living with Dean and the cling-on-to-the-apron-strings son.*

She wished she and Dean had another one or two children. *Maybe then I would have a kid I could feel proud of and love.* James was a terrible disappointment to her because she could only see Dean in him and their shared personality traits, not James in his own right as an individual person.

Their home town of Newdon boasted a nice shopping centre, and a newly pedestrianised area. Plenty of hours could be lost in the shops trying on clothes and chatting to friends over coffee and snacks.

Her new man was what she thought she wanted. A real career guy with ambition. Jake Hunter wanted Denise.

He was trying hard to get on in life but was missing the intimacy of having a partner after his last girlfriend dumped him for paying more attention to the office than to her. A good career was the priority for Jake.

Denise started flirting with him at work, and before long, he fell for her feminine affections. She asked him what his favourite perfume was, and he dropped the name of one that was on the television adverts. Denise then wore it every day.

Jake didn't have to chase her much or try too hard to win over her affections; he felt like he could've just clicked his fingers and she would've been there in an instant. *Can't say I blame her, I'm good looking and not always broke.*

They rushed to move in together less than six weeks after their first date. Over the next few months, Denise became besotted with Jake, yet he grew distant from her full-on affections and attention seeking behaviour. The fact Denise was going over the top in her efforts to keep him was making him feel suffocated. *We are a couple, she doesn't need to keep acting like she is trying to get me to fancy her.* After work one day, he asked her grumpily, 'How do you expect me to pay you more attention and be with you more when you want me to be successful at work too?'

Denise looked at him with wide eyes. 'I got the impression you were better than the other men and were doing well without having to try too hard.'

'Sorry, I've had a hard day at work.' *Maybe I'm just trying to adjust to being in a relationship again, I'll give it a few more weeks.*

It made Denise wonder if she was looking at history repeating itself by living with a partner that put themselves first and didn't care about their partner's wellbeing.

****

James' job was handed to him on a plate with a good management career path. His dad had been at the warehouse since leaving school, so a good word from him on behalf of his son went a long way. Dean was different at home to how he was at work, where he always made an effort to try and impress his boss.

It turned out that James was good at his job and had progressed well from being an office assistant. He was now one of the shift managers in charge of the day-to-day running of the warehouse. The next step would be a move to regional management, which he expected to be inside the next twelve months.

****

James liked to watch other people and wonder what it would be like to look at life through their eyes and have their thoughts as his own.

To think of the things he would be able to do if he became another person and was able do what he wanted with no real comeback on himself. He could then just pop back into his own body as if someone had pressed a pause button on his life in a way indiscernible to anyone else. It would be like he had continued on an autonomous path with everything decided by his unconscious mind, using his past decisions as a metronomic guide.

How about if he could just do things that *he* would never normally do, and then just switch back into his own shoes and not regret a thing? Maybe, just a petty thing like walking past an expensive car and digging a house key into the paint. The sound of the metal on metal would screech, but it would still be fun to do. A long, glaring line of bare metal standing out, causing a lot of problems for the owner, not to mention money lost on insurance claims and a sense of immense satisfaction for James. Why should he be bothered about stress in others' lives?

Perhaps he could do something more exciting, like squeeze a woman's arse in a shop. Any woman, it didn't need to be an attractive woman. A minger would be just as good; the outrage would be worth it. Then, he'd just vanish before their eyes so they'd think they were going crazy. Even better, he would pretend to be a plumber and install hidden cameras in bathrooms. The thought of watching a woman taking care of her personal needs, assuming she was alone, really turned him on. Whether in the shower or soaking in a luxurious bubble bath, he couldn't think of anything better to observe. He kept these thoughts to himself, as he knew they wouldn't be acceptable to anyone with normal morals. That made the actions he dreamed about seem even better.

He enjoyed playing make believe with what would happen to people he saw from time to time.

He looked out of the window of his identikit warehouse office window, the type of building that was replicated in thousands of other places around the country. He saw a boy of about fifteen walking a jolly looking dog. The boy thought he was cool. Styled hair, trendy clothes, expensive trainers and an arrogant air, walking with his chin jutting out like he was the bee's knees.

It wasn't even a rainy day; the weather was nice, if cold. James saw a car in his mind's eye, a vivid red Fiat 500, whiz around the corner. A huge puddle appeared in the gutter; filthy and simply aching for a car to plough through it and splash the water over a passing victim. James' imagination did not disappoint. He chuckled to himself as he saw the kid sodden and shaking with the shock. Probably now with squeaky soled shoes and a bollocking when he got home. The dog remained chilled out, untouched by the fictional wave of puddle water. James blinked to clear the vision and turned away from the window to go back to the real world.

****

Dean had been gutted by Denise's disappearance to her new flat, even more so by her inviting another man to live with her. He still saw her as a possession rather than a loved one.

It was already too late by the time he'd realised not only what he had lost, but also that he should have picked his game up and put much more effort into the relationship than just a bunch of flowers and a box of chocolates for special occasions. Although they squabbled, they did love each other, and he had assumed that was enough to keep them together.

The day she told him she was moving out, he pretended to not care, assuming she was merely posturing. She left with just a suitcase of clothes and a holdall containing cosmetics and other things she couldn't live without.

A taxi pulled up outside the house and sounded its horn. Denise opened the door with a self satisfied grin across her face. 'See you later, Dean,' she said. 'I hope you're happy now you've driven me away.'

Dean's eyes narrowed, feeling annoyed at her saying he had driven her away, but also feeling panicked when he realised she really was leaving him. 'Come on, Denise, give us another chance. I promise I'll change.'

She patted his upper arm and smiled what appeared to be a sympathetic smile. 'Sorry, Dean, it's too late. Goodbye.'

Without further ado, she left the house and was driven away in the taxi without even a look back at the marital home.

Dean felt numb, like a total loser, something that had not happened to him before.

James found himself living alone. Not long after his mum left, Dean died.

He could have found himself a new housemate if he really wanted to. The internet played quite a big part in his life, but being in his thirties, he just about remembered a time when people didn't stare at a screen at every opportunity like some kind of robot; especially if staring into a screen meant they didn't need to risk making eye contact with a fellow human. To him, it seemed like these days, people were too easily addicted to their electronic devices when there was so much life to live and so many books to read.

The house was just as it had been for the last couple of years. James didn't see the point in decorating because it was already finished to what the estate agent would call 'a very high standard.' The only thing he considered changing was the colour of the paint on the walls; the beige bored him.

Having no children meant his pay cheque wasn't swallowed up with nappies or budget price clothes that would soon be too small.

His house had no mortgage because Dean 'Bastard' Dean, as James called him, had done the sensible thing and taken out life insurance.

****

The car crash had knocked James and Denise for six.

Dean thought he was a great driver, but he was not. Despite this, James enjoyed the enthusiastic lifts into work. It happened just a year earlier, a couple of months after Denise had left, while on their way home from work. Dean braked for a ninety-degree bend just a second later than normal, driving ten miles per hour faster than every other day.

'Eat your heart out, Jenson Button!' shouted Dean as he yanked the steering wheel of his blue fifteen-year-old Ford Mondeo to the left.

'SHIT!' shouted James as he flinched and curled into a ball.

'You are such a nobber,' Dean yelled as the Mondeo flew out of the bend, waving his hand with exuberance to push his point home. 'I have never crashed yet, son!' He mashed the spongy throttle pedal down as far as he could towards the floorpan. As he did, something went wrong. He grabbed the steering wheel with both hands and tried to force the car to follow the bend round, but his speed was too high and his strength couldn't stop the old banger from under-steering onto the wrong side of the road. The whole weight of the car seemed to fight against him, and his biceps felt like they were going to pop.

A pungent smell of tortured rubber poured into the car along with the screech of under inflated tyres. Less than a second after a lurid slide, the back wheel hit the high kerb and before Dean or James knew what had happened, the Mondeo began to roll over and over as if they were doing a stunt in a Hollywood movie. Glass and plastic shards shattered and flew in all directions as tortured metallic screams filled the air.

By the time they stopped rolling and came to rest with the driver's side of the car on the road, Dean was already dead. His head had hit the road hard and been pushed sideways past the point of no return, snapping his spinal cord in the process. Dean never fastened his seat belt because he believed it would strangle him to death one day. He wasn't worried about getting a fine for not wearing it.

The final fatal slide meant that a part of Dean's skull was chamfered, like it had been pressed onto a deadly sanding belt. Blood and gore sprayed far and wide, splattering across every surface nearby. James vomited when he realised a small chunk of his dad's face had landed on his lips. The metallic smell of blood rose above the stench of burning rubber and petrol fumes as various bodily fluids dripped from above like a huge paint pot of gore had exploded inside the car.

The smell was not one that could be replicated anywhere else but at a trauma scene; it was a disgusting fetor. His puke splashed onto his dad's face, while some projected onto the exposed road through the smashed glass. Some came to rest on Dean's face and returned to his open mouth, where it mixed with saliva and blood to make a terrible cocktail. James escaped the crash with just a few scratches and a drenching of his dad's blood. It's no wonder James was unstable and lived increasingly inside his dreamland. Although he wouldn't go to the doctor for help, he probably had some form of PTSD.

****

During the reading of the will, Denise expected to get everything.

Jake was about to walk away from her after the crash, where her loser ex, whom Denise was so fond of sneering about, died such a gruesome death.

He saw that Denise obviously still missed Dean.

Then, he had second thoughts. *What kind of heartless bastard would do that? Walk away and break the heart of a vulnerable, if not annoying and materialistic woman.* No, even he couldn't do that. Good job he hadn't, he had smirked to himself. Denise let slip, after a cocktail or four, about the inheritance.

She was sure Dean wouldn't have gotten around to changing his will; he was too lazy to do anything important like that. The house, a life insurance windfall to pay off the mortgage and even his beloved record collection would all be coming her way.

****

She sat in the solicitor's expansive office, wearing an expensive outfit bought specially for the occasion. A luxurious aroma dominated the air. It was cloying in James' throat. She knew he was not a fan of perfume that had been over-applied by the wearer. How she had done herself up, she told herself, was to say 'screw you' to James.

Who did he think he was? Even bothering to turn up. The sad loser should be grateful she let him stay; he would get jack shit.

Still, seeing him squirm before walking away empty handed would be fun.

The solicitor was well dressed although plain Jane in looks. 'Mr Dean. Mrs Dean,' she started. She was out of her depth. *But why?* thought James. He knew his mother would get the lot.

Shit. It flashed through his mind he'd need to find somewhere to rent so Denise wouldn't get the satisfaction of turfing him out.

Mrs Lawson looked at the expectant pair, knowing the mood was about to change somewhat. Mrs Dean sat there, looking smug. Mr Dean looked like his entire world was crashing down around his ears.

'Go on, Mrs Lawson,' smirked Denise, readying herself for a very nice windfall. Lawson coughed. A smoker's cough, which she restrained from progressing into a full on hack. James looked around the office, trying not to make eye contact, trying not to cry. He knew his mum would tell him to man up, so he looked at the paintings hanging on the walls to push the tears away.

'It is a concise and very clear will,' continued Mrs Lawson.

Denise shot a sideways look at James, then another wide-eyed glare at Lawson. *What the fuck?* She thought. She and Dean had been to Lawson & Lawson a decade ago, when times were much better. The wills they had laid down were simple, but long and verbose, with small gifts to various charities. The cherry on the cake, if either of them should die, was that the other would get everything of real value. Well, except the stupid record collection; James was welcome to that. Who even has a record player these days apart from the one that was so beloved of Dean and James?

Mrs Lawson looked back at Denise. *What was that look? Pity? Cynicism? Humour? Is the cow laughing at me?*

Lawson blushed a little. She almost leaked urine she was so nervous. *Better get on with it.*

James hadn't noticed the awkward moment. He wasn't listening much. The sound and smell of the god awful crash was intruding into his conscious mind. He tried to keep it blocked out. *Who the hell pukes onto a dead man?* James was glad his mum didn't know. Mrs Lawson politely cleared her throat again and said, 'James?'

James came round quick. The solicitor sipped some water before continuing. 'Everything I have, I leave to my son, James Dean. Nothing is to go to any charity, nor to my estranged wife, Denise Dean.' She poured some more water from a glass jug and took a sip, seemingly to compose herself. 'That's it, Mr Dean. Mrs Dean. Thank you for coming today. James, I'll be in touch.'

James was speechless. Contrary to Denise, who dissolved into an aggressive monologue upon realising Dean, for once, had actually pulled his finger out and changed the damn will. 'What the actual hell, Mrs Lawson? James! Say something, you shit. Did you have something to do with this? That house and everything belongs to me! Sod the will, I'm having it anyway. Mrs Lawson, rip that up, put it in the bin and find the original will. Please? Please. I'm begging you.'

'Mrs Dean—'

'Please!'

'Mum,' started James, but stopped when he saw the mix of fear and hatred in Denise's eyes.

'Mrs Dean, it is binding. You can instruct another solicitor to appeal, but I'm afraid your chance of winning is zero. The will is watertight.'

'Screw you.'

'Please leave. I won't have anyone behaving like this in my office. Go. Now.' A flush of red crept across her neck, spreading up towards her pinched face. Denise stood.

Trying to appear respectable again, she cleared her throat and said, 'Goodbye, Ms Lawson. I won't waste my time appealing. I have a life to live.'

Without a second glance at her only child, she walked away.

****

The morning after Denise had left him for a new life, Dean had called the solicitor and asked for an urgent appointment.

'You're in luck. Mrs Lawson has had a cancellation this afternoon at three. Would you like to take it?'

'Yes please. I'll leave work early.'

He arrived at five to three, and Mrs Lawson was waiting for him. 'Welcome, Mr Dean. Please, come into my office.'

He entered the spacious room and sat with a sigh. Mrs Lawson smiled in anticipation of what could have brought Dean to book such an urgent appointment with her. 'How can I help, Mr Dean?'

Dean tried to smile, but his heart was sinking like a dinghy with a large hole. 'My wife has left me.'

He looked at the carpet, his head seemingly too heavy to lift and make eye contact for the moment.

'I'm sorry to hear this. Can I get you a drink? Maybe tea with sugar?' Mrs Lawson spoke with her best sympathetic voice.

'I'd like that, thank you.'

The solicitor lifted her telephone handset and spoke to someone, ordering a sweet tea. Almost as if this had been anticipated somehow, there was a knock on the door a minute later. 'Come in!' called out Mrs Lawson. The receptionist came in and set the drink on the table by Dean's chair.

He looked at her with a warm smile, but his eyes gave away his true feeling of sadness. 'I can't let her get away with this, just walking away. I want to change my will.'

Mrs Lawson interrupted him. 'Don't you think it's a bit soon to be doing things like this? Denise might well come back to you.'

Dean squinted, his brain ticking over as he thought about what Mrs Lawson had just said. He took another sip of his tea and nodded his appreciation. 'No, it's not too soon. She's moved out and shacked up with another man. She deserves nothing of mine. I mean, I'm not planning to die, obviously, but you don't know what's around the corner. Might get run over by a bus tomorrow.' He chuckled with a glint in his eye.

Mrs Lawson smiled pragmatically and made some notes on a pad of paper. She cleared her throat and tucked her hair behind her ears. 'Alright, Mr Dean, I'll prepare the paperwork and email it to you. Sign it electronically and send it back.'

Dean was already moving to stand up. 'Thank you for your time today. I'll send it back as soon as I get it.'

'Very well, thank you once again for your business.' Mrs Lawson held out her hand for Mr Dean to shake. She had perfected the 'limp lettuce' handshake, which Dean wasn't impressed with, but he didn't let it show. He walked out of the office with a spring in his step, feeling good that he had taken control of something for himself.

No sooner had he got into his house, he opened his laptop to find the email already in his inbox. Smiling to himself, he muttered, 'Screw you, Denise.' He pressed the enter key to dispatch the reply with a firm prod. *Time for a beer. I think I deserve it.* Dean padded through to the kitchen in his bare feet, wrinkling his nose at the sticky floor. He opened the fridge door and let out a self satisfied sigh as he reached in for a can of Guinness. *I could get used to this, not having to ration how many beers I can stuff into there.*

****

James' mobile vibrated on the coffee table. *Mum.* 'Not reading that,' he muttered under his breath.

He tucked into his Chinese takeaway. Even though it smelled great, he could smell himself over it. James needed a shower, but he hadn't felt the motivation to take himself to the bathroom. He was still numb from the crash, and more so now his mum had walked away. Without looking at the message, he knew the gist. He knew that Jake would have told Denise to leave when he found out the eagerly anticipated windfall had blown out of reach.

The pressure in James' head was unbearable. He didn't want to face the choice of letting her come back or telling her to jog on. James had the feeling that if he said no to her, he'd regret it with a feeling of terrible guilt and she may well disappear. The image of her walking away in the Lawson & Lawson office had burnt into his mind. He pressed delete on the message without reading it.

With the belief he would soon get turfed out of his home, cleanliness hadn't come high on his list of priorities. *Shit, the funeral is tomorrow. Best get ship shape.*

James paid a local catering firm to supply a buffet; he couldn't face having the wake in public like in a pub. He finished at ten thirty. *Not late enough for bed.*

What to do? He thought. The only untouched place was the garage. *Sod it.* There is a door into it from the kitchen. *It is cold in here, but not too messy.* James made a mental note to dispose of the chest freezer that was standing against the brickwork of the cobweb-encrusted back wall. It hummed. 'Best see what's in there, and then call the council to take it away,' he muttered to himself.

He opened it and faced nothing. Well, not quite. A frozen baby carrot and a thick layer of ice crusted around the rim. James allowed himself a small, wry chuckle. Dean had eaten everything in there and not bothered to refill it. Maybe he had left it switched on to wait for the never-ordered ASDA home delivery. *What a waste of power*, thought James as he turned it off.

The day of the funeral arrived and James woke early. Well, early compared to the rest of the week. He felt numb, and it was a struggle to summon enough energy to crawl out of bed. It was nine in the morning when he turned on the shower, which was still as good as new. Dean and Denise had done a lot of DIY a couple of years before. James set the temperature a little bit hotter than usual, but not enough to scald. He relished the almost burning feel, which made him feel more awake. In the here and now rather than in his dream world. He wanted to look good, even if he didn't feel it. He didn't want Denise to have a reason to make nasty comments to him. The Debenhams suit was a good fit for him. He had bought it a week before the crash for an interview. James allowed himself a wry smile as he looked at his reflection in the mirror. Still no grey hairs. With all the recent wrenching events, he half expected a white streak.

Dean's funeral service was held at Saint Peter's Church. The building was impressive; a typical Gothic style like so many churches in England. It was cool inside, the lit candles giving a welcoming and comforting glow. James was not a regular churchgoer. Hatch, match and dispatch described his attendances at St Peter's. The massive pipes of the church organ hummed the whole time James was there, but the old hymns were sung with little gusto by the assembled mourners. Dean, despite all of his faults, was popular. James noticed about a dozen people from work there too. *Good job I made an effort. Maybe, once the funeral is over with, I'll get my head back to normality.* He wanted to break out of his weird fantasy world. At the same time though, James could not see how to clear the mental fog that clouded his cognitive processes.

The family was not extensive. James was an only child. Still, at least that meant no arguments about Dean's possessions. He spotted Denise, and James got a feeling he had never experienced before towards his mother. *What was it?* He couldn't put his finger on it. James wanted to hug Denise and tell her he loved her. To say, *please come home.*

A feeling of reality was gnawing at the pit of his stomach. The ship had sailed; she had walked away without looking at him. James felt a conflict of emotion when he realised where she was sitting. At the front. The pew had a small placard hanging from a fraying piece of string, bearing the legend 'Family Only Please'. Pleasure, that she wanted to make that human contact on such a sad day. Resentment, that she had the cheek to sit there when it was her that had given Dean the metaphorical middle finger when she shacked up with Jake.

'Mum?' James whispered. Denise sat silent. She wore large sunglasses, even though the lighting in the church wasn't dazzling. She was dressed in black from top to toe and had obviously made a big effort to look smart despite Dean being her ex.

Maybe she was hiding tears, betraying her feelings towards Dean. Denise didn't respond. 'Mum?' James repeated.

Without turning her face, Denise replied in a monotone voice, 'James, thank you for allowing me to come. I still love you, and I'm sorry about how I behaved at the solicitors. I was shocked.'

Me, me, me, James tried to parrot in his mind, but his heart overruled his head. 'It's okay, Mum. I didn't read your messages, I thought you wanted nothing to do with me.'

'Oh, James, I am so sorry. Forgive me. Please.'

More begging, but James couldn't help himself. He thought about telling her to leave now and never contact him again. *Maybe, she would top herself though.* He tried to stop his mind from visualising her standing on the nearby train tracks. He imagined it was winter, and people could see her from the road. The bushes and trees naked. She stood there with a determination that suited her pigheadedness. His mind snapped back as he heard the imaginary noise of an approaching train, the rails whooshing and rattling. Not yet in sight.

'James? Are you okay, James? You seem distracted.' Denise looked at him through her oversized sunglasses.

'Sorry, Mum. I'm just struggling to believe this day is here. I wish I'd told him to slow down. I could have made him not die. Maybe I should have got him to check his tyre pressures the week before, and then maybe he'd still be here now.'

'It isn't your fault. You know, my gran once said we all have a number, and when our time is up, there is no changing it.' James couldn't help a single tear from winding down his cheek. The pressure in his temple made a vein throb.

He had a rare moment of clarity. 'Mum, come round to mine and stay after the wake. Let's have a coffee.'

'Thank you.'

The rest of the funeral passed by with a depressing familiarity that being an adult brings. It was nice. Pat Poole's Catering did a lovely spread. Sandwiches and quiches. A buffet always goes down well, and the mourners seemed to enjoy it. James couldn't help smiling at their neighbour's young son who piled his plate high with crisps, sausage rolls and pickled onions.

'Thank you,' said James to Pat, with genuine gratitude.

'My pleasure, James. Your dad would be proud of you.' James wondered how Pat knew Dean, or whether her apparent familiarity was just a throwaway comment. Pat smiled sympathetically and said goodbye. She left, leaving a pleasant aroma of food and a hint of perfume in her slipstream. Not the awful cloying smell that Denise used at the solicitors, James reflected. That annoyed him; he tried to push the thought away.

****

After the lethal crash, Jake became more nasty than ever to Denise. Their relationship hadn't been long at all before he changed. He had become jealous of Dean, even though Denise had left her husband. Instead of trying to talk to Denise about it and work a way through to a bright future, he internalised his feelings. That can never be healthy.

The day before the funeral, Denise had been reflective and naturally sad. Even though Dean had been nasty to her, he would never have dreamed of being physically abusive. There had been good times in the past, and Denise wondered if she had been so wrapped up in looking for a perfect future that she could no longer see the positives of the relationship she had with Dean. But, then she thought of all the times he had been mean about her appearance or ambitions and had laughed at her. 'Really, Denise, come on, you know people like us should be happy with what we have and just make the most of it, rather than stressing ourselves out by trying to be someone we aren't,' was one piece of logic she remembered well from Dean.

She sighed out loud and took another glug of her coffee. Jake couldn't quite stop himself from making a comment. 'Bit common that, Denise.'

She came out of her daydream. 'Pardon? What do you mean?'

'Slurping your drink like that, it's a bit common, love.'

She looked at him with confusion, scrunching up her face. 'That's uncalled for, Jake. Sorry, I was just in a world of my own.'

'Thinking of Dean again?' he asked, not able to conceal his sneer. Jake looked down on him and James, and he made his feelings increasingly plain as each day went on.

'Actually, yes, I was. It is his funeral tomorrow, it would be weird if I wasn't thinking about him.'

'But you have me now,' glowered Jake, blood rising to his head and making his neck veins start to throb. He knew from being a child he had a jealous streak, but he thought it was under control. Despite wanting to leave Denise, he couldn't bear the thought of her thinking of another man. Even if they were dead.

'I know. I love you, Jake. You know that, you're the best thing that's happened to me.'

'So why are you thinking of Dean? He is history now, literally.' Jake knew he had overstepped the mark, but he simply couldn't help himself.

The devil on his shoulder was whispering, 'Go on.'

'Oh, Jake, I was married to him for a long time, and we had a child together. How can I not look back when it's the funeral tomorrow? I think I need to pop out to the shops, it'll give you a chance to cool down.'

'Cool down? Cool fucking down? Who do you think you are talking to? I am not some petulant child.'

'I know you aren't, sorry if I offended you, but I think you're taking it out of proportion.'

'You need to appeal that will. Do it, or I'll knock you out!'

'What? Why would you bring that up now? Leave. Now.' Denise tried to push him towards the door.

The blood that was rising seemed to break through the dam of self-restraint, and he raised his fist to her face.

'You wouldn't dare. Hit me, and you are history.'

Jake punched her, and as she doubled over and grasped her face with both hands in desperate pain while stars popped in her vision, he pushed her over.

'Bye then.'

He walked away, leaving her alone and crying in pain, lying on her carpet. Denise was shocked and devastated. *I didn't deserve that, what a monster.*

****

'Coffee?' James called.

'Yes. Please.' He came back towards the lounge and saw Denise remove her sunglasses. She set them down on the coffee table and looked at him.

'Mum, what the hell happened?' James exclaimed. 'That is a bad black eye! No wonder you were wearing shades.'

'Jake happened.'

'What?'

'I told him I would get nothing. He told me to appeal. I told him I wasn't going to.'

'He gave you a black eye because of that?'

'Yeah.' She laughed ruefully. 'He says he didn't mean to. But he did. The bastard told me to appeal, or he'd knock me out.'

'Arsehole.'

'I know. I said he had to leave and tried to push him out, but he hit me.'

James felt a sudden wave of anger that scared him. 'I'll go and show him why he shouldn't hit a woman!'

'James, no. Please. It'll only make things worse.'

James and Denise cried and hugged. James hoped things were changing for the better between him and his mum. The thought of hurting Jake, really hurting him, kept elbowing into his conscious mind. James couldn't shift it. It was almost 10 p.m. before Denise went home. James felt emptiness, happiness and grief, and a wonder of what the future might hold. Feeling fed up of being suited and booted, he went to his bedroom and changed into jogging trousers, a tee shirt and a cosy hoodie. It wasn't cold enough to switch on the heating. Another coffee and normal television was in order. *Please*, thought James, *please, God, if you are listening, make my life back to normal.* That was what James wanted, to be back to the routine of work and home. He was reflecting with pleasure about previous journeys in Dean's car, and realised there would be no more lifts to work. The black cloud rolled back into his mind. Sleep descended into the quiet house. The television turned itself off after two hours.

It was dark and quiet. James slept deep, but at about one in the morning, all that changed.

****

James loved his dreams, those he remembered at least.

His unconscious mind was telling him it was time to make things happen. Stop being a passenger in life and do something that would feel good. That gave him a sense of having a kind of power.

Dean shouldn't have died; he had a life to live. Perhaps others need not live. Maybe their existence served no purpose. James felt a rush of determination. *Someone must die at his hand. Tonight.*

He walked into the kitchen with a sense of twisted mischief spreading through his body. The ornate magnetic knife rail had several knives displayed. James picked the one he used to carve chicken for Sunday roast. He knew who he should look for.

Someone who wouldn't be missed, except by other people who society frowned down upon. James decided to walk. He knew the risk of his car being caught on CCTV was too high, so he stepped out into the cold, late night air on foot. At least the fact he was wearing a hat and a hoodie with a scarf pulled over his face wouldn't stand out as looking odd. The wind was light, just a faint breeze. The quietness of the night was stark compared to the hubbub of the day James was used to, as was the supermoon lighting the streets of Newdon.

It wasn't far to the park next to the town centre. The green space was the pride of a community group, whose volunteers worked tirelessly to keep it looking good. Graffiti never stayed for more than a day, and the flower beds were immaculate. It provided an outdoor area for everyone to use.

The local Facebook page always displayed long threads of people complaining about how the rough sleepers should be banned from the area. Some people felt sorry for them and proposed that the community should help, so a small group of volunteers were starting a charity to provide a night shelter for the homeless.

It was late enough for there not to be many people around, and no office or shop workers wandered the park on breaks or lunches. James walked with quite a slow pace, but not slow enough to draw attention to himself. He looked around, checking it was safe to cross and that an imagined villain wasn't about to mug him. Cameras were what he was looking for. He spotted one high on a pole, pointing down the high street. That was the opposite direction to where he had come from, but he knew it could swivel at any moment and capture him.

He could make out the form of a man sitting on a bench by the switched off fountain. There was a bag on wheels next to the bench. It was tartan; the kind much loved by elderly ladies to go shopping with and use as a walking frame. This one was dirty, with multiple stains making the pattern look irregular.

The man was of an indeterminable age. Maybe even a vintage, judging by the odour of god knows what alcohol carried on the breeze. His hair was more like an ill-kempt animal's coat. The colour was literally dirty blond and stuck to the man's jacket, which looked at least twenty years old. It wasn't, but a life on the streets had been cruel. His face had more lines than a roadmap; the ravages of being outside in all weathers made it look like old leather.

This is the one. Who will miss him?

James nonchalantly walked by in an attempt to work out if the man would try to fight or escape. He was fast asleep with a bottle of cheap vodka resting on its side under the folds of his coat. 'Perfect,' muttered James beneath his breath.

This has to be the one. A stranger that no one will miss.

A compassionate thought passed through James' mind. *At least the bloke is self anaesthetised.*

A final look round to make sure there were no other passers-by, he stepped behind a magnificent oak tree next to the bench. If anyone came by, he'd look like he was about to urinate. As if controlled by an unseen force of nature, James stepped over a knotted root that sprouted through the earth behind the bench. He retrieved the knife from his belt. With one swift, fluid move, he hooked his left elbow under the fetid tramp's jaw and pulled his head back so the skin over his neck was taut. The tramp made a guttural choking noise. James felt invincible and pushed the blade against the man's throat. He had no idea how hard to cut, so he cut with as much force as he could summon.

A bloody gurgle emanated from the man's lips, and he went limp just as James was deciding if he needed to make the cut deeper. He looked down and saw the man had bled out. The blood looked unreal in the deep shadow afforded by the tree. A feeling of intense satisfaction and cold-hearted determination seeped into James' soul. He wiped the knife with the fabric top of the shopping cart. *Best not leave the knife here.* In a leap of disconnected reality, James was back at home. He walked into the house, thankful there were no sleeping people to try and not disturb. He placed the knife into the dishwasher. James had already filled it after the wake, placing a dishwasher tablet into the tray and selecting the seventy degree programme so it was ready. *That should do it.*

****

Saturday saw James awaken, still on the sofa. He was aching.

A strange feeling passed through him. *No,* he thought to himself, *nothing is amiss.* He wandered into the kitchen and chose the porridge. No bowl in the cupboard. *Shame that Pat Poole's Catering didn't do the washing up too, as well as the food for the wake.* He opened the dishwasher and selected a bowl and a spoon. The knife glinted on the top rack, a witness sworn to secrecy, clean. Porridge was James' favourite comfort breakfast, topped with banana, blueberries, blackberries and kiwi fruit.

Soccer AM was playing on the television, the default Saturday morning viewing. *Same shit, different day. At least Man United will not win the title,* he thought with a smirk. *That tosser, Jake Hunter, supports them.* James flicked through the channels with no real interest. The news came on. James liked watching the news, to Denise's approval. Dean didn't see the point of keeping up with current affairs and would always turn the channel over when it came on. He'd say something pathetic to try and wind them up like, 'What's the point in watching the news? The government do what they want anyway, and who cares about some war in Syria when we have real problems like running out of milk?'

There was a brief item on the local news about a homeless man called Patrick O'Leary being murdered. His throat cut wide open while he slept, he was found by an early morning dog walker. 'Jesus,' muttered James under his breath. *Some right nutters about. But what is it with dog walkers? They always find the bodies.*

The rest of the day passed by in a blur while washing clothes ready for work. He decided he should go back to work and get back to normal. Try and show his mum that he had become an independent, strong man. *Sod it, might as well watch football on the television. No one here to tell me not to.* In an act of defiance to no one in particular, he cranked the volume up to twenty.

His mind drifted in and out of consciousness, thinking about this and that while paying zero attention to the match.

He was fantasising about killing again. His soul felt the renewed satisfaction of power and told him he should do it again. 'Go on,' it whispered into his mind. Without even pausing or connecting to his conscious mind, he agreed. The autonomous robotic element was taking over.

With a jump, James realised someone was knocking on the door. He forced himself up from the sofa. *Doubt it is anyone I want to see. Maybe it's the postman.*

He opened the door, and two people greeted him with a smile. Jehovah's witnesses. There was a man, about sixty years of age, and a younger female perhaps approaching her fortieth birthday. The pair were dressed well. The man wore a smart, albeit musty and well worn suit. *Not threadbare, but a pair of leather elbow patches might improve it,* thought James. He was tall, maybe five foot eleven, but thin. He reminded James of a coat hanger with a protruding Adam's apple. The female was wearing a dowdy trouser suit and flat soled shoes. Like the man, her clothes were a few years old. She had a pleasant face, albeit vacant. 'We are here to tell you good news,' said the man. The female nodded. 'Tell me, sir,' he continued, 'do you have a belief in God?'

James looked at him. He'd had no company apart from his mum on the day of the funeral. 'I don't know,' James truthfully answered. He looked again at the pair. *Father and daughter? There was some kind of connection there, but not chemistry. Odd.* 'Why don't you come in? It's cold out there today.'

The man shot the woman a quizzical look. They were surprised. 'Thank you,' said the man as he ushered the woman into the house.

'Have a seat.' James motioned to the large leather sofa. That sofa was one of Dean's pride and joys, one he had saved up for a long time to purchase.

James had that now familiar, but intimidating dark cloud rolling through his mind.

To cheer himself up, he asked the pair if they would like a whiskey, presuming they would be offended by the offer of alcohol.

'No, thank you,' said the man. 'I'm Tom Jones. This is Val Hawley.'

'I don't believe it!' exclaimed James. 'I'm James Dean.'

A hint of amusement twinkled in Tom's sharp looking eyes. 'Ah, you too are a famous-named man. It's quite something, isn't it?'

James didn't miss the real Tom Jones' catchphrase and grinned, clearly enjoying himself. 'Say that again!'

Val sighed and rolled her eyes as if she thought no one would notice. *Maybe she'd had her fill of people making Tom the centre of attention.*

She reached into her handbag and pulled out a dog-eared bible with a well loved patina. Tom smiled and slipped his hand into his leather satchel. James liked the bag. *Damn, an old boy Jehovah bloke has better taste than me.* James imagined just taking the bag from Tom and pretending to steal it. It amused him for a minute or two. James tried to shake himself out of the creeping onset of his daydream world, telling himself to concentrate and make the most of the encounter.

Next week would be his return to work, and James knew he was more than ready to go back. As much for a distraction as anything else, and to get back into the old nine-to-five routine.

He was losing the will to talk about religion as the image of Dean with his head twisted against the unforgiving tarmac wormed its way into his mind alongside the deafening screech of metal. *So screwed up,* was James' opinion of his mind's ability to put a downer on everything.

'Fancy a cup of tea and a biscuit?' he heard himself saying.

'Oh wow, this never happens,' Val enthused. 'Normally, people just tell us to go away.'

'Well, to tell you the truth, I was feeling lonely. I rarely invite strangers in.' James was now regretting asking Tom and Val in, but he was still grateful for someone paying him attention. 'Tea? Coffee?' he asked with a broad smile, which belied his inner feelings.

'Tea for both of us, please. Milk no sugar,' said Tom.

James wondered why Tom had just spoken for them both. Maybe Tom liked to be a father figure or more likely just took the lead as the man. James stood up, his body a little stiff from sitting down for a long time. He looked across at Val and Tom and felt a creep of loathing. *Why, though?* It was the same loathing that Jake Hunter invoked in him. James tried to justify it by thinking maybe Tom was a pervert who lusted over Val. The murderous feeling gestated in his belly, an overwhelming urge, and James forced himself to put the thought into a box at the back of his mind.

The kitchen wasn't far, but it was round a corner from the lounge, so the interior wasn't visible from the sofa. James found himself in the kitchen, having walked there in a daze. *What's happening?* thought James. It was a weird feeling, not unlike a déjà vu.

'Tom?' James heard himself say, almost like his voice was being borrowed by an unseen entity. 'Can you come and help me carry through the tea and some biscuits?'

'Okay, be there in a jiffy,' said Tom.

It took less than a jiffy for James to pick up a heavy pan he used to cook steaks. As Tom trotted into the kitchen, James swung the pan in a fast upwards swipe at Tom's face. It struck Tom on the temple. Very hard. He fell to the floor with a strange look in his eyes. Was it fear? Bewilderment? Who knew, but James had a visitor in a barely conscious state on the floor. James was on autopilot. He picked up the boiled kettle from the granite work surface. *What am I doing?* His unconscious devil had taken over again. He tipped the kettle and watched with great satisfaction as the boiling-hot water poured into Tom's eyes, instantly causing Tom to let out a bloodcurdling scream.

From the lounge, a timid voice called bizarrely, 'Is everything okay?'

'Yes,' James called back. 'Tom just scalded his finger, no biggie.'

James looked at Tom and decided he had to die. If he lived, he would go to the police and James would be imprisoned. Which, obviously, meant Val must die too. *Leave no witnesses*, thought James, chuckling to himself at the play on words.

He reached for the kitchen roll. In a swift flick of the wrist, James ripped off fistfuls of it. A second later, he was stuffing Tom's mouth with the roll. He rammed in as much as he could with one hand, while pinching Tom's nostrils together with the other. Tom felt his life slipping away, but he didn't put up a fight. He felt a sense of relief and happiness in knowing death was close, and he knew he would soon be with his God. Tom went limp, and James was elated.

How do I get rid of a dead body, never mind two? Val had to die too, as she would certainly tell the authorities if she escaped. James looked around. His eyes settled on the chest freezer in the garage. He opened the lid. With a grunt and feeling like his joints were on the point of dislocation, James heaved Tom into the freezer.

As he returned to the kitchen, Val wandered in from the lounge. 'Where is Tom?' she demanded, with a wobble of fear in her voice.

'Oh, he's just in the loo. Do you mind helping me to clean up this water please?' He tossed her some paper towel. An annoyed look flashed through her eyes for a moment, which made her look much more attractive. *Shame*, thought James, *she'll be in the freezer soon.* As she knelt down with the paper towel, James felt the irresistible urge. He struck her on the back of her head with the same instrument that had felled Tom, with the same amount of viciousness.

As she slumped the short distance to the vinyl flooring, a wave of tiredness passed over James' body.

Killing is tiring.

He was sure Val was dead. Her body was not as dense as Tom's by a long way. She was much easier to lift from the floor and place into the freezer. As he laid her body over the top of Tom's, Val took a sharp intake of breath and her eyes opened with an brain injured look, failing to focus. James was amused. He closed the freezer lid and said, 'Sleep well.'

With the power turned back on and the temperature turned to the coldest possible, their death sentence was complete.

James returned to the kitchen and mopped up the remaining water. He was relieved and delighted there was no blood spatter to clean up. *Keep the blood evidence away,* he grinned to himself.

If he were in his conscious state with both feet firmly placed in reality, he would have been horrified. As it was, Soccer AM was still on the television and he sat down with a cup of tea. *Cold, but drinkable.* The Jehovah's Witnesses were now not even a memory, almost as if his actions had never even happened.

****

James felt his return to work was going as well as could be expected.

His heart wasn't in it at first, but as the weeks and then months rolled by, he settled into the rhythm of daily life.

He was not thinking of looking for love.

The past few months had been full of grief, and he missed Dean more than expected. James figured that a girlfriend would be too much for him, so he concentrated on work and looking for a pastime to enjoy at the weekends. Denise visited the house a few times in the months after Dean's premature death. She and James were getting on better than ever, but there was still a je ne sais quoi that neither of them ever got over.

James was waiting for her to ask if she could move back in, but that never happened. He wouldn't be surprised if she did, though, sometime in the future.

****

'Listen in.' Sergeant Laura Love raised her voice to get the attention of the officers sat in the small and stuffy briefing room. There were a handful of faces peering back at her.

'Okay, Love!' smirked PC Hooker-Wolfe. Sgt Love shot her a funny look as everyone relaxed.

'Today is the six month anniversary of Mr O'Leary's murder.'

She sipped water from a plastic cup, letting her words float in the air. 'To be blunt, we have nothing. Today, you lucky lot will do a door knock. Ask residents if anyone from that address either saw anything or suspects anything. On your way out of here, pick up some leaflets to hand out. It has a picture of the deceased on it. Good luck.'

James was just getting out of the shower when someone knocked on his door. Something about that sound rang a faint bell far in the depths of his troubled mind. *What now?* With a towel tied around his waist, no chance of his modesty being compromised, he opened the door.

He didn't expect cops. 'Er, hi,' he said, bewildered, to the two female officers standing on his doorstep.

Hooker-Wolfe handed him a leaflet with the photo of Patrick O'Leary printed on it in glossy magnificence. 'We're going door-to-door today, reminding people about the recent murder of Patrick O'Leary.'

'Huh, okay.'

'Do you know anything that may be of help, sir?'

That uneasy feeling again. 'No, no, I'm sorry. I wish I could help.'

'It was you, wasn't it?' asked Sgt Love.

'Yes, it was me!' James laughed and swung a punch at her.

As quick as a flash, Hooker-Wolfe shrieked, 'Spray, spray, spray!' as she lifted her canister of incapacitant spray and pointed it at his face, discharging the torrent of PAVA into his eyes.

James rubbed his face. 'Thank you for your help, sir.'

'Thank God for that,' chuckled James as he closed the door. *His imagination had played a blinder,* he thought. *Almost fooled me for real.*

As if I'm capable of murder. He shrugged his shoulders almost imperceptibly. Dean came back into his mind's eye. All that crimson blood and the stench of gore floated through his mind.

****

Much as they had expected, the door canvas had revealed nothing of use. 'Come on, time for home,' said Sgt Love.

PC Hooker-Wolfe sighed as she put her incapacitant spray back into her personal locker along with her radio. Night shift had started their tour of duty; nothing more she could do today. Something was nagging at her thoughts as that famous copper's nose sniffed through the events of the day.

'That guy with the towel around his waist when he opened his door was a weirdo.'

'Yeah, I thought that too, but that doesn't make him a throat slasher,' chuckled Sgt Love as she placed her radio with care on charge inside her locker. 'Come on, let's go home and have that bottle of wine.'

'Okay, but let me do an intel report just in case.'

****

Denise felt lonely after Dean's horrendous death and her awful liaison with Jake. Perhaps many people would be put off relationships because of events like that, and who would blame them?

The pangs of loneliness haunted her; she couldn't even contemplate living alone for more than a short time. Every time she turned on the television there seemed to be nothing but dating website adverts, all purporting to be the best thing in town.

Denise worried about what kind of man she would attract. The last thing she needed was another man like Dean or Jake. A slobby bully or a well-dressed bully. *I'm sure something will turn up, I must be due some good luck.*

She was grateful for her friends. Living in the same town for so many years meant she had more than a few. Some of them had stable relationships and were happy with their place in life, kids still at school and family around them.

There was one friend in particular who had been around forever. Donna Miller. Even from when Denise had been pregnant with James, Donna had been a steady shoulder to cry on. When they were younger, Denise thought Donna was a bit dull. The steady life of living with an average family and being happy in life didn't appeal to her, but now she understood the attraction. A happy family to go to every day; sure, there were ups and downs, but that was perfectly normal to Donna.

After Jake left, Denise spent more time keeping in touch with Donna, hoping to keep attached to everyday life and not sink into a depression or become too self-critical.

Surely time will be a good healer. There have to be some old wives' tales that are true.

Denise decided she wanted to thank Donna somehow for being a good friend and confidant.

They were enjoying a chat before Donna had to go to collect her daughter from the after-school ICT class. Denise looked across at her friend sitting on a chair with her feet tucked under her bottom. 'Donna, are you free in a few weeks for a weekend away?'

Donna's eyes swivelled round to Denise, away from the television. Cocking her head to one side as a curious look spread over her face, she asked, 'Why's that, Denise?'

Denise shrugged, self doubt pecking at her. 'You've always been an awesome friend. I think you deserve a treat.'

Donna turned her body and looked at Denise. 'Oh? What do you have in mind? A romantic weekend in Paris maybe? I like the sound of that.' She grinned at Denise and raised her eyebrows, waiting for a response.

'I ain't that loaded, Donna!' Denise protested, looking at her nail polish closely. 'I was thinking more of a day at a health spa. Let us have some pampering.'

Donna's face was a picture of amazement and happiness. 'OMG, really? That would be amazing. I've always wanted to do that but never thought about actually getting around to it.' Her eyes sparkled. 'Thank you so much.'

Denise felt herself grin wider, and more genuinely than she had for a long, long time, years even.

A sly smile crept onto Donna's face. 'Have you ever been on a blind date before?'

She let that hang in the air for the time it took Denise's face to change into a shocked and curious expression combined.

Her good friend screwed her face up as if she was working out the cooking time for her dinner. Her voice went up half an octave. 'No, never! Hang on, what are you up to?'

Donna looked up at the wall clock and gasped. 'I have to go and collect Olivia from school. Do you want to come?'

It wasn't far to the school, just around the corner. The two women hurried, along with plenty of other mums and dads rushing in the same direction.

'So, what's this about a blind date?' Denise looked at Donna sideways. Her curiosity had gotten the better of her, and she couldn't wait any longer to find out what Donna had in mind.

Donna grinned. 'I wondered how long it would take you to ask. I knew it would be before you left to go home.'

Denise smiled. 'Well, you obviously know me so well...now, spill the beans.'

'I have a friend who works at Newdon hospital. He's a chef.'

Denise pulled a grimace. 'A chef at the hospital, isn't that an oxymoron?'

Donna tittered. 'He's a lovely bloke, but he never has chance to meet anyone. I know a lovely lady...' She looked at Denise and winked.

'Hmm, I'm not sure. I might be better off looking online.'

Donna sighed, and with patience said quietly, 'You've had some bad luck with men. At least come out to Nando's and see if you like him. Me and Jack could come too?'

Sod it, could be fun. It'll get me out of the house.

'Yeah, why not,' Denise beamed,

Donna did a fist pump, which wasn't like her. 'Brilliant! I'll sort it out. How about Friday night, sevenish?' She had a smug look on her face as if she had a plan she'd been working on for a while.

Cocking her head, Denise asked, 'You look so smug, Donna. I guess that's a good thing and he is a decent person?'

Donna nodded. 'Yeah, he is. I think you'll get on like a house on fire. We need to wait here for the kids to come out of the classroom.'

****

It had just gone past 6 p.m. on Friday when Denise gazed in the mirror in her bedroom and looked at the woman she saw.

God, life has been hard the last few years. I hope tonight might be the start of something new.

She had made an effort to look good, but not too much because she knew Donna wouldn't be dressed to the nines.

For the next few minutes, she just messed about with her hair and makeup and called for a taxi at 6:30 p.m. Denise arrived at Nando's a few minutes after the others, who were waiting outside the door. Donna said with a grin, 'Denise, this is Paul. Paul, meet Denise.'

Denise was impressed that Paul had not looked straight at her breasts before her eyes, and he was dressed well too, but not over the top. He seemed to be a couple of years younger than her, which she liked.

A slightly awkward and mumbled 'hello' from both of her friends and Donna, with a satisfied smile, led the way inside the restaurant.

The friends enjoyed their meal and went to a pub afterwards. Before they knew it, the landlord was ringing the bell and shouting, 'Time, ladies and gentlemen, last orders please.'

The group said their goodbyes and made their own ways home.

Denise felt thrilled she'd had a lovely night out and that she hadn't wasted her time. She wanted to see Paul again, and wondered if he felt the same way.

Only one way to find out…

****

Donna's phone beeped to signal she had a text message. *I bet that's from Denise.*

Hi Donna,' she read out loud, 'thanks for a great night out. Denise is great, do you think she's interested in seeing me again? Give her my number. Smiley face. Kiss.'

Another beep.

'Heard anything from Paul? I had a good night. What's his number? Kiss, kiss.'

Donna couldn't help but burst out laughing. *These two must be psychic or something!*

She worked her fingers over the keypad, sending a message back to Denise: *Yes, he loved it, and he wants me to give you his phone number. He texted a minute before you did.*

Donna didn't even bother to text Paul back, as she knew Denise would send a text straight away. She wouldn't wait long enough for her nerves to build and risk putting her off.

Less than half an hour later, Donna had a text back from both of her friends to say thank you and that they were going to meet up again during the week. She had a tingle of excitement and crossed her fingers, hoping this was the start of something special.

****

Denise and Paul did indeed meet up again during the week. It was a very positive experience for Denise. She was used to being bullied or belittled, but Paul did neither of those things. Compliments came easily from him, and Denise could tell he meant them.

Over the course of the next few weeks, they met up several times, and Denise felt herself falling for Paul.

****

Denise popped round to Donna's house for another meet up before she had to go on the school run.

She sat back in the comfort of an armchair, cradling her coffee. 'I can't thank you enough for introducing me to Paul. He is amazing. I didn't think there were any true gentleman left, but he's proved me wrong.'

'Sounds like you might even be in love with him,' grinned Donna with a triumphant spark in her eyes. 'You really deserve a turn in fortune, and I think this could be it. So, when should I buy a wedding hat?'

Denise almost spluttered her coffee out and chortled, 'Hilarious...you only said that to make me spit out my coffee.' She adopted a serious face. 'I just hope that James takes to him.'

'I'm sure he will, besides, it's not up to him who his mum falls in love with,' said Donna with a kind smile.

That seemed to really cheer Denise up. She felt a lot more positive about how James might feel about Paul.

'Yes, you're right. I feel like this is the best thing to have happened for me in years.'

****

James got a WhatsApp from Denise on his mobile phone. *Hi, can I bring my fella, Paul, round for Sunday dinner?*

He typed back, *Yeah, sure ;-)*

James had been hearing quite a bit about Paul Edwards from Denise.

He was wary at first and wanted to make sure he wasn't another arsehole like Jake. Paul seems alright. Like James, he hated Manchester United. Paul was cagey when he first met James, and he guessed it was for fear of getting off on the wrong foot with his partner's son.

It turned out that Sheffield Wednesday was his favourite football team. *Suppose that is okay,* thought James. *At least they wouldn't be winning any trophies soon.* Paul had apparently been introduced to Denise through a mutual friend, and he went on to explain how he'd worked at the hospital for many years as a chef. James was surprised that his mum had gone for a normal, blue collar guy. *Hopefully this one will pay her a lot more attention than Jake ever did. I really hate that arsehole.*

Sunday came, and the dinner was nice. Pleasant chat filled the evening, and Paul even did the dishwasher duties, which impressed James.

James leant towards Paul and slipped into the conversation in a conspiratorial tone, 'Hear what mum's ex did to her?'

Paul curled his top lip in disgust, looking a bit like Elvis Presley. 'Slapped her about, I heard. What a tosser. Who would even think about doing something like that, especially to a special woman like Denise?'

As the evening rolled on by, Paul and James were getting on like old friends. *Paul actually seems like a nice guy. I hope Mum doesn't put him off by being too much of a diva.*

It was getting late, well after 10 p.m. when Denise announced she was going home because she had work the next day and would leave the two men in her life to socialise.

Denise and Paul had a quick smooch by the door. She whispered in his ear, 'See, I told you that he'd like you.'

James saw them kiss and felt a prick of anger. He realised that Paul wasn't guaranteed to not hit Denise, despite seeming like a really nice guy. James felt that like a hard punch in his solar plexus. The anger gave way to a murderous feeling. By now, logic and reasoning had gone, but he somehow kept a temporary lid on his explosive temper. 'Fancy a kick about in the garden, Paul?'

'It's dark though, and it's too cold, mate.'

'That doesn't matter. I have an outside light in the garden. Come on, it'll be a laugh.'

'Huh, alright then, fella. I have to warn you though, I'm a ninja with a ball.'

As soon as Paul's left foot took a step out of the house onto the patio, he slipped on a patch of ice and hit his head on the hard, unyielding flags. Some blood leaked out of his scalp. Not much, but enough to tell James that Paul was out cold and in trouble. Calling for an ambulance did not occur to him. The garden was not overlooked by other houses, and tall trees provided a barrier between his house and the neighbours.

How long does it take to kill a man?

He sauntered into the kitchen, whistling the theme tune to Kill Bill under his breath. There wasn't a samurai sword to fetch. *Pity*, thought James. He sniggered as he looked at his new collection of knives on the magnetic strip bolted to the wall. James' lips curled as he selected the sharpest looking one.

A moment later, James was on his knees trying to find a pulse on Paul's neck. He failed because Paul was already dead. 'You bastard,' muttered James. He felt a little sad that Paul was dead, but satisfied nonetheless that Denise couldn't be harmed by her new love.

A new evil thought wheedled into his mind from the depths of his wicked soul. He dragged Paul near to the drain beneath the downpipe from his integral garage and double checked that the heart had stopped beating. He positioned the knife on the skin underneath Paul's left ear and made a cut right across his still-warm throat. Blood flowed out like water from a garden hose, glinting under the streetlamp that stood behind his garden wall.

James wasn't satisfied with simply being responsible for Paul's demise, and set about seeing what else he could make himself do. *Only one thing for it.* He pulled Paul's head as far back as he could, making sure the eyes were closed; he didn't want to be stared at by a head as it was being severed. It wasn't too hard to cut right through the neck. In fact, James didn't need to. He cut through just over halfway, then grasped Paul's head and twisted it with a violent jerk. The head came off in his hand.

In a flash of inspiration, James dragged Paul's headless body onto the lawnmower and arranged the Honda's tarpaulin over the top of it. He didn't want blood in the house, so he went back inside, leaving the head on the grass.

It didn't take long for James to recover what he was looking for in the cupboard under the sink. Strolling back into the garden, he placed the lifeless head into the black bin liner he had retrieved. James decided he would think about what to do with the rest of Paul tomorrow. For now, he was out of sight under the bulging tarpaulin.

Nonchalantly making his way to the black wheelie bin, he dropped the head inside. It came to rest on top of a packet of gone-off meat and sent a cloud of vacuum cleaner dust into James' face before he could close the lid. James put Paul's coat into the Salvation Army clothes collection bag that had dropped onto his doormat the previous week and left it out by the kerb. He pushed the wheelie bin onto the path too, ready for collection the next day.

The dishwasher again swallowed a dreadful secret into its metallic gut.

****

Justin Rae was playing football in his garden with Craig Kadish, his best friend from primary school. They were just nine years old and loved doing what boys all over the UK do in their spare time.

Craig wanted to be goalkeeper and stood between a pair of jumpers that were being used as goalposts. He crouched in position, ready to spring and save the penalty that Justin was lining himself up to take.

Craig pointed at his mate, who was blowing into his hands to try and warm them. 'You're going to miss this, Justin! There is no way you'll score past me.' He'd learned that Justin was easily teased and was putting this to good use in an attempt to put him off.

'Shut up, Craig! Concentrate on trying to save my shot, which you won't even see 'cause it'll be too fast for you,' retorted the aspiring football star.

Justin placed the ball *just so,* and took a dozen steps back. Without taking his eyes off the ball, he sped forwards and powered his boot through it.

Miss! The ball sailed over Craig and right over the wall separating the garden from their neighbour's.

Craig bellowed with laughter, 'See! I told you that you were going to miss! Justin, you're shit at footy.'

'Not as shit as you, Craig. You'd better go and get the ball back, or your dad will kill you!'

Justin mumbled something Craig couldn't hear, but he guessed Justin probably questioned his parentage. The shorter of the two boys set off on his mission to get the ball back from the man next door. Craig wandered around his friend's garden while he waited for Justin to come back. He heard the neighbour's door being knocked upon and someone say, 'Hello, you okay?'

Justin wasn't a quiet speaker and boomed, 'I've kicked my football into your garden…can I get it back please?'

The owner of the other voice laughed. 'Yeah, sure, just don't get any mud on my floor. Go on, through you go.'

Justin wiped his feet on the coconut doormat several more times than he really needed to. His neighbour was huge, and a bit scary too, especially to a nine-year-old schoolboy. He nervously looked at the floor in the desperate hope he could avoid dropping any mud from his trainers. 'Thank you.'

Justin wandered through to the back door, the layout being the same as his own house. It wasn't locked, and he was looking for the ball before even stepping over the threshold into the garden. The ball was a fluorescent yellow colour, so it wasn't hard for him to spot it resting beside something hidden by a cover that bore the legend 'Honda'. The boy jogged over to the ball, eager to get back to the game with Craig in his garden.

It was then he saw it. He blinked in disbelief, and looked again. A greyish coloured human hand was protruding from under the cover. Filled with horror, he grunted another thanks to the neighbour and left the house as quickly as he could without running. As soon as he arrived back home, he told Craig about the human hand. Craig just stood there with his mouth wide open, looking like a Madame Tussaud's wax work.

'You better call the cops quick!' Craig squealed. 'I bet they'll come with guns and everything.'

****

'What have you got there, boy?' asked Ray Stigall, the sixty-something-year-old council manager. His unkempt but friendly mongrel dog, Trev, looked back at him. Trev was free to roam the landfill as and when he wanted. Ray couldn't care less; he was in charge of the landfill site. Arriving refuse trucks chugged along the service road and weighed in, and again on exit after they'd dumped their cargo. The cantankerous and dirt encrusted computer spat out a receipt showing the difference and hence the weight of the disgorged load, which was then recorded for the people who cared about that kind of thing.

It was a filthy, dusty job. Perfect for Ray, as the council office desk jockeys never wanted to come down to see him or his workspace. He chain-smoked in the office and had a calendar of topless women displayed with pride; it really was a relic of a bygone era.

Seagulls made the cry that evoked seaside memories as they circled around the tip, scrapping over god knows what items they had found.

Ray looked out of the window and frowned when he saw the scabby cat he let roam alongside Trev scratching at an already ripped open bin bag. The seagulls were trying their luck against the cat to get into the bag too. Trev thumped his wagging tail on the metal filing cabinet as he looked at Ray and put his wet nose into Ray's outstretched hand. Ray realised that Trev was trying to give him something.

'Give,' said Ray. Trev complied, and immediately dropped a human eyeball into Ray's palm. 'What the fuck!' he yelled, in a much higher pitch than he'd achieved before. Shocked and trembling to the core, he'd also set Trev off barking.

Ray ran out of the office door and up the heap of refuse to where Pam the cat was scratching around. The climb was quite steep, about seventy feet, but the adrenaline surged Ray onwards and upwards.

The seagulls wheeled up into the air in a cacophony of noise, protesting at the interloping human. Ray's boots slipped, and he slammed face first into an old barbeque. As the wind returned to his lungs, he looked up to see where Pam was. 'Oh my fucking God!' he proclaimed, having spotted what the creatures were competing over. An actual human head in a bin bag! The head didn't have much face left; the cat had scratched most of the flesh from the skull.

The eyeballs were both missing. One of which was no doubt rolling around on the floor somewhere in his office; a seagull was trying to eat the other one. The tip's noisy murder of crows were flapping at some of the gulls. Blood trickled from Ray's eyebrow towards his eye, but he barely noticed it.

Unsure whether to leave the head where it was or to retrieve it, he placed the battered barbecue over the top of it instead. *There*, he thought, *easy to find again and the damn seagulls shouldn't be able to uncover it.*

He picked up Pam, grimacing and trying not to gag as he noticed some kind of foreign gunk in the cat's fur. 'For God's sake, you minging moggy,' he muttered, straining his head away from a piece of skin with a few what looked like beard hairs attached, hanging from the edge of Pam's mouth. Ray tucked her under his arm, intending to wash her in the grimy sink in the office cloakroom. He descended the huge heap of stinking trash on unsteady feet, his well-worn rigger boots offering minimal grip with their almost-slick soles.

Pam wriggled and extended her claws. *Who does this human think I am, carrying me like a disgusting lap dog?* With a growl, a screech and a flash of a claw that dug into the wound Ray already had from the barbecue, Pam leapt like a wild cat away from Ray.

Ray wasn't prepared for Pam's hasty escape, and the sudden move coupled with the pain from the claw made him lose his footing. As the pain shot through his ankles from the unnatural torsion, his body collapsed and he rolled to the side, his boots having sealed his fate. With no control of his own body soon becoming a victim of gravity, Ray somersaulted and flipped his way down the face of the tip.

Cathy Bonham was proud to be a trucker. In her mind, she was a figurehead for women. After all, if the men can drive a truck, then damn right she could do it better. Cathy had spent too long away from her family while driving trucks all over Europe. She loved it but needed to be nearer home. It also meant she would have more time to ride her beloved motorcycles as often as she could.

Karen Lyon-Mace sat in the crew seat, with some kid from the agency squeezed in the middle. They had just turned off the main road. Cathy was persistently underwhelmed by the truck's brakes when it was loaded, and sure enough, she couldn't stop in time for the turning and had to reverse back up the road. 'Fucking shit brakes,' she cursed.

'Oi, watch your language, our new teammate isn't old enough to know words like that!'

Cathy cackled, as she knew Karen was just having banter with her to make the lad uncomfortable. It worked. The lad's pasty white skin under his mop of ginger hair turned a deep shade of beetroot. Cathy looked into the mirror mounted onto the door of the truck and admired the huge cloud of dust in her wake. *Shame it isn't the red soil of the Australian outback behind a road-train rather than a rusty, dirty, shitty refuse truck.*

'Watch out!' squawked the ginger kid.

Cathy and Karen whipped their heads round to face the boy in utter shock. It was the first time they had even heard Scott Walker speak, never mind shout.

They glanced at each other with a look that only good friends who are almost psychic share. Cathy looked out of the windscreen, past the numerous chips and dead insects.

Suddenly, she saw Ray. He was falling, tumbling like a rag doll. With limbs flailing round in all directions and trash being tossed in the air along his path of descent, Cathy shouted, 'Shit!' He was about to hit the road. 'Bollocks!' she squealed, standing hard onto the brakes. Really hard. Still not good enough; there was just too much weight in the back.

First, the truck hit Ray with its front axle wheels, then the second and third axle wheels. Bump, bump, bump. Just like driving over sleeping policemen.

Scott projectile vomited over the dash like a combine harvester and ended up more or less upside down in the cab, his top half bouncing off the transmission tunnel while sliding under Cathy's feet. 'For fuck's sake, you ginger twat! You owe me some new boots.'

As the truck came to a halt, the two women and the young man jumped out to see how badly hurt Ray was, and to find out what had caused him to be tumbling down the steep side of the landfill site in the first place.

****

Denise sat on her sofa and looked out of her lounge window. A blackbird pecking at the leaves caught her attention as she tried to not think about Paul. But, the harder she tried to not think about him, the more she did so. She took a sip of her cold drink and shook her head with sadness. *I wonder what happened to me and Paul. It seemed to be going well. He was so nice and I felt so safe with him all the time. I just don't get how he's just vanished. Maybe he's been injured or taken ill or something. Perhaps James will know something.*

James picked up his phone and realised he had a new text from his mum. *Hi James, hope you're okay. I don't suppose you've heard from Paul, have you? I haven't spoken to him since he came round to your house the other night. I'm just really worried about him. Did he say anything to you about if there are any problems or anything?*

A weird hot and cold feeling passed over James' skin as his hairs all stood on end. He couldn't understand. It was the weirdest feeling he'd ever had. *What the hell is that about?*

Something was wrong, he could feel it. *I hope everything is alright. He seemed like a really nice guy as well.*

****

Inspector Sarah-Jane Rutherford was looking forward to the end of her shift. A neighbourhood meeting with residents moaning about dog shit and feral youths wasn't what she had signed up for when she joined Newdonshire Police. She was thinking of pressing a button on her radio to signal she was now off duty, but something stopped her. The screen lit up, as did everyone's when there was a transmission, and she heard Mildred Bird's voice speaking out her collar number from the force control room. 'Six, six, six.'

'Six, six, six,' Rutherford replied.

'Ma'am, we have a report from a young person getting his ball back from a neighbour. He saw a human hand sticking out from under a tarpaulin in the garden. Can you attend?'

The inspector was excited. *A dead body under a tarpaulin? Hell yeah! Best not be a shop dummy.* 'Assign Sergeant Love and PC Hooker-Wolfe too. Make it grade one and get me CSI on standby.'

'Yes, ma'am,' said Mildred.

Sarah-Jane smiled to herself as she imagined Mildred being busy organising people like an earnest Miss Marple.

'Three, six, four, four, nine,' spoke Sgt Love into her radio.

'Three, six, four, four, nine,' echoed Mildred.

'Show me and three, two, two, three, seven as ten-five.'

'Received.'

Sgt Love started the engine of her police car and hit the button bearing a sticker with '999' printed upon it.

The blue lights strobed into action and the siren began to wail. PC Hooke-Wolfe exclaimed, 'Hang on, this address is where that weird guy lives who we met when we were canvassing about O'Leary.'

'Best get there fast then, you might like to see him in a towel again!' Sgt Love enjoyed trying to wind up her partner. The cantankerous old station gates seemed to take an age to draw themselves apart. As soon as there was a gap big enough for the car to squeeze through, she gunned the throttle and chirped the tyres on the tarmac, revving the engine ever closer to exhaustion.

****

James had decided on a new hobby.

He'd thought for ages about something like fishing. Every day, while looking out of his window at work, he saw a motorbike with a wonderful sonorous noise sweeping around the corner where the imaginary Fiat had soaked the boy. That looked much more fun than sitting by the side of a body of water waiting for a bite.

He looked up how to get a licence and bought a brand new Ducati Scrambler. Yellow was the only colour that caught his attention apart from the famous racing red, so yellow it had to be.

Denise's mobile sounded to tell her she had a new WhatsApp message. It was from James. *Hi Mum :-) want to meet me at mine at 6 this evening? The motorbike is being delivered to my house then.*

She smiled, delighted that James felt like her beloved son now, rather than a burden.

James was standing on his drive, waiting for the Ducati to arrive. Denise was driving to his house. The weather was nice, the sky a gorgeous blue without a cloud in sight, and it was warm despite the season. She wasn't far away, in fact, just a street away.

Two police cars shattered the peace and screamed past Denise's VW Beetle, which rocked in the slipstream of chaotic air. *What's the rush? Someone died?*

It occurred to James that he hadn't made space in the garage for the bike. Casually turning around, he sauntered up the drive to the integral garage door, lifted it and smiled as he remembered he had indeed tidied it up some time ago. However, something wasn't right. That same weird sensation ran through his body again.

There was a loud 'toot toot' a short distance away. James was irritated; he hated people honking their horn without a good reason. Realising it was the delivery van from the Ducati dealer, he smiled at the noisy arrival.

That nag was back in his head though. His stomach churned. He started to sweat. *Why, though?* A déjà vu feeling passed through him and bolted straight into his soul. He glanced back at the garage, eyes scanning the interior. The green light on the freezer gazed back. An accusatory stare. Another cold shudder passed through him just as the distant blare of sirens came into earshot. 'No. No, it can't be,' whispered James as an image of his front door opening and a pair of Jehovah Witnesses looking back at him flashed through his mind. Followed by a man on a bench. *Shit*. The awful, evil truth of realisation dawned on James' conscious mind. The gruesome image of Paul Edwards' severed head burned into his eyes in a terrible flashback.

'It can't be true,' he uttered in desperation.

James found himself drawn by an unseen force to the freezer, terrified of what would face him under the lid. *Shit*. His entire concentration being focussed on the freezer, he didn't hear the police-issue Hi-Tec Magnum boots marching up the drive. He didn't hear the trio of cops shouting, 'Police!'

The inspector shouted at him to stop where he was. James didn't hear and took another stride towards the makeshift frozen tomb. He lifted the freezer lid. *Oh fuck. Two dead people. No fucking way!* A small red dot flickering across the freezer lid brought his mind back to the here and now. James spun around, and Sgt Love pulled the trigger of her Taser X26. Realising his thick jacket and sweater had stopped the Taser prongs from reaching his skin, he yanked out the wires and tossed them down.

Denise's voice shrilled. 'James!'

He broke into a run, his crazed state not registering the baton as it struck him across the back. James burst out of the garage, which seemed to have compressed in time and space. The fresh air slapped him back to reality, and a fresh wave of panic built through his chest as the shriek of more sirens filled the air. His brand new, bright yellow motorbike sat on the kerbside, gently ticking over for its new owner as steam billowed from the exhaust.

Autonomy took over James again. The delivery guy stared wide-eyed in disbelief as James ripped the new helmet from his hand. Ignoring the high-pitched orders being screamed from the growing crowd of police officers, he jumped on the bike, pulled in the clutch lever and prodded the gear lever down into first gear. Without so much as a look back at Denise, he roared away into the distance.

The End

DEATH DOLLS

Chapter One

Benjamin McGuinness had a passion for life, and he was outgoing and clever enough to keep his ominous dark side hidden from the general public.

His last birthday was his thirtieth.

Time for The Plan.

Benjamin was many men to many people. To his family, he was lovable Benjamin, always polite and rang his mum, Delia McGuinness, every other day to make sure she was all right. The phone call was always the highlight of her day, and he sent her flowers at least once or twice a month. When she had her birthday, and at Christmas, he always got her a great gift. Last year, he bought her a cruise holiday. She'd hinted about it for years. The holiday was amazing; she flew out to Florida and hopped on a ship that took her around the Caribbean. His father had died from cancer when Benjamin was a boy, but he remained close to his younger sister, Lisa, who always encouraged him to follow his dreams.

He kept himself in decent shape with visits to a gym twice a week. Benjamin wasn't bothered about being muscle bound, but he was vain about his appearance. *No way am I going to let myself get fat.* His arms and torso were plastered with colourful tattoos; he would have liked more but time wasn't abundant for him to use. Standing at five foot ten and of average build, he could have blended into any crowd if he wanted to, but his personality meant that he preferred to stand out. He loved to talk to anyone and everyone at length, especially when he was at work.

To the folks at the nearby airfield, he was a faultless aviator. He didn't yet own his own light aircraft, but he always made sure that the planes he'd hired were returned to their owner cleaner than when he'd rented it. Owner pilots had made quite a lot of cash out of all the times he'd rented a plane from them. Despite the many times he'd thought about buying his own plane, the cost of hangering and maintenance put him off. Besides, it was always nice to use different machines. Benjamin had passed all the exams to be a private pilot a couple of years previously, flying through the tests, and a Piper PA-24 Comanche caught his eye on eBay. *Only ninety thousand pounds. When this venture takes off, I might get that.*

The clients at his popular tattoo shop, Dr Tattoo, loved his artistry and skills with the tools of his trade. He operated from a previously abandoned courtyard of units on a remote farmyard, about fifteen miles from the town of Newdon, deep in the English countryside. It was perfect for his desires, and for people who wanted a Dr Tattoo masterpiece and didn't mind that it was a trek from Newdon by car—it was impossible to get to by public transport. Farmer Wright had been delighted to lease the units to Benjamin. He had thought the buildings would become ruins after he became too old to do the upkeep; he loathed to ask others to do any maintenance for him.

Who wouldn't want to get a fabulous tattoo while looking out over archetypal English countryside of rolling hills to take their mind off the pain? His clients didn't have to deal with members of the public walking by, gawping through regular shop windows as they sat at a tattoo workstation, usually half naked; that's how it would've been if Benjamin had leased a shop in the town centre. Besides, the management of most town centres had really ramped up the cost of rent, so it probably wouldn't have been cost effective.

For Benjamin, the location was perfect, and he could repair the buildings to any spec he wanted. *Perhaps the old boy will let me buy them one day.*

With arable fields all around, even the trunk road dual carriageway in the distance that pushed its way through several counties and carried thousands of cars and trucks each day, couldn't spoil the peaceful picture. The occasional police car pierced the air with sirens, but not enough to disturb the tranquillity. Birds of prey appeared in the sky from time to time, diving to catch their lunch. Benjamin loved to watch the kestrels hover above the fields before swooping down and vanishing in the crops.

Several other businesses populated the farmyard. These were:

SkunkWorks Leather

Original Organic Piggery

Ashes to Ashes Unique Dispersal

All of them belonged to the charismatic Benjamin McGuinness, apart from the ashes business, which he co-owned with his sister, Lisa.

The ex-farmer, Mr Wright, got paid more than enough rent to turn a blind eye. He didn't pry into Benjamin's businesses. Benjamin had made sure that the farmer wasn't the nosey type before agreeing to rent the units from him, so he was more than sure that Mr Wright wouldn't interfere. The leather shop was his latest venture; after the piggery had taken off, it seemed to make sense to move into other avenues. Location wise, the leather shop was perfect too; plenty of chemicals were used for the tanning, so he had more than enough secure storage space.

Although not very noticeable to visitors, the final unit housed the workers. There was no sign saying 'private,' so it just looked like an unused building. That suited the workers just fine. 'Slaves' in a very loose sense of the word. They all wanted to be there and wouldn't want to live anywhere else. There were two gender specific sleeping rooms, with a shared living and dining space. Benjamin paid them decently, more than minimum wage, and each of them did exactly as he told them to. They were afraid of being cast out of the farmyard because they didn't have the confidence or ability to look after themselves. Their colleagues were also their family.

Chapter Two

About two years or so earlier, Benjamin was enjoying one of his regular visits to his mum's place. The sole business that he owned at this point in time was Dr Tattoo.

Benjamin pulled up outside his mother's house, noting with pleasure that the gardener he paid had been and trimmed the lawn. The flower tubs were all neat and tidy too, with some daffodils already growing.

He got out of his car and rang the bell before letting himself in. His mother, Delia McGuinness, sat in a wingback armchair. She stood up, slowly, and pottered over to the hall where Benjamin was taking off his coat. He hung his coat up on a hook affixed to the wall and then hugged his mother and kissed her on the cheek. *You are looking more frail by the month, Mum.*

She had made a roast dinner for them, the smell of which wafted through from the kitchen. Benjamin said, 'Mum, that smells so good! Shall I do the honours?'

'If you don't mind, my hands are hurting a lot. I should go and see the doctor really.'

'Oh, Mum, make sure you do go and see Dr Green. He'll make sure that you get the right pills. It sounds to me like it's arthritis. Please make sure that you go next week. For me, Mum. Promise?' Benjamin said, while making a praying sign with his hands pressed together.

Delia smiled lovingly, 'I promise! Now, get in the kitchen and sort out the dinner.' She play smacked Benjamin's bum as he walked past, and they both laughed. Ten minutes later, as they sat facing each other over a small drop-leaf table, Benjamin made sure that Delia had the best cuts of beef on her plate.

'So what do you know, Benjamin?' asked Delia. She had never shortened his name and, as a result, no one else ever called him anything other than Benjamin.

He pointed to his mouth to indicate he had a mouthful of mashed potato. There was no way he would speak, especially to his mum, with food in his mouth. He swallowed then said, 'Actually, Mum, the tattoo shop is doing really well. I will look for an assistant soon. I'll probably look for someone who can live in; there's plenty of room in the unit for other people. It'll be nice to have some company too.'

Delia smiled, 'That is so well deserved, son. I am sure people will be queued up for the job. Who wouldn't want to work for you? Make sure you pay them properly and sort their holidays out right. There's no quicker way to make bad feelings than messing up people's money and holidays. Remember to talk to me if you need any advice.'

Now Benjamin could get a word in sideways, he said, 'Don't worry, Mum, I'll treat anyone who works for me right.'

They spent the rest of the day nattering and drinking endless cups of tea.

Benjamin hugged his mum and promised to keep her informed with his progress in recruiting an assistant.

He advertised on his Dr Tattoo website for a worker.

WANTED DEAD OR ALIVE!

LOYAL TATTOO ARTIST

ACCOMODATION PROVIDED

TOP RATES OF PAY FOR THE RIGHT PERSON

EMAIL BENJAMIN FOR DETAILS

Five applications arrived into his inbox. One he rejected because it was barely legible. A second because the 'artist' attached images of their work, and to say it was terrible would've been kind. It was a portrait, and the child in the picture had one eye bigger than the other and the shape of the face was more potato than human.

That left three applicants, and Benjamin intended to interview each of them at the studio.

The first was a woman called Susan Claymore. After ten minutes, Benjamin got the impression that the landmine may have been named after her explosive temper. He just had the feeling that she wasn't suitable, so she didn't get the job.

Next was Zack Miller. Benjamin was surprised to see his name in the hat. Zack had been a regular in most of the industry magazines, and he regularly won competitions at conventions, both in the UK and overseas.

On the morning of the interview, Zack pushed the door open into the studio.

He was much smaller in build than Benjamin; if he were a woman, he would be described as petite. Zack was dressed smartly, but in comfortable clothing that allowed him to move freely while tattooing clients. His beard was neatly trimmed, as was his short mousey hair. He clearly took some pride in his appearance, but he was nowhere near as vain as Benjamin. Zack appeared to live on his nerves; his fingernails were well chewed, and a cigarette packet sat in his shirt breast pocket. The inside of his fingers were stained a light yellow, but Benjamin didn't take too much notice of that. After all, the black gloves worn by tattoo artists would hide that from customers.

Benjamin said to Zack, 'Come in, Zack. How are you?'

'I'm good, thanks. I need a change and saw your advert. Bournemouth isn't where I want to be anymore.' Zack looked out of the windows into the distance, deep hurt visible in his eyes. He took a cigarette out of a packet and stuck it behind his left ear.

'Coffee, mate?' Benjamin asked, wanting to give Zack a moment to compose himself.

Zack looked back at Benjamin and pursed his lips in contemplation, 'Yes, strong and black please.'

Benjamin made them both a coffee. He preferred his white with two sugars. Sitting back and taking a sip of his hot drink, he said, 'I can offer accommodation too, Zack, right here. It's the perfect escape from the rat race. I ain't going to patronise you and ask you to do a tattoo—you're the best. I can't believe that you're even contemplating working for me.'

Zack smiled wryly, 'I've heard great things about your studio. I've seen the tattoos on your website, and I'm happy enough that you ain't gonna bring my reputation down.'

He drained the last of his coffee, retrieved the cigarette from behind his ear and started to fiddle with it. Smoking in the studio would be a big no-no. Standing, Benjamin requested, 'Come with me, we'll go into the yard and you can smoke that if you like.'

Zack stood, grateful for the chance to have a nicotine fix. As they went out into the yard, Benjamin looked on with envy at Zack's tattoo on his forearms, smiling to himself that he'd landed a scoop by getting the smaller man to work with him.

Zack finished smoking and ground the stub under his trainers into the gravel.

'Where's the accommodation? I'd like to look at it please,' Zack asked with a calmer air.

'I think you'll love it. Come with me.'

They meandered across the yard to the anonymous looking door. Benjamin unlocked it and opened it inwards. Zack peered into the room inside. His eyes lit up when he saw the excellent furniture and huge TV.

'Do you like it?' asked Benjamin, trying to decide if he had read Zack right.

Zack replied, 'It looks bloody wonderful, pal. When will I hear back about if I've got the job?'

Laughing, Benjamin said, 'Mate, I'd be honoured to work with you. If you want the job, it's yours. I'll just cancel the last interview…'

Running his hand through his hair, Zack replied, 'Well, I'd best get a diary sorted out. I'll move my shit in next weekend and start the week after that.' He glanced over to his new boss, 'If that's ok, that is.'

Benjamin clapped him on the back, almost knocking the new employee over. 'Thank you so much. You won't regret it!'

Zack punched the air, 'Thank *you*. This is a life saver. I don't really want to talk about my ex, but moving away will be so good. I'll do you a tattoo for free, if you like, when I'm here.'

Benjamin's mouth dropped open, 'Thanks, that's amazing!'

He pulled his mobile phone from his jeans pocket and sent the last candidate a text to cancel them. Sighing, he added, 'I wouldn't normally do something shitty like that, but it would waste his time and mine.'

Chapter Three

'Hi, Mum, what's cooking?' Benjamin sniffed the air when he walked into Delia's home.

Delia smiled at him, 'Spaghetti Bolognese of course, it's your favourite!'

Benjamin grinned. Of course he knew what was cooking. He leant down and kissed his mum on her cheek. 'You're the best mum ever!' He gushed and sat on the chair he always sat on when he visited Delia.

Delia frowned as if deep in thought and said, 'How's that lovely new man Zippo getting on?'

Benjamin couldn't help laughing, 'Mum! Zippo is a lighter...Zack is the new guy at work.'

He really did love his mum dearly, but he had noticed lately that she was becoming somewhat forgetful.

'Oh...Silly me!' Delia chuckled.

'Don't worry, Mum. He is so great, I can't believe he really works for me.' Benjamin looked out of the window; a yellow Ducati motorcycle whizzed by and a police car followed with blue lights flashing. *Wonder what that's all about?*

He rubbed his stubble, 'He's loving living in too; it's give him the break he needed away from his ex girlfriend.'

'That's nice. You are so kind, giving him somewhere to live.'

Benjamin waved a dismissive hand. 'Oh, you know me, Mum, all heart!' *Well I do love it when things make me more money…it's nice to have the start of a kind of tribe too.*

'I've had a great idea. I'm going to open a totally different business at the yard —'

Delia interrupted, 'Oh, before I forget, I've taken out one of those prepaid funeral thingies so you don't need to worry if anything happens to me. Carry on.' She smiled at him as if she hadn't just dropped some kind of bombshell.

Benjamin was shocked, but he recovered enough from the revelation to continue speaking, 'I'm going to open an organic piggery at the yard and look for some new people to come and live with me and Zack, like some kind of family. I'll, well, they'll rear pigs and then make them into sausages and whatnot. Everything will be done properly, and I think there is a decent gap in the market for it.'

'How about buying some rare breeds?' Delia said in a flash of genius. 'You know, like a Newdonshire Black Spot?'

Benjamin looked at her wide eyed.

'Mum, that's a brilliant idea!' he exclaimed. 'I think that will seal the deal.'

'Don't forget to let Lisa know how you are doing; she always talks about you. Are you going to open that bottle of wine in the kitchen?'

'Lisa already knows. I text her every day and talk to her a couple of times a week. You do know that, Mum. I don't know what I'd do without the two ladies in my life.'

Delia waved a dismissive hand, 'Yes, of course, I keep forgetting things these days.'

As the mother and son enjoyed their meal, Benjamin was mulling over his new plan. *This is a great idea. I'll ask Zack if he knows anyone who might like to come on board.*

****

Before they opened Dr Tattoo for the day ahead, Benjamin asked Zack, 'Hey, Zack, do you know any people needing work? I'm looking for people to live in with us. I'm going to start an organic piggery and raise rare breed pigs to make foodstuffs like sausages and things like that.'

Zack sat back, clasped his hands behind his head and put his feet up on his desk, then caught himself and put them back underneath instead. 'Actually…well…maybe…'

Benjamin picked up a mug and pretended to chuck it at Zack. 'Come on, son, don't hold back. Is it some south coast freak?' He smirked, feeling that the reference to where Bournemouth was might tease his employee.

Zack lifted a middle finger up to his boss and laughed. Shaking his head, he said, 'You might not thank me for it, but I just might know the perfect people. You'll have to find enough work for them though *and* make a girly bedroom in the unit.'

That made Benjamin sit up straight, 'Girls? Them? Come on, man, spit it out!'

Zack pulled out a cigarette packet, put a cigarette between his lips and pretended to take a drag. He chuckled and said, 'You are going to think I am mad…'

'Go on...'

'I know a family from Bournemouth, the girls are actually triplets. Two are identical and one isn't. Their parents want them to move out; they can't cope with the hormones or something. Mind you, they are twenty-five like me, so maybe their parents are ready for some peace and quiet in their life.'

Benjamin's eyebrows shot up so fast they were in danger of taking off from his face, 'Go on.'

Zack shook his head a little, 'I don't know...They do everything together, so they can't find jobs because who would want to employ three people for one job?'

'Actually, I think with working in the piggery and the admin, *and* if we find a third business to go with this tattoo studio, then they could be ideal.'

'They are kind of cuckoo though, Benjamin. I'll warn you now, they never take no for an answer if they get something in their head. And they have this terrible laugh like a cackle. It makes the hair on the back of your neck stand up,' Zack smirked, knowing that Benjamin's interest was well and truly piqued.

Benjamin wafted his hand and laughed, 'Well, your recommendation is as good a reference as any. You don't need to be mad to work here, but it helps. How do you know them, anyway?'

'School,' Zack said, rolling his eyes. 'We go back for donkey's years. Shall I tell 'em to come up for an interview?'

'Yeah, sod it, why not?' Benjamin stood. 'Tell them they can start next week if they want to. I can't be bothered with interviews again.'

Zack raised an eyebrow in surprise, 'Well, only if you are sure, boss…'

'I'm sure.'

Chapter Four

'Boss?' Zack said, trying to get Benjamin to stop daydreaming when they were supposed to be cleaning the tattoo studio.

'Sorry,' Benjamin looked across at Zack. 'What's up?'

Zack smirked. *Ben ain't gonna know what's hit him.* 'The girls, Helena and Tilly who are identical and Franchesca who is the third triplet, but she prefers to be called Chesca, are coming tomorrow...'

Benjamin looked at Zack, seemingly hearing about the girls for the first time, and shook his head as if trying to clear his mind. He smiled and replied, 'Ah yes, of course. Sorry, I was just thinking about my mum, she seems to be getting forgetful. I think I might have to take her to the doctors.

'As for the girls, well, I don't need to interview them. What time are they coming?'

Zack pondered for a moment and chewed a fingernail, 'Ten in the morning. They'll drive themselves here; they don't like public transport because of germs.' Zack made air quotes with his fingers as he said the word 'germs'.

'I don't blame them at all, many people are filthy animals!' The two men laughed as if it were the funniest joke they'd ever heard. 'Thanks, Zack, I needed that laugh. Can I leave you to the rest of the cleaning? I need to ring my sister and talk to her about Mum.'

Zack smirked again; he loved the chance to wind his boss up, 'Yeah sure, boss, I don't mind being your cleaning bitch. Your sister is fit by the way.'

He laughed so much at his own comment that it set him off coughing.

Benjamin shook his fist in mock rage, 'I hope you choke to death, you knobhead! If you weren't so good at your job, I'd give you the sack!' It was clear from his face that he wasn't cross at all, but all the same, he left Zack to finish the cleaning up.

****

He walked across to the accommodation block, let himself in the door and sighed with relief. *It's always nice to be home.*

His sister answered on the second ring, 'Benji? What's up?'

'Only you can call me that and get away with it, Lisa,' the smile in his voice was almost audible.

'That's because you love me so much. Anyway, is everything alright?' The almost psychic connection that some siblings have was strong between them. There was no point trying to go around the houses in getting to the point, so Benjamin simply put his cards on the table.

'I am worried about Mum. Have you noticed that she seems to be getting more forgetful? The other day, she called Zack, Zippo.'

Lisa laughed and wiped her face with a palm. *That makes sense, Mum hasn't been right for a few months...* 'Now you come to mention it, she has seemed a bit strange. I just put it down to it being around Dad's anniversary.'

Benjamin said nothing for a moment. *That hadn't occurred to me.* 'You could well be right. Tell you what, let's both go there on Sunday and see how she is.'

'See you there at twelve-thirty. Love you, Benji,' Lisa almost whispered, worry tainting her voice.

'Love you too, sis. Bye,' Benjamin cut the line and released a long, drawn-out breath.

****

As Zack and Benjamin sat drinking coffee, Benjamin glanced at his wrist watch; it was only nine-thirty. He drained his cup and asked Zack, 'How are you enjoying your time here at Dr Tattoo?'

He studied Zack's face for any visible reaction, but there wasn't much of a response beyond Zack sucking the froth from his top lip.

Zack glanced across at Benjamin before looking at his shoes. 'It's good, thank you. I'm really liking not having to see anyone apart from the customers. It's perfect, to be honest with you,' sweat glistened on his forehead. 'I don't cope well with people, but at least I have something in common to talk about with people getting a tattoo from us...'

Poor man really has been saved by me! Wonder if the women are going to be the same.

Something caught Zack's attention, and he looked up out of the window. 'I think they'll be here soon. I saw something shine, which could have been the sun on a windscreen down the lane,' he stood and walked up to the window. As he did so, an old car made a rather rapid entrance into the yard. It stopped inches

186

away from the building that Benjamin had just ordered fridges and butchery equipment for.

Zack looked over his shoulder and grinned at Benjamin, 'That'll be the girls; I bet Helena is driving.'

Benjamin stood and put a paternal arm around Zack's shoulders. He said, 'We had better go and greet them. I hope their work ethic is better than their driving skills.'

The two men laughed at the eternal joke about women's driving and walked out to meet the newcomers.

Benjamin wasn't prepared for the triplets' immense energy. The three of them bounded over to greet Zack and took turns to embrace him tightly. Chesca squeezed him so tight that Benjamin was sure he heard Zack squeak, and a bone pop. When he managed to get his breath back, Zack introduced the women to Benjamin.

'Chesca, Helena, Tilly, this is Benjamin," he announced. "Benjamin, meet the girls. Thank me later.'

Benjamin held out a hand to shake with each woman in turn. They had other ideas.

One by one, they hugged him just as tightly as they'd hugged Zack.

Helena quipped, 'Well, we're here now, boss. What do you want us to do?'

Benjamin sighed nervously. *Why am I getting a bad feeling about these three? Better give them the benefit of the doubt now they are here. After all, they've travelled a long way.*

'Well, ladies, let's get a coffee and talk about it. I want you to run the piggery. Come with me and I'll tell you all about it,' he instructed.

****

Benjamin took the trio over to the piggery, where a pair of sows and a boar happily slept, covered in a crust of mud. No piglets had been born yet, but he explained that he hoped there would be piglets in due course. They had only been purchased a few days earlier in anticipation of the new workers coming.

Chesca cooed at the sows, 'They are so cute! I'll take the job of making the website.'

'Website? Oh yeah, good idea, Chesca. I should have thought of that myself,' Benjamin admitted. 'Do you have any experience in website design?'

Chesca made a weird laughing noise, which came out in a tone that Benjamin had never heard before. It made a chill run down his spine and he shivered involuntarily. He hoped that no one else noticed, but he saw out of the corner of his eye that Zack was smirking at him.

Benjamin smiled, 'I can see that you three could be a handful. It's probably best if I leave you to your own devices to sort this business out. Do you need me to recruit a butcher, or can you take care of that too?'

Tilly said, 'No, we'll recruit someone. I'll be wasted here, but I can make leather things you know. I can make belts and purses, things like that. Bear it in mind...it is profitable. I've done a course and everything.'

She adopted a haughty face.

Chesca poked her, 'Do as you're told, for now. We have to be good, remember?'

Benjamin's head was spinning slightly at all the back and forth involved in having a conversation with the triplets. The women had more energy than he had, by far, and he felt like he'd had more than enough of them already.

Benjamin walked out into the yard and looked across at the empty unit opposite. *I might as well use Tilly's skills and make even more money. Make her prove herself first...*

Stroking his chin, he offered, 'Tell you what, make the piggery pay and I'll start up a leather business. I think that's fair enough. You'll have to sort out the process and all that though, I don't know anything about it.'

Helena let out a weird noise, a grunt mixed with a sigh, 'You'd better pull your weight, Tilly, not just daydream about handbags!'

The women did indeed recruit a butcher—Aled Price. He excelled with his knife skills and everyone was happy with him. Aled lived in Newdon, making him the only employee that didn't live at the yard with everyone else. He didn't talk much about his family, although Benjamin knew that Aled had got married just the previous year. Goodness knows what he thought about the triplets; Benjamin thought he must either have the patience of a saint or be able to ignore their skull-piercing laughter and teasing antics.

****

Nine months to the day after the piggery went under the stewardship of the triplets, Skunkworks Leather opened for business.

Tilly stood with great pride when Benjamin gathered the workers in the yard and placed the ribbon that he'd affixed across the door to celebrate his new business opening between the blades of a pair of scissors.

'Thank you all for coming,' he joked. That generated some laughter from the crowd, all of whom lived in the accommodation on site, so it wasn't hard for them to be there.

He grinned and continued, 'I am honoured Zack brought you women into my life. The business wouldn't have prospered without you. I declare the Skunkworks...open!'

A round of applause rippled around the workers, and a real ambiance of celebration settled over the group. Tilly hugged Benjamin tightly and whispered into his ear, 'Thanks a million. You won't regret this, I promise.'

'You're welcome. You three have been a total pleasure to have on board,' said Benjamin.

Tilly tucked a strand of hair behind her ear and looked up at Benjamin, 'You know, it has been so hard in the past. No one has wanted to give all three of us a chance together in a job, but we can't cope with being apart. This is so great, and I have more plans for the business.'

'Oh, what's that?' Benjamin said, an eyebrow lifted in curiosity.

Tilly looked over his shoulder into the distance and said, 'Oh, never mind for now, we'll talk about it another time. Let's not run before we can walk.'

Benjamin shrugged, 'No worries, you can talk to me at any time, you know?'

Tilly hugged him again and kissed him on the cheek, 'You're the best boss ever, Benjamin McGuiness.'

His cheeks flushed a deep shade of red, which was something he never normally did. Zack and the other two sisters smirked.

Tilly laughed that awful sound that the trio seemed to enjoy. It was almost as if they knew they sounded like a coven of witches. Zack lit up a cigarette and puffed out a huge plume of smoke into the sky. Tilly pointed at him, 'Don't even think of smoking anywhere near this place, Zack. There are loads of chemicals here and I don't wish to risk a fire, mate! Anyway, see you lot in a bit, I have work to do.'

She sashayed into her new workshop and got on with preparing for hides to arrive. Zack and Benjamin returned to the tattoo studio, and the two remaining women made their way back to the piggery.

Chapter Five

Delia pottered around her home. She paused at her sideboard and picked up a framed photograph of Benjamin and Lisa. They were stood with Benjamin's arm around Lisa's shoulder, and hers around his waist. Their smiles stretched from ear to ear. The photo had been taken on a normal Sunday, under the apple tree in her garden, not a special occasion. *I'm so blessed to have such wonderful children.*

She peered at her wristwatch. It was almost eleven-thirty. Delia mumbled to herself, 'Better put some water in a pan and start warming it up for veg.'

The smell of beef cooking in the oven was heavenly. Delia smiled as the odour hit her senses.

She put a pan on the electric hob and used a jug to fill it. The pan itself would've been too heavy to lift full of water. *The kids can drain it when they are here.*

When a wave of fatigue washed over her, she mumbled to herself, 'I think I'll sit down for a moment.'

It took a minute, but she sat in her comfy chair. *Just five minutes can't hurt.*

Delia was asleep inside twenty seconds.

BBC News 24 was on her television, and the time in the corner of the screen read 10.20am—she had misread her watch.

In the kitchen, a corner of a tea towel was pinned underneath the rapidly heating pan.

Delia didn't smell the material singeing. The towel ignited, and flames began to lick up the side of the cooker and over to a roll of kitchen paper sitting on the worktop on its holder. In no time at all, the whole kitchen was alight, and the sound of the smoke alarm screamed through the house.

Delia didn't awaken.

Choking, cloying plumes of black smoke spread rapidly through the house. Delia died in her chair from smoke inhalation before the fire brigade could reach her.

Chapter Six

Benjamin's mobile rang just as he'd started to dry himself from a shower. He glanced at the screen and frowned.

'Hi Lisa, what's wrong? You don't normally call before we meet up at Mum's.'

'Sorry, Benjamin. It's about Mum...'

'What? Is she okay?'

'Benjamin...I don't know how to say this. She's died at home...There was a fire—'

'No, it can't be true!'

'I'm sorry, but it is true, Benjamin. I am outside the house now, the firemen are dampening it down. Meet me at the hospital.'

Chapter Seven

Benjamin sat with Lisa in the lounge at the farmyard. He took a sip of his coffee and sighed as he placed the red-hot drink back on a coaster.

'It's a shame that Mum didn't have a conversation with us about what she wants us to do with her ashes,' said Lisa. 'I know she had paid up for a funeral plan though.'

Worry lines creased her face, stress written in her eyes. Benjamin laughed with sadness, 'The funny thing is that I was talking to her the other week about an idea I had for a business, and she thought it was great.'

Lisa looked at him through tear-stained eyeliner, 'Do tell. I can't wait to hear this.' She sat forward on the edge of her chair, eager for something to cheer her up.

Benjamin shook his head, 'It sounds silly really. We were talking about one of her friends who died, and the family chucked her ashes overboard from a cruise near Denmark or somewhere random like that. So I said maybe I should take relatives up in a light aircraft, to scatter their loved one's ashes out over the sea.'

Lisa's eyes widened.

'Benji, that is inspired!' she exclaimed. 'We should do that. The cremation is next week, so how about the Monday afterwards?'

Benjamin smiled as though a huge weight had just been lifted from his shoulders. He sat back in his chair, 'I'll hire a plane. Two weeks is plenty of notice for one of the lads to lend me something. You haven't been up with me for a while either. It'll be good. I reckon we should fly out over Skegness; Mum loved going there for the market.'

He sent one of his friends a text.

Hi buddy, Any chance I can borrow your plane pls week on Monday for an hour or two?

Almost immediately, his phone pinged with a reply:

Yeah sure, I'll leave the keys in the control tower.

He smiled and looked up at Lisa, 'Bingo, make sure you bring a sick bag.'

Lisa threw a cushion at her brother, which he caught deftly, 'Shut up, Benji!'

They hadn't noticed Tilly had come in the door, but she cottoned on to the shortened version of his name and smirked.

'Hey Lisa, hi Benji!' she taunted slyly, and a cackle slipped from her lips.

Benjamin looked at his sister and shook his head, 'Oh my God, what have you done?'

Lisa couldn't help herself from laughing, 'Oh, Benjamin, you shouldn't mind it so much. It'd be one less stress for you.'

Benjamin didn't laugh though. He pointed at Tilly and swore, 'Never call me Benji again or you'll get the sack!'

Tilly stood open mouthed, and Lisa chuckled.

'Don't listen to him. He's always got his knickers in a knot over his name...God knows why.'

Benjamin half-heartedly held a hand up, 'Sorry, Tilly, it's just that I was teased at school about my name. People used to say that Ben is a dog's name. That's kinda stuck in my head.'

Lisa stood, 'I have to go now, speak soon, *Benjamin.*'

He walked over to his sister and kissed her on the cheek, 'Love you, sis.'

****

The allotted day came, and Lisa sat next to Benjamin in their borrowed plane. She gazed out of the window, enjoying watching the countryside slide by under the wing. There were a few clouds around, but not enough to spoil the flight. Before she knew it, Benjamin pointed out of the windscreen and said, 'Look, Lisa, there's the sea on the horizon. This is such a nice day for flying.'

Lisa couldn't resist clapping her hands in excitement, 'This is more fun than the big wheel. Shall I get the urn ready?'

Benjamin looked across at her through his Ray-Bans and simply nodded.

Lisa sighed as she looked at the urn and said, 'We love you, Mum. Hopefully, we'll meet again one day.'

Benjamin reached over and put a hand on her arm, smiling sympathetically. By now, they had reached the coast, and he banked the plane until they were following the coastline. Lisa prised the lid off the urn, slid open the window slot and held the lip up to the narrow gap. With a whisper of, 'We love you, Mum. Rest in peace,' Lisa tipped the urn and poured out the ash. The slipstream of the plane whipped the ashes away, and they gently rained down to the waves of the grey North Sea below.

She peered into the urn and, satisfied that it was now empty, replaced the lid and shuffled in her seat until she was comfortable again. The siblings looked at each other and Benjamin blew Lisa a kiss.

'I don't know about you, sis, but that felt right,' he admitted.

Lisa nodded thoughtfully, 'You know what? It was perfect. Mum would have loved what we did for her. I definitely think you should offer it as a service. I bet people would pay, like, three or four hundred pounds.'

Benjamin looked down at the countryside, smiling as they flew straight over a traffic jam caused by a slow-moving tractor. He replied, 'I have the space at the yard for a respectable quiet office. All I need is a computer, and maybe a little storage room in case anyone wants me to put their loved one's ashes to one side before the appointment to scatter them. Do you want to go into partnership, Lisa, and we can share the profits in memory of Mum?'

'Yeah, I'd love that. I'm sure Mum would too.'

Within six weeks, Benjamin had set up Ashes to Ashes Unique Dispersal. Lisa created the website, and they soon had bookings for relatives wishing to scatter the ashes of their loved one from a plane. Occasionally, relatives couldn't face it themselves, so Benjamin and Lisa did it for them. Either way, they always treated the ashes with utmost respect, as if it were their own relative.

Chapter Eight

After a long day at work, Benjamin, Zack and the triplets sat eating a curry that Chesca had made for them.

Benjamin's face was slightly red, and a few beads of sweat gathered at his brow. He drank a little milk and looked suspiciously at his workers. *Why is no one else sweating?*

Chesca sniggered and looked towards the television. Zack smirked and looked only at his food. Benjamin dropped his fork into his curry and said, 'Okay, good joke, Chesca!'

Chesca fluttered her eyelashes at him and said, 'No idea what you mean, boss!'

'I ain't going to give in, no curry will beat me,' Benjamin grimaced. *My bloody pride…*

As it was Saturday night and no tattoos were done on a Sunday, Zack looked in the fridge and pulled out a can of beer. He asked, 'Anyone want a drink?'

Everyone had more than one alcoholic beverage of some kind over the next hour.

Tilly pondered, 'So, Zack, tell me something that I've always wondered about tattoos.'

'Oh God, what are you going to say?' Zack rolled his eyes, bracing himself for a stupid question.

'What's the *rudest* place you ever did a tattoo?' She asked, smirking. *That should make him squirm.*

Zack chortled and set his beer down as he and Benjamin exchanged glances. Zack sat on the edge of his seat and looked around at the expectant faces waiting for a story.

'Well, just yesterday, a man came in with his girlfriend. They had just got back together again after he played away. She *insisted* that he got her name tattooed on his...um...*penis!*' He laughed.

'No!' shrieked Tilly. 'Benjamin, that isn't true. Is it?' She looked at Benjamin wide-eyed in disbelief.

Benjamin grinned, 'Not only is it true, the poor guy was so scared that his cock looked like a button mushroom! It couldn't have gone any smaller, I'm sure, and Zack here had to try and write 'Melanie' on it. He gave up after 'Mel'.'

The group laughed so much it wouldn't have come as a surprise if one of them had wet themselves.

More alcohol lubricated them all, and the chat followed the same lurid vein.

The talk later turned to business, something that they all held in common.

Benjamin looked over at Tilly, 'You're doing so well with the leather shop. What were you telling me about a new interest? You know, to move things forward, you were saying at the opening of the business that you had a good idea.'

Tilly looked to her sisters for moral support. Chesca and Helena gave her a thumbs up.

She took a sip of her drink and started, 'Do you know that human leather is very in demand?'

Benjamin's jaw dropped, 'You what? Are you crazy?'

Shaking her head, Tilly said, 'Far from it. It's perfectly legal, and people will pay a lot of money for it - many times the usual price for things like belts. Twenty-five pounds for a cow-leather belt, ten thousand pounds for a human skin one. Think about it. I bet you'll sell so many, you'll be a millionaire from this business alone.'

Benjamin popped the ring pull on a fresh can of beer and drank it in one go. He crushed the can between his hands and realised that everyone was looking at him.

He narrowed his eyes at Tilly in contemplation, 'I can't believe I'm saying this, I really can't, but let's give it a trial. Put something on the website, you know, price on application or something. Shit, where will we get the skin from?' *It must be the beer going to my head.*

Tilly put a hand to her mouth, seemingly in deep thought. She finally said, 'Three ways. First, from people who send their relative to us for skin harvesting, and we pay them for the skin. A regular human has a lot of skin I can use, on its abdomen and back. Secondly, and I don't know how this would work, but we could get corpses from the undertaker and pay someone there, get the skin, then send the stiff back to the undertaker for burial or whatever. Thirdly, well, have you ever wanted to bump someone off?'

Benjamin gasped, 'Yes, I mean, who hasn't? But you can't be serious, surely.'

Helena was the next to speak, 'The butcher who started working for us when we set up the piggery, he wants to leave the business unless he gets a pay rise. We could start with him.'

She tilted her head, as though she were a sparrow listening to a faraway sound. Benjamin scratched his chin and then his head. He looked over at Zack, who shrugged. Benjamin did a double take and said to Zack, 'You knew about this, didn't you? You don't seem shocked.'

Zack swigged more beer, 'Yes, we have spoken about it a lot. Ever since me and the girls started at school, we have been the outsiders. People bullied us, people hated us. We were different. No one would ever know. Come on, Benjamin, you feel the same as us. At the end of the day, everyone dies at some point. We might as well help them die or just make money from them. They don't need their skin anymore anyway.'

Benjamin sighed, 'Sod it, why not? You're in charge though. As far as the business goes, the less I know the better. No, I want to know everything! Just don't talk about it in front of the butcher. I want Aled to stay, he's superb for what peanuts I pay him. I'll give him a little pay rise to keep him happy.'

Tilly had a huge grin on her face.

'You're the best! I have another idea too.'

Groaning, Benjamin said, 'I dread to think what you're going to say next. Go on.'

'I think items with a tattoo on them would be awesome. Think of it as every item is unique. Purse with a swift tattoo on it? Yes please.'

Zack clapped Tilly, 'You are inspired! I think Benjamin should give us all a pay rise 'cause of all the new income that's coming his way.'

Benjamin almost choked on his beer, 'Dream on, I already almost bankrupt myself paying for and homing you misfits!'

Laughing, Zack said, 'No harm in asking.'

The triplets joined in laughing; the noise was almost deafening.

Benjamin, in a moment of clarity, sent a message to Lisa.

'Come round tomorrow; need you to get a job at the undertakers!'

Chapter Nine

Lisa arrived at Dr Tattoo at five thirty. Benjamin was still about twenty minutes from finishing a tattoo for a client, so Lisa sat on a bench in the yard while she waited for him to complete the body art.

She had just finished a coffee when a middle-aged woman left the studio looking thrilled. The woman got into a Nissan Micra and drove out of the yard slowly, followed by a cloud of dust thrown into the air by her tyres. Lisa knew that the wind could swirl and blow the dust into her face, so she stood and went into the studio.

She embraced her brother and waved over to Zack, who was cleaning a mirror. There were no more clients in the shop. Lisa looked quizzically at Benjamin and asked, 'So what's this about you wanting me to get a job at the undertakers?'

Benjamin screwed his face and rubbed his stubble. Zack boasted, 'This is genius, Lisa. It's about Tilly.'

Lisa looked closely at her brother and said, 'You aren't going to kill her, are you, and get me to dispose of the body?'

Benjamin shook his head. 'No—'

'I was joking!' Lisa said, hitting him on the upper arm.

Benjamin made himself a coffee, 'More coffee, Lisa?'

'No, thank you. Come on, I want to hear this. Must be good, as you're trying to avoid the subject now, and I came out here to the back end of nowhere to see you...' She peered closely into his eyes, until he blinked first and averted his gaze.

After a deep intake of breath, Benjamin began, 'Tilly is making leather goods over in one of the units. Anyway, she's had an idea. Bloody genius idea to be honest, and it's gonna make me a millionaire.'

Lisa rolled her hands, 'Go on.'

'Leather goods made from humans,' Benjamin closed his eyes and took a drink from his coffee. Lisa stood with her mouth wide open, for once lost for words. He explained, 'It is legal, and people will pay a damned fortune. I'll make a, well, the girls will make a website offering big payouts for people letting us take skin from their dead relative before they are buried or cremated...Which is where you come in, sis. If we get short of skins, then you could bring corpses for flaying, or whatever it's called, and take 'em back to the funeral home before the sun rises again. It's going to be easy money, and I'll give you cash for it too. It's not like the dead person needs their skin anymore, is it?'

'No way, not a chance,' Lisa refused. 'You must be off your rocker with this madcap idea.'

Benjamin refilled his coffee cup, 'It could be very lucrative, sis...I'd give you a couple of grand for less than a night's work. You wouldn't need to do anything beyond transporting them. You can't even say that it's immoral.'

Lisa stopped in her tracks, 'A couple of grand, you say?'

'Minimum. Maybe a bit more if they are...statuesque.'

Zack and Lisa both laughed at that statement, and Zack accused, 'You mean fat, don't you?'

Benjamin laughed and held his hands up in mock surrender, 'Whatever you say.' *There is no way she'll refuse now; she loves a few quid in her pocket. Just like me.*

'Let me think about it,' Lisa said pensively. Benjamin smirked; he knew Lisa well enough to know that she would say yes. She looked out over the yard, shaking her head slightly as if disapproving whatever was going through her mind.

Benjamin whispered to Zack, 'This is going to be so good. Have you got any contacts at a funeral home?'

He winked at his colleague.

Lisa stomped a foot and span round to face the two men. Her eyes drifted up to the banners dangling from the roof, 'Tell you what. Benji, if you pay Zack to do a tattoo for me on my foot, then I'll join in your madcap scheme.'

'Can you fit her in, Zack?' Benjamin asked, a smug smile settling on his lips.

'Sure, come and have a seat,' Zack motioned to the plastic-covered chair. 'Let me just have a quick smoke and I'll do it for you now.'

Lisa giggled, 'Thanks, Benji, I love you.'

Zack popped out of the door and sat at the same spot that Lisa had been occupying not so long before.

He smoked his cigarette, puffing out smoke rings into the now still air. When Lisa saw him coming back into the building, she took off her trainers and socks.

She already knew what tattoo to get—Delia's name surrounded by stars and ribbons. Zack took great care, as he did with all his clients, to execute the tattoo immaculately. It took about two hours, falling dark before he finished.

'There, I love it. Let me get a handheld mirror so you can see it properly,' Zack murmured with a smile curling his lips.

He held the mirror so that Lisa could see the tattoo. She almost burst with excitement. 'Oh my God, it's so perfect, Zack! Thank you so much!' She half looked over at her brother and warned, 'Don't try and wriggle out of paying Zack for this, it is awesome!'

Benjamin smiled lovingly at Lisa, 'It's lovely. I'm sure Mum would have loved it.'

Zack wrapped the tattoo with plastic film and handed Lisa an aftercare sheet to tell her how to look after her new body art.

'Make sure you follow this; I'd hate for you to get an infection,' he directed.

Lisa stood and pecked Zack on the cheek. She promised, 'I will…scout's honour. Anyway, I have to go home now and put a CV together.' Turning to her brother, she added, 'I'll ring you later in the week.'

They hugged, and Benjamin helped her to get out to her car because she couldn't put her sock and trainer back onto her foot.

Chapter Ten

Almost two months passed by from that day when Lisa agreed to try and get a job at the undertakers.

Finally, she noticed an advert online for the local independent funeral home, Jo Hawley Funeral Services. Excitement filled her, and she printed a copy of the advert.

Following the instructions, she wrote a short application letter. The funeral home was only half a mile from her home, so she cycled to hand the application in rather than posting it through the Royal Mail.

Lisa fastened her bike to a lamppost with a cycle lock and, with a slight feeling of apprehension, she pushed open the door. A bell attached to the door sounded with a tinkle.

From somewhere within the building, Lisa heard footsteps approaching. A moment later, a chubby woman with short cropped hair and thick-lensed spectacles appeared. She looked to be about fifty years of age. Noticing the envelope in Lisa's hand, she smiled kindly, held out a hand and said, 'Hello, I'm Jo Hawley. Have you come to apply for the job?'

Lisa shivered a little inside. *God, if you are real, please forgive me.* She took Jo's hand, which was surprisingly warm, and shook it.

'Yes, I'm Lisa McGuinness. Here is my application.' Somehow, Lisa made eye contact with Jo and smiled brightly.

Jo tucked the envelope into a drawer.

'Thank you for coming in, Lisa. I will be in contact with you later this week, regardless of whether or not I offer you an interview. I believe very much in proper manners,' she smiled at Lisa, a curious gesture that looked polished after years of practice.

Lisa got the hint and left saying, 'Thank you, I look forward to it.'

Lisa didn't have to wait long in the end. Twenty-four hours on the dot later, her mobile rang; she had already programmed the funeral home's telephone number into the device, so she knew if they were calling her.

'Hello? Lisa speaking.'

'Jo Hawley speaking. Are you free to come to the office today for an informal chat?'

Lisa looked down at what she was wearing. *Better get smartened up a bit.* 'Absolutely! I can come in forty minutes, is that okay?'

'Perfect, see you then.'

Jo didn't wait for a reply and cut the connection. Lisa rushed around, brushed her hair and teeth and changed her clothes into a blouse and work trousers. Pulling on a coat, she pushed her bike out of her hall and onto the path. Lisa had decided to not wear her cycle helmet, to avoid developing the dreaded 'helmet hair.' But, as she cycled, not having it on made her feel somewhat vulnerable; she wished that she hadn't been so vain and just put it on anyway.

Her legs powered the bike as fast as she could muster without breaking into a sweat. Upon arrival, she fastened her bike to the lamppost again and tottered up the ramp to the door.

Lisa gently pushed the door open, noticing that it opened quietly and easily as if the hinges were regularly oiled. The bell tinkled it's quaint ring. Jo was already in the reception area, dusting the desk.

A feeling of apprehension gnawed at Lisa's stomach, and she felt her cheeks redden a little. *I wonder if this is such a good idea after all. Still, I suppose dead people aren't as antisocial as some live ones. Ugh, I guess I can always just give it a try if she offers me the job.*

'Are you alright, Lisa?' Jo asked, with a look of concern. 'You look quite flushed.'

Lisa smiled, 'Yes…yes, I'm fine thanks. I've cycled here…you know, doing my bit for the planet.'

'Ah, I see, too energetic for me. Anyway, would you like a drink perhaps?'

Lisa felt herself warming to the woman. Jo reminded her a little of her mum; seemingly always trying to look after other people. 'Yes, I'd like some water please. I should really have brought a drink with me.'

Jo went somewhere into the depths of the building and reappeared with two glasses and a jug of water, balanced on a silver tray. She set them down on a small table that Lisa hadn't noticed before and sat in a chair.

'Have a seat, Lisa,' she invited.

Jo poured them both a glass of water as Lisa lowered herself into the chair and quickly looked around to see what else she had missed. There was a grandfather clock in one corner, reminding her how she'd always liked those imposing timepieces.

Jo spoke, which made Lisa jump a little, 'I love that clock too, it was a gift from a client's family. We do get a lot of repeat business from some families. Tell me, what is it about this place that prompted you to apply for the job? It is quite a change from an office job.'

Surprising herself, Lisa spoke from the heart—a far cry from the reasons she'd fabricated in preparation for the interview. She explained, 'Well, it's a business that will always be in demand, as long as there are humans around. I think it's a lovely opportunity to help people when they are at a low point in their life, losing a loved one.'

Jo nodded and took a sip of water, 'You are right, in the main. There are some people we lay to rest that have no family or friends. And, yes, it's always a bit sad, but we treat all of our customers with utmost dignity at all times. Sometimes, relatives can appear uncaring about their departed relative and just want us to put on a basic funeral to keep up appearances. People are mostly very vulnerable when we are dealing with them, when they are grieving. You'll find also, that some people can be a bit rude, but take it with a pinch of salt. It's not *you* that they have a problem with. Rather, it's their grief that makes them be a bit...short.'

Lisa sipped her water and wondered if she had heard correctly; it seemed that Jo was offering her the job. She waited to see what the woman would say next.

Jo settled her glass back on the tray after she had emptied it. She looked at Lisa through her thick glasses, which served to magnify her face somewhat, and only turned away when the phone on the desk rang. Jo moved with effortless speed to answer it.

'Jo Hawley Funeral Service. Jo speaking. How may I help you?...Uh-hmm...Yes. Sure. Come in at two this afternoon and I can take you through your options…Thank you and see you at two.'

Jo rested the handset back onto the cradle and turned to Lisa. After a moment, she said, 'So have you seen a body before?'

Lisa thought about it for a moment before gently shaking her head, 'No, never. Well, apart from on telly of course.'

She subconsciously looked at the door leading back out to the street.

Jo chuckled, which caught Lisa's attention as it seemed so abstract given the location. She must have looked surprised, which amused Jo even more.

'Don't worry, most people in normal walks of life haven't. Come with me; I'll give you a tour of the place.'

Lisa tried to not think of the prospect of coming face to face with a corpse.

'This way," Jo instructed. "Right, you've seen the front office. I'll show you the facilities first.'

They found themselves in a comfortable kitchen with a fridge, kettle and microwave. A small table and a trio of chairs finished off the room along with a pin board displaying the 'Health and Safety at Work' poster. Lisa was pleasantly surprised to note that there were no dirty mugs sitting in the sink. Jo pointed to a cupboard and announced, 'That's your cupboard, Lisa. Store anything in there; no-one will touch it. I provide milk, coffee and tea bags.'

Lisa stopped in her tracks, 'So, um, have I got the job?'

'Oh yes, that's why I asked you back down here,' Jo revealed. 'Sorry, I should have said. I assume that you accept?'

With a huge smile, Lisa said, 'This is awesome…of course I accept! Thank you so much.'

As they continued their tour, they passed the toilets on their way to a huge garage that contained a van and several coffins on metal racking. Jo saw Lisa's surprise at the vast space. 'We have to keep the van inside, so we can transfer bodies in and out of it away from prying eyes. People don't mean to be nosy, but they become morbidly curious when the opportunity to stare at body bags and coffins arises.' A hearse and a pair of limousines completed the gaggle of vehicles.

The garage had two connecting doors leading out of it, one of which led back to the reception area. A single coffin was displayed in the centre of the garage, and Lisa couldn't help but notice it didn't have a lid on to hide its contents. She peered inside but saw only a plush silk lining and a small cushion at the head of the casket.

Inadvertently letting out a sigh of relief, Lisa smiled to herself with relief.

'Right, one last place to go now. It's what I call the laboratory, but really, it's where we do embalming. Just to let you know, there is one body on a work trolley. Don't be scared, you'll soon get into the swing of things.'

Jo pushed open a double door and entered the embalming room. Lisa took a deep breath and followed her in. As promised, there was a body on the trolley, with a light sheet draped over the top of it. A massive industrial fridge took up most of the opposite wall.

It was not as Lisa expected, yet there seemed to be nothing more natural than the scenario in front of her. She let out a sigh of relief.

'Ready?' Jo asked, as she stood by the head end of the deceased.

Lisa nodded. *Oh my God…is this really happening?*

Jo took care in folding back the sheet, just to the body's chest. It was an elderly man. Lisa looked at his face and felt a sense of relief. The moment changed her whole outlook on life and death. The end of life was laid bare in front of her, and it was no longer something to be afraid of.

Jo re-covered the man and smiled kindly at Lisa, 'Are you alright, Lisa? It can be a shock seeing a body for the first time.'

Lisa smiled more genuinely than she expected. *This is actually going to be a good job. Thanks, Benji!* 'Yes, I am fine. It was nowhere near as bad as I feared it would be. I guess there's going to be a lot of training,' something suddenly occurred to her. 'Where are the other workers?'

Jo sighed, 'There was only me and Tom. He left to live with a woman, in Wakefield of all places!'

Lisa looked blankly at her new boss, 'Wakefield?'

'Yes, Wakefield. All I can say is that I hope she is worth it!'

'Sorry to hear that, were you married for long?'

Jo laughed, 'Sorry, I must have given you the wrong impression! I'm actually gay; Tom was my long-suffering colleague.'

'Oh! I'm so sorry that I jumped to such a conclusion. Er, when should I start training?' Lisa asked, attempting to swiftly change the subject.

'Monday…be here at nine sharp. You can bring your bike into the garage; it'll be safe there. Then we'll sort you out uniform and do the boring stuff like payroll. It'll just be me and you in the main, apart from on funeral days when I have some casual staff come and help with pallbearer duties, etcetera.'

Lisa felt her cheeks cooling to their normal colour, 'Thanks so much for giving me this opportunity. You won't regret it.'

'See you Monday.'

Chapter Eleven

Benjamin sat in the office in the piggery, suddenly feeling glad that he'd splashed out on air conditioning after Chesca and Helena had nagged about it for months.

The numbers on the spreadsheet in front of him showed a business in rude health, even if it meant the women and the butcher were run off their feet. He took in all the posters and information sheets affixed to the walls in the office. With a smug smile he realised that Zack had found him a goldmine of employees.

But something was bothering Benjamin; he just wasn't sure what it was. He stood and strolled over to the door. Looking through the window, his eyes settled on the butcher, Aled Price. Helena and Chesca must be in the back of the unit with the pigs.

The portly man was expertly cutting up joints of pork. A radio played Newdon DAB at a loud volume. That didn't matter; there were no neighbours to worry about. Benjamin was satisfied that Aled was wearing the correct protective clothing; if environmental health came knocking, there would be no issues.

There was an issue with Aled, though. Benjamin was sure he wouldn't approve of the human leather. He didn't know why, maybe a sixth sense.

Benjamin put on his best good-boss-face and went out into the butchery room. Aled had a saw in his hand, so Benjamin avoided making the man jump. *This is no time for an avoidable injury.*

He walked round the table to face Aled. The butcher, realising that Benjamin was watching him, looked up and smiled.

'Hi, Benji, you alright?'

'My name is Benjamin. I don't like being called Benji.'

Aled did a double take and frowned, 'The girls call you Benji all the time. Sorry.'

Benjamin relaxed a little. *Maybe I shouldn't be so precious about my name.*

'Don't worry about it, mate. How are you liking working with Chesca and Helena? I believe that Tilly helps sometimes as well when she has time.'

'They are…unique,' Aled smiled. 'Tilly is always boasting about her leather goods. Credit where credit's due though, the stuff she makes is excellent.'

Benjamin agreed, 'It certainly is, and it's proving really popular. Maybe she should think about other leathers too.'

Aled looked up through his eyelashes, 'You mean like kangaroo and ray skins?'

'Something like that…'

With a strange laugh, more of a snort, Aled straightened up and pointed the saw at Benjamin. 'I hear that, in some places around the world, they like using human skin,' he took hold of the piece of meat he was working and rasped the saw into it. 'I think that sounds awful. Even if it were legal, I don't think it's ethical. I mean, really? Come on!'

Benjamin waited to see what Aled would say next.

'If I ever got wind of it that Tilly was going to use human leather, I would quit and report her to the police.'

Chesca made both men jump. They hadn't noticed her come into the room, 'What are you two talking about?'

'Oh, nothing, darling, just about how well Tilly is doing with the leather shop,' Aled replied.

Chesca smiled sweetly at Aled, 'Yes, she is a star really. Benjamin has given her the green light to use human flesh you know, to make into leather.'

Aled instantly dropped the saw, which clattered loudly on the stainless steel. 'No way!' he looked at Benjamin wide eyed. 'That isn't true, is it?'

Benjamin smirked, 'Maybe, maybe not.'

'Everything okay? I heard a loud noise,' Helena said, jogging in with beads of sweat running down her face.

Chesca laughed the terrible triplet laugh that made Benjamin's skin crawl. She teased, 'It's okay, just Aled being a butter fingers and dropping his saw. He doesn't like it that Tilly is going to use human flesh to turn into leather goods. He almost cried.'

Aled looked again at Helena, shaking his head. He picked up the saw, 'Helena, please tell me that these two jokers are kidding, right?'

Helena looked into the corner of the ceiling and tilted her head, as if in deep thought. She licked her lips and said, 'Sorry, Aled, but it really is true. Do you know what the best thing is?'

Aled looked at her, unaware that his jaw was dropping open. 'The *best* thing? How can anything about this be a best thing?' He laughed maniacally like he had suddenly thought of the funniest thing in the world.

Helena clapped her hands together twice, and Aled stopped laughing as though someone had pressed a pause button.

'The best thing is that YOU are the butcher,' Helena pointed at his chest. 'YOU are going to be the one removing the skin from dead people! Benjamin might even give you another pay rise.'

She winked at Benjamin, who smirked at her. *The poor lad is being tipped onto the verge of a breakdown by Helena…*

Aled took off his butcher's hairnet and hat and threw them onto the floor. His shiny bald head shimmered with sweat. Next, he removed his apron. That went onto the floor too.

When Benjamin held up a hand, Aled halted. Benjamin barked, 'What are you doing, Aled?'

The butcher threw up his arms in exasperation.

'Until you crazy bunch tell me you're joking, I'm out of here. I can't cut people's skin off! What sane person could even do that?' Without pausing for an answer, he continued. His face flushed bright red, a neck vein bulging dangerously, 'I have a good mind to drop into Newdon nick and let the cops know what depraved act you're going to do!'

His volume and pitch increased with every word.

Benjamin quietly said, 'Aled, calm down. You're going to have an aneurysm or something, mate. I would never ask you to do anything illegal…'

The butcher's eyeballs bulged, 'I don't give a flying fuck if it's legal or not! It's not right. Who the hell is going to give a relative or a friend to you to be turned into a leather item? No one, that's who! You have to be planning something nefarious, and I ain't never going to have anything to do with it.'

Chesca interrupted, 'That's a double negative, Aled.'

Aled stopped in his tracks. 'What the hell are you on about? We're discussing chopping up *people*, and you want to correct my grammar?' His voice had now descended to a hoarse whisper.

Benjamin stepped towards Aled, who tried to retreat, but hit his back on the table. The boss said, 'Aled, here's the thing. You *have* to take part in the project now. By being here, you have agreed, whether you like it or not.'

Aled and Benjamin stood close together, close enough for Benjamin to smell Aled's breath. All either man could see was the other's eyes; nothing else in the room came into their focus.

Aled blinked first and stepped to one side. Everyone else, who seemed to have held their breath, suddenly exhaled a collection of deep breaths around the room.

'I'm going now,' Aled announced. 'Send my P45 in the post.'

He hadn't noticed that Helena and Chesca had grabbed a sharp butcher's knife each and held them behind their backs while he and Benjamin were nose to nose. Aled took a long stride forwards, and the two women rushed towards him. He stopped in his tracks and stared in surprise, his hands groped around his midriff.

Helena grunted as she pulled her knife out of Aled's groin. Blood pulsed out of the stab wound, spraying Helena from head to toe. Aled tried to step forward, but he could only stagger.

Benjamin shoved him, causing him fell onto his left side. Chesca's knife stood proud from the right-hand side of his ribcage. Benjamin pulled the knife out with all his might; it felt stuck somehow and made a sucking noise as it teased out. Rolling backwards, his head missed the table by a hair's breadth, leaving only his pride with the worst injury.

Chesca and Helena laughed at him.

'Shut up!' Benjamin barked. 'How did this happen?' He looked down at the motionless man on the floor. *I think he is dead. Shit! Shit! Shit! Shit! Shit!*

A blood puddle surrounded the man, the viscous fluid trickling towards the drain under the centre of the cutting table. Neither Chesca nor Helena tried to stem the bleeding, neither did Benjamin. He seemed to be beholden by an unseen supernatural being to not attempt to save Aled's life.

Silence descended over the room, and the loud music faded into nothingness in Benjamin's conscious mind.

'Benjamin, are you alright? You look rather green,' he realised that Helena was holding his shoulder and peering closely at him. 'I'll get you a glass of water.'

Benjamin closed his eyes tightly. *When I open them, maybe Aled will still be sawing a joint.*

He reopened his eyes. *Damn!* Aled was still dead.

Helena came back into the room and handed Benjamin the drink. He nodded a quick thanks and guzzled it down in one go. Benjamin gasped; the cold drink brought his mind back to the present.

Benjamin looked again at Aled, then at Helena.

'You should go and shower. Throw those clothes in the garden incinerator. I'll burn them later,' he blew out a lungful of air and watched Helena leave the room. 'I didn't think you lot were serious when you said that killing someone was a way to get human skin for leather.'

Chesca shrugged, 'I wasn't. I don't think the other two were either. I think we just got used to the idea, and when the situation came up…it just happened.'

'We can't exactly call an ambulance for Aled, can we? We'll be in the police cells before we know it. Shit. What a fucking mess,' Benjamin sighed.

'I'll go and get Tilly from the leather shop and between us we should be able to lift Aled onto the table,' Chesca said. Benjamin, seeming to have lost his ability to talk, simply blinked and looked down at Aled again.

Chesca walked out of the room and left Benjamin alone with Aled's body. He whispered, 'Mate, I'm really sorry about this. I really am. You'll be pleased to know that you're going to be the first donor to the leather project. Damn, I hope you're proud, mate.'

Tilly bounded into the room, so excited that she was jumping up and down. Benjamin looked at her wide eyed, 'Why are you so happy? We've killed a man here.'

Tilly grinned.

'He should yield plenty of skin. That will make us *tons* of money,' she suddenly frowned. 'Is the farmer's old forklift still behind the unit? I saw it there recently I'm sure...'

Benjamin poked Aled with a foot, 'I'll go and get it, and a pallet to move Aled. We can't risk lifting him by hand, you're right.'

Ten minutes later, Benjamin was coaxing the door to the unit open. It hadn't been open for months; the triplets only used the personnel door.

The door eventually yielded and wobbled open with a shriek of protesting metal. He stepped on the gas, and the forklift belched a cloud of dirty diesel fumes out of its exhaust stack. Inexpertly, he lowered the forks so that the blue wooden pallet rested on the floor next to the butcher's body.

With much grunting and groaning, Chesca, Benjamin and Tilly shoved Aled onto the pallet. Helena came through the doors with a look of satisfaction on her face, her freshly washed hair tied back into a high ponytail.

She glanced over to the tattoo studio, glad that the interior of the piggery still wasn't visible through the open door.

Benjamin hopped back into the truck and lifted the forks. With another splutter of exhaust fumes, he moved forward a little, so the pallet was above the table. He tried to lower the forks with care, but the unmaintained machinery juddered down and bounced the body off the pallet onto the table top.

He then backed the forklift truck out of the building and pushed the door closed.

On re-entering the building, he hoped in vain that the scene he'd left behind moments earlier might turn out to have been just a nightmare.

Unfortunately, that was not the case. Chesca was already cutting off Aled's clothes with a huge pair of scissors. She passed them to Helena who in turn dropped them into a yellow 'hazardous waste' plastic sack.

Tilly whispered, 'I'm glad that you murderers didn't stab him in the back or higher in the abdomen. That would've ruined the skin, a waste of potential leather.'

Benjamin glanced at Tilly, 'You really just said that? That's horrific. We've just killed a man and you can only think of the leather?'

'Shut up! We've been thinking of this for a long time. Just think of the money. That's what you're all about anyway,' she snapped back.

Benjamin stepped back and held his hands up in protest, 'Calm down, Tilly. We have to keep cool headed; Aled's family will be looking for him in a few hours.'

'You are right, but he had to die. It's his own fault though. He should've been happy for the new opportunity,' she looked around for a particular knife and made a triumphant noise when she found it. 'Huzzah!'

Helena dumped the sack of clothes by the door. *I'll burn it later.*

Benjamin couldn't help but watch as Tilly drew the knife around Aled's corpse. The act was morbidly fascinating. She lifted the section of skin off Aled's back with an expert touch, and deposited it in a huge bucket that Helena had fetched from another part of the unit.

'We need to roll him,' Tilly said matter-of-factly. She stood back as her two sisters and Benjamin turned Aled onto his back. 'Good,' Tilly declared, and cut his abdomen and chest skin off with great skill.

Benjamin gawped at Aled's naked and flayed body. He had become a grotesque representation of the human form. Chesca cleared her throat, 'We should cut him up and feed him to the pigs, there will be nothing left...'

Benjamin felt like he was some kind of robot or humanoid, controlled by someone else. *This makes no sense. I have to be dreaming.*

Without thinking about what he was actually doing, he grasped the saw that Aled had been using not long beforehand. He put the blade into Aled's armpit and commenced sawing. It was surprisingly easy for Benjamin to saw the arm off. *Is this real? Am I in a violent dream?*

Something occurred to Benjamin, and he stopped sawing. He turned to Chesca and said, 'We will have to hide his car. Maybe we should burn it out. What do you think?'

'I think we should just park it inside one of the unused barns or something. If we set fire to it, where would we even do that?'

Benjamin sighed and commenced sawing the other limbs off. He tossed them to the side of the table, where they rested higgledy piggledy. Looking round, he waved the three women over to the table.

'I ain't going to be cutting his head off; that's just...wrong,' he balked.

A low laughter went around the group, which slowly petered out into a sombre silence.

Tilly grabbed Aled's right arm by the wrist and took it to the pigs. She tossed it towards the sow and returned to the table. The left arm went next. Her sisters took a leg each. That left the torso and head. None of them took the lead for the final task; they could barely even look at each other.

Benjamin coughed quietly, 'We have to move his body. Jeez, I can't believe what we've done...but it's done now, and we have to protect our secret. I will hold his body by the hips, Chesca you take his shoulders. Tilly and Helena, just help as best you can, okay?'

The triplets nodded; no more words were needed. Benjamin grasped the large man and heaved him up with all his strength. Where Aled's legs had been attached to his body, now dripped with blood and hunks of gory raw meat. It appeared to be slick, and not a place to grip.

Benjamin tried not to take any notice of Aled's genitals slapping about as he gripped him. Chesca shoved her arms under Aled's shoulders.

'Next time, leave the arms on. It'll be easier to lift the body if I have armpits to shove my elbows under.'

Benjamin grimaced, 'My God, I hope there isn't a next time. One murder is bad enough, but more? No...We must work on chasing up *willing* donors, and then we can just give the bodies back.'

Tilly glared at him, her eyes boring a hole into his. She prodded, 'I don't think any of us like it, but now we have made this first step, it can only get easier.'

Benjamin shrugged, at a loss as to what he could say next. *I guess she is right…wow, this is insane. I thought I'd cope better than this.*

The group made it to the pig pens and tipped Aled unceremoniously over the concrete wall. He hit the ground with a thump; his head bounced and made a sickening dull thud as it came to rest.

A pig trotted over to the body, its ears bouncing around in a comical manner.

'I can't watch this,' Benjamin admitted. He left the piggery, and then the unit as fast as his shaking legs could carry him. The fresh air hit him in a rush, causing the boss to bend at the waist and vomit. *I'd better go back in there or the triplets will think I'm soft.*

Helena had a hosepipe in her hand, washing the remaining blood towards a drain, while Chesca wandered in with a bottle of bleach, a bucket of hot water and a mop. As Tilly picked up one bucket containing Aled's skin and headed off out of the unit, Chesca pointed to the second bucket and said, 'Off you go, Benji, make yourself useful and take that over to the leather shop. Then come back to help with the clean up.'

Benjamin nodded, his normal status of being the boss seemingly put to one side.

Over the next hour, Benjamin felt numb, like a spare part as he watched the women sort out the crime scene. When they'd finished cleaning, the gleaming tiles and stainless steel benches spoke nothing of the horrors they'd showcased earlier.

Tilly put an arm around Benjamin's waist, 'Try not to worry. Nothing will go wrong; it isn't possible. I'll get Aled's car and you follow me in your car.'

Benjamin couldn't argue, he just followed Tilly out to where Aled's car waited for an owner that would never return.

****

Tilly drove with care out of the farmyard. Her speed didn't rise above thirty miles per hour for around ten minutes.

'Come on, Tilly, where are we going?' Benjamin mused.

He didn't have to wait long. A gap in the high hedge marked an entry point into a field. Tilly swung off the road and stopped Aled's car on the grass before Benjamin left the tarmac. She lowered her window and shouted to Benjamin, 'Don't drive off the road; you could leave tyre prints for the cops!'

He pulled up the handbrake lever and got out of his car to follow her on foot. He pushed open an unlocked five-bar gate and she drove onto the field, coming to a stop about twenty feet into it.

Benjamin opened the passenger door, and looked inside the car. There was nothing of value in there, nor anything that could have identified it as Aled's. He noticed that Aled had nice floor mats. Benjamin crouched by the car and fished his cigarette lighter from his jeans pocket. He lifted the edge of the mat and held the lighter under it. With a flick of his thumb on the harsh metal lighter wheel, a small flame appeared and flickered. It took just a few seconds for the mat to ignite. Benjamin pushed it underneath the seat which in turn soon burned bright, sending billows of smoke into the sky.

'Come on, let's get out of here,' Tilly advised.

Benjamin nodded, and they both left the field and got into his car.

He glanced into the field, satisfied that the Peugeot was on the journey to car heaven. No words were spoken on the way back to the yard.

Benjamin turned off the engine after he parked. 'Now is when the real hard work starts. Lying to Aled's wife. Lying to the police,' he rested his forehead on his car's steering wheel and let all the air in his lungs whoosh out. Sitting back in his chair, he stated, 'Come on, let's go and find some food.'

Chapter Twelve

Tilly and Benjamin sauntered over to the living quarters as if nothing had happened. They entered the unit and found the others eating toast and drinking tea. Benjamin inhaled a deep breath through his nose, 'That smells heavenly!'

Helena and Chesca were telling Zack about what had happened to Aled. Benjamin smiled when he saw that Zack had gone very pale, like a blank piece of A4 paper. *They must be pulling no punches...poor lad looks like he's going to puke.*

Zack stood. 'Want some tea and toast?' he asked Benjamin and Tilly.

Benjamin put on his best smile, 'Yeah, go on, mate. Marmite for me, please.'

'How can you feel like eating?' asked Tilly. 'Not for me, thanks, Zack. And I need a stronger drink than tea.'

Zack smiled at her, 'Stick with tea for now. I'll put two sugars in to help with the shock.'

Silence settled, a comfortable one where the group could just sit with their own thoughts.

Breaking the quiet, the toaster popped and the kettle clicked off. Zack made himself busy by refuelling everyone who wanted more toast and tea. Benjamin took a sip and turned to Zack, 'Tell me, how's the afternoon been in the studio? Sorry I didn't come in to help with the cleaning...'

Zack enthused about the day in the studio, telling the group how a tattoo virgin had been in and had a large portrait of their recently deceased nephew tattooed on her leg. He described in length to Benjamin about how he'd made the client happy.

When Zack stopped talking, no one else took up the opportunity to speak, which was not the normal state of play.

Zack drained his tea and sat back with his arms crossed. Benjamin noticed and asked, 'What's up, mate?'

'We need more staff. My diary is jam packed.'

Benjamin stroked his chin and looked thoughtful, 'Hmm, perhaps you are right. But I don't know where I could recruit, you know, *those* kind of people...someone I could trust with our secrets.'

Chesca, who was always more forthright than her siblings, chipped in. 'It has to be someone to live in with us, to be a part of our little community. Aled was an outsider, and we couldn't trust him to not blab to the authorities.'

Shaking his head, Benjamin wondered, 'But where would I find a talented tattooist? Zack is the best there is, and I am shit-hot, obviously.'

That statement seemed to break the ice, albeit unintentionally. Tilly laughed, 'Oh my God, Benjamin, how big is your ego? You're right though. I have to say that I could do with another pair of hands in the leather shop. The piggery is too busy to keep asking Chesca and Helena to come and help out. It's well busy, and if this human leather takes off, it'll be insane. Maybe even a new person to float between the two and help out where needed would be a good idea.'

Benjamin sat back and looked at the ceiling, seeming to avoid eye contact while he thought, 'Alright, let's see how the human leather takes off. I'll definitely put low-key feelers out.'

Benjamin's mobile phone rang. He looked at the display and groaned, 'It's Aled's home number.' Pressing the display, he answered the call.

'Hello?...No, Aled isn't here, he left work at the usual time....Hmm, odd...he didn't mention he was going to call anywhere on the way home...Sorry I can't help, let me know when he turns up...Okay, bye.'

Benjamin sighed and shook his head, 'That was shit. Aled's wife sounds like a nice person. I hate lying.'

Zack put a brotherly arm around Benjamin's shoulder, 'As long as we all stick together, it'll all be alright.'

'I hope so, I really do. We could be in so much shit...'

Chapter Thirteen

PC Hooker-Wolfe stood in the small kitchen opposite the office waiting for the microwave to ping. It was the first chance that she'd had to grab a bite to eat during her twelve-hour shift. Her radio lit up just as the food was ready. With a sigh, she answered the transmission. Sgt Love was making a cup of tea and listening in.

'Can it wait? I'm 10-4 hot refs...Thank you...' she asked, using police radio code for a refreshment break.

'I don't blame you, it's been manic,' said Sgt Love. 'I'll come with you if you like; taking a missing persons statement is always difficult for the family.'

****

Sgt Love rapped on Holly Price's door. After a couple of seconds, it swung open and a short plump lady stood before her.

'Mrs Price?' she asked. The woman half nodded and stood back just enough to let the two police officers to enter her home. They all stepped into the small living room.

Holly gestured for the two officers to sit. She sat on the edge of an uncomfortable looking armchair and grasped a sodden tissue. Sgt Love looked around the room, noticing that there were more than the average number of photographs of the couple together.

PC Hooker-Wolfe introduced them both, 'I'm Emma, this is Laura. I understand that your husband didn't come home after work today. Can you tell me more?'

Holly's bottom lip wobbled a little, but she composed herself enough to speak, 'Aled always comes straight home after work. He doesn't *expect* it, but I always have something in the oven for him. He's so dependable.' She dabbed the tissue on her eyes, scooping up a small streak of mascara.

Sgt Love spoke with an unusual softness to her voice, 'I'm sorry, but I do have to ask you if you know of any reason why Aled may have chosen to not come home?'

When Holly began to sob, Emma sat next to her and put a reassuring arm around her shoulders.

Holly looked up through her tears, 'No, we are an ordinary boring couple. He works hard and is tired out when he comes home. We've only been married a year…this isn't happening.'

Sgt Love said, 'Alright, tell me his workplace address and phone number and we'll see what we can find out. Try not to worry too much, hopefully there will be an explanation.'

Holly seemed to steel herself, and smiled slightly, with hope etched in her eyes.

Sgt Love took the details and said, 'Here's my card. Call me any time if there's anything I can help with.' She handed Holly a business card with her phone number and email address on.

'Thank you, and good luck trying to find him,' said Holly, seemingly detaching herself from her emotions.

The officers stood, made their goodbyes and left.

****

PC Hooker-Wolfe and Sgt Love pulled into the farmyard. As they were about to get out of their car, the sergeant was called from the control room. Mildred Bird, the earnest controller, spoke in her ear, 'To advise you, Mr Price's car has been found burned out in a farmer's field. No trace of Mr Price nearby.'

'All received,' Sgt Love replied. She said to PC Hooker-Wolfe, 'That's interesting. Let's go and see what Mr McGuinness has to say for himself.'

Holly had told them that Benjamin and the other workers lived together in a unit in the yard. Sgt Love glanced around the yard and pointed to the living quarters, 'They must live in there, it's the only building that's not a business.'

They sauntered over to the unit and Sgt Love rapped on the door. Benjamin answered the knock. He opened the door and greeted the officers, 'Have you come about Aled? Please, come in.'

When they got into the room, Zack made coffee for them.

Sgt Love took the lead, 'As you know, Mr Price did not go home after work. Did he say anything to anyone about his plans?' She scanned the faces of those around her; they all shook their heads and looked puzzled.

Benjamin said, 'No, nothing. He really loves his missus, so we can't understand it.'

'Did Mr Price say anything unusual or act different to normal in any way at all? Even the smallest thing could be useful to us,' asked PC Hooker-Wolfe.

Benjamin looked over at Chesca and Helena. 'You two work with him most…'

The sisters exchanged shrugs. 'We just had a normal day at work, that's it really,' Chesca lied.

Sgt Love sighed and stood. PC Hooker-Wolfe followed suit. The senior officer said to Benjamin, 'Thank you for your help. Here's my card, if any of you think of anything at all, please call.'

Benjamin took the card from her and read it with care before slipping it into his wallet.

'I hope to hear something soon; hopefully he's alright,' Benjamin said and set his mouth into a line, not quite managing a smile.

The two officers said goodbye and left the building.

Sgt Love looked over to her colleague, 'What did you think, Emma?'

'Strange set up, like the Banana Bunch or whatever it was called.'

'I think you mean the Brady Bunch. Anyway, I meant do you think there was something shady there?'

'Don't think so, how about you?'

'Not sure. I really don't know. The girls' body language was a bit strange, but maybe they aren't used to talking to the police...'

'We were right about that James Dean bloke, though, remember him?'

Sgt Love sighed, 'How could I forget that man? One day we'll get him behind bars. Something here...ugh, there's nothing to put a search warrant in our hands. All we can do is hope for a break somehow. I'll update the file when we get back to the station.'

Chapter Fourteen

A month passed.

Benjamin's phone rang as he sat to tattoo a client. He glanced at the screen. *Shit, better answer it.*

'Holly. How are you?'

'Been better. Has Aled been in touch?'

'No. You?'

'No. The police came around again and said there's nothing more they can do. There was no evidence from the remains of his car or anything,' she sighed deeply. 'Looks like Aled wanted to leave. I'm sorry, you'd best get a new butcher.'

She started to cry, 'I'm sorry, Benjamin, I am heartbroken.'

'It isn't your fault, Holly. All the best for the future, yeah? Try and move on when you can and put the past behind you.'

Holly sobbed and cut the connection.

'Sorry about that,' Benjamin said to his client and turned off his phone. He shook his head as if to try and dislodge something. 'Now, where were we?'

****

The rest of the day passed in a blur, and Benjamin threw all his energy into creating the best tattoo that he could for his client.

After the end of the work day, Benjamin took a long walk around the country lanes for well over an hour before returning to the living quarters. He sighed as he put his hand on the door handle to enter his property.

Zack and all three sisters were sat watching the television.

Tilly looked round and asked, 'Are you alright, Benji? You look like you've seen a ghost.'

Benjamin switched on the kettle.

'Yes. No. I don't know…Aled's wife has been on the phone. The cops have closed the case. I guess that means we are in the clear. This feels wrong. Maybe we should confess. What am I talking about?'

Tilly walked over to the kitchen and put a hand on his arm, 'It's alright, Benjamin, you're in some kind of shock, I think. It's all too real now, and Aled is gone. Sit down and I'll make you a drink.'

Benjamin sat in his favourite chair, not really feeling present, at all; so much so that he jumped when Tilly put his drink next to him.

She peered at him, 'I know what will cheer you up.'

'What?' Benjamin said, eager to be distracted from his down mood.

'Aled has been sold. All the human leather is gone.'

'Gone? Already?' Benjamin asked with wide eyes.

'Yup…now we have a waiting list for more stuff. It is amazing, it really is. How's Lisa getting on with her job? We really could do with more skin you know.'

Benjamin felt energised, he felt the weight of Aled's demise lift from his shoulders and turn into excitement. He answered, 'She sent me a WhatsApp yesterday actually. She's doing really great there. She actually said that she feels more like a partner in the business now than just an employee. I'll ask her to bring a corpse round this week,' Benjamin's eyes shone as he said those words to Tilly. He sipped some more of his drink and added, 'I will look harder for new employees now. Promise.'

Benjamin pulled his phone from his pocket and sent a text message to Lisa.

Lisa, are you alright? We need a body from you. This week. Love you! Xxx

Less than a minute later, his phone beeped with a reply.

Jo is going out to her friend's 50th party on Friday night. I'll be round about 9pm x

'Guess what, Tilly?' Benjamin said to his employee, beaming. 'Lisa is gonna bring us a new body on Friday.'

Tilly smiled with satisfaction, 'Good. I hope she brings us one next week too. It's amazing how many people want a human leather product. Purses are the best seller at the minute; I can't make enough. I'm hoping that she brings someone with some tattoos or something so I can make some unique stuff. We'll get plenty of cash for that.'

Benjamin nodded along; the whole leather manufacturing was beyond him. The sight of the various vats in the unit gave him the creeps, and knowing that human skin passed through them fired off his vivid imagination. He'd had a dream a few nights ago that someone's skin had crawled out of one of the vats and smothered him to death. *I ain't going to tell Tilly about that, she'd take the piss relentlessly.*

Chesca called Benjamin's name and waved at him to get his attention. She offered, 'Benjamin, can I make a suggestion?'

He made a show of rolling his eyes while the other sisters laughed at Chesca.

'I think you should get a couple of big fridges, you know, to store the corpses.'

Benjamin looked puzzled, but Chesca continued, 'If we *accidently* cause other deaths or something, we can store the body until it's needed for flaying. Or we can store spare limbs if the pigs don't need feeding and then give them the body part another day to eat. We don't want to keep them out of a fridge 'cause of the flies and shit.'

'Good idea,' Benjamin agreed. 'I'll leave it up to you to order them; there's more than enough cash in the piggery accounts to buy them.'

Tilly grinned at Chesca then planted a kiss on his cheek. 'Thanks, boss, you're the best.' She gave Benjamin her best smile, showing off her straight white teeth. *That girl is getting under my skin. No way I want to get into a relationship though.*

****

More months passed by and business was brisk. To Benjamin's amazement, the human leather trade was exceptional in its profitability. Purses, in particular, and belts featuring tattoos and birthmarks sold very well.

The piggery now boasted a diverse range of different breeds, and Benjamin had to rent more land from Mr Wright, the farmer, to accommodate the animals.

In addition, quite a few more people had opted to fly with Benjamin to disperse ashes, so he was finding his bank account becoming rather fat.

****

Zack was just having a single day's rest from work each week to try and stay on track. One day when he was extra tired after work, he said to Benjamin, 'Mate, I can't keep up. My quality is starting to suffer from fatigue. From next week, I'm going to have to have two days a week off or I'm going to have to leave.' He looked at Benjamin with as much defiance in his expression as he could muster.

Benjamin looked back with concern, 'I wish you'd have told me before. But of course! I love us doing as many tattoos as possible, but the family's health matters more.'

'Family?' said Zack, doing a double take.

With a broad grin, Benjamin said, 'Yes, that is how I feel about you all. More like family than employees.'

Zack pursed his lips, 'In that case, you should be paying us all more. Anyway, I've seen how you look at Tilly; wouldn't that be incest if you got with her?'

'Piss off!' Benjamin laughed and threw a cushion at Zack's head. With a serious tone, he added, 'I really will need to find more people to work and live here. Do you know anyone else? Oh, and no more weird sisters either.'

Zack thought for a moment and said, 'Sorry, boss...um, Dad... no. No one.'

Chapter Fifteen

PC Emma Hooker-Wolfe pulled into a parking space in the car park at Newdon Police Station.

She sat for a moment, just to have a brief respite before whatever job was coming her way next arrived. A look out of the windscreen at the pouring rain didn't fill her heart with joy. She sighed and pulled the zip on her fleece jacket right to the top.

Stepping out of the patrol car, she dashed across to the main building. A swipe of her warrant card across the card reader by the door made the lock release, and she hurried inside out of the rain.

Apart from Sgt Laura Love, the office was deserted. There were just three more officers on duty, and they were all out of the building.

Emma grabbed a plastic cup from a tube attached to the water cooler and gulped two full cups.

'Don't make yourself comfy,' the sergeant said. 'There's a truck at the industrial park, and when they opened the trailer up, they found some people inside. We need to go now and see what's happening.'

Emma groaned, 'Has the control room sent an ambulance too?'

'Yes. Let's go.'

Chapter Sixteen

Aleksandr and Dmitri Sokolov were Russian brothers, at the end of their long journey across Europe.

Both had their hair cropped closely to their large block shaped heads. Dmitri was more unfortunate than Aleksandr in the looks department. His face was ravaged by acne, which had left at least two dozen pockmarks, maybe more. They both had piercing blue eyes and big noses. The brothers were unmistakable as twins, standing tall at six foot two.

They looked at each other as the trailer moved again, slowly, in reverse.

The family they had found themselves with had huddled together, the mother with plain fear in her eyes. The father tried to look determined, but fear gave itself away in his eyes too. Their two children sat on top of a stack of tomatoes, mostly unaware of the implications of what was happening. Their faces were streaked with dirt, the wear of their journey showing as fatigue.

Aleksandr and Dmitri didn't understand what the family were saying to each other; they spoke a foreign tongue and looked at the twins with apprehension throughout the journey. The trailer they'd found themselves in was noisy; a fridge unit sat on the bulkhead, running and filling the space with cold air. The fan whirred round constantly. A tiny digital readout by the back doors read '5°c'.

Suddenly, the trailer stopped and the small kids almost toppled off their perches. A second later, the loud hiss of air brakes reached the refugees.

The twins prepared themselves when they heard the long bolts being moved. Light blinded them as the barn doors swung open; a large man wearing a high-vis jacket and a grubby baseball cap peered in from outside. He yelled out, 'Security! There are people in here!'

Dmitri jumped down first, Aleksandr followed him like a shadow. The man, who had to be the truck's driver, stepped back to give them space. He asked, 'Are you guys okay? It's cold in there.'

Dmitri just nodded at the man while looking for the way out of the yard. He spotted the gatehouse, a single-story glorified brick shed, about fifty metres away. Pointing at the gate to freedom, he and Aleksandr soon found themselves jogging. As two men marched out of the gatehouse, the taller one shouted, 'Oi! Stop here till the police come!'

The twins increased their pace and ran out of the yard to freedom. They didn't know where to go, so they just picked a direction and kept walking along the roadside through uncut long grass, brambles and nettles. A police car sped past them, heading towards the warehouse they had just left. Thankfully for the twins, it paid them no attention.

****

They had been released from a prison camp six months earlier and smuggled themselves into the UK. Their journey had been terrible and arduous, and they had to rely on their wits and guile to make the journey across the continent. Awful weather tried to put a dampener on their spirits with sleet, hail and bone-chilling winds throughout the trek. Several weeks had elapsed from leaving to reaching their destination. The final part of the journey from Calais was in the back of an articulated truck, in a trailer destined for the warehouse of a national supermarket. A fixer in the port town had arranged for a truck to slow down just enough for them to jump into the trailer from the dark roadside.

The expensive load was rejected because of human contamination; not that this minor detail mattered to the refugees.

The family, from who knows where, stayed in the yard to be looked after and taken to the hospital for a much-needed check over.

****

They eventually found other illegal immigrants at a roadside car wash in Kettown, Newdon's nearest neighbouring town.

Hand car-washes had popped up all over the country, usually manned by hard working Eastern Europeans. Some were known as centres for petty, and not so petty crime. Drug dealing, thefts from vehicles and money laundering all took place at many of these establishments, but still they were popular with people looking to get their car washed by someone else. The one that Benjamin liked to use had been raided by the immigration service the previous week, and most of the workers had been detained by the authorities.

Benjamin had bought an eight-year-old Porsche from a dealership a couple of weeks before this eventful day and had decided to take a break from the tattoo studio for the afternoon. *I'm the boss after all.*

He spotted the car wash and, on a whim, decided to have his new car cleaned.

Both Dmitri and Aleksandr sported intricate prison tattoos on their hands and necks. It was a freezing day; the winter had been long and cold with record snowfalls over several days. Hot and soapy buckets of water scalded their numb hands as they worked; like it had done every day since they started there.

Benjamin had dressed for the weather—comfy woollen tracksuit trousers and a thick bubble jacket topped off with a hat with a ridiculous bobble and gloves.

Steam billowed from the buckets and the squeegees dribbled streams of soapy water onto the wet concrete. A fat man wearing a woolly hat and gloves sat on a plastic chair that buckled under his weight. He didn't seem to do much beyond yell at the workers and peer at his smartphone while chain-smoking cigarettes. Benjamin nodded to him. *Keep the boss sweet.*

Benjamin tried to strike up a conversation with the twins. 'Nice tattoos, lads. Did you do them yourselves?' he asked, smiling widely as he peered at the ink work.

'Yes. Why?'

'Where are you lads from?'

'Russia.'

'Did you do those tattoos in prison?'

'Yes. Why?'

'They are fantastic, despite the obvious use of, um, basic tools,' he leaned closer, out of earshot of the boss. 'Come and work for me at my studio, Dr Tattoo. I'll give you a good wage and somewhere to live. I'll come and collect you later, at six, if you're interested? Show you the set up.'

Benjamin wasn't used to people saying 'no' to him; it simply never happened.

'Okay. Bye.'

They aren't too talkative...perfect.

****

Benjamin drove across the yard with care. *Don't want stone chips.* He popped into the Dr Tattoo studio just as Zack was about to finish working on a huge back piece, which was almost complete after several sessions.

Benjamin called to him across the studio, 'Zack, I'm bringing two guys in later for an interview.'

Zack's face lit up, 'Great, hope they are good!'

'I have an inkling they are shit hot. Anyway, catch you later."

Benjamin jogged across to the piggery and then the leather shop to inform the sisters. They were as pleased as Zack.

It had already been dark for over an hour when he collected the twins at six o'clock. They were stood waiting by the side of the road. The atmosphere in the car was thick, matching the odour of hard work, cheap deodorant and roll up cigarettes. Benjamin could tell they were hardened men, and he wondered what had happened to them in Russia to lead them to a grubby car wash in Kettown.

It didn't take long to travel to the farmyard, just twenty-five minutes, but it seemed like a million miles away from the drudgery of the car wash and even further away from their old life in Russia.

They had been sharing a semi-detached house in Kettown with seven other people; their shared bedroom had once been the living room. The bathroom was best described as grotty, with a never-cleaned toilet and mould all around the windows and grout. The food in the kitchen was all tins, nothing fresh, and the bin overflowed onto the dirty floor.

As the trio entered the Dr Tattoo studio, Benjamin gestured at a seating area and told the men to take a seat until the last client left.

'Coffee?' he asked, and retrieved a handful of mugs from a cupboard under an expensive looking machine. Without asking what everyone wanted, Benjamin jabbed the button marked 'Cappuccino' and filled each mug before handing them out with a small biscuit in a red wrapper.

The Russians sat on the bright green trendy sofa with stainless steel legs, and watched Zack finishing a tattoo with watchful gazes, grateful for the free hot drink.

When he'd added the final touch, Zack instructed the client to admire the new tattoo in a large mirror hanging on a far wall. She looked at the intricate mandala that had just been applied to her shoulder blade region. The expression of pure delight plastered on her face gave away her true feelings. She looked at the twins and said, 'You've come to the right place to get a tattoo. This is just awesome!'

They nodded politely at the woman and smiled their approval.

When the client had paid and practically skipped out of the door, Benjamin turned to the Russians and spoke, 'Alright, you are probably wondering why I have brought you all the way out here. I'm Benjamin McGuiness. I own this tattoo studio, and this is Zack. He is the manager here, and an award-winning tattooist. He's been in all the trade magazines.'

The assistant smiled, albeit seemingly nervously. Benjamin picked up a fresh tattoo gun, waving his arms around to take in the airy space.

'This is the *best* tattoo parlour in the country, but Zack and me can't keep up with the work. We could fill our diaries three times over. You know how to use this?' he asked, holding the tattooing instrument out towards the twins. It was plain that he was inviting the Russians to make a tattoo to show off their skills.

'Yes, I'll make something on Dmitri,' Aleksandr didn't wait for an answer from his brother. Instead, he moved swiftly to sit in the artist's chair and motioned with a huge scarred hand for Dmitri to sit by the table. He took the tattoo gun from Benjamin with a surprisingly light touch. Without discussing what design his brother may like, Aleksandr commenced work. He looked closely for a patch of suitable skin, shaved away the mass of dense black hair and wiped it to make sure it was clean.

The needle buzzed as it unloaded ink into the man's skin. Aleksandr's intense blue eyes never left his twin's shoulder the whole time he was working. A few minutes after starting, he noted, 'This machine is superb. I think top of range.'

'Of course, only the best will do at Dr Tattoo,' Benjamin boasted.

Dmitri never flinched or pulled away as the needles filled his skin with fresh ink. It must have felt like his skin was being invaded by a hot electric hob, but he either didn't seem to care or he was used to pain.

Zack and Benjamin watched patiently while Aleksandr completed his art. After all, quality takes time. It took about two hours to complete. The finished piece was a Russian doll with a skull instead of a girl's face. A large black heart sat in the centre of the design.

'What do you think, Benjamin?' Aleksandr asked with pride, a wide smile dancing on his lips.

'Fucking hell! I love it. You have a job here if you want it. And free accommodation too. Shit, man, you did it freehand,' gushed Benjamin, genuinely impressed. *This man is going to make me a fortune.* 'The quicker you can start, the better, to be honest with you.'

Aleksandr looked again at the design with pride and smiled before turning back to Benjamin and stating, 'Dmitri does not tattoo. He is not good with people. If I stay here, then so does he. Deal?'

Aleksandr found a roll of cling film and snapped off a length before applying it over the art he'd drawn on his brother.

Benjamin nodded with enthusiasm, 'I'm sure I can find something for him here; he looks tough enough to handle anything.'

'He is. Since we were in prison, Dmitri cannot talk, except to me. I talk for him. The prison was terrible place, too much violence and torture.'

'Okay, can I call you Aleks? I would like him to work in the leather shop and piggery. No need to communicate after he has learned the job if he doesn't want to. It is a bit monotonous, but the work is never-ending.'

'Aleks is fine. Can we see quarters, then decide?'

'Follow me,' said Benjamin, who stood and took the lead.

The band of men walked across the dusty yard to the final unit, their footwear crunching on the rough gravel. To the left of the unit was a barbed wire fence. Beyond the fence sat a wheat field that stretched across the horizon to the boundary of the next field. Traditional hedgerow marked that field's limit, thick with prickly branches and providing a haven for small creatures. It wasn't uncommon to see creatures like foxes and mice darting around the yard, typically after dark. Benjamin thought about getting a couple of farm cats to keep the rodent population down, but he hadn't got around to it yet.

CCTV cameras sat in metal cages attached to each of the buildings, pretending to keep constant watch, but they were all fake.

The units themselves had been built in the style of railway arches—large and imposing. Stark red brickwork framed huge weathered timber gates. Only the tattoo parlour had a friendly facade with floor-to-ceiling glass windows and exposed metal framework. Inside the brickwork, large banners sported Dr Tattoo's artwork on a variety of body parts. Amongst the everyday people were celebrities, sports people in particular, including several international footballers. Their toothpaste-advert white smiles beamed down on the staff and clients.

Inside the housing unit was an extra large bright and airy sitting room. To the Russians' surprise, the side of the unit had a substantial triple-glazed window that stretched to at least twenty-feet long. The space was warm and inviting. Several sofas and a sixty-inch television made it a far cry from their dismal expectations. At the far end of the window was a kitchen, complete with a substantial cooking island, expensive looking kitchen units and various pans hanging from hooks. The room was painted in relaxing pastel colours. An air conditioning unit kept the space at a perfect temperature, even in the height of summer.

'Nice. Can we check the sleeping area and bathroom now?'

'Sure, this way.'

Benjamin and Zack led the way to the rear of the unit. Separated from the rest of the unit by plasterboard walls, were three bedrooms. One was locked, a blue wooden sign on the door said 'Benjamin McGuinness' Quarters', with a ship's anchor and rope motif on it.

The other door was propped open with a wooden stop wedged under it.

Inside were four sets of Ikea bunk beds. Only one bed had bed clothes on, the rest were waiting to be neatly made and readied for their resident.

Zack pointed at the one made-up bed and said in a determined voice, belying his timid disposition, 'That's mine…I ain't moving, lads.'

Aleks smiled. Without even looking at his brother, never mind conferring, he decided, 'Yes, this is good. Me and Dmitri accept.'

'Great. I'll take you to your old flat later to collect your belongings,' said Benjamin with a satisfied smile.

The twins nodded in agreement. Their aura was that of relief and satisfaction.

'There's another bedroom for the women, which is the same as this one. I daren't show you in there; the girls are protective of their privacy. Want to see the bathroom?' He didn't wait for an answer and led the way.

The bathroom was more modest, with a standalone roll top bathtub and a toilet. A hand sink finished off the facilities, apart from a set of shelves that carried rows of beauty products and a stack of fluffy towels.

'No shower? I don't like the bath,' Aleksandr cringed.

Benjamin gestured to another door, 'Yes, there's a shower between the bedrooms.'

That door was painted in black and wasn't noticeable at first glance. Aleksandr looked inside the room and was very pleased to see a double sized shower with a huge showerhead and trendy tiling. Another stack of towels to match the pile in the bathroom rested on a shelf, with a number folded over a heated towel rail.

Aleksandr inhaled a lungful of air, 'Where are the women you talk about? It smells like lots of perfume in here.'

Benjamin laughed and his eyes sparkled, 'You know how girls like their pampering, right? They've gone to the nail bar in town; they go like clockwork every other week. Anyway, they work in the organic farm, and the leather shop is the kingdom of one of them. They love looking after the pigs and doing the paperwork.'

'How about the leather shop? What do you make there?'

'Ah, that's where I want Dmitri to work, well, there and if the other girls need a hand, he could help in the piggery. We take animals and make them into leather. Cow leather, but also kangaroo and stingray. And another very...um...special product.'

Aleks spoke to Dmitri in Russian. Neither Benjamin nor Zack understood a word so instead relied on the twins' body language to tell if they were pleased. Not that their awkward stances gave much away.

Dmitri nodded a lot, seemingly in a happy way, which was in stark contrast to his previously intimidating rock-hard stares.

'The ashes shop, what is this about?'

'I work in there myself. People come to me after someone has died, and I scatter their loved one's ashes. Often, it's because they can't face it, or sometimes I can do things that they can't do themselves, such as scatter them out of an aircraft.'

'Is that allowed?' Aleksandr asked, his voice rising half an octave, his eyebrows shooting up and giving away his surprise.

'No one has told me it's not,' Benjamin replied, laughing. The concept of being told not to do something amused him.

Benjamin put a hand on Zack's elbow and said, 'Zack is my second in command, and he is your manager. Any problems, talk to him first, okay?'

Dmitri and Aleks nodded. *So, he understands English.*

'Right, lads, let's go and feed the pigs.'

Benjamin grinned before turning on his heels and striding towards the apartment's exit door, not waiting for the other men to follow him.

Headlights swung with some speed into the courtyard. An MPV crunched across the gravel before pulling up outside the piggery with a slight skid.

'Be glad it's not been too dry, the rain has kept the dust on the ground. In the summer, you have to watch out for clouds of it when vehicles drive into the yard. If it gets into your eyes, it really stings,' said Benjamin, as if telling a state secret.

The twins nodded, keeping their gaze fixed on the floor to avoid being dazzled by the headlight glare.

The headlights faded once the driver turned off the ignition. Three doors opened and the women got out, leaving the engine to tick and ping as it cooled down.

'Hello, Benjamin, Zack. Who are these two hunky men?' one of the women asked while looking the men up and down lecherously.

'Helena, meet Dmitri and Aleks. They have come to live with us. Lads, meet Helena and her sisters.'

Aleks did a double take, 'Are you twins and a sister?'

'We are triplets. Me and Tilly are identical. Chesca is the outsider.'

Tilly and Helena tittered together and Chesca shook her head, 'Them two are stupid...I'm the superior triplet. Obviously.'

Chesca looked at Benjamin and tilted her head to one side, her dark shoulder length hair lightly ruffled by the breeze that had started to pick up. She said in a light voice, 'Do they know what we do here?'

Benjamin sighed, 'Not yet. Me and Zack are about to show them the piggery. Want to join us on the tour?'

Chesca and her sisters nodded and let Benjamin take the lead.

The assembled crew followed him towards the piggery. The Russians followed Zak, and the girls brought up the rear.

Benjamin breathed warmth onto his right index finger and pressed the digit onto a fingerprint scanner. A pair of beeps and a click followed. The heavy personnel door, which sat in the frame within a much larger cargo door, swung open with ease.

Inside, to Aleks' surprise, there was no front counter. Benjamin saw his puzzlement and explained, 'Online only. We don't want outsiders shuffling around.'

'Why? What is there to hide? Can I see pigs?'

'This way,' Benjamin instructed before taking off with long strides.

The rearmost part of the unit had several pungent pig pens with mountains of hay lying scattered around. Three sows lay on their sides, each with four or five piglets greedily suckling from their mother. The walls had been painted with thick whitewash that had plainly been applied a few years previously. It was faded and large chunks peeled off.

The girls cooed at the pigs.

'So cute!' exclaimed Chesca.

'Be cuter in a breakfast!' Aleks grinned.

'Aleks!' Chesca punched him playfully in the chest. 'You can oversee slaughter, mate. Us girls are too girly to keep having to kill piggies.' She and the other sisters shared amused glances.

Benjamin coughed, 'Excuse me. So, it looks like Dmitri is the hands of death now...'

The Russians laughed and Chesca blushed. 'My girls will still be in charge of the website though.'

'Babe, I doubt that the average customer can read Cyrillic,' said Benjamin with mock scorn.

As they backtracked through the unit, Aleks noted the five huge stainless-steel fridge-freezer units humming away, 'That's a lot of storage. Surely you don't use them all?'

'Ah, we keep a back stock of meat. We can't disappoint the customers now, can we?'

'Is the butchery done here? Who does it?'

'Yes. Now it is Dmitri, and you and Zack can help too. The last permanent butcher, well, he wanted to leave.'

The girls and Zak all chuckled like school kids. Helena rearranged her hair into a scrunchie, 'That didn't go down too well, did it, Benny?'

'Don't call me Benny or you'll get the same redundancy package!'

He laughed, and Helena rolled her eyes at him, 'Yeah, yeah, of course!'

Dmitri and Aleks exchanged puzzled glances; they were yet to understand what the inside joke was about.

Benjamin walked between two of the humming freezers, 'This way, lads.'

He pushed open a knackered looking door with the door frames showing a lot of scrapes and gouges as if knocked by trolleys. Inside was a large steel table with drainage holes in each corner. On racks attached to the wall sat a selection of shelving, and several saws hung next to cleavers, sharp knives and scissors.

The floor was bare concrete, with a trough around its perimeter and a further large drain hole in one corner. A hosepipe and tap were the final items. The smell was peculiar—cleaning chemicals mixed with the metallic tang of blood.

Zack stepped in front of Benjamin and leant over to the drain hole in the floor. He retrieved a small piece of meat, 'Might as well chuck this to the pigs.'

Aleks saw what Zack was holding.

'Is that what I think it is?'

'If you think it is a little finger, then yes, it is,' Zack laughed.

The digit had a bruised black nail with tendrils of connective tissue dangling from it.

Dmitri laughed, which was the first sound that anyone but Aleks had heard him make. The sound of his laugh made everyone except for Aleks feel uncomfortable; it was the sound of a disturbed individual, which made the hairs on the back of Benjamin's neck stand on end.

'Is Dmitri alright with cutting people up?' Benjamin asked, matter of factly.

Aleks smiled, 'Yes, he has previous experience, in Russia. He had to kill, or be killed. This is like, how you say...Busman's holiday.'

'How about the pigs? People buy cuts of pork online, sometimes they get pork, sometimes a substitute if we are running low on stock.'

Dmitri and Aleks cackled a dark laugh in unison, 'Meat is meat, what happened to the rest of the body?'

'His body is with the pigs; his skin is over in the skunkworks. That's where we'll go next. Tilly is in charge there.'

The twins were stunned. Tilly was barely five feet tall and had a petite build. Her makeup was immaculate, as was her hair. She couldn't have looked less like a manual worker if she had tried. She led the way to the leather shop and opened the door by using another fingerprint pad. Inside the workshop was a small office.

Smiling her gap-toothed smile, she nodded at the luxurious office chairs and desk.

'Here is where our clients look at the leather samples. We use cow skins, pig skins and human skins. Only a tiny number know about the human leather of course, at least for now until we publicise it more. Our current customers have to find us via a Google search.' She looked at the twins and waited a moment to see if there would be a reaction.

The twins' faces remained blank, giving nothing away.

Tilly continued talking, 'What things do we make here? The usual belts and wallets, and other items by request, which people can do on the website. Last month, I made leather to send to someone who makes saddles for custom motorbikes. Let's see the workshop itself.'

Aleks looked into the office and noted the photographs on the wall. The celebrities that featured in the Dr Tattoo studio were here too. The difference: accessories were the focus, not the tattoos.

The group went through another fingerprint-protected door.

'Fuck! Motherfuckers!'

Everyone looked at Dmitri. Aleks was open-mouthed and said, 'Dmitri! You have your voice back...amazing!'

Aleks followed Dmitri's gaze and his jaw flopped open. Against the far wall, several hides were stretched out on racks to cure.

Two were cowhides. The other three skins—human.

Hooks pierced the skins and held them in place; the exposed membranes left nothing to the imagination.

'I am always amazed by how far the human skin can stretch. It's the largest organ of the human body,' Benjamin mused.

A large bucket contained a fourth skin soaking in a chemical solution.

Unlike in the piggery, there was no metallic stench of blood and death.

Aleks nodded to the bucket, 'Unhappy customer?'

'He couldn't leave,' Tilly grinned the gap-toothed smile again.

Helena and Chesca giggled in unison, proving their undoubtedly close bond as sisters. It made the hairs on the back of the twins' necks stand proud, the sound akin to nails being dragged down a blackboard rather than the sound of hilarity.

'Who are the others?' Aleks asked as he and Dmitry stared at the skins. They noted that the first one was covered in stretch marks and scars, with the kind of deep tan that only spending many years outside in all weathers brings. Almost a mahogany.

Benjamin looked respectful and held a hand over his heart, 'That is Mrs Stein. She was my biology teacher at school. Bitch will be a millionaire's cushion. If it was up to me, I'd use her as bog roll.'

Tilly made a mocking face and puppy eyes, 'Poor old Benji got a D.'

'Fuck off, Tilly.'

Dmitry and Aleks looked at each other, confusion once again etched on their faces, 'What's a D?'

'Ignore Tilly, she thinks she is being funny. I didn't pass my exam for biology at school. That's a while ago now though.'

Benjamin turned his attention back to the skins, 'You see the other two have tattoos on them?'

The twins looked at the artwork, and there was no doubt that it belonged to the Dr Tattoo studio; the quality of work was exemplary.

'Bastards thought they could have tattoos and not pay. The one next to Mrs Stein, she said that it's not like we could repossess the goods. I would've let her off, but she signed her own death warrant by saying that.'

'The other one?'

'That, God rest his soul, is a donated skin. When he died, his family respected his wishes for his skin to be turned into leather products...they got paid a lump sum to keep them quiet though. It isn't something that needs to be general knowledge.'

'What happened to the rest of his body?' asked Aleksandr, fascinated by the grizzly sight in front of him.

'The undertaker brought him here, we skinned him, and they collected him in a coffin for a regular burial.'

'This is fucked up.'

'Yes, Aleks, it is. But you and your brother are part of the team now,' Benjamin looked at the skin in the bucket and shrugged. 'Whether you like it or not.'

Aleksandr frowned. *Was that some kind of threat?*

'What about the ashes workshop? Can we see there too?'

'All will be revealed in time. There's nothing to see in there except a computer desk and a storage cupboard. Let's eat, you guys must be starving.'

'Yes, but no pork for me.'

Benjamin slapped Aleks on the back. 'You are hilarious. I didn't know that Russians had a sense of humour. I'm guessing there will be a pie of some description on the menu. Anyway, that was a joke about sending human meat out. That would be too sick.'

****

As the smell of Zack's shepherd's pie wafted around the building and set stomachs off rumbling, the colleagues all sat round a large table ready to tuck in.

They had been eating for about five minutes before vehicle wheels crunched over the yard and headlights swept across the window, catching Benjamin's attention.

'It looks like the undertaker has arrived, Zack.'

Zack nodded and pushed his chair away from the table. Benjamin follow suit. The Russian twins also stood, and all the men put on their coats and shoes.

The men walked across the darkened yard to what turned out to be a black undertaker's van. Zack unlocked the door to the piggery and opened the hefty vehicle access doors. A slim woman climbed out of the driver's seat. She hugged Benjamin and gave him a kiss on the cheek.

She looked at Dmitri and Aleks, 'Who are these men? Your new workers?'

'Boys, meet Lisa, my sister.'

The Russians looked at Lisa; there was no denying that she was Benjamin's sister. They had similar facial features, even similar noses. She was a foot shorter than him but they were both dressed to impress.

Lisa wore a black suit, complete with a waistcoat and watch chain. A delicate fragrance drifted from her, an expensive perfume.

'Who have you brought for me today, sis?'

'Mrs McCafferty. She has the skin tone that you asked for. Mature and weather worn, and that's being kind. Your client will be thrilled. I'm sure that you can make a belt and a matching purse from her, you will have plenty left over.'

'About time, sis, Mrs Jones is annoying. She rings every day asking if we have found a suitable skin donor.'

Lisa smiled sweetly and put her fingers on the handle to the tailgate, underneath the bottom of the window sticker that said 'private ambulance' in fluorescent yellow writing. All the windows were blacked out. She pulled on the handle and the tailgate hissed open on hydraulic rods.

When a strip of soft LED lights illuminated the interior of the van, a huge body on a gurney in a pink body bag came into view.

Lisa gripped the end of the trolley and pulled it out of the van, the extendable legs dropping to the ground with a clatter.

Benjamin whistled. 'Wow, I see what you mean. We will probably get two or three purses and matching belts from her body,' he glanced at the assembled men. 'Let's get her flayed and back to the chapel of rest before somebody realises her body has gone. She'll be ready for her cremation and for her family to say their last goodbyes.'

'Lisa, you work in chapel of rest? How perfect for you, Benjamin.'

'Yes, Aleks. Perfect, like you say, but her employment is by design not by accident. We've been planning this for a long time. It took patience to get Lisa a job in the undertakers; a few months in the end.'

After Zack and Dmitry had pushed the trolley into the piggery, Benjamin closed the huge doors behind them to keep the cold outside.

Benjamin turned to one twin and said, 'Okay, Aleks, let's see your skills with a knife. I want you to score all around the body with a scalpel, and then me and Zack will show you how to remove the skin. There shouldn't be too much blood; she has been dead for over twelve hours. Remember to put on a pair of disposable gloves.' He nodded to a trolley with a box of latex gloves sitting atop it.

Benjamin grabbed a yellow rubber handset, which was attached to a robotic looking machine by a thick black cable. He pulled out the red emergency stop button with a click to reset the machine and then pressed a button, standing back slightly as a metal arm swung out from the top of the machine. Attached to the arm was another arm, rocking from side to side with its own weight. At either end of the arm was a bracket with two metal carabiners at each corner. The Russians looked on with fascination as the arm kept swinging until it was over the body bag laying on the trolley.

Benjamin pressed another button, and the arm with the carabiners lowered towards the mountainous body hidden inside the fabulous pink bag. When the arm was a couple of centimetres from the bag, Benjamin stopped it.

Zack stepped forward and attached the carabiners to the small metal eyelets at each corner of the body bag. He stepped back and nodded to Benjamin.

'It's a crane!' Aleks exclaimed.

Benjamin nodded. With a deft jab of a button, the crane whirred, and the arm raised until the cords had taken up the slack. Groaning with the strain, the crane lifted Mrs McCafferty clear of the gurney. It swung round, following Benjamin's inputs on the controller, before he lowered her down to the table. Zack stepped forward, unclipped the carabiners and pushed the crane arm back to its stowed position.

He unzipped the bag and then, with help from Benjamin and Lisa, tugged it from under the cadaver. Mrs McCafferty lay naked on the table ready to have her skin removed. She smelt strongly of decades of smoking like a chimney.

Benjamin removed a scalpel from a drawer set into the wall and handed it to Dmitri.

No words were necessary.

Dmitri moved so he was standing next to the deceased. He hesitated, unsure where to cut.

'I have a marker pen here somewhere. I'll draw where I need you to cut, I've watched Tilly do it before.' Benjamin opened the same drawer that the scalpel had come from and retrieved a fat black permanent marker pen. Dmitri took a step back from the body to allow Benjamin space to work.

As Benjamin's other hand grabbed a large cloth, he pushed the drawer with a swift hip movement and it thudded shut. The others watched as he took the lid off the pen.

'Don't want that bitch watching me work,' Benjamin muttered.

He placed the cloth over her face, hiding her eyes and grotesquely agape mouth. Benjamin scribbled on her shin until the ink came from the nib.

Starting at her collarbone, he applied a firm pressure and drew a freehand line, which looked much like the collar on a tee shirt, down towards her armpit and, as straight as he could manage on the fleshy, bumpy terrain, down to her hip. Turning a right angle, he left a pen trail across the bottom of her stomach over to the opposite hip, then up past her armpit to her shoulder and back across to the collarbone.

He stepped back with a smile on his face and replaced the lid onto the top of the pen.

Dmitri lent over, and a look of relief passed over his solid facial features when he looked at Mrs McCafferty and noted the cloth over her face.

With a deep breath exhaled, he took the scalpel and pushed it onto the tanned skin by her collar bone. The skin resisted, but with increased pressure, the blade pierced her elderly flesh. Dmitri tensed as if expecting the corpse to object or cry out in pain.

He wrinkled his nose and muttered something in his mother tongue.

Benjamin looked at him and raised an eyebrow.

'He says that she stinks,' Aleks explained.

Benjamin's lips curled into a peculiar smile. 'All the dead have their own individual smell. I'd call that pound store toilet water and cigarettes,' he laughed at his own joke, oblivious that no one else laughed along.

Dmitri shook his head a little and resumed the cutting. He followed the black line with precision, even when fat flowed over his wrist. With a flourish, he completed the circuit. Mrs McCafferty looked as though she were wearing an apron made of skin.

Benjamin and Zack nodded their approval as Lisa lifted a spatula from the rack and gave it to her brother. He slid it under the skin and with a side-to-side motion, loosening the skin away from the muscle with a terrible tearing noise.

Zack took hold of the loose bit and lifted until it became taut, affording Benjamin more space to push the spatula around the apron edge. It took about ten minutes to complete the circuit around the flap of loosening skin and muscle.

Lisa took the knife and stood to one side as her brother and Zack tugged the skin away from the body. If any bits remained stuck, Lisa swept the spatula underneath with an expert touch while the men held the rest of the skin up.

Removing the section from the body, the men placed it into a large bucket. All that remained was fat and flesh, congealed and massive.

Zack pulled Mrs McCafferty's right arm as far across her body as he could, and Benjamin did the same with her leg.

'Alright, more hands needed here. Let's roll her onto her front.'

All the men assembled and rolled her over with plenty of grunts, the process made harder by the onset of rigor mortis stiffening the woman's body.

Once on her front, Benjamin nodded at Dmitri, who took the knife from Lisa and repeated what he had done to Mrs McCafferty's front.

Ten minutes later and the huge back skin sat in another bucket next to the front skin.

Benjamin nodded his approval, 'Excellent work. Take her back to the undertakers. Lisa, can I add an arm from the freezer?'

Lisa laughed darkly, 'Sure, why not, it's not like her bulk won't hide it.'

Zack disappeared for a moment and reappeared with a woman's arm.

'It's from the girl who tried to avoid paying,' he explained, with a grin that suggested he was apparently amused by his actions.

Aleks nodded sombrely, respectful even, despite the action being far from respectful.

Between them all, Mrs McCafferty was soon back into her body bag. Benjamin then used the crane to put her back onto the gurney. Without being asked, Dmitri and Aleks pushed the gurney back through the building, over the gravel to Lisa's van and loaded the body back inside. Zack closed the rear door and bowed his head once.

The others laughed at him.

'Show some respect at least,' he said before laughing too.

Lisa climbed into the driver's seat and gave Benjamin a wave before driving away, leaving a slight dust cloud in her wake.

Benjamin signalled for the men to go back to the living quarters.

They walked back in silence, none of them in the mood for small talk.

Chapter Seventeen

The smell of food was tremendous. The triplets had finished making the dinner for them all and Benjamin and the other men sat down to eat. The ladies had already demolished their servings.

'Tell me, Aleks, is there anyone that you would love to see dead?'

Aleks ran his open hand back and forth over his stubble, his mind in overdrive.

'Yes, the guy who runs the car wash. He promised that me and Dmitri would be treated proper and paid cash...that never happened. Mikael always found reason to not pay like fucking car needed filling with petrol, or that car wash not busy enough. That was garbage, there was always a queue. He thought I didn't know, but I saw him selling cocaine to customers. And he made us steal shit out of cars, like gifts for kids. I hate him. So does Dmitri. I tell him to come for free tattoo and we kill him.'

Benjamin grinned with mirth, his eyes lighting up at the idea, 'Tell him you'll do your brand logo tattoo; you know, the doll with the skull face and a black heart. I think that's awesome and would love to use it as a design on the leather. Can I?'

'Yes. Mikael deserves to die, no one will be sad to see end of that bastard,' Aleksandr virtually spat out the man's name; his hatred plain to see.

'Do you know his phone number? Ring him now if you like. Tell him that you have a waiting list but you'll put him to the front of the queue. I think the brand should be called Death Dolls.'

Benjamin's face had hardened. He looked like a man with murder in mind. He passed his iPhone X over to the Russian, and Aleks' fingers flew across the keypad as he dialled his old boss; he didn't need to look up the phone number.

Mikael answered on the third ring, and he spoke with Aleks for about five minutes. Benjamin tried to understand some parts of the words that Aleks spoke but with no success.

Aleks hung up, his mouth set in a line and his expression determined; his eyes had Russian fire in them.

This Mikael character is going to feel pain!

'What did he say, your old gaffer?'

'He comes tomorrow. At two in the afternoon. He's excited.'

****

The next day, Benjamin and Zack telephoned all of their clients that were due to come that afternoon and cancelled them, telling them that there was a sickness and diarrhoea bug in the shop and they wanted no one to contract the illness unnecessarily.

Mikael arrived at one thirty on the dot, keen to get his free tattoo. He parked his ten-year-old black 7 Series BMW as close to the doors as he could, ignoring the sign indicating where visitors should park their cars.

Benjamin glanced at the car, noting the dark tint in every window and the air freshener hanging from the rear-view mirror. He was warmly greeted by the twins when he entered the shop, with much backslapping and pumping handshakes.

Benjamin got the impression that Mikael was trying too hard to be friendly with Aleks and Dmitri. The body language being given off by the twins indicated they were firmly pissed off with the new arrival, but Mikael didn't seem to pick up on it, or if he did, he didn't show it. *He's an arrogant prick; no wonder the lads hate him.*

After a gobful of rapid-fire Russian, Aleks turned to Benjamin and said, 'Mikael loves the death doll. He wants for me and Dmitri to start gang with him, have it as our symbol. That's a huge honour for us to be asked by him.'

Aleks winked at Benjamin who had to look out of the window over the bucolic scenery to avoid smirking too much, or laughing.

After Mikael had sat where Aleks signalled him to and rolled up his sleeve, Aleks nodded and started tattooing his ex-comrade. Benjamin noticed that Aleks was pushing harder than necessary, which amused him, and he couldn't help but chuckle.

'What are you laughing at, man?' said Mikael, with menace in his voice.

'Oh, nothing, mate, just thinking about a guy who came in earlier and asked for a unicorn on his chest.'

Mikael snorted, 'That is fucking funny. Did you do it?'

'Yes, of course. With a rainbow coloured cock!'

'You English are funny. In Russia, he would have got beaten.'

'Live and let live, Mikael, live and let live.'

Benjamin couldn't help but burst into laughter at the irony of telling the condemned man to live. He took a moment to compose himself, then asked, 'Coffee, lads?'

He returned a few minutes later with coffee for all the men and looked with genuine admiration at the tattoo that Aleks had crafted on Mikael's shoulder.

That will look awesome on a handbag.

'I've put two sugars in your drink, Mikael. Keep your energy up, mate.'

'I'm not English pussy. Tattoo does not make me faint.'

Benjamin shrugged. *Maybe, mate. You're brave now, but not for long.*

Aleks finished with a proud smile and pointed at the long mirror, 'Take a look.'

The newly inked man did as directed, and a massive grin broke out on his face, 'Shit, man, I love it. You were wasted at car wash. Can I take you all out for drinks?'

Aleks grinned, 'No, thanks, I'm washing hair tonight.'

Dmitri put his hand behind his back and took out the cleaver tucked into his belt at the small of his back, carefully hidden by his sweater. He held the handle with both hands and lifted the weapon high above his head.

The cleaver started its swing down towards Mikael's crown, Dmitri throwing all his weight behind it at the critical moment. Milliseconds before impact, Mikael saw the approaching threat in the mirror, but fear had him rooted to the spot.

In less time than the blink of an eye, the blade smashed through Mikael's skull and wedged itself in his brain. A sickening crunching noise bounced around the parlour, dampened by a squidgy noise from the brain and other cranial tissue. Mikael's eyes rolled into the back of his head as blood poured out of his skull like a crimson waterfall. The viscous river pumped ferociously at first but then slowed as his heart came to a stop. He collapsed to the floor like a discarded ragdoll.

Benjamin suddenly felt ill and only just made it out of the door into the yard before he vomited.

'What is wrong, Benjamin? Don't you like sight of blood?'

'Fuck off, Aleks. I don't know why I puked, but that was fucking brutal *en excellence*. I loved it. I'll get the mop and bucket to clean up that blood.'

He heard the Russian twins laughing at him. *I don't give a flying fuck…that was fucking awesome. The brand is going to make a killing. Literally. It ain't like we're not used to murder here, but that…*

****

The men took Mikael's body over to the piggery in an old shopping trolley that Benjamin had found one day behind the studio. It wasn't easy going over the gravel, so they took it in turns to push.

'Cremation for this fucker or eaten by the pigs? It's up to you, he's your enemy,' asked Zack.

'Pigs. Harvest skin then cut him into pieces. Feed him to the swine; he'll be many meals for them,' Aleks chose; his lips curling into a nasty sneer.

'No need to cut him up. The pigs don't give a shit,' said Benjamin, his face betraying disgust as he looked at Mikael.

Although it took a while longer than if the triplets had helped, the three men skinned Mikael without too much difficulty.

With his skin heaped inside a large bucket, Aleks laughed, 'Thank God for hose clean flooring. Comrade cunt is better down drain than making miserable Russians. I have one final favour for him.'

Benjamin looked at Aleks quizzically.

'Watch this. You will love it,' said Aleks.

Aleks selected a large pair of scissors and grinned at Benjamin. 'Get out your camera, boss.'

With one gloved hand, he grasped Mikael's penis and snipped it off with the other. Blood ran freely from where the base of the penis had been moments earlier.

Gingerly, he held it by the end and tilted his head towards the door.

'Follow.'

Benjamin and Dmitri followed Aleks through to the pigsties.

'Take photo of me feeding cock to fat pig.'

Aleks looked like he was about to burst with pride as the pig brought her snout towards the penis. Benjamin took a photo when the snout was a few inches away, perfectly framed.

Aleks dropped the penis and the pig ate it in one bite.

'That, Aleks, was fucking gruesome...I love it! What are you going to use the photo for?' asked Benjamin.

'Mikael has reputation as bad motherfucker. Someone no one dare fuck with. When my people see I feed his cock to pig, then me and Dmitri will be kings.'

'Remind me to not piss you off!' Benjamin laughed.

Chapter Eighteen

Benjamin looked at his watch; in five minutes, it would be ten o'clock. Not long until lunch.

He frowned, searching his mind as to where he should be. A Ford Fiesta bumped across the yard and parked outside his Ashes to Ashes Unique Dispersal office. The penny dropped and he quickly walked across to the unit. A middle-aged trim woman got out of the car as he approached.

'Mrs Fletcher, how are you?' Benjamin said, holding out a courteous hand to shake.

'I'm okay, thank you. Gerald would be so excited,' she said, nodding to the wooden box that she held in a firm grip. 'Thank you for giving me this opportunity.'

Benjamin realised that Mrs Fletcher had no intention of shaking his outstretched hand. *She probably hasn't even seen it, poor cow.*

He smiled with his best sympathetic approach, lines creasing at the edges of his eyes. 'Let's jump in my car and go to the airfield. Are you ready, Mrs Fletcher?' Benjamin placed a caring hand on the tip of her elbow.

She smiled up at him, vulnerable at this moment of grief, and nodded with sadness.

Benjamin drove with care. *I can't risk scaring Mrs Fletcher on Gerald's last journey.* He took the bends at about half the speed he would normally.

Ten minutes later, he and Mrs Fletcher arrived at the airfield. He jumped out of the car and lifted the barrier, so he could drive onto the car park.

'How are you feeling, Mrs Fletcher?' he asked quietly.

'Strangely excited,' came the short reply. 'I have never been up in a little plane before. The last time I flew was in one of those new fangled double-decker planes.'

Benjamin gave her a strange half-smile. 'Come this way. I've hired that Cessna today,' he said while pointing to a blue and white aircraft with a propeller sitting on the nose, and the wing sitting high.

He looked into the sky, noting with pleasure the lack of fluffy white clouds. Sunshine was welcome after the last few weeks of seemingly endless rain and gloom. They walked over to the plane, and Benjamin held the door open for Mrs Fletcher to clamber in. Once she had sat, he helped her to secure her seat harness and passed her a set of earphones with a boom microphone. He then got into the pilot's seat and went through the pre-flight check with slick efficiency. Soon, he was ready to get going. The plane jolted as it traversed the grass airfield to the end of the runway. It vibrated as Benjamin asked the engine for enough power to escape the grip of gravity; Mrs Fletcher gasped with delight as the plane gained height.

After he had levelled the plane into a casual cruise, Benjamin looked over to Mrs Fletcher through his Ray-Ban Aviator shades. She was looking out of the window, smiling as she recognised landmarks here and there. With a pointed finger, she exclaimed, 'I can see my house!'

'Cromer?' Benjamin said to the bereaved woman. She looked across to him and gave a determined nod of her head. No more words were needed, and Benjamin concentrated on navigating over to the Norfolk coast and the seaside town. The small plane held a steady course, bobbing around a little as the wind increased and decreased. Thirty minutes later, the coast came into view.

Mrs Fletcher surprised Benjamin by speaking without being spoken to first, 'Thank you, Benjamin; you are so kind. Shall I slide the window open?'

'Yes, Mrs Fletcher, that would be good.'

The woman slid the window open with a bit of difficulty, and noise increased inside the cockpit. They were both thankful for the protection that the earphones afforded.

A moment later, the coastline slipped under the fuselage and the plane was over the sea. Benjamin looked at Mrs Fletcher and gave her a thumbs up. The predetermined signal prodded her into action. As she took hold of the lid and gripped it hard, her knuckles turned white with the effort. With a twist, the lid came off. Mrs Fletcher looked into the box and very quietly said, 'Your dream is coming true. I love you, Gerald Fletcher.'

She held the box up close to the window and tipped it, gingerly at first, and then with determination. Ashes poured out of the box and were whipped away from the aircraft by the rushing air outside. It didn't take long for the entire contents of the box to be sucked out into the slipstream and scattered into the sea. *Thank God none blew back into the cockpit and landed on her face.*

Mrs Fletcher put the box back onto her lap and secured the lid back onto it. A single tear trickled down her face, until she wiped it away with the back of her hand.

'Are you alright?' Benjamin asked, with his best sympathetic smile.

Mrs Fletcher fought back sobs and nodded. She retrieved a small packet of tissues from her handbag, 'Yes, I feel very relieved, thank you. Let's get back home.'

She slipped on a pair of retro sunglasses, which could well have been originals from twenty years ago. Benjamin tipped the plane into a gentle bank until he was pointing back towards the airfield. The rest of the flight passed by with no more chat between the pilot and passenger; the silence was comfortable for them both. *Easy way to get my flight hours up...* The landing was smooth, despite the runway being bumpy grass.

Mrs Fletcher wasn't the only one with plans to scatter loved one's ashes over the sea. In fact, it came as a pleasant surprise to Benjamin when he totted up that he'd made the same flight with thirty other people over the past eighteen months.

After landing, he discreetly paid an airfield groundsman twenty pounds to power-wash the aircraft to make sure that no ashes had clung on. He drove Mrs Fletcher back to her car, and she thanked him with a kiss on the cheek before departing.

Chapter Nineteen

Another month passed, and Lisa was feeling more guilt with each body that she took for flaying. She was sat in the kitchen, drinking coffee and staring into space when Jo came into the room.

'Are you okay, Lisa? You haven't seemed yourself lately,' asked Jo as she made herself a drink.

Lisa sighed and heard herself say, 'I'm fine. Well, there is something wrong, but I can't tell you what.'

'Oh? Whatever could it be? You can tell me anything, you know. I promise I won't be judgemental. Tell me your secret, and I promise I won't tell even the customers in the fridge.'

The internal torment that Lisa had been building up had pressurised itself so high that she felt as though she might burst like a volcano if she didn't say something. *But what should I say? Think, Lisa, think.*

'You might have seen the new trend of buying items made from human leather,' Jo watched her employee and friend with intrigue and waited for her to continue. 'Well, I...shit...I'm sorry, I have to quit.'

Lisa stood and fished her coat from a hook. Jo screwed up her face in confusion. 'What the Dickens are you waffling on about? You ain't quitting, so sit down and tell me—'

Lisa sat and buried her face into her palms, 'I'm so, so sorry, Jo. The leather is coming from here.'

'I don't understand...'

'The cat is out of the bag now, isn't it?" Lisa sighed. "My brother owns the shop that makes the leather, and he pays me to provide a donor. I take the corpse over there, he and his worker skin it, then I bring it back ready for the funeral or cremation.'

She started to cry, the stress and self loathing that had built up over her greed for money breaching the dam of emotion. Jo pulled her chair closer to Lisa and put a comforting arm around her, 'I know.'

Lisa sat bolt upright and looked at her boss with wide bloodshot eyes, 'How? I mean —'

'CCTV attached to motion sensors on the garage doors. I wondered for a few weeks why you were taking the van out from time to time after hours, so I put another hidden camera up to cover the inside of the garage and the other rooms. I saw everything; you taking bodies and bringing them back. I checked one a few weeks ago and saw the skin was missing.'

Lisa was stumped for words, so much so that she looked like she had just put her finger in a plug socket.

'I didn't know what exactly was happening to them,' Jo added. 'But I said nothing because I knew that you'd tell me in good time.'

'Aren't you angry?' Lisa said, mascara painting a map of black lines on her face.

'I wasn't too happy, but I can't lose you as my worker. You are far too good at your job, and the clients' families all love you. I guessed that the dead didn't need their skin anymore...'

Lisa puffed out her cheeks, 'Are you going to sack me or tell the police?'

'What for? You can't have your skin stolen. At least, I don't think you can. It is very immoral, yes, but fucking hell, if it got out then the business would be history.'

Lisa sat back, 'So I've been worrying over nothing.'

'Not exactly, but I'm sure your brother will be willing to pay more for a corpse's skin now that I could inform the authorities...' Jo smirked at Lisa, well aware that they both had each other over a barrel if push came to shove.

Lisa agreed, 'I'll tell him to pay more because you found out.'

Jo patted Lisa on the back, 'Awesome, we'll be quids in. Anyway, how much does he pay?'

'Seven hundred quid each,' Lisa lied. *Trying to blackmail my family, Jo? Might as well profit more myself.*

Jo looked towards where the bodies were kept and lowered her voice as if she were worried that one might reveal their secret. 'We'll be able to send more of them across to be skinned and make even more money. There's always some relative who irritates me. Yes, that would be just desserts,' she grinned. 'Anyway, get the kettle on; I make it coffee o'clock.'

Chapter Twenty

Benjamin's phone buzzed, the tone telling him that an email had come in. He took it out of his pocket and flicked through to his inbox. He broke out into a huge grin, pleased with himself.

'Zack, Aleks, we've just had an order come in for five Death Doll satchels. We have enough leather. Mikael was a fat bastard.'

The two other men laughed, but Dmitri was impassive as usual. *I wonder what it would take to get a reaction from him.*

'We need more bodies to harvest skin from. This trend is going to take off like crazy! One order has even come through from a parliamentary email address. Isn't that amazing? It's clear on the website where the leather comes from and that it's legal, but can you imagine the shit storm if it came out that a front bencher of the governing party had a satchel made from human leather? I can see blackmail in their future, once it's been delivered that is. In the meantime, I must get Lisa to bring another *donor* round later. It's a shame that we've only had white skins so far. I'll have to remember to ask her to bring round some non-whites, and soon.'

Benjamin's phone buzzed again, this time with the jolly ringtone for his Ashes to Ashes business.

'Hello, how can I help?... Pardon? I'm not sure I heard you right...Of course, sir, that wouldn't be a problem. See you in a bit.'

There was silence. Zack looked at Aleks, and they both looked at Benjamin who was staring into space.

'Benjamin, what have you agreed? I've never seen you look shocked before.'

'Huh? I'm not shocked, just trying to think how to do it.'

'Do what? Come on, man, spill the beans,' prompted Zack.

'Fella on the phone, his Great Dane called Kaiser has been cremated.'

'So?'

'He wants me to get his dog's ashes into human food, so he can serve it to his family without them knowing.'

'Easy. Give it to the girls to incorporate into a Bolognese, freeze it, and then he can just reheat and serve with spaghetti and loads of herbs. Sounds tasty to me.'

'Zack, you're not just a pretty face. I love it.'

****

An hour later, a tatty old Ford Mondeo estate rolled into the courtyard and pulled up outside the Ashes to Ashes office. Benjamin opened the office door and welcomed Mr Hickman.

The man smiled sadly and put a casket on the countertop.

'Kaiser, I presume.'

'Yes. Thank you for accepting my request. I couldn't face doing the cooking myself.'

'Do you mind me asking why you want to serve your family your dead dog's ashes?'

'It's fine, I don't mind. They hated Kaiser. They wanted a fucking Chihuahua. I ask you, a Chihuahua? They deserve to eat cremated dog. I will fake a migraine, so I don't have to eat the food. Greedy cunts will gobble it all up.'

'Our on-site chef will be delighted to assist. She is going to make a Bolognese with plenty of 'secret ingredient' spices. Can you come back tomorrow at noon?'

'That's fine. Can she freeze it, please?'

'Of course, Mr Hickey.'

'Hickey? It's Mr Hickman. I hate being called Hickey.'

'Sorry, Mr Hickman. I'll see you tomorrow.'

Benjamin nodded towards the door. Mr Hickman didn't need prompting twice. He left with a festering rage, which Benjamin found highly amusing.

He lifted the casket and held it under his arm before walking with long strides over to the piggery.

'Here you are, ladies, one cremated dog to make into Bolognese. Oh, put in some extra garlic too, it'll help mask whatever ashes taste of.'

Helena sprang over to the kitchen. Tilly was already there making coffee.

'I think that Mr Hickman might be made into leather too. Old chap almost had a cardiac arrest when I called him Mr Hickey. I was only messing about,' Benjamin chuckled.

The two sisters laughed their signature weird staccato noise that made them sound somewhat insane. A shiver ran up Benjamin's spine and the hairs on his arms stood erect.

'Where's Chesca the third evil sister?'

'Evil? How rude! She's in our bedroom...with Dmitri,' said Helena with a dirty smirk.

They cackled even more, and Benjamin felt as though his brain was about to implode, 'Alright, lucky for them!'

He walked backwards at speed, unable to get out of there fast enough.

Chapter Twenty-One

Benjamin decided to go to the tattoo shop to see Aleks and Zack, and whoever was having a tattoo. He was pleased to see both men making intricate body art on clients.

It seemed to be that lions were the choice tattoo of the year; Zack's customer was having a massive one inked on his back. Benjamin gazed at it, intrigued by the photo-like image.

'Hey, Mr Burton, great to see you here again today!' Benjamin cried, genuinely delighted to see an old face.

'Mr McGuinness, what a pleasure to see you too. Zack here was telling me that you have a new brand called Death Dolls or something,'

'Yes, thanks to Aleks. It will be the must-have design before you know it.'

'Really? Wow, Zack, can you put me in your diary for one next month?'

'My diary is chock-a-block for at least three months, mate. If I get a cancellation though, I'll ring you, is that alright?'

Aleks looked up, 'Hey, Burton, doll is my idea. I'm new, so no waiting list. Come in tomorrow okay, and I'll do real original Death Doll on you for seventy-five pounds.'

'Oh, that's amazing! Thank you,' Mr Burton grinned.

A feel-good ambience settled in the studio, all the men happy with what they were doing.

'Ok, fellas, I'll catch you later. Call if you need me,' Benjamin was at a loss as what to do. Dmitri and one of the triplets were 'busy', the terrible two were cooking Dead Dog Bolognese and the other two were tattooing.

He decided to go to the Skunkwork leather workshop to catch up on his paperwork.

That kept his attention for about ten minutes before he was bored and went back to the studio to admire the art that Zack and Aleks were putting on their clients.

Chapter Twenty-Two

Monica Lashley sat in her lounge, browsing on her tablet and looking for a new purse. It had only been a few weeks since her Aunty Zoe had passed away, and Monica had decided to treat herself to cheer herself up.

She looked on eBay first, then Amazon, but nothing really caught her eye. Monica tapped her finger on the arm of her chair, 'Hmmm, what should I type into the search bar?'

Her cat, Zed, looked at her and winked, purring in contentment.

In a lightbulb moment, Monica jabbed *Unique leather purse, Newdon* into a search engine.

The processor delivered thousands of results to the device in less than a heartbeat.

With a keen index finger, she pushed the display up the screen. *Huh? What's that?*

Monica paused and peered at the purse. It was unique; she had seen nothing like it before. The item had what appeared to be a tattoo of a mandala on the back of it. *That's awesome.*

She stroked Zed again absentmindedly, who butted her hand for more fuss. Monica pressed on the link to see more items, 'Look at this, Zed, they have purses made out of human skin! I bet it isn't really, Zed. That couldn't be allowed, could it?'

She peered closer at the screen, 'Must clean my glasses, Zed. I'm glad no one can hear me talking to you, they'll think I am going crazy. You don't care though, do you, baby?' Zed meowed at Monica as she cleaned her specs. She stroked the cat again and put her glasses back on. 'Right, let me have a closer look at this purse. It says new in,' Monica zoomed in again on another purse. Confusion passed through her mind. 'Well, would you look at this, Zed, Aunty Zoe had a tattoo just like that. I've seen no one else with a tattoo of an emu. I don't understand...Zed, can you think of anyone else with a tattoo of an emu with a prosthetic leg?' Zed winked at her again and kept purring. 'I just don't understand it, it can't be possible...'

Monica felt like her head had been filled with a load of marshmallow. She poured herself a glass of wine, a large one, and sat down back next to her feline companion. With a sigh, she picked up her mobile and rang 101, the UK non-emergency police telephone number. It was answered after three or four minutes.

'You might think I'm crazy, but I'm sure I've just seen a purse online made with not only human leather but from my Aunty Zoe. She was only buried the other week; they must have stolen her skin or something,' Monica, shrouded by a deathly cold, felt like the walls were closing in on her.

'I'll send an officer around to talk to you, Miss Lashley. They'll be with you in the next couple of hours,' the kind voice on the other end of the phone replied.

An hour later, Sgt Laura Love rapped on Monica Lashley's door and stood back in anticipation of someone opening it. In her left hand she held a large leather folder containing papers and forms for every conceivable occasion.

A large woman answered the door, holding a huge ginger cat in her arms. The woman looked shell shocked.

Sgt Love said with an official voice, 'Miss Lashley?'

'Yes, call me Monica, please. Come in,' Monica stepped back to admit the officer. The door opened straight into Monica's lounge, which was sparsely furnished, but what furniture there was looked to be high quality and well cared for.

There was a pregnant pause, so Sgt Love broke the ice, 'Who's this handsome chap? I love cats.'

Monica seemed to come alive.

'This is Zed. He's three. Isn't he gorgeous?'

'Yes, he is a smasher,' smiled Sgt Love. Sitting forward, she began, 'I believe that you found a purse made from one of your late relatives?' *I've come across some weird shit in my time, but this is something else.*

'You'll think I'm insane, or a crazy cat woman...' Monica looked at her shoes, full of doubt.

Sgt Love shook her head, 'Not at all. In my years on the force, something new always comes up. Go on...'

Monica seemed to steel herself, 'Zed and me were looking for a new purse to cheer me up. My Aunty Zoe died a few weeks ago and I've been really down,' she sighed and continued. 'I wanted something unique, and I found a shop that makes leather stuff out of human skin. I thought it had to be a fake or a wind up, but I looked through the stuff for a laugh and...'

'Go on...'

'I found a purse with a tattoo,' Monica dabbed her eyes with a tissue and started to cry more. Through her tears, she pointed at an item on the tablet screen, 'That tattoo is an emu with a prosthetic leg. Aunty Zoe had that same tattoo for a joke last year. She was bonkers.'

Zed purred and butted Monica's hand to be stroked again, which seemed to calm the woman.

'Let me see that,' said Sgt Love. She frowned as she peered at the item. *What the fuck?* 'Do you have a photo of your aunt's tattoo?'

Monica's eyes lit up. 'Yes!' She picked up a Samsung Smartphone from a coffee table. Sgt Love watched the woman prod and swipe the screen. 'Here, look, she made me take a photo right after it was done. I went with her for moral support.'

Sgt Love looked at the photo, and then she looked at the image of the purse. And back again. She squinted and rubbed her eyes with the backs of her index fingers.

'They do look remarkably similar. Can I ask you, who was next of kin?'

Monica stroked Zed again as another tear trickled down her cheek, 'Me. Aunty Zoe didn't have any family of her own, and she asked me if I'd do all the funeral stuff and all that.'

Sgt Love put a calming hand on Monica's wrist, 'I'm so sorry, but I have to ask you this. Did you give permission for Zoe's skin to be used to make leather products?'

Monica could only shake her head and squeak, 'No...' before breaking down into floods of tears.

'Let me take some details and I'll look into it. I'll write a short statement in my notebook and get you to sign it. If I need a full statement at a later date, I'll make an appointment with you.'

Monica nodded sadly and spoke to Zed, 'I'll make myself be strong. For Zoe.'

Sgt Love retrieved a notebook from a pocket in her jacket and spent the next five minutes writing down the details of their interview. Monica signed it with a sigh, 'Good luck, Sarge. I hope you get a good result.'

'So do I. I'll be in touch,' said Sgt Love as she stood and made her way to the door.

Chapter Twenty-Three

Upon her return to the station, Sgt Love knocked on the door of her new boss. Inspector Beth Lightowler had joined the Newdon Station roster six weeks previously. Already she had impressed the officers by not being glued to her office, and went out on jobs to help out when she could.

'Come in!' she called when she heard the knock.

'Ma'am, can I have a word please?' Sgt Love asked.

Inspector Lightowler waved a hand at a chair opposite her desk. 'Take a seat,' she removed her specs from her nose, the nose pads leaving a reddened dent. 'I was having to do one of those damned online training programmes.'

She sighed and ran a hand through her short bobbed brunette hair, 'Anyway, how can I help?'

Sgt Love took a deep breath, 'Ma'am, I need some advice. I've just visited a woman on a scheduled appointment. She's found an online company selling leather goods made from human skin.' The sergeant paused for a moment before continuing, as if she could barely believe it herself, 'She found a purse, embellished with a tattoo.'

The inspector found her full attention fixed upon the sergeant.

'Here's the thing. The tattoo was of an *emu with a prosthetic leg!*' She emphasised this by tapping a finger on the desk with each word. 'A fucking emu. With a false leg. I wish I was joking...'

'And?'

'Sorry, yes, the thing is that her aunty, who only died a few weeks ago, had that same weird tattoo. It cannot be a coincidence, in my opinion. The thing is, ma'am, that I would like guidance as to what to do next. This is a new one on me.'

The inspector screwed up her face, thinking hard. 'The first thing is that humans, dead or alive, cannot be property. There have been some cases about body parts, but nothing like this as far as I know. Hang on…' She turned to her computer and prodded various buttons. Menus and submenus flashed up so fast that Sgt Love couldn't keep track.

'Here,' said Inspector Lightowler, 'this is Regina versus Kelly and Lindsay, 1998. Hmm, right. This is about the theft of body parts that were being kept as anatomical specimens. Not quite what we are looking at here. That is assuming that there has even been a theft. There could be an innocent explanation, such as the tattoo belonged to someone else who donated their skin. Let me have a good look at the Human Tissue Act 2004 as well.'

She sighed and put her glasses back on, 'Tell you what, go to the premises and talk to the staff; see what you can find out. I have a meeting with the boss that I can't swerve. Take Emma with you; she's doing scheduled appointments but I'll get the control room to rebook them all. Report back to me when you get back.'

Sgt Love said, 'Thank you, ma'am. I'll be back shortly.'

She stood and left the office. PC Hooker-Wolfe was nowhere to be seen, so the sergeant called her on the police radio.

'Go ahead, ma'am,' the officer answered.

'Get yourself back to the station asap. We have a job to do.'

'Received, be there in ten.'

Sgt Love was waiting in the car park when her colleague pulled in through the creaking automatic gates.

The constable hadn't even yanked up the handbrake when Sgt Love opened the door and piled in.

'Remember where we went ages ago about a missing butcher, out in the sticks?' Sgt Love said as she pulled on her seatbelt.

PC Hooker-Wolfe looked across with a hint of a frown, 'Yeah, with the weird sisters and the blokes who do tattoos?'

'That's the one. I'll fill you in as we make our way over there.'

****

Benjamin looked out of the Dr Tattoo studio windows as a police car crunched over the gravel. He groaned when he saw it was the same two cops who came to investigate Aled's disappearance. Zack spotted the officers too and smirked at Benjamin, knowing that his boss could be in for a grilling.

Aleks looked to see what his colleagues were peering at. When he saw it was the police, he put his head down and stared at the tattoo he was working on.

Sgt Love took the lead and pushed the door to Dr Tattoo open.

'Hi, how can I help you?' Benjamin greeted them smoothly, while displaying his best smile, trying to contain his nerves.

Sgt Love asked, 'Is there somewhere we can have a word please? In private.'

'Of course,' Benjamin said, still with a smile in his voice. 'Follow me.'

He led them to the accommodation unit. *I hope they are impressed...*

'Come in, ladies, make yourselves at home.'

The officers sat next to each other on the edge of one sofa. Sgt Love took out her notebook and asked, 'Mr McGuinness, can you explain to me please how you procure skins, human skins, to make into leather?' She hadn't realised, but she'd turned up her nose a little when she said 'human skins.'

Benjamin thought, she ain't a fan then, best keep it simple and get 'em out of here.

He frowned a little, 'Of course, there's no secret, Sergeant. People, before they die, contact us and arrange for their body to come here after they pass away. We then flay, that is remove the sections of skin that we can use, and then send the corpse back to the undertaker ready for the funeral.'

PC Hooker-Wolfe fixed Benjamin with an intense stare, 'And the tattoos? I'm under the impression that the goods are worth more with a tattoo for embellishment.'

Benjamin cocked his head to one side, 'Well, sometimes, skins come in with tattoos in situ. Sometimes, we get a special request and we do one post-mortem; I mean on the skin after it has been removed.'

The two officers continued staring at him and he could feel himself squirm. He couldn't help himself from talking, 'You'd be surprised what people ask for. The most popular thing is the Death Dolls—we can't do enough of them.'

'Who does the tattooing?' Sgt Love asked, tapping her biro on the notebook.

'Sometimes me, sometimes Aleks. Zack isn't keen, so I ain't gonna make him.'

'Tell me about the purse on your website, the emu with a false leg,' demanded Sgt Love.

Benjamin's eyebrows furrowed towards his nose, his forehead creasing, 'I don't see all the patterns to be honest. Tilly, one of my workers, runs the shop and sees to the orders and all that kind of thing.'

'So, in summary, you don't know anything about that product?'

'That's right.'

Sgt Love sighed, 'Right, me and Emma will speak to her now. I'll be in touch, *sir*.'

The two police officers stood and left with no further pleasantries. *They aren't very friendly. The sooner they leave, the better.*

Sgt Love and PC Hooker-Wolfe didn't speak to each other as they walked across the yard. They knew each other so well that words weren't always necessary. With a terse knock, they entered the Skunkworks shop.

Tilly had her back to the officers and said, 'Take a seat, I'll be with you in a minute.'

Sgt Love said, 'Police. We need to ask you a couple of questions.'

Tilly finished what she was doing but didn't rush. When she was ready to talk, she smiled and apologised, 'Sorry about that. If I'd dropped everything, that hide would have been ruined. What's up?'

She seems a lot more normal than the boss. He was trying to impress me and Emma.

'Benjamin indicated that you could advise me on an item with a unique tattoo,' Sgt Love started. 'You have for sale a purse with an image of an emu with a prosthetic leg. Where did the leather come from?'

Without a pause for thought, Tilly beamed and said, 'That is a most excellent one, isn't it? Aleks from the studio made that tattoo on a donated skin a few weeks back.'

'Can I see it?' asked Sgt Love.

'Of course!' Tilly smiled again and opened a drawer in a filing cabinet. She reached in and grasped a purse from inside a small plastic sleeve.

Tilly handed it to the police officer. Sgt Love peered at it, 'Can I take it out of the plastic? I want to look closer at it.'

'Sure, no problem,' Tilly smiled widely. *I don't think she has a clue what she's looking at.*

Sgt Love looked closely, 'Very nice. I wouldn't have known that it's made from a human...Emma, have a look at it.'

The constable took the purse and admired the quality, 'I love the lining...yes, it's really lovely. How much would you sell this for?'

'Eight hundred for that one. It is unique, the graphic is different. I doubt it will take long to sell.'

Sgt Love crossed her arms, 'Why did the tattooist choose that particular graphic?'

Tilly laughed, sounding like nails dragging down a blackboard. 'We often talk about fun logos in the evening. I said as a joke, 'Hey, why not do a disabled emu with a false leg?' Zack thought that was hilarious...and there's the result.'

Emma slid the purse back into its sleeve and handed it back to Tilly. She glanced at her colleague, an unspoken word passing between them. Together, they stood and Sgt Love summoned her sweetest smile, 'I think that is all for today. Thank you for your generous assistance.'

Tilly smirked. *Clueless, these two. Couldn't catch a cold, never mind serial killers.* 'Lovely to meet you, officers. If you want to buy anything in the future, let me know and I'll arrange a discount.'

'Thanks,' said Sgt Love, who smiled broadly but it never reached in her eyes. She and PC Hooker-Wolfe lingered no longer, and departed the unit to get back into their car.

Once they had started the drive back, Sgt Love asked, 'Is it just me, or did that tattoo look quite old? I don't get why it's done as a real tattoo and not just printed on.'

Emma thought for a moment, watching the bushes whizz by in a hypnotic blur. She sipped some Lucozade then replied, 'That woman must think we were born yesterday; there is no way on God's earth that tattoo was freshly done. Complete crock of shit. What the hell is happening there? I was thinking of getting one of those Death Doll tattoos, they are so cool, but not from there!'

Sgt Love chuckled. 'I can't imagine a lady like you getting a tattoo...' She sneaked a look across to see Emma's reaction, which turned out to be a raised middle finger. 'When we get back to the station, we'll be going to look through the missing persons lists and see if anything jumps out.'

'Something isn't right there, is it?'

Sgt Love just nodded in reply.

****

'Ma'am?' Sgt Love knocked on Inspector Beth Lightowler's office door.

The inspector looked over her glasses at the sergeant, 'Come in, have a seat. What did you find out?'

Sgt Love sighed. *I need a holiday soon.* 'Me and Emma are going to have a good look through the missing persons files. It might be clutching at straws, but it's a good place to start.' Rain started to patter on the window, making the room seem more gloomy. 'The tattoo photo I saw from today's appointment was too similar to the purse to be a coincidence.'

Inspector Lightowler sat forward and leant on her desk. A photograph of her son playing football for his school team caught her attention for a second but didn't distract her completely. 'Report back to me what you find from the missing persons list. I need to know about any correlation with what they were meant to have been doing on the day they disappeared to the tattoo studio. Also, look at products on the website and see if any distinctive tattoos match descriptions of tattoos from the missing persons.' The inspector looked at a point above Sgt Love's head, deep in thought. 'Aha!' she exclaimed. 'Get back to your appointment contact; tactfully ask them where their loved one was buried or cremated and get their funeral director details. Don't contact the funeral parlour yet; let's see what turns up in the missing files first. Alright?'

Sgt Love nodded eagerly, 'Yes, ma'am. There is something here, I'm sure. I don't know what yet, but my instincts are almost always right.'

She left the inspector's office with a spring in her step and briefed Emma.

They spent about an hour cross-referencing missing persons and tattoos. Sgt Love jabbed her computer keys more harshly as the time ticked by. Not one missing person from the last year had that detail of the tattoos they had noted on their files.

'Damn!' Sgt Love thumped her desk and the keyboard jumped a little. 'Emma, this is so frustrating. We *know* there is something afoot, but *proving* it enough is being a pain in the arse. I'll ring Monica Lashley and get the undertaker's details.'

Sgt Love punched the telephone keypad with Monica's digits. Monica answered on the second ring. 'Hello?' she answered cautiously, as if worried about who could be calling her.

'Miss Lashley, it's Sergeant Love calling. I came to see you earlier.'

Monica interrupted, 'Oh, hello, nice to hear from you already. Have you found anything out?'

Sgt Love managed to subdue a groan of frustration at the lack of progress. She said, 'Nothing to get excited about yet, but we are putting together a fact sheet to see what we know already. Can you tell me which undertaker you used for your aunt?'

'Jo Hawley Funeral Directors. Do you think she has something to do with it?' said Monica with tears in her eyes.

'I doubt it very much. We are just gathering as much evidence as possible.'

'You think that the tattoo is from Aunty Zoe, don't you?'

Sgt Love put her head in her hands. 'There isn't any evidence either way at this moment in time. It would need expert analysis, so I wouldn't like to speculate. Sorry,' keen to cut off any further conversation, and the inevitable awkward questions, she ended with, 'I have to go now; I'll be in touch.' She pressed the catch on the telephone to terminate the call, and absentmindedly tapped her temple with the receiver.

Chapter Twenty-Four

Chesca stood in the kitchen, stirring a barely bubbling pot of curry. The day's meat of choice was goat. She loved cooking for the colleagues, and her food was always popular. Her sisters watched Eastenders, Zack was watching too but pretending to read. Aleks and Dmitri stared at their smartphones and talked to each other sporadically in their mother tongue.

Benjamin was out for the evening, visiting Lisa. They had been meeting more regularly since their mother passed away; her death had galvanized their relationship and their need for family.

Helena looked across to Chesca as the credits rolled on the soap opera. She asked, 'Need a hand, sis?'

Helena plopped a ladle of rice on each plate while Chesca completed the serving with wonderful aromatic curry.

'Penny for your thoughts,' Helena gently said to Chesca as they sat with their food.

Chesca poked her curry around her plate with a fork, 'Have you *seen* Benji's Porsche?'

Zack wafted his spoon, 'It's a bit of a beast, innit? Must have cost him quite a bit of coin.'

Chesca pointed her fork at Zack.

'Precisely. You three in Dr Tattoo seem to be busy permanently, the piggery is mental busy, especially with the rare breeds. Tilly, how's the Skunkworks?'

Tilly cocked her head, twirling her fork as she chewed a mouthful of curry. When she had swallowed, she muttered, 'Now you come to mention it, the business is going great guns. I physically couldn't do more than I am doing now. I'd burn out if I took on much more. Benjamin has had a few ashes trips in his friend's plane lately too,' she took a swig of coffee. 'He must be raking it in.'

The twins put down their devices; the conversation in the room was more interesting than whatever social network they were looking at.

Aleks added, 'The death doll tattoos are extremely popular. I do five a week, minimum. Benjamin is thinking to ask Helena to make website to sell things like tee shirt with death doll.'

Chesca gazed at Aleks, 'Are you thinking what I'm thinking?'

'You think we demand pay rise and shares?'

The woman nodded once and looked around the room at her sisters and the three men. She saw them all nod with determination. She enjoyed a few more mouthfuls of the delicious meal. *I wonder where Dmitri got the goat from.*

Zack played a bit with his flat cap until he was happy with its position on his head. 'The thing is, granted, he gives us free lodging, but without us he'd be lost. I mean, Tilly runs the Skunkworks and has made it a huge success,' he looked at the other two sisters. 'You pair run the piggery, which he couldn't do, not forgetting Dmitri. And it's only because of Aleks that the Death Doll brand exists at all.'

Chesca pointed out, 'Don't omit yourself, Zack. You are world class at tattooing. I'm sure some people come here just 'cos you're here.'

Dmitri spoke next—he had, in the months since joining the organisation, been able to increase his vocal contribution. He wasn't verbose by any stretch of the imagination, but it was no longer a shock to hear him speak, 'We ask nice, then if Benji say no...we take anyway.'

Tilly and her sisters tittered, making Zack squirm at the noise. 'I think we just keep asking and asking,' rebuked Chesca. 'How can he keep saying no? We always have the option of blackmail. I'm sure he wouldn't like a rumour going out that people have died here for their art.'

Helena chipped in, 'And if we wear shorter skirts and lower tops when we ask him...well, he is male after all. And I think he holds a light for Tilly.'

Everyone was amused by that old-fashioned saying. 'Good. That's decided then,' Chesca finished.

****

Lisa sipped a glass of wine, her feet tucked under herself. Benjamin only drank tea; he was driving home later.

'I'm amazed that your boss has joined in with the project,' Benjamin said.

Lisa sighed, 'So am I. It seems that money really does talk, doesn't it?' The rest of the glass of wine poured down her throat in one glug.

'It's a shame that Mum isn't here to see our success. I wonder if she would have bought a human leather purse?' Benjamin mused.

Lisa threw a cushion at his head.

'Don't be an idiot! There's no way she would have one, but she would still have been proud. I could see her with a kangaroo leather product though.'

Looking across at Benjamin from the corner of her eye, she teased, 'I see that you and Tilly are getting on well...' Benjamin rouged a little, which was unusual for him, 'I'm right, aren't I?'

'I think she is smart, and good looking too.'

'Are you sure it's not how she dips the skins in and out of the chemicals?' smirked Lisa.

Benjamin shook his head, knowing that Lisa was teasing him and despite himself, he blushed, 'Jesus, Benji, you've gone redder than a fire engine!' *I'm gonna get some mileage out of this!*

'I don't think I'll pursue her though; don't want to make her sisters jealous,' Benjamin said, drinking his tea and trying to avoid Lisa's gaze. 'Besides, it's never a good idea to mix business and pleasure.'

Lisa prodded further, 'Whatever, bro, you'll be shagging her before long.'

'Doubt it. I'll leave that to Dmitri and Chesca. I think I'm happy being single and not having to worry about a relationship. Anyway, you going to get us a couple more bodies this week? I think the stock in Skunkworks is getting low. Try and get us something Chinese and something black.'

'Something? Something?' Lisa hissed. 'These are *people*, you know, not items. Remember that when you are counting your pennies.'

'Sorry. I think sometimes, because I don't really deal with the bodies much, I do forget,' Benjamin looked shamed and gazed at the prominent veins on the back of his hand. He shook his head. 'Maybe I should be paying Jo more. She's at the sharp end.'

'I wouldn't bother. She's as bad as you really, and she's happy with the deal,' Lisa bit her lip. 'Maybe you should withdraw from human goods...it is distasteful and I'm hating it more all the time.'

'You could always leave the funeral home. I'm sure Jo would give you a good reference. I could teach you tattooing skills if you like?'

Lisa scoffed. 'I do love you, Benjamin McGuinness, but I don't think I'd be able to work with you!' The icy atmosphere broke; it wasn't often that a frost thickened between the siblings. 'I do know that Mum was proud of you for making a home for your workers, and I think she would have really loved that you gave jobs to a sibling group, so they could stay together for a long time. It's been a couple of years now, hasn't it?'

Benjamin sighed heavily.

'Something like that. Time flies, Lisa. Mum's been gone for too long,' he glanced at his watch. 'Wow, look at the time. I'll toddle off now. Need my beauty sleep.'

'Ain't that the truth!' giggled Lisa.

Chapter Twenty-Five

Inspector Beth Lightowler sat with her fingers steepled under her chin. The curious case of the human leather was bothering her. She had full faith in her sergeant. Although they had only recently begun to work together, it felt like they'd been colleagues for many years. *That has to be a good sign, like a litmus paper.*

Beth stood and gazed at her reflection in the window; dark had fallen unnoticed from her side of the desk. A pile of paperwork and another damned NCALT e-training package had occupied her time for a couple of hours. *Bloody training on the computer; it's a waste of my time. Should be a proper day in the classroom. Why is there so much grey coming through in my hair? I must find some time to get that sorted soon.*

Beth found herself sat at her desk, punching the phone number into her handset for Rachael Rose, her friend of many years. Rachael wasn't a cop, but she worked at a science research laboratory in Newdon University.

'Rachael speaking, how may I help?' a posh voice on the other end of the phone said.

Beth smiled to herself at how officious her friend sounded, despite knowing that Rachael spent her spare time walking her dog, always via a public house to sample as many single malts as possible. 'It's me, Beth. I'm ringing to pick your brains.'

'Oh, God,' groaned Rachael, 'I still haven't worked out how to turn water into wine from the last time you asked me a question...'

'Very funny, Rachael,' Beth giggled. 'It's more serious than that I'm afraid. I can't go into details, as you know, but are you as well versed in DNA as I believe?'

'Yes, I'm an expert. Go ahead,' Rachael said with a slightly bossy air. 'I hope that you're going to pay me for my time.'

Beth laughed, 'Nice try, Rachael. I have less and less budget every year, so you haven't a hope in hell.'

'You can't blame a girl for trying. What's up?'

Beth paused, composing the question in her mind, 'If, hypothetically, one had a new purse and wanted to check that the leather was genuine, could a DNA test prove it?'

'Well, just a check under a microscope should be okay for that. Come on, Beth, I know you...'

'Could it be proven what kind of animal it came from?' Beth squinted, anticipating her friend's reply.

'You mean like cow or goat? Yeah, someone did a test on chamois leather to see that test through and it worked a treat.'

'Human,' Beth blurted. 'And could it reveal the identity of the human in question?'

Rachael was momentarily stunned, silent for what felt like an eternity.

'Rachael? Are you there?'

'Yes, sorry, Beth,' Rachael sighed. 'That I don't know. I guess it would depend on if the DNA was robust enough to survive the tanning process and whatever chemicals were thrown into the mix. Marine chemicals are often used. Let me think for a minute.'

A comfortable silence ensued for a short time before Rachael said, 'Send me a sample of this shit awful stuff and I'll see what I can do.'

'Thanks, Rachael, I owe you one.'

'Whatever, Beth. I'm sure your local Morrisons has single malt whiskey...Balvenie. Nothing less.'

'I'll get onto it and send you the sample by the week's end. Thanks.'

Beth cut the call, breathed out deeply and turned back to her computer.

****

PC Hooker-Wolfe pulled up the handbrake on her patrol car, wincing at the creaking noise that came from somewhere under the chassis. She got out of the vehicle, as did Sgt Love and Inspector Lightowler. All three women glanced at each other with a determined expression and headed up the ramp.

The bell tinkled as the inspector opened the door into the funeral directors. Lisa was sat at a computer, doing admin chores. She did a double take. *I wasn't expecting police officers at eight o'clock in the morning.* She stood to face the visitors.

Summoning her best smile, Lisa said, 'Good morning, officers. How may I help you?'

Her struggles to make eye contact gave away her nerves. 'I'm Inspector Lightowler, and these are my colleagues, Sergeant Love and PC Hooker-Wolfe.' The two other officers nodded tersely. 'Are you in charge?' Beth asked.

Lisa shook her head, 'I'm just the assistant here. Jo Hawley is my boss and the owner of the establishment.'

'Where is she? I need to speak with her, now,' demanded Beth. Her no-nonsense demeanour was striking to her officers, who were only used to her behaviour while in the police station office environment.

Lisa stammered, 'I-I-I'll get her for you now. She's dressing a deceased ready for their funeral.'

'Take me to her, please,' Inspector Lightowler exchanged a glance with Sgt Love.

'I'm really not sure that I'm allowed to take visitors behind the office,' Lisa said, trying to sound defiant, but her bottom lip started to wobble. The inspector raised an eyebrow, and that was enough.

'This way,' Lisa instructed.

It only took a few seconds to reach the room where Jo was dressing a corpse. The body had a pair of smart suit trousers on, and a shirt that was as yet unfastened. A male, a black-skinned man, lay in his coffin. The sight of a man missing his abdomen skin was a shock to the police officers. All three of them were experienced professionals; a dead body was nothing new to them. Even tragic events such as a car collision, although sad, was no longer a shock to the system. *This* was something else though. The setting was peaceful, but the missing skin was like a cross between medical and medieval.

'We need to talk,' Sgt Love said, filling in the silence.

Jo blushed and then blanched, 'Come with me to my office. It is quite small…'

'It'll do,' the inspector snapped. 'You stay where I can see you, and then we'll speak to you if we need to,' she addressed Lisa.

Jo trudged through the building to her office, the officers following in single file. Lisa sat back at the reception desk and pulled her kindle from a drawer. *No way I'll be able to concentrate on any work.*

PC Hooker-Wolfe was the last through the door, which she closed with care. Inspector Lightowler was pleased to note the large glass panel, through which she could see Lisa. She sat in the comfortable office chair, relegating Jo to a plastic chair that she retrieved from a short stack of five.

With no further pleasantries, the inspector said, 'Why had that man in the coffin got no skin on his abdomen?' She fixed Jo with a fierce glare.

Speaking in a hushed tone as if talking to a relative, Jo said, 'After his death, his family donated his skin to a leather goods manufacturer for handsome compensation. It is all above board and at the family's request.'

'Really? I am struggling to understand this. You are saying that relatives give permission for their dearly departed to have their bloody skin peeled off? Bollocks,' she spat out the last word, making everyone jump. 'Show me the evidence.'

Jo had a bead of sweat forming on her forehead, despite the air conditioning. She wiped it away with the back of her hand. From an old-fashioned filing cabinet, a free standing one with four huge drawers, she pulled out a thick lever arch file with what appeared to be over a hundred sheets of paper tucked inside. Her hands shook a little as she opened the file, removed the top piece of paper and handed it to the Inspector.

Jo Hawley Funeral Director

Contract for Leather Goods

I hereby give express permission for the Funeral Director to take the recently deceased _____ for:

Donate their skin for the purpose of making leather goods. I will be compensated, as next of kin, to the sum of £_____

Date:

Signed:

Printed:

Relation:

'This is blank, Miss Hawley.' Inspector Lightowler glared at Jo.

'Shit, sorry,' said Jo. She took out the next sheet and handed it to Beth. In the spaces, she saw the name Vincent Palmer and the sum of £2500. The date was from three days previous, and signed by Liz Palmer, wife. 'Is Vincent the unfortunate man in the coffin who you were dressing?'

'Yes, yes, he is,' Jo said with a resigned air.

'Hmm, let me see the file,' Inspector Lightowler barked. She made a show of looking at each sheet in turn, but slammed it shut after looking at about half a dozen. 'I'll be in touch,' the inspector said and stood. The other two officers, neither of whom had sat, followed their inspector out with no further words.

Jo trotted into the reception where Lisa was staring at her Kindle. She hadn't been able to read one page. Jo looked perplexed, 'That was fucking weird. Rude woman; who does she think she is, waltzing in here and looking at my stuff then walking away with no explanation? I have a mind to complain to her boss.'

Lisa laughed bitterly, 'Really? On what grounds? If you make waves and rock the boat, they'll only want to look closer at what's really going on...then we'll really be in deep water.'

'I'd normally laugh at those metaphors, but I'm in no mood for that,' Jo put her head in her hands and then on her hips. 'Put the kettle on, and let's hope we never see them again. I'm just glad that I made that file of contracts from relatives signing their loved one's skin over to Skunkworks.'

****

Sgt Love and the inspector sat in the back of the car while Emma drove them back to the station. 'What did you see in that file?' asked Sgt Love. 'As if I need to ask.'

'Pure bullshit, that's what. To my eye, all the signatures were done by the same hand, just different names. I got down to a contract signed by Monica Lashley, donating the skin of her aunty, Zoe Lashley,' Beth looked out of the window at the dreary suburban scenery and grunted in frustration. 'Are you positive that Lashley wouldn't have signed her aunt over for skinning?'

'A hundred per cent. There's more chance of seeing an emu with a prosthetic leg walking down the high street in a pink tutu than her lying,' Sgt Love laughed sadly.

The inspector turned her body so that she was facing the sergeant. She pulled a small notepad out of a pocket in her Newdonshire Police issue fleece and opened it to the first fresh page, 'Right, let's see what we know. Fake contracts from the funeral director. Did you see the name badge on the assistant?'

Sergeant Love nodded, 'Lisa McGuinness. It seems too much of a coincidence, doesn't it?'

'I'd put a fiver on her being related to Benjamin McGuinness at Doctor Tattoo. I think that funeral director and Miss McGuinness are selling the corpse skins to Benjamin,' Beth poked the paper with the nib of her pen. 'Where does that leave the butcher? Aled Price, if I remember right. Do you reckon they killed him there, for whatever reason, and took his skin?'

'Who knows. Damn it…if they did kill the bloody butcher, that was a long time since. I wish we'd nailed them then,' Beth said, waving her hands about. She frantically wrote some notes with the neatness of the average family doctor.

'When we get back to the station, let's have a good look at their website again. I bet they'll have Instagram and Facebook pages too. There has to be some clues on there,' Beth raised her voice a little to catch PC Hooker-Wolfe's attention. 'Emma, I want you to liaise with our neighbouring forces and see what tattooed missing people they might have. If we're lucky, they'll have a photo of a distinctive tattoo on a missing person that matches something on their website.'

Sgt Love frowned, 'Ma'am, with all due respect, we have a good case to get a search warrant. Even without Mr Price's body, I'm sure that, with the fake contracts, Miss Lashley will no doubt give us a statement to the effect that she expressly did not agree to her aunt's skin being sold. That gives us something around fraud. We have the image online of that purse with the emu tattoo; we'll ask Miss Lashley if she has any photos. If we seize the purse, we can send it for DNA extraction to prove the origin of the leather. What's bugging me is what they could be doing for the disposal of bodies that they have gained themselves, not from the funeral home.'

From the front of the car, PC Hooker-Wolfe said, 'There is a piggery in that yard. That might belong to McGuinness too. And I believe that pigs will eat human remains. I read about it once.'

'This is horrific,' gasped Inspector Lightowler. 'I'll liaise with the Chief Inspector on this; it's going to be a major operation. There has to be a fraud of some sort around the skins from the funeral director, probably murder too. It can't be too big a leap to imagine killings there at the piggery. I'm sure the number of contracts at the funeral home can't equate to the number of goods on sale, even allowing for several products per body. We'll have to arrange a joint operation for the funeral home and the Skunkworks at the same time. And the other businesses there. The firearms department are going to have a wet dream.' She sighed and put her notebook away.

They were still about ten minutes away from the station. Sgt Love fiddled with her mobile phone, looking at the screen with close attention.

'Ma'am, there might be another set of offences too,' she glanced over at her boss, who made a 'go on' gesture. 'The tattoo studio, there are photos of Benjamin tattooing, a guy called Zack, and then another man called Aleksandr. When we visited the studio before, he always studiously avoided eye contact. I wonder what his status is...'

'He could be a Brit. You can't presume going by a name,' Beth admonished the sergeant. 'But you are right; we need to look into it. We could get Immigration to join us on a raid. Oh, and not forgetting the CSI crew.'

Chapter Twenty-Six

Benjamin had blocked out Wednesday from his diary so that he had a day off from tattooing. He looked out of the window and saw that it was raining heavily. With a sigh, he muttered to himself, 'No flying for me today…shame.'

Coffee, thick and black, oozed out of the coffee machine into an espresso cup. He stirred a sugar in, and then another. A small sip and he was satisfied that the coffee was just right. Just outside the window sat his new car; an upgrade to a two-year-old Porsche. Benjamin gazed at it; he had always dreamed of getting such a great car and status symbol.

'This won't get the baby a new bonnet,' ha chuckled. *Mum always used to say that.*

He pulled a rainproof jacket over his tee shirt and fastened his trainer laces. Benjamin opened the door and peered at the clouds. *Still raining.* He jogged up the yard, keeping close to the buildings to minimise exposure to the precipitation. A moment later, he was dashing through the piggery door and into the building. A radio was blasting out a pop music station. He grimaced; the charts didn't fill him with enjoyment these days.

'Benji!' Helena and Chesca squealed.

'Are you going to help us make sausages today?' Chesca asked.

He scoffed, 'Like hell I am. Don't get me wrong, your sausages are lovely, but I'd dent the profits if I tried to make them.'

Dmitri was standing at the cutting up table, expertly making cuts of meat from a pig laid out on the work surface. He saw Benjamin and smiled, waving a cleaver around as a greeting.

'Hi, Dmitri. Great work, mate.'

Benjamin opened the doors of the person-sized fridge and glanced at the three bodies inside. With a feeling of satisfaction, Benjamin closed the door, 'Those bodies in there, did you three kill them all?'

Chesca nodded, 'Yep...another two trying to avoid paying for a tattoo. They tried to get past Aleks. Bad idea.'

'What about the other body?' Benjamin asked.

The two sisters exchanged glances, 'That's Helena's ex-boyfriend. He came to see her but didn't get to leave again.'

'Great work, keep it up,' he decreed. *I didn't even know about those three. How could they have been so blasé?* 'I'm just going to go through the books. I'll be in the office if you need me.'

The books were doing amazingly well. They hadn't been cooked, yet they were still giving a much better profit than Benjamin had imagined. Chesca slipped into the office, closely followed by Helena and Dmitri.

'You three come for coffee?' Benjamin smiled. 'I don't mind making it.'

'Yeah, coffee would be great,' agreed Chesca. A silence settled in the office, the radio seemingly faded into the background. The four people sat on chairs, looking at each other. It felt a bit awkward, like everyone was waiting for someone else to speak.

'What's up, Chesca?' Benjamin asked, peering at her through the steam coming out of his coffee cup.

'Benjamin. You know how much we love you, right?'

'Yeah,' he drawled out the word to at least twice its normal length.

'It's a clear fact that your businesses are very successful. The Death Doll brand has gone more or less viral—it's everywhere online. That creepy doll with a black heart is pouring out of computer screens and on clothing. I'm outsourcing about fifty mugs a week,' Chesca sat forward to close the gap between her and her boss. 'But we're the people who have made the success happen and, well, we all feel that we should all have a pay rise at the very least. And some shares too.'

Benjamin sucked in a sharp breath that made a whistling sound around his teeth. He glanced at the three friends in front of him.

'I dunno. I think it's best to keep wages as they are, as I still have plenty of overheads,' he babbled, desperately trying to buy time to think of other reasons to not open his wallet. *Cash should always flow to me.*

Dmitri scoffed, the noise made Benjamin jump. He fixed Benjamin with an ice-cold stare, which filled Benjamin's vision even though he was a few feet away, 'I'll think about it. There might be some wriggle room. I have to go; a migraine is starting. I'll be in my room. Keep up the good work, guys.'

He almost ran away from the piggery, his feet scrabbling for grip on the gravel.

'He pay us more now, I know,' Dmitri grunted with a satisfied smile.

Helena smirked, 'No doubt thanks to your interpersonal skills.'

Chapter Twenty-Seven

PC Hooker-Wolfe sat at a computer in the police station, scowling at the screen. She had called the Dr Tattoo studio website up and was flicking through the menus.

'Resident Artists. Hmm, let's see.' *Aha!* She scrolled past Benjamin and Zack to a photograph of the third tattooist. Like a butterfly flapping in her stomach, a rare flutter of excitement started as something caught her attention. Emma knew this was always a good sign that something was about to go her way. She clicked on his face, which then filled the screen. A quick flick of the mouse's wheel, and the page scrolled up the screen. Her scowl softened to a small smile that lifted the side of her mouth.

'Right, best make some notes...'

In less than a minute, Emma had written:

Aleksandr Sokolov - DOB unknown.

Twin Brother. Tattooist, founder of Death Doll logo and tattoo.

From Russia.

It took her a moment more to check the voter's register. *He isn't registered to vote.*

'Laura?' Emma called across the office to the sergeant.

Sgt Love padded across the room and pulled across a spare office chair to sit next to Emma, 'What have you found out?'

'The Aleksandr guy is Russian, *and* he has a twin brother. I wonder where the twin is? Maybe back in Russia.'

'Get onto the control room and get them to run a person's check on him. Let me know what they say,' she stood and went back to her computer to continue her own work.

Emma grabbed a beaker of water from the cooler before sitting and lifting her telephone handset.

'I'd like a person check, please...Aleksandr Sokolov, Newdon. Date of Birth unknown...Thanks, bye.'

The sergeant saw Emma replace the receiver and looked across the office expectantly.

With a disappointed expression, Emma said, 'No intel at all. Damn.'

'That doesn't matter. It just means he isn't currently in any records for misdemeanour or being a victim. How about those women? If Doctor Tattoo's website lists all the staff, then maybe the piggery and Skunkworks have decent websites too. Have a look; hopefully it'll stay Q for a minute,' she was careful to not use the word 'quiet' itself, as it was seen as bad luck in the police and would no doubt result in a flurry of emergency calls.

Emma didn't waste any time in looking at the other business websites. 'Someone has been really proactive in making these sites.' The officer squished her nose to one side with a lopsided grin. 'Probably a woman. I can't see a man being as slick as this.'

'It's alright you being cheeky. That's an out-of-order comment. I have half a mind to send you for more diversity training!' laughed Sgt Love. 'Anyway, what's what?'

'Give me a chance, ma'am,' Emma looked studiously at the screen and made notes on a jotter pad.

Ten minutes later, Emma waved her hand towards her superior. Sgt Love strolled across the office space. 'Whoever's bag this is, move it! It's a trip hazard,' she shouted in her most officious voice as she kicked a large black patrol bag to the side of the room.

'Ma'am, look at this. There's a Dmitri Sokolov listed as working in the piggery. That can't be a coincidence. He's the odd one out, though; everyone else has a photo. There are three women, all with the same name. I think two are twins, as they look virtually identical, and the last woman I'm sure has to be a sister. Francesca, Helena and Tilly Hawkins. I'll run persons checks on them all. Oh, and look, it says that the leather stuff is made to order, but they have sold over a hundred products with Death Doll motifs on. That's a shit load. I think it's amazing that so many people want human skin products,' Emma shivered. 'Ugh, I think one of the dead has just walked over my grave! Hang on, that means they must have more bodies go through there than the undertakers admit.'

Ten minutes later, her queries were complete.

'Clean as a whistle, Sergeant. Not even a parking ticket between them all. Dmitri is unknown too. The females are all on the voters register. What do you think we are we going to do?' Emma raised her eyebrows and waited for Sgt Love to respond.

A PCSO, Andy Smith, answered a ringing telephone and called Sgt Love over, 'Ma'am, a PC Williams from Northamptonshire Police is asking for you.'

'Thanks, Andy,' Laura said as she took the handset from him. 'Sergeant Love,' she addressed the caller.

Laura Love nodded, said a few 'yeses' and 'uhuhs' before hanging up the telephone with her eyes as wide as dinner plates.

'Emma, we need to meet in the inspector's office, right now.'

Sgt Love knocked once with a raised knuckle and peered into Inspector Lightowler's office over a notice affixed to her door. 'Come!' came the reply. Beth hadn't even looked up from a stack of forms.

'Ah, Laura, Emma, what delights have you come into my office with? Coffee?' Beth smirked, knowing that Sgt Love hated being asked to make the drinks.

'You are not going to believe what I have just found out...Northants have just taken a missing person report. A man called Michael Hendry; his boyfriend says that Mr Hendry was going for a Death Doll tattoo yesterday at the Dr Tattoo studio, and he never came home. PC Williams and a colleague spoke to Benjamin McGuinness on the phone, who confirmed that Hendry did indeed attend for a tattoo and left in good spirits.'

Inspector Lightowler squinted, and after thinking for a moment said, 'That's the straw that broke the camel's back. I was aiming to seize that purse with the Emu on to send to Rachael Rose for analysis, but if I do that, then McGuinness is going to be suspicious.'

She held out a clenched fist and then counted the fingers off, 'One, suspicious circs surrounding missing persons including Hendry and Mr Price. Two, there has to be a fraud case regarding the dead relatives. Three, where are all those dead people coming from? I reckon there are grounds there for suspecting murder. Shit, this has come to a head now. Oh, and not forgetting the alleged illegal immigrants. We won't wait for immigration to come with us, it'll take too long to arrange. I'll get onto the chief right now and lay everything out. Be ready.'

Chapter Twenty-Eight

PC Hooker-Wolfe sat patiently outside the magistrate's courtroom on an uncomfortable plastic chair. She had spent a pleasant ten minutes catching up with an old colleague who was also waiting to see the magistrate.

'Come in,' a bodiless voice called from within the adjoining room. Emma stood, said goodbye to her colleague and entered the courtroom.

A woman who appeared to be in her seventies, and a man of similar vintage sat behind a mahogany desk. The woman looked to have come straight out of the hairdressers having had her hair set in perpetual animation of largeness. Bluish in colour, it set off her lavender scent and pastel cardigan. 'Hello, dear, what have you got for us today?' the man asked, whilst holding out his hand for the wad of paper that Emma had taken with her.

'Oh my!' the man said, echoed by the woman as she read the warrant papers. 'Denying a rightful burial, murder, fraudulent activities: my word, these are quite some allegations.'

The woman sighed, 'Will there be any dogs or children on site that you know of?'

'No, Ma'am,' Emma replied, very familiar with the verbal tango involved in getting a search warrant signed off by the court.

The steel haired man took off his designer glasses and smiled. 'Still, it makes a change from all those drug dealers, doesn't it?' He laughed at his own joke, seemingly not noticing that no one else shared his mirth.

'Very well, you know what to do now,' the magistrate said to Emma. *Why do the magistrates always seem to be so old?*

Emma took to the witness stand and read out an oath, as she had done many other times in the past. A clerk took care of the paperwork, which the magistrates both signed and gave back to Emma. 'Thank you, see you soon,' she said before jogging out of the court to speed back to the station. Before starting the engine, she keyed Sgt Love's number into her radio and gave a short message. 'Done, ma'am.'

****

PC Hooker-Wolfe pulled into the station yard; Sgt Love was stood waiting for her. The inspector jumped into the back of a marked Police BMW X5—Armed Response. A second identical vehicle started to move as soon as the first one pulled away.

'We can't risk anything less than taking AFOs with us, especially as we know there is a good chance that we'd be outnumbered without the backup,' Sgt Love sighed.

Another three patrol cars, each double-crewed, joined the convoy, one with a PCSO in the back for good measure. A van marked 'Territorial Support' contained another six cops, which latched onto the end of the column of cars. 'Good job the chief has sent a few cops from Kettown to backfill, or Newdon would be bereft of law keepers now,' Sgt Love smiled ruefully. 'Still, it'll be a piece of cake for these lads and lasses; Kettown is much rougher. Beth has sent a pair of cars round to the funeral home. They are to enter the premises at ten-thirty hours, which is the same time as our ETA at Dr Tattoo.'

Emma laughed; the banter between the towns was decades old.

****

The day was overcast, for the first time for months, and Benjamin was feeling low but couldn't work out why and blamed it on the weather.

'I can't believe the weather is so shit, lads,' Benjamin said, looking out over the courtyard and noticing that there were no clients in for a tattoo for the first time in as long as he could remember. There were a couple of people due in, but they hadn't yet shown up.

'Yeah, something is up today. I can feel it in the air,' Zack pondered, while he stabbed at a button on the coffee machine.

'You're right, Zack. I thought it was just me,' mused Benjamin. He lifted his mug. *I've got time to drink this before the guy comes for his bolognaise at long last. I must remember to not call him Hickey. Hickman, Hickman, Hickman. I can't believe I had to ring him to remind him; we've only had it in our freezer for six months.*

He looked over the yard, taking in the faded signage at the piggery. *I'll sort that next week. There might well be no shop there, but that's no reason to be slack.*

'I'll tidy up the Death Dolls merchandise stand as well, it looks like it's been ransacked."

Benjamin glanced over at Zack's words, 'Yeah, you're right. At least it means that merchandise is selling well.'

'I tell all my clients, it is condition of Death Doll tattoo that they buy tee shirt and mug,' Aleks grinned.

'That's a brilliant idea, Aleks, keep it up.'

Benjamin was genuinely impressed.

Crunching pebbles caught his attention; the rusted Mondeo drove at a slow speed and pulled up outside the tattoo shop.

'Hey, Aleks, I think I should tell him to park that shit pile around the corner. It's bringing my image down,' Benjamin glowered.

Aleks smirked as if he was thinking of a wisecrack to come back with, but instead, he looked back at his untidy workspace and continued cleaning up.

'Nice wrist action there, Aleks,' chuckled Benjamin. Aleks merely shook his head and sighed at his boss.

Mr Hickman walked into the tattoo shop wearing a cowboy hat and a long black leather coat. The look was completed by boots that looked to be straight from the set of a movie. Zack quietly whistled a Wild West tune, as if a duel was on the cards, and the other two men struggled not to laugh.

'Mr McGuinness, I'm here for my bolognese. It's kind of hot food weather, don't you think?'

'It is, Mr Hickey, I agree with you.'

'What the fuck did you just call me?'

'Mr Hickman?'

'I warned you. Never call me Mr Hickey,' his carotid artery throbbed dangerously in his neck, as though it were trying to escape his body.

'I'm so sorry, I won't do it again. I was trying too hard to not say it and it just came out.'

'You will never, ever say it again.'

His tone of voice hung thick in the air.

In one smooth motion, Mr Hickman put his hand in the back of his coat and pulled out a sawn-off double-barrelled shotgun.

Before he could raise the weapon to fire, Aleks leapt into action. He flew from his station in a strange sort of rugby tackle, leaving time to almost stand still as he dived across the studio and slammed into Mr Hickman. The gun flew into the air. Benjamin and Zack froze in their positions, watching as it reached the apex of its arc and plummeted to the floor. An ear-splitting boom exploded around the studio and the huge windows blew out a mosaic of glass into the yard.

'Oh dear, Mr Hickman, you're now going to be the recipient of a death doll tattoo,' growled Benjamin.

'Isn't that a good thing? They are must-have nowadays,' Mr Hickman said, weirdly calm considering what had just happened.

'Not for you; your tattoo is going to feature on a trendy satchel.'

'What the fuck you talking about?' Mr Hickman said, confusion etched on his weather-worn face.

'Zack, Aleks, you know what to do.'

Aleks and Zack manhandled Mr Hickman into a chair at Benjamin's workstation and bound his wrists and ankles to it. Benjamin couldn't help but smile as he punched Mr Hickman, splintering his nose and sending a shower of blood across his face.

Aleks nodded with approval and picked up his tattoo gun. It didn't take him a great deal of time to tattoo the death doll onto Mr Hickman's expansive abdomen. He'd had a lot of practice in perfecting his design over the previous year or so.

'I think that is your best one yet,' Benjamin complimented Aleks, nodding his approval.

Aleks picked the shotgun up from the floor and ejected the two used cartridges. He patted Mr Hickman's trouser pockets. Smiling, he plucked the remaining two shells out and reloaded the weapon.

'To the piggery I think,' Aleks said with menace, his glare drilling into Mr Hickman.

Benjamin nodded. The prospect of killing Mr Hickman made his eyes shine. Zack untied Mr Hickman and Aleks ordered him to follow Benjamin, using his bulk to make an unspoken threat.

The trio marched across the yard to the piggery. Benjamin bellowed as he passed the housing unit, 'Dmitri, get your arse out of there and to the piggery right away!'

Dmitri joined them just before the group reached their destination.

With his face turning ashen as they entered the building, Mr Hickman turned and tried to run but came face to face with Aleks and his own shot gun.

The men forced Mr Hickman into the butchery room and secured him to the top of the stainless-steel table with thick rope. Dmitri retrieved the freshly sharpened scissors and removed Mr Hickman's clothes with ease. He tossed them into a jumbled pile on the floor before turning back to face the condemned. Laughing wildly, he pointed at Mr Hickman's penis and then at the scissors. The penis shrunk back into his body until it resembled a tiny button mushroom.

'That's far too small for the pigs, don't bother cutting it off,' laughed Benjamin with genuine amusement.

Summoning all his strength, Mr Hickman tried to free himself but quickly realised he was no match for the restraints. All he achieved was some bruises to his head and a copious drenching in his own sweat.

Dmitri selected a scalpel and pushed into his victim's flesh with relish. Mr Hickman unleashed a terrified scream, which fell only on deaf ears. Within a few seconds of the blade gliding smoothly across the surface of his plump body, Mr Hickman choked on his own vomit and passed out.

When the slab of flesh with the Death Doll on had been removed and dumped into a bucket, Benjamin grinned and nodded his silent approval.

Aleks stood tall and looked at Benjamin with a renewed hardness. He cleared his throat and brought up a dark green mass, which he promptly spat into the drain. *What the hell is happening? If looks could kill, Aleks...*

'Benjamin, your profit is boosted by my ink skills and Dmitri's muscles. Zack and the girls, too, make you very much money. It's time to give us many shares of the company, and big pay rise.'

Benjamin's eyes widened, betraying the fear he so desperately tried to hide, 'No. Not yet anyway. If it wasn't for me, then you'd still be cleaning cars.'

'I tell you again, it is time.'

'No. You're fired. Please leave.'

'I asked you nice, now I take everything with Dmitri,' The menace in Aleks' voice was now not so subtle and tinted with hatred. He squared up to Benjamin, who was dwarfed by the Russian.

As Benjamin lost control of his bowels and bladder, shit and piss flowed down his trouser leg and pooled around his feet.

Aleks' eyes glazed over as he raised the gun and aimed at Benjamin's knees. The noise was catastrophically loud in the enclosed space when he pulled the trigger.

'I asked you nice.'

Benjamin's wounded knee pumped blood over the floor tiles, merging in a slick stream with his excrement as it flowed freely towards the drain, 'You're crazy!'

Dmitri and Aleks laughed and held the gun out towards Zack.

'Kill him, you will enjoy. We all take share. Or, if not, then I kill you.'

Zack looked ecstatic and took the gun from Aleks. He ejected the shell and held his hand out to the Russian for the last remaining round.

Aleks obliged and Zack reloaded the weapon. Placing the end of the barrel barely an inch from Benjamin's temple, he placed a finger on the trigger, mentally bracing himself to pull it.

****

'Did you hear that?' Emma said to Sgt Love as they climbed out of their patrol car. Before she could answer, four other officers rapidly exited the premium BMW vehicles and ran to the back of their cars. 'Get down, get down in cover!' one male officer hissed at them while retrieving his Heckler and Koch G36 carbine firearm to compliment the Glock 17 handgun in his leg holster.

'Sounded like a gunshot to me,' frowned Sgt Love. 'Come on, let's see what's going on!'

Inspector Lightowler pointed at her sergeant, 'No way! Remain out here. In fact, you and Emma can check inside the tattoo studio for suspects.'

She delegated the other cops to search the buildings, and the PCSO to tape across the access point out to the main road, 'No one in, no one out, got it?'

The inspector couldn't hear the radio traffic from firearms but called into her radio for more AFO and unarmed reinforcements. The duty inspector from the Force Control Room came to life with a crackle on the airwaves, 'Lightowler, I've tasked NPAS 75 to fly across and provide air support. You are Bronze Commander in the field; Gold Command is convening in the control room imminently.'

'All received, the helicopter is overhead,' Inspector Lightowler allowed herself a small grin. *This is going to be Gold for my C.V.*

Sgt Love urged Emma, 'Come on, let's get into the Skunkworks. I'm going to seize that purse and send it to Rachael Rose for analysis. I want to find out for Monica Lashley if it is her aunt or not.'

****

'PUT DOWN YOUR WEAPON!' PC Dyer yelled at Zack, who looked wide-eyed and open mouthed at the sight of a deadly rifle pointing straight at him.

Zack squatted and put the loaded shotgun on the floor, and then stood up straight and lifted his hands high into the air, revealing a sizeable sweat stain under each armpit. The Russian brothers and Benjamin followed suit, the four of them standing like statues.

A moment later, the officers ordered them to lay face down in the various bodily fluids coating the floor, with their arms behind their backs and their wrists secured with plasticuffs.

Chapter Twenty-Nine

<u>Seven Hours Later</u>

A new team came to the farmyard to relieve the exhausted officers at the scene. Inspector Lightowler, PC Hooker-Wolfe and Sgt Love climbed into the same car to drive back to Newdon Police Station.

The location had been a hive of activity after the sound of gunfire blasted into the yard.

CSI had seemingly summoned every operative from the force's resources, along with a few more from neighbouring forces on mutual aid, to the complex scene. Men and women in white suits busied themselves, tents had popped up, and yards of tape sealed off the piggery from all but essential personnel to prevent scene contamination as much as possible.

Outside the farmyard, on the road that was sealed off from the location, two TV news trucks were parked with satellite dishes standing proud on their roofs.

'Give it a wee while, and they will multiply,' Beth muttered. 'I'm glad we're escaping before we end up on the news. Great job, ladies. There'll be a hell of a lot of work coming our way from this, so don't leave the country.'

The three women laughed, content that they had finally brought down the kingdom of Benjamin McGuinness.

Epilogue

'Miss Lashley, can we come in please?' Sgt Love said softly. Monica nodded with sadness and stood to one side. The police officer and Emma entered the living room and sat.

'It's true, isn't it?' Monica said, not lifting her eyes to meet Laura's.

Sgt Love nodded, 'I am very sorry, Miss Lashley, but the purse was made from your aunt's skin.'

'I knew it. Those bastards; I hope they rot in hell!' Monica broke down in tears.

'We'll do our level best, trust me. I'll keep you updated as often as I can. Are you willing to testify in court?' asked Sgt Love with hope.

As Monica steeled herself, a determination lifted her shoulders, 'Too fucking right.'

****

After a lengthy investigation, all three women and all four men were charged with a number of offences, including murder. It took the CPS several months to determine what offences had been committed, so the 'family' were kept in custody whilst the case was put together.

The human leather caused them a particular headache because humans can never be property, dead or alive, so theft would never be classed as an offence in this case. Rachael Rose analysed almost a dozen leather items; DNA was extracted from ninety per cent of those. As a result, five missing persons cases were closed, including that of Aled Price.

Jo and Lisa were also arrested and charged in relation to fraud offenses.

Life sentences were handed down to the residents of the unit, in addition to individual fines totalling many thousands of pounds.

Lisa and Jo escaped a sentence after the case was eventually dropped due to insufficient evidence. Jo's business initially suffered, but trade is once again picking up.

The Streets of Newdon are once again safe.

For now.

THE END

DR PODALIRIUS

Chapter One

25th September 2000

Robert Podalirius, son of Elaine and Eddie, was born in a blur of blood, sweat and tears.

He was the first child of the 70s in the family; the christening saw relatives come from Greece and an epic party. Eddie had no idea who most of them were. His parents had come to England in the 1960s and joined the ever-expanding Greek community in the outskirts of Newdon. After settling they opened an authentic restaurant with Eddie's uncle and aunt. Business was brisk, to start with. Every Saturday night the restaurant burst at the seams with clients. There was the occasional dork who smashed their dinner plate after they finished their dinner, but they always got told in no uncertain terms to not do it again.

Fads come and go, and in the summer of 2010, the eating out trend swung from Greek to Italian. That, combined with a client maliciously telling the local newspaper that he had found a pubic hair in his moussaka, saw business plummet. Social media fuelled the local grapevine as it twisted its way through the suburbs.

By the autumn, the restaurant owners decided to close. It was a hard choice to make, but the hate meant that the decision was out of their hands.

On the last day, Eddie shook hands with his uncle and walked away. His head wasn't in the clearest of places. He came to the edge of a road, but neglected to look out for traffic and stepped out into the busy wayfair.

The coroner said that Eddie wouldn't have suffered much after being struck by a fully-loaded articulated truck.

It was certain that the eyewitnesses suffered trauma. They saw Eddie disappear under the front bumper, heard him rattle under its chassis over the sound of locked up tyres tearing against the hot tarmac and saw his head being ripped from his shoulders before the force of momentum fired it sideways and through the window of a newsagents.

In the blink of an eye, Elaine became a widow and a single parent. The terrible trauma hit her hard; she had several breakdowns in the following years. There was no doubt that she had some form of PTSD, but she never sought help, nor did anyone think to try and get her to ask for it.

Years passed her by, barely noticing that Robert was growing up as the adult in the home. He made sure that the cupboards and fridge were stocked, and that the bills were paid. The experience of being a young carer was tremendously hard but helped to toughen him up in preparation for adulthood.

On a particular day that formed the rest of his life, Robert tuned in to see Children in Need. Clip after clip showed kids and their grown-ups, most of them had the audience in tears, digging into their pockets to donate hard cash for the great cause.

Robert was particularly touched by the films showing other young carers; it made him realise what a great job he was doing with his mother, who he loved so much.

But, it was the films of young lives being torn by the curse of cancer that spoke into his heart. A mission was born, a deep calling that awoke an ancient soul. He was going to be a medical doctor. There were so many kids with so many terrible diseases that he knew he had to help.

Podalirius was reborn.

Chapter Two

The medical school didn't know what had hit them.

Robert was a star pupil at high school—being a young carer hadn't held him back. Somehow, he had wrinkled time itself, and fitted caring and studying and socialising together with ease.

Never in the history of Newdonshire University had someone ripped up the rule book and passed with the highest grades possible; a year early!

Despite his poor upbringing, Robert made the Hall of Fame. A prize that only ten people had claimed in the last century.

Dr Podalirius, or Dr Pod as he was known to his colleagues, was ready to make amazing changes to the lives of sick people. He decided to specialise in paediatric medicine; children especially shouldn't have to suffer.

Chapter Three

Jake Oaks was an ordinary twelve-year-old boy. He liked school, but his love was playing football. Between the sticks he was king of the school; no other boy got picked to be goalkeeper when Jake was in the game.

'Mum, I don't want to go to school, football is cancelled because of the weather,' Jake said one particular Monday morning while moping about in the kitchen.

'You can't stay at home from school because it's raining darling,' his Mum, Claire, said.

'My head is banging though. I'm serious Mum, my head really hurts.'

Claire sighed, 'Alright, I'll ring the sickline, but I'll know if you are swinging the lead.'

'Thanks Mum, I'm going to lie down on the sofa,' Jake said, his eyes failing to focus.

It wasn't long before he was asleep.

I hope he is alright, he isn't normally ill.

By Wednesday, Jake still had his migraine. Claire rang their doctors' surgery and made an appointment for him to see a medic.

'Jake Oaks?' Dr Green smiled at Jake and Claire as they stood from their chairs in the waiting room.

He's easy on the eye! Thought Claire, *damn, I shouldn't be having thoughts like that when Jake is poorly. That looks like a fresh tattoo on his arm; must be a Death Doll.*

Dr Green sighed as if Jake was the ninetieth patient that day, 'How can I help today?'

Claire replied, 'Jake has been having a migraine for a few days now. I'm worried, it isn't like him at all. He loves playing football, but didn't feel able to go to school even though he had P.E. today.'

'Hmm, ok,' said Dr Green with obvious concern 'Let's check you out and see what we can do.' He smiled warmly at Jake, who eventually began to relax. His tension seemed to melt away, a burden lifted from his shoulders.

Dr Green did a few tests, checking Jakes ears and blood pressure. With a smile to Claire he said, 'So far so good, I'm just going to look in his eyes, and that will be us done.' He scooted his chair closer to Jake and leaned in with his instrument.

The doctor continued to look for what seemed like an age. Claire knew that something was wrong. 'What is it, what's wrong?' Claire said, a feeling of panic rose inside her, its hands grasping her throat.

Dr Green had to force himself to make eye contact with her; he hated giving bad news to anyone, let alone a parent of a young child.

'There appears to be a problem in the back of Jake's eye. I can't tell exactly what it is, but I'll ring the hospital and ask them to see you in the drop-in ward. That's called PAU, so you know what to look for when you get there.'

'PAU?' said Claire

'Sorry, it's the Paediatric Assessment Unit, on the Children's ward.'

'Alright, thanks for seeing us Doctor,' Claire said. She stood, as did Jake, and they left the surgery to go to the hospital.

Jake was scared, but not as much as his mother. Claire just knew, call it mother's instinct, when Dr Green sent them to the hospital that something was seriously wrong with Jake.

Chapter Four

Dr Pod had yet to have a day where he hadn't helped someone. Whether that was a kind word to an anxious parent or dealing with a kid that had been involved in a car crash, it didn't matter to him. It mattered to him that he worked his hardest and made a difference in people's lives.

Other department managers tried to get Dr Pod to join their ranks, especially Dr Goodenough from the cardiac team. But the more that they tried, the stronger that he became in his vision and ambition for the paediatric department. Something bothered him though; there wasn't a neurology specialist in the paediatric department at Newdon.

He put his heart and soul into getting the qualification to be a neurologist. The training was terrifically difficult, but Dr Pod, of course, passed with top grades. Somehow, he negotiated hard with the hospital management. Within the next two years, he had a bustling department with another neurologist that he had recruited from Great Ormond Street children's hospital, and an epilepsy nurse specialist.

Chapter Five

Dr Pod called out into the clinic's waiting area for Jake Oaks.

Jake wasn't on his list of patients, he was on his colleague's, but Claire had emailed him five times a day and rang his secretary twice a day, every day that week since being told that Jake had to see a neurologist. Jake's story hit a chord with him, and he felt that he could help him get back into his school's football team. Dr Pod smiled warmly at Jake and Claire as they walked towards him across the waiting area. *His gait doesn't look too good, I wonder what's going on.*

They drifted down a long anonymous corridor, past the numerous posters about washing your hands and various other clinical curiosities.

Once inside the consulting room, they were greeted by a nurse called Eloise. She seemed to be there to take notes, and support the doctor. Once pleasantries had been exchanged, they each took a seat, and Claire poured out to Dr Pod all her worries and what she knew about Jake's health issues.

The doctor took great care to record everything that was said to him, and then conducted a thorough examination of Jake. Consulting his impressively thick BNF textbook, he wrote a long prescription of painkillers and ordered an urgent MRI scan for Jake.

****

'Hi, good to see you again, come in,' Dr Pod ushered Jake and Claire into his consulting room, 'please, take a seat.'

The nurse, Eloise, sat in the same place as before. Dr Pod steepled his hands under his chin and he said, 'I'm afraid it isn't good news. The test results are in—you have a Medulloblastoma. It's the most common type of childhood brain cancer.' He paused for a moment, and adjusted how he was sitting slightly, as if he had sat on something uncomfortable. 'Conventional medicine says that it is cancerous, and you have a poor outlook. *However*, I am sure that I can do something about it, and I will try my damnedest to make you well again Jake. I want you to be back in goals again by this time in six months, but promise me that you will set your mind to help. If you don't believe that you can be cured, then it will be much harder. Is that ok, Jake?'

Dr Pod looked gently at the young man, waiting for Jake's response. Jake lifted his face to make eye contact with the doctor, and nodded, 'Yes. Let's do this!'

'Great, I have a very good feeling about your case, Jake. Come back and see me in two weeks, and we'll see where we are then. Is that ok with you Mum?' Dr Pod looked over at Claire, whose eyes were welling up.

'Thank you so much, I know that Jake is going to be ok!'

'I can't promise that, of course, but I am optimistic. See you in a fortnight...'

Claire and Jake took their cue and left the clinic with fresh optimism.

Chapter Six

Exactly two weeks later, Claire and Jake attended Dr Pod's clinic.

'Come on in guys, take a seat,' the young doctor said as he gestured towards the hard plastic chairs.

'How do you feel in yourself, Jake?' Dr Pod asked with concern.

Jake squirmed a little, intimidated by the doctor's authority and said, 'Never better sir.'

'No need to call me sir, young man,' the doctor smiled, 'Alright, let me examine you.' The doctor spent twenty minutes examining Jake with plenty of 'hmm' noises and blowing out his cheeks.

Claire finally asked, 'What do you think, Doctor?'

Dr Pod smiled cockily, 'I think he's healed!

Claire couldn't hide her joy. She jumped up, throwing her arms around the doctor, 'Thank you so much! I don't know what you did or how you did it, but I knew that I was right to have faith in you. This is nothing short of a miracle,' she gushed with a huge grin plastered over her face.

****

On the following Friday, Dr Pod telephoned Claire, with the results of Jakes MRI. The phone only rang once, then Claire's anxious voice came through the handset, 'Hello?'

'Hi Claire, it's me, Dr Pod. I'm just ringing to confirm what I suspected at the appointment. Jake is completely cancer free. Congratulations. Thank you for bringing him to see me, I'll make an appointment for Jake to see me in six months to follow up...'

'You are amazing! I can't thank you enough.' Claire's excitement was palpable.

'No problem, bye for now,' said the doctor, as he hung up the phone with a great feeling of satisfaction.

He opened a locked drawer in his desk, eased it open and retrieved a notebook. Finding the thin lacy bookmark, he opened it, found Jakes name and drew a large tick in black marker pen. With a thin smile of satisfaction, he put the notebook back into the drawer and relocked it. He couldn't resist a quick sniff of the marker pen before putting it back into the pen holder. With a smile, he remembered his school days.

Over the coming months, hundreds more children gained the same large tick in his notebook. None were marked with a thin red cross, to signify death or declining health despite Dr Pod's treatment.

Chapter Seven

It didn't take long until the chatter on social media picked up, and the national media heard about the marvellous Dr Podalirius.

He appeared on breakfast programmes and the evening news; soon everyone wanted a piece of him. His face was on the front of all the newspapers, fame had landed squarely on his lap.

One particular morning, a letter dropped through his letterbox from the royal family asking him to become the Queen's personal physician. Dr Pod was astonished and delighted in equal measure. He sat at his dining table, and hand wrote a letter to Buckingham Palace.

Your Majesty,

I was delighted to receive your letter today, asking me to be your personal doctor.

I am unable to accept your invitation, as I am committed to treating children through the NHS.

Yours faithfully,

Dr Robert

He pondered writing some kisses in the bottom of the letter, but thought better of it.

Feeling happy, he posted the letter that day in a red post box near his home. As he did, his memory popped brightly with images of children like Jake who he saved from the ravages of illness.

As he walked home, the fresh scent of cut grass filled his nose, and he admired the blooms on the trees lining the pavement.

Turning into his street, his stomach suddenly turned. Outside his home sat a line of trucks with satellite dishes on their roofs. 'Dr Podalirius! Is it true that you are going to be the doctor for Her Majesty?' Screeched a blonde-haired woman who looked vaguely familiar. The penny dropped when he saw the microphone in her hand with a bearing the logo 'Sky News'. *Oh God, news travels fast! I'll have to try and be professional.*

He smiled and waved at the camera's, 'Hi, nice to see you!' And he scurried past as quickly as he could to reach his front door. Relief flooded through him as he shut the door behind him and locked it. Walking into his lounge, he realised that the cameras were pointing through his window. With a cheery but uncomfortable wave, he gave the metal pole a half turn to close the blinds.

From the kitchen, he made himself a hot chocolate, sat in his comfortable lounge and turned on his television. The last channel he had watched was Sky News. For a moment, it puzzled him why his house was on the screen, and then he realised that *he* was on the headlines. 'Miracle doctor, curer of thousands, invited to be Queen's medic' scrolled across the bottom of the screen.

His guts churned, *I never asked for this,* and he chugged his hot chocolate in one go. 'Right then,' he said to no one in particular before getting up. He put on his smartest jacket, and went back out of the front door.

Questions were being yelled at him, the camera lights burned into his retina and he felt the colour draining from his face. Smiling at all of the cameras and presenters, he said, 'Thank you all for coming today. I can confirm that I have been offered the job at Buckingham Palace. However, I have taken great thought and rejected the offer from Her Majesty. I am humbled, but I am needed by children whose parents can't afford to fund private treatment. They are my priority.'

More questions were fired at him, but Dr Pod was feeling dizzy from all the attention and the pressure, so he waved thanks and returned inside his house. Once more he sat and gazed at his television. He was still the main focus of attention. *They must be getting bored of the Russian poisoning in Salisbury.*

Dr Pod found that news crews seemed to be everywhere that he went; only the hospital and his home seemed to be safe from the intrusion. Nothing could prepare him for what he saw next on the news. Sat on an expensive looking sofa were a pair of intimidating looking women. Both of whom wore a t-shirt with his face on, and a slogan underneath declaring, 'Jesus Is Back!'

Dr Pod couldn't believe his eyes. The presenters gave their best smiles to the camera, and interviewed the women. They seemed normal, except for their belief that he was the messiah. He shook his head sadly, knowing full well that these women would be encouraged to be on many programmes and that other people would be jumping on the bandwagon.

Within a week, his phone hadn't stopped ringing with interview requests, so much so that he bought a burner phone. Of course, the shop recognised him, and it didn't take long before that phone started ringing non-stop too.

The pressure of being so famous started to wear him down; it felt unfair to him that he should be under the glare of the spotlight when all he wanted to do was make sick children well again. He didn't look at social media much and had to change his personal Facebook account to use a pseudonym that only his closest friends and family knew the details of. After one particularly difficult day at work, he logged on and couldn't believe the following that groups declaring their love for him had. Most of them that he saw had well over two thousand followers. He wished that he hadn't seen one of the groups when he scrolled through the photographs. It was named 'Dr Robert Podalirius is Jesus Risen!'

There were scores of photographs of him in various places, most of them had a halo superimposed on his head. He was astonished when he saw images of him asleep in his bed. Dr Pod ran into his room to rip it apart, find the camera and destroy it. *It has to be around the drawers, from the camera angle.*

He looked closely at every item on his chest of drawers, there were a couple of teddy bears that had been given to him by grateful patients, deodorants, and aftershaves. *There is nothing suspicious here.* Short of destroying things, there was nowhere that he could see that a camera could possibly have been hidden.

Wait? What's that?

Looking closely at a Steiff teddy, he noticed something about the button in its ear... a tiny lens. 'Argh, how bloody sly!' he yelled. *But it can't have been the child or parent. That means that someone has been trespassing in my home... Oh my God! Where else have they hidden cameras? It's a good job I don't have a partner here; I'd be livid if their photos appeared in public.*

Dr Pod felt grubby knowing that he had been spied on. He ripped out the lens from the bear's ear. Going into the bathroom, he threw the button into the bin and ran a sink of hot water. When it was full, he plunged his face into it and held it under the water for as long as he had enough breath, and then stood straight, holding onto the side of the sink while looking into his shaving mirror. *My God, I look like I have aged ten years in the last ten minutes!*

What the hell should I do now? Maybe I need to employ a security team; not on my wages!

Chapter Eight

Fuck it, might as well have a beer, Dr Pod said to himself, as he left his bathroom. His feet fell heavily on each stair as he descended downstairs with a series of thuds. He looked up, making sure he didn't bump into the door frame as he entered his lounge. It was then he saw three heavily set men sat on his sofa.

With a sigh, he looked at them, all wearing smart suits with army style haircuts. Each of them had a pair of aviator style shades tucked into their shirt pocket, making them look like triplets. They stood in unison, Dr Pod said the first thing that came into his mind. 'Have you got an appointment, chaps?'

One of the triplets extended a hand, and he said, 'Dr Robert Podalirius, pleased to meet you. I am Darren Small, from Porton Down.' Despite himself, Dr Pod guffawed.

'I know right, a guy my size called Small,' grinned the man.

'I guess that you aren't here on a friendly visit?' The doctor fiddled with his shirt in a failed attempt to hide his nerves. He sighed deeply and sat.

Darren gave a tight smile, a dark glint twinkled in his eye. 'You are to come with us. We are from Her Majesty's government, and she requires you to work for the greater good of the nation.'

'But, I already posted her a letter to say that I am not going to quit my job at the hospital...'

The other two men stiffened their postures, looking like coiled springs ready to pounce. Darren made a small dismissive hand gesture, and they subtly relaxed their bodies. He cleared his throat and said with a hint of menace, 'There appears to be a misunderstanding, Doctor. We are not here to take you to the palace. You're coming with us to Porton Down, you'll be fully debriefed on arrival. Pack a bag with the essentials, underwear and toiletries. You have ten minutes.' He looked at his Breitling watch to make it plain to Dr Pod that he had no choice.

It didn't take him ten minutes to pack a bag; he always travelled light. *No point trying to fight the goons, I'll be the only loser. Shit, I'd better ring work.* He patted his pockets to check that he had his wallet and phone. No phone. *Ugh, I bet that Small has it already.*

With a knot tightening in his belly he returned to the lounge. Darren grinned, Dr Pod noticed he had a gold tooth, which seemed odd.

'You saw my tooth? It's an old war wound,' the muscle-bound man said.

'I'm ready. Do you have my phone?' Dr Pod asked, knowing the answer already.

'Yes. Couldn't have you calling the authorities now, could we?' His eyes flashed dangerously, making the doctor feel more uneasy with every passing moment.

'Let's go,' Darren said. Dr Pod was not going to argue. All three of the 'visitors' put on their shades, making them look like mafia henchman.

His guts clenched, and he felt like he was about to shit himself, but he managed to ward it off. Going outside, he was surprised to see that the media had disappeared, leaving one tatty Transit van. One of the big guys strode ahead and opened the sliding side door. As Dr Pod approached the van, Darren pointed to the door and grunted, 'In there, mate.'

So we're mates now are we?

Dr Pod stepped up into the van and shuddered when he saw a large vat of cleaning chemical with a large, well-used yard brush wedged into it. Darren saw him staring and chuckled, 'That's for cleaning out the van if any blood is spilt...'

Blood!? Dr Pod laughed nervously and sat on one of the four seats bolted to the floor. He noticed a cage by the back door, like in a police van. *Good thing I didn't resist.*

****

Two silent hours passed until sleep descended on him. Three hours later, he awoke with a start as the door was vigorously opened.

Rubbing his eyes, struggling to focus, Dr Pod saw that they had come to a stop inside a large garage with its massive metal doors already rolled down.

'Robert. Come with me,' a fresh-faced man said from outside the van.

'My name is Dr Podalirius. Or Dr Pod if you must shorten my name,' he said through gritted teeth. *Who does he think he is? Only my secretary gets to call me Robert.*

The man laughed, a weird high-pitched noise more suited to a schoolgirl than a fully-grown man. Dr Pod's skin crawled, he had taken an instant dislike to this man. He picked up his bag, and stepped out of the van, blinking at the bright light after the gloom of the van.

'I am Mr Stannington, Robert. You have to be nice to me. It's my job to make sure that you are *comfortable* during your stay. Do I make myself clear?'

'Yes, *Stan*,' quipped Dr Pod, knowing that would rankle the other man.

'Come, follow me,' Mr Stannington said as he spun around and walked towards a door that presumably led into the building's belly.

Darren and the other two men followed Mr Stannington, ushering Dr Pod forwards, ensuring that he didn't try to escape.

They walked up and down seemingly endless corridors, painted in a brilliant white that hurt Dr Pod's tired eyes. Finally, they arrived at what was to be his living quarters. He looked around, taking in the comfortable furniture and expensive flat screen television, *It's not that bad after all*, he said to himself.

Mr Stannington grinned glibly, 'Better get used to it Doc, this is your home now. If you behave yourself over the next few days, I might arrange for your belongings from your old house to be brought here. We are grateful for your large financial donation to the government by the way, what a nice thing to do with the proceeds of the future sale of your property.'

Dr Pod gasped, 'What the hell do you mean? Am I a prisoner here or what?'

Darren laughed, there was a cruel edge to his voice. 'The press thinks that you were found hanging from your bannister, your suicide note tells them that you couldn't cope with the pressure of fame. Sad really.'

'This is insane, you can't do this to me. I won't be cooperating with you until you make it right. The public will be very upset about this! They won't stand for it.' Dr Pod said, desperately trying to get out of the situation he found himself in. He did his best to remain composed, but this revelation was a shock.

One of the men had a large chin like Jimmy Hill, Tony, or Cockney as he was known, at last spoke in a heavy accent, 'Mr Stannington is right mate; we'll leave you in peace until tomorrow at 9am sharp. Then you will have your induction. Don't try anything silly though Doc, you're on candid camera 24/7.'

The three men nodded curtly at him and left as abruptly as they had arrived into his life.

****

Sunlight burst through the window, waking Dr Pod. He looked at his ancient Rolex, memories of his father from before the fateful day when he had so cruelly died. Eddie had spoken often to Elaine about selling the timepiece which had belonged to his grandfather. She wouldn't allow him to part with it. *Memories are worth more than money*, Dr Pod could hear his mother's voice in his head. He gasped with the sudden realisation that his mother would now believe that he was deceased, with all the heartache that entailed.

The time read 08:30. *Shit, better get ready quick. Those goons won't like it if I'm late.*

Dr Pod entered his bathroom, smiling at the wonderful walk-in shower which was at least twice the size of the one at his home. *What was my home...*

Wasting no time, he showered and shaved, grateful that he had remembered to pack his new electric shaver. It didn't take long to lather up some shaving gel, which he lathered over his already wet face, and manoeuvre the shaver expertly around his face.

He had *just* finished getting ready and had slipped on his pair of expensive shoes when there was a rat-a-tat at the door. *Funny that knock came precisely when I was finished getting ready. They must have been watching me.* Looking around, there was no sign of a camera, but he knew that they were there, which was more disconcerting.

With a sigh and a slight shrug he called, 'Coming,' and walked casually to the door to his quarters as if he owned the place.

Mr Stannington was on the other side of the door, 'Morning Stan.'

With an impatient shake of his head, Mr Stannington said, 'Good morning Doc. Come with me, I'll show you the canteen where you can get lunch after meeting some VIPs.'

This took the doctor off guard, 'Oh? Who's that?'

'You'll have to just wait and see,' grinned the abductor with a cruel glint in his eye that Dr Pod really didn't like, especially as he was used to working with children. *They always have the upper hand. I'll have to try and get them to show me some respect, seeing as they obviously want something from me.*

'Follow me,' the man said as he started walking down the corridor. Dr Pod soon became disorientated, each corridor looked the same as the previous one. They passed several labs, which to Dr Pod looked well maintained and kitted out with up to date equipment. He was daydreaming so much that he almost walked into the back of Mr Stannington when he halted outside a room that had a slider on the door, signifying 'Free' or 'Occupied'.

Mr Stannington knocked once, and an impatient voice from within the room called, 'Come!'

He opened the door and ushered the doctor in ahead of him. An even bigger and more dangerous looking man stood, pulled a chair from under the table and indicated for Dr Pod to sit. He sat without question. A familiar looking woman gazed at him before saying, 'Welcome to the programme Dr Podalirius. Thank you for agreeing to take part,' she said with a mean look at him, as if daring him to say anything other than the fact that he was there voluntarily.

She continued to speak, 'I am Prime Minister Veronica Edwards.

Of course!

'And this is the home secretary, Felicity Peacock.'

Dr Podalirius had to try hard to suppress a snigger. Stressful moments tended to bring out the immature side of his personality.

Ms Peacock nodded curtly, 'Thank you Veronica,' and peered at the doctor over the top of her glasses, which were secured around her neck by a pearl chain.

'So, you may be wondering why you are here, Robbie,' she looked across at him with a smirk on her face, as if she were a parent playing games with a small child.

Robbie? he thought. *Best not to say anything.*

'You are here for the greater good of the nation's well-being. Whatever it is that you do to cure all children who come to you, you are to replicate and produce it into a chemical that we can introduce into the drinking water supply nationwide. It will save the country billions in NHS spending, and make us billions when we sell it worldwide. As a government, we will crush the opposition. Thank you.'

'What if I don't want to?' said Dr Pod.

Veronica laughed, tossing her head back exposing a mouthful of rotten teeth covered in grey fillings. 'Not an option Robbie. Not an option at all. As you may know from school, when the Greek demigod Podalirius died, animals were still healed by him. So even if we have to beat you up to and beyond the point of death, you will still be of use to us. I'm sure that you don't want to find out how nasty Mr Stannington and his cronies can really be. The last I heard of a dissenter, they had the soles of their feet whipped with a rubber hose until they were crossed with bleeding fissures.'

Dr Pod couldn't help but wince at the thought of this. 'When do I start?'

The PM smirked, as if she was used to getting her own way, 'Get some breakfast Robbie, and then Mr Stannington will introduce you to the team of scientists here. Goodbye.' She nodded at the door, and Dr Pod felt the giant man tugging on the back of his chair.

Their manners really are poor. He rose, said goodbye, and left with Stan to find the canteen.

Chapter Nine

After a hearty full English breakfast and a couple of steaming hot mugs of tea, Dr Pod and Mr Stannington made their way to a lab. 'Stan, I hope there is a decent gym here; too many of those belly busters and I'll be a right porker!'

Mr Stannington laughed, the ice had seemingly been broken after spending time together at the canteen.

He still kidnapped me, I'll have to keep an eye on him.

'We're here,' Mr Stannington said, and entered into a lab without knocking first. This looked different to the other labs that they had walked past; the wall backing against the corridor was made of glass with a huge door. All of the other hundreds of labs were regular looking rooms, not goldfish bowls.

The other difference was a huge MRI machine, in one corner of the room. Dr Pod gasped, this room was ginormous. A man and a woman both wearing white clinical coats appeared from a side room. They came over to Mr Stannington and Dr Pod, and in turn, shook hands with them both.

The woman introduced them both, 'I'm Doctor Scarlett Hammond, and this is Doctor Justin Davies. We are the most senior clinicians here at Porton Down,' she smiled coyly, 'You must be wondering what is going on, but please don't worry. After all, you are of most use to us when you are cooperative.' She looked at the male doctor, who took his cue, 'There is clearly something extraordinary happening with you. We have examined the prescription charts of all the children you healed, and there is nothing there that explains your amazing success. No medications prescribed, no procedures. I am not a person who is used to using superlatives, but with you and your gift, there are no substitute words that are appropriate. Now then, today we shall give your brain an MRI scan and have an in-depth interview and analysis of what you are able to tell us. On top of the scientific analysis, we have a special forces interrogator and depending on how the day goes, other guests could see you too.'

Dr Pod's face fell at the last revelation, 'I hope that waterboarding isn't on the menu today.'

Scarlett laughed warmly, 'No, nothing like that. Not at this stage anyway, but I'm sure that you are going to cooperate and not leave us with the necessity to interrogate you as an enemy of the state.'

Despite the intensity of the situation, Dr Pod felt himself relax. *Maybe this isn't going to be so bad after all, it is good to be with fellow medics again.*

She spoke again, stopping his mind wandering, 'Rightio, let's start. Get yourself changed into a gown and we'll scan you.'

****

Half an hour later, Dr Pod was back in his regular clothes and sat in the radiographer's booth, gazing at the images alongside the two other doctors. He shook his head in disbelief, there was no explanation for what was on the screen.

Justin spoke first. 'I have never ever seen anything like this. You have double the brain mass of a normal person. It appears that you have in effect, two brains in one. One brain is a regular one, albeit very well utilised. The other is, from what I can see, old…mummified almost. I can see the word Ellas carved into the tissue. Justin pondered for a moment. 'That's Grecian.'

'That is amazing, I am of Greek descent.' Dr Pod interrupted.

Justin raised an eyebrow at being interrupted. 'I know everything about you remember... Your name, Podalirius, do you know where that comes from?'

Dr Pod looked out into the corridor and furrowed his brow, thinking hard, 'No, should I?'

Scarlett spoke next. 'It is a shame that you don't know; Podalirius was a Greek demigod.' She paused to let the train of thought sink into Dr Pod's head.

'So, what you are saying is that I have somehow obtained a second brain?' Dr Pod's head was now spinning. *How could this be possible?*

'I don't know,' said Scarlett, 'One thing is for sure though, that your seemingly magical powers have to come from the ancient part of the brain. Now we just have to work out what to do...'

Justin pressed a button set underneath the desk, and Mr Stannington arrived a moment later and took him back to his quarters.

'See you in the morning,' Mr Stannington said, then left, leaving Dr Pod somewhat bemused.

****

After another good sleep, Dr Pod felt good. He hadn't set his alarm, waking when his body had slept enough. For the first time, he really noticed the windows in his room. They were huge, and gave lovely views of countryside... beyond the impenetrable-looking fences and barbed wire.

He washed and dressed, then did a double take when he looked at his watch. It was almost 11 am; but as yesterday, there was the unmistakable knock on the door of Mr Stannington at the same moment as Dr Pod slipped on his shoes.

'Nice of you to join us Sleeping Beauty,' Mr Stannington greeted him with an amused twinkle in his eye. 'No breakfast today, come with me.'

I don't have a good feeling about this.

The two men walked for what seemed like twice as far as the day before to the lab. Dr Pod immediately saw what wasn't there the day before. An operating table. He broke into a cold sweat and looked at the man who seemed to have become a comfort blanket, hoping he might offer some way out.

Mr Stannington avoided eye contact and said, 'Wait here, mate.'

So, I'm his mate now? He left the room, locking it behind him leaving Dr Pod alone. *This is the first time that I have felt vulnerable in my adult life. What's happening?*

A team of several men dressed like surgeons and nurses appeared thirty minutes later, along with Mr Stannington and his two goons. Dr Pod's face drained of all colour. *Looks like shit's about to get serious!*

Mr Stannington cleared his throat, held out some hospital clothing and said, 'You need to put on this gown, Rob. This is Mr Quentin Jefferson. He is the chief surgeon at St Albert's Hospital in Westminster.'

'Wow, I am pleased to meet you. I've followed your work closely Mr Jefferson, you are an inspiration.' It was safe to say that Dr Pod was starstruck.

'Quite. I am not so pleased to see you, Doctor, I should be having whisky at my golf club, but the damned government have forced me to be here.'

Dr Pod felt as though he had been hit in the guts with a hammer. *What the hell is going on? Talk about never meeting your heroes.*

Mr Jefferson seemed to sneer at Dr Pod, 'Still, at least I don't have to wait for you to fill out a consent form, nor do I need to spend time explaining to you the risks and benefits of this surgery. I take it that you do know that you are about to be operated on?'

'Well, I did get that impression. But, what if I don't consent?' Dr Pod looked past the team to the door towards freedom.

The third man, Justin, or Geordie as he was known to his friends, spoke in a broad Geordie accent, 'You don't want to be silly mate. Either you get changed and have the operation and everything will be ok, or you can try and escape, fail to get past me and Mr Stannington, get knocked out then be operated on anyway.'

'Well now I have the choice, where do I get changed?' Dr Pod said in a high-pitched voice that surprised him.

'Just here will do,' Geordie said with a grin.

With a feeling of resignation, Dr Pod stripped off all of his clothes and changed into the gown while the assembled medical team made sure that all the necessary equipment was present and correct.

Once changed, he lay on the operating table. In a slick well-rehearsed dance, pads were attached for cardiac monitoring, and an O2 sensor was placed onto his forefinger. One nurse sank a cannula needle into the back of his wrist. Dr Pod whispered to her in a fear-soaked voice, 'What's the operation?'

With a sympathetic look, she replied, 'Brain dissection. Mr Jefferson is going to remove a portion of the ancient brain for analysis.'

A small amount of urine leaked from Dr Pod and trickled onto the floor, which no one seemed to bat an eyelash at. One of the team simply cleaned it up, washed their hands and continued with their task.

One of the doctors who hadn't introduced themselves yet said, 'Try to relax Dr Podalirius. You are in very experienced hands here. I'm the anaesthetist. Soon you will be unconscious. See you on the other side.' His voice was very soothing, Dr Pod felt himself relax more and more until he was indeed unconscious.

The anaesthetist inserted a breathing tube, other team members inserted catheters and put tape over his eyes. Mr Jefferson manoeuvred Dr Pod's head into a three pin Mayfield skull clamp and tightened it to secure him for delicate brain surgery.

Mr Stannington and his colleagues sat as far away from the action as they could; they had a feeling that it wasn't going to be a pretty sight. They watched uneasily as a male nurse shaved one half of the doctor's head and jumped a little as the razor was tossed into a metal bin with a sharp clang.

Monitors beeped loudly, so Mr Jefferson asked for Spotify to be turned on to cover the rhythmic noise of the heart monitor. After cleaning the scalp with iodine, he made a small incision. With close attention, the surgeon peeled back scalp and muscle. He picked up a drill, with a burr bit and carefully placed it over the mark that he had made on the side of Dr Pod's head. The sound of the drill was intensely loud, like a dentist drill played through a loudspeaker. As he began drilling into Dr Pod's head, a small amount of smoke wafted from the skull. Fluids being suctioned, people talking, and the music made it a noisy place to be. Mr Stannington, Geordie and Cockney were on the brink of sensory overload, so they snuck out of the room and went to the canteen.

Once Mr Jefferson had opened the dura, the brain's protective covering, he demanded silence while he examined what was in front of him. It was unlike any brain he had ever seen. The organ in front of him was dry looking and shrivelled, like an old walnut. His face slipped into a cunning, hateful sneer as he prepared himself to do something which had never been attempted in the realms of legend, never mind reality. The surgeon picked up a biopsy punch, placed it against Dr Pod's brain and with pressed it into the ancient matter with a satisfactory squish. Pulling it out, with a peculiar sucking noise emanating from inside the skull, Mr Jefferson placed the ancient particle of brain onto a stainless-steel tray.

He reversed the process of opening the head, closed Dr Pod's skull then left the rest of the operation to the other doctors present to complete. He handed the tray to Scarlett and Justin who took the sample away into the belly of the top secret building.

****

Six months after the operation Dr Pod remained in a coma. When Mr Jefferson's unprecedented operation would in all probability never be repeated again. The doctors and anaesthetist were baffled as to why Dr Pod remained in a coma; it was as if a part of his soul had been taken away.

If he were conscious, Dr Pod would probably have been surprised that Mr Stannington and his sidekicks visited him every day.

'It's a shame, I was getting to like this guy,' said Mr Stannington while sadly shaking his head, 'He was genuine in what he did, making sick kids better.'

Geordie agreed, 'You're right there, he didn't deserve to be incarcerated in here. I bet when he wakes up, if ever, he won't be the same as before. They stole a bit of his brain for God's sake!'

****

In the laboratory, a discovery had taken place. A fragment of the tiny brain piece had sat under a computer controlled microscope that imaged the sample. Something that had never in the history of science been seen before; the brain tissue was still alive after being removed from the patient.

The scientists carried out further tests, isolating the atoms that made the miraculous healing possible. They managed to replicate and bottle the unique proteins in the brain.

They quickly moved onto the animal testing phase, starting with rats, rabbits, and eventually, a horse. All of them, without fail, were cured of cancer by drinking water supplemented with the mixture made at Porton Down.

Later, the scientists used it on twenty human volunteers, who were compensated handsomely for their time and potential harm to their body.

It was a real eureka moment when it was proven beyond all reasonable doubt that they held the cure for cancer in the vaults.

Chapter Ten

The government had indeed found the cure to cancer, and many other illnesses. Most people would say that they had a moral obligation to use it to heal those living with disease in all its forms.

However, most people would have been wrong; it was kept secret and sold to the major party donors who gave millions to the ruling elite.

Some things could never be kept secret; whoever thought at the upper echelons of power that this cure could remain under wraps was very much mistaken. When news of the treatment leaked, it was patented and guarded fiercely by the prime minister.

****

A year to the day from the operation, Mr Stannington and his two friends continued to visit Dr Pod daily. 'It's sad mate, you would be proud knowing that you are the cure to cancer…' Cockney said.

Geordie held his hand up to silence his friend, 'Wait! Did you just see that?'

Mr Stannington said, 'If you saw his eyes flicker open, then I saw it too!' The excitement grew in the room, heightening when Dr Pod's eyes flashed open. In a fit of confusion, he pulled the breathing tube out of his throat. Geordie pulled the alarm cord hanging from the ceiling by the bed to summon a medic.

Scarlett and Justin sprinted in through the door, an intensive care nurse in hot pursuit. Despite being out of breath, Scarlett said, 'Can anyone tell me what's happened?'

Mr Stannington said, 'Well, us three were visiting, as we always do every day.' Jerking a thumb in the general area of Geordie, he continued, 'He spoke to the doc and told him that had got the cure for cancer and other illness', and then he opened his eyes and yanked out that pipe!'

Justin said, 'Awesome, let's see what's happening.' He pulled out a small torch from a shirt pocket and grasped the stethoscope that was hanging around his neck. It seemed that Dr Pod was asleep, but breathing on his own.

Geordie, Cockney and Mr Stannington looked on, not realising that they were holding their breaths while they awaited the verdict from the doctor.

Eventually, Justin slung his stethoscope back around his neck. He said, 'It looks like good news. He isn't in a coma anymore. I guess that all we can do now is to wait for him to come around and see how he is.'

Scarlett spoke to the nurse in a low voice, no one else heard what she said, but it was plain from their body language that they were all relieved. She spoke to the other people in the room, 'Ok, we don't need to be here at this point in time. Nurse Matthews will be keeping a very close eye on him. See you all later,' she beamed, delighted at the doctor's surprising recovery.

A day later, Dr Pod was sitting up in the hospital bed. Mr Stannington had come to see him, alone this time because the other two were on other duties.

Dr Podalirius was sucking water from a plastic beaker using a straw; it was going to take time to recover from lying flat for so long. His muscles had wasted; a private sector physiotherapist was due to come and start working with him that afternoon.

With barely a whisper Dr Pod said, 'What happened to me, Stan? I hear that they did something with my brain or something.'

Mr Stannington pulled his chair as close to the bed as he could and spoke in a low voice to try and avoid any eavesdroppers hearing his words. 'Yes, they took out a tiny bit of your brain, and the scientists have done their magic and made a cure for cancer and other illness'. It's a miracle.'

Dr Pod's eyes lit up, and for the first time since reawakening, he was able to absorb the information. 'So, in other words, millions will be cured! How amazing is that?'

Mr Stannington avoided eye contact with him.

'What is it, Stan? What's wrong?'

Staring at the flow and shaking his head, he said, 'The bloody government have patented it and kept it for themselves and the elite, especially party donors who have given massive donations to them. The news is being kept from the man on the street.'

The doctor's eyes lit up with raging fire, 'No! That's crazy!'

'Shh, keep your voice down mate, people could be listening,' Mr Stannington said fearfully, expertly looking around the room for hidden microphones and cameras.

'I can't let this happen,' whispered Dr Pod, 'You must help me to escape and get the word out.' Dr Pod's eyes glowed the colour of blue marble, and his skin appeared pale and smooth, almost like alabaster.

The doctor seems to be getting more like a Greek statue every time I look at him.

Mr Stannington sighed, *I really have to help; although it could be the death of me.* 'Leave it with me, mate,' he said before pushing his chair back and getting ready to leave. 'See you later, either me or the lads will come to see you, ok?'

Dr Pod nodded, *I think he is on my side...*

Mr Stannington left the room, but not until he looked at his reflection in a mirror and straightened his tie.

Chapter Eleven

'Are you crazy? We'll be crucified by the state!' said Cockney, 'but then again, the status quo is wrong...'

'Aye man we have to do something.'

'Yeah, or it makes us just as culpable as the state,' said Mr Stannington. The three men were sat in the canteen, their heads almost touching as they sat around a small table, nursing their bitter tasting strong coffees.

Silence followed for a minute or two as the men thought hard about what they could do, the air conditioning making their shirt sleeves flap.

Geordie swigged his drink, including the granules at the bottom of the cup. He wrinkled his nose at the gritty texture and looked straight at Mr Stannington. 'Have you seen the news today? There's a new presenter on Sky News, she looks like you...'

Cockney grinned with a naughty glint in his eye, 'Alright mate, just 'cos you fancy him...'

Mr Stannington adjusted his tie again and took his phone out of his pocket. He looked up the Sky News app, expertly working the screen with his thumb looking for the 'contact us with your story!' tab. It didn't take long; thirty seconds later his phone rang with a cheerful tune.

'Hi, can't talk here, send me an email, and I'll reply,' he said curtly and terminated the call. 'I see what you mean lads, she is almost as good looking as me!' he guffawed, and not taking his eyes off the screen navigated to his email server.

Geordie and Cockney watched his thumb swiping this way and that way over the screen, smiling as he punched the 'Send' button.

****

An hour later, their earpieces burst into life, a remote voice dropping each of them the same message: 'All guards to the gatehouse'.

Clearly, there was a mole in the Sky News camp, because outside the main gates to the secretive facility were news vans from all the major networks.

Mr Stannington was taken somewhat by surprise. 'Shit, I ain't seen that many since the Russian geezer was poisoned a few months back!' he said.

As one, the three men secured their impenetrable shades onto their faces and stood waiting to spring to action at a moment's notice.

In front of them, a representative of the facility stood to attention, his boots and shaven head reflecting the shine of the sun like a well-polished mirror. His voice boomed, 'Thank you all for coming. There is no truth in the rumour that Dr Podalirius is living here. As you know, he committed suicide at home.'

A highly strung bottled blonde woman ordered an answer to her question. 'Why is it that there are so many reports of rich people being cured of serious illnesses by drinking a potion invented here with a portion of Dr Podalirius' brain? What *is* going on?'

'Thank you for coming today, goodbye!' The man who Mr Stannington knew to be Graham McLean, head of HR, left the scene so quickly that his heels almost sparked against the concrete.

The assembled news crews refused to move; they were going nowhere…

Mr Stannington and his two colleagues looked at each other, an unspoken word passed between them. They briskly made their way back to Dr Pod's hospital bed.

To their surprise, the doctor was not sitting in his bed. He was standing by the window that flooded the room with natural light. Without turning, he pointed to the wire fence and the news crews beyond. 'They are here for me, aren't they?'

Mr Stannington said, 'Yes. Somehow the news got wind of you being here. No idea how that could have happened…The HR boss has been out to tell them that you can't possibly be here. They ain't buying it.'

Dr Pod turned to face his three unlikely friends, 'What's the plan, Stan?' He said, turning his palms to face to the ceiling while shrugging his shoulders.

Mr Stannington scratched his temple, deep in thought. 'I know what to do. The government fooled the people; now the people will fool the government.'

****

A black Transit van wearing a sign reading 'PRIVATE AMBULANCE' edged out of Porton Down. To the casual onlooker, it was just another journey for a corpse before it reached its final destination.

****

'We interrupt this programme to bring you breaking news.'

In homes around the nation, people eagerly looked at their screens to see what news had interrupted Emmerdale.

The elder statesman of British television news, Trevor McDonald, sat behind a desk. He turned towards the camera and said, 'Tonight, we have incredible news to bring you. Contrary to government reports, Dr Podalirius, the man who formulated the ancient Greek cure for cancer, is in fact *alive*. And he is here with me tonight for an exclusive interview.'

The camera panned to the left Dr Pod, who was sitting on a leather chair next to Trevor, smiling at him triumphantly.

THE END

About the Author

Simon was born in Doncaster, South Yorkshire, England. He is proud of his Yorkshire roots. This can be seen by how much Yorkshire Tea he drinks!

He has lived in various places, and went to the University of Derby and gained a HND and a BA (Hons). Since then, he has lived and worked in a few more places before finding the love of his life.

He moved in with his wife, got married and had three kids. Our home is shared with Missy the cat and Skeddie the Pink Tongued Skink. They have lived in Corby since 2005 and love living there.

What an adventure; it started fifteen years ago when we met.

Since then, Simon is proud to have served as a Special Constable in Northamptonshire. He wanted to join up to be a full time police officer, but life had another plan. At the time, he was working for a major national supermarket as a HGV (large truck) driver, which he did for over a decade. He became ill in 2011, but the illness never went away. Now he is disabled with various chronic illnesses, which resulted in him losing his day job about four years ago. Fibromyalgia and Psoriatic Arthritis are the main culprits.

He wondered where life would take him next.

Mark Nye, a superb writer and a friend, asked for submissions for an anthology. Simon wrote a short story called Famously Ordinary. To his delight, Mark told him that it was a good story. By then, he had caught the writing bug!

The anthology was never actually published, so Simon made it into a novella and the series Newdon Killers was born.

Get in Touch

Website: www.farrantfiction.com
Email: Simon@farrantfiction.com
Facebook: www.facebook.com/simonfarrantofficial
Twitter: @asfarrant
Newsletter: https://www.subscribepage.com/FarrantFiction

Other Work by Simon Farrant

Standalone:

Anathema: A collection of short horror stories, co authored with Mark Nye, and a bonus story by Matt Hickman.

Coming soon:

Too Early for Death, The Right time for Death and Never Too Late for Death,

These books are a low fantasy trilogy.

…..and a fourth Newdon Killers book.

If you have enjoyed this book make sure that you join my mailing list to keep up to date with news. I send a regular email about every 2 weeks, and promise to not spam!

There is a FREE ebook for all subscribers called Black Cat. https://mailchi.mp/8b69a296ff09/farrantfiction